BABYDADDY

"THE GOOD, THE BAD & THE SEXY"

BY
GERMAIN
MAURICE GREEN

Contact information
NULyfebooks@gmail.com
Facebook Germain Green

NULyfe books
P.O. Box 7339
Portsmouth, VA 23707

ISBN - 13: 978-0-9840811-0-3

Printed in the United States of America
Signature Book Printing, www.sbpbooks.com

SPECIAL THANKS

To my mother Billie, and sister Stacy, for reigniting my soul on the days I felt lonely insignificant and forgotten, like Anita Baker sang *'You Bring Me Joy'* where would one be without family?

A very special thanks to my Petersburg family. Continue to free your mind until the physical can catch up. I thank you all for critiquing my projects and pushing me to be more than just better but to stride toward greatness...

To my roaddog, Brandon Grimes, thanks for having my back, hitting the road to pick up these cars with me.

Thanks to those that supported me by purchasing a car or obtaining personal training services from me, and yes bootcamp will still go on Ladies and Gents good health never stops.

To Keysha Johnson thanks for retyping *"BABYDADDY"* no doubt you jump started it all with your effortless help.

To my nephew T'isson Green he put that cover together for me and took me out of the ice age and into the PC world. Continue to do your thing at Virginia State and Uncle G gotchu, don't worry you still got that honda accord coming....and no it will not be a 2000 nothing..lol maybe next year.

Much love to Kimberly Richardson Blunt for putting together my first book release party.

To my two barbers Rob and Bar, thanks for making my photo look extraordinary, GQ Magazine here I come.

To my facebook family thanks for all the support.

To Phil and his staff at Signature Book Printing, much love. I handed you guys the baton and you took *Babydaddy* across the finish line. No doubt Nulyfe Publishing look forward to future endeavors with your company.

And most importantly to the Babymomma / that I dreamed about so many nights, you are the very woman that gave birth to the many thoughts of a perfect love. I took that same desire and created a unique tale. That Babymamma is now my wife. Thank you for that inspiration.

To Shonda, thanks for putting together my website. Can't wait until it's complete.

To Fiasha Girmay aka Fish, thanks for looking out, fixing my cars.

To Steve Cooper, good looking out. I love the way you conduct your business. I will send anyone looking to buy a car to you. Definitely a car dealer people can trust.

Table of Contents

CHAPTER 1

It was mid fall; gloomy skies were blocking the half–moon from its light glisten over the streets of Richmond. The autumn leaves had prematurely blanketed the capitol, while a chilling air swept through bushes and trees during the freezing night. This chilling mist was Tony Gangsta. Tony Gangsta was a short, stocky light skinned brother, 27 years of age, though his deceptive naked face made him appear much younger.

He and his longtime brother and friend, Killa, waited in a stolen van, dressed down in all black designer trench leather. As soon as the avenue was clear of traffic, Killa jumped out of the black caravan. He glanced up and down Georgia Ave, and then moved swiftly across the street, leaping over a small rose bush to the back yard of Big Ike's gambling and bootlegging spot.

Big Ike was a tall 330 pound ex-gangster from Norfolk, turned gay the sixth year of his eleven year prison bid. Every Saturday he hosted the largest cee-lo game in Virginia. It was no secret that lucky ballers sometimes walked away with a million in cash from Big Ike's.

Tony Gangsta turned the screwdriver in the ignition until the engine cranked up. With the van running, he stepped out onto the street and slammed the door shut, then double checked to make sure he hadn't locked himself out. He reached inside his trench coat, smoothly disengaging the safety on two 357 Desert Eagle Magnums velcroed on his bulletproof vest.

Then, pulling out a pair of Cartier wood grain glasses, he diligently covered his eyes before tilting his Burberry hat to the side. Feeling like a superstar, he checked himself over using the caravan's window reflecting as a mirror.

"Tony", Killa called over the two way. "Tony its' time." Tony Gangsta reached in his coat pocket for the radio, "Yo!, I'm moving now. Remember, twenty minutes....no more, no less you hear me nigga? I'm out." Tony Gangsta turned the radio off the tossed it back into his pocket as he pimped across the street.

Before ringing the doorbell, he scanned the front yard once more. As far as he could tell, there was no one sitting in any of the cars that occupied Big Ike's front lawn. He took in a deep sigh, and then checked his Movado watch for no reason at all. It was a habit he'd picked up from frontin and bling-blingin in the club for so long.

He rang the bell, and in seconds the door opened. "Yo wussup Tony Gangsta, welcome to the party. Come in shawty." Porkchop has done 16 years in Greenville State Penitentiary for the first degree murder. During this bid he'd earned a reputation from all the heads he split and guts he put a shank to. When he came home, all the young hustlers worshipped and respected him, and every female wanted to make his acquaintance. Porkchop had been with a man the majority of his bid, and big feet, mustaches and hairy asses were all he had known the past decade and a half. So he stayed with the one thing that he'd grown to love....men. Though he lost respect from most of the hood, the fact remained; Porkchop was not to be fucked with.

Tony Gangsta's plan was fool proof. Still, he felt something was out of place. He joined the other ballers in the back room. "Trips..fo...five six! "A side better yelled over the dice. He quickly counted the heads there, then slid a bar stool up to the pool table. Reaching in his pocket, he pulled out 50 grand, all in one hundred dollar bills, and then sat down on the stool to join the huge Cee-Lo game.

Tony Gangsta had become a regular at Big Ike's. Everyone thought he was running an ecstasy ring in Charlotte, North Carolina. That was word in Churchill. Never had he made any moves in the city. Street rumors spread that he didn't do business in Richmond because his drug status was too large.

Five minutes in the backroom and tony Gangsta was sipping on his second Corona. He'd just lost twenty grand, but that was just a deposit. He planned on leaving with half a million dollars strong. His main objective right now was to scan the room, checking out the other shot callers. Being as everyone had pistols, it was imperative that he keep track of all movement. Tony Gangsta couldn't help but wonder how Porkchop answered the door so fast. But he brushed the thought away, figuring he was just being over cautious and paranoid as Killa so many times suggested.

Two houses down, across the street from big Ike's crib sat Slim, Porkchop's lookout man, in an old MPV that hid in a driveway behind a row of bushes. Slim used to be the neighborhood crack dealer in the early 90's.

After his Mother passed away, he suffered a nervous breakdown. Years after he rebounded from the illness, he found himself a new friend.....HEROIN. Slim hustled small time, mostly to support his dope habit. On the weekend, Porkchop would pay him five hundred dollars to watch while the Cee-Lo games were in progress, his job was to report anything that looked suspicious, such as loiters and the police. He also was told to call whenever anyone made way unto the premises.

Slim had called Chops informing him that Tony Gangsta was approaching the door. He hadn't noticed Killa running across the street five minutes earlier. Slim was preoccupied, moaning out to Londa, the neighborhood crack head, about how good her pussy was. After he reached his climax he tossed her out the van by her long nappy weave, along with a 20 piece of crack. Disregarding her plea for another hit, Slim got back down to business, watching out for Big Ike.

Killa made his way to the back door of the house. After peeping through a window, he patiently waited until the back door opened. Killa ducked behind a boat near the shed, drawing an AK-47 from under his trench coat just in case someone spotted him. He realized it was Big Ike letting his 2 Boston terriers out for a late night yard disposal. Ike stood there for a moment, wondering why the backyard motion sensor lights hadn't lit up as usual, he quickly assumed the bulb had burned out. Ike shrugged, turned around and strolled back inside the house.

"Right on time. Just as Tony Gangsta planned," Killa mumbled to himself. He sat the AK-47 down on the frozen grass. Quickly retrieved a plastic bag from his inside coat pocket, he lured the dogs with its contents. The two pit-bull terriers immediately raced over to the other side of the boat toward the goods. Killa pulled two Cornish hens covered in inches of peanut butter and tossed them to the ground for the dogs to eat. After the dogs devoured the bait, Killa slowly lifted the rifle. Just as he started to make his way to the back door, the bigger of the two dogs let out a vicious growl.

Killa sighed, lowering his assault rifle to the grass once more. He slowly reached under his pants legs to retrieve a ten inch hunting knife he kept to maim unwillingly dope dealers fingers off. Killa adored his Kenneth Cole slacks, and the last thing he wanted was to get them all bloody. "Damn mutt insists on being a good guard doggy" he whispered under his breath. As he pulled the knife out, he stood up on his feet in a crouch. Before the dog could let out another peep, Killa swung the mini sword into its neck partially decapitating the kennel champion. Blood sprinkled and splashed everywhere.

The dog fell along the boat dying instantly. The other tried to run, but Killa's reflex was just too fast. With the flick of the wrist he hurled the knife at the dog striking it in the ear, causing it to collapse to the ground. Cautiously, he looked around the yard then toward the back door, hoping he hadn't alerted anyone in the house. He grabbed the AK, tiptoeing toward the dying dog, then pulled the knife from its neck and wiped the blade clean using the canine's skin as a rag. Killa pulled up his pants leg, easing the blade back in its holster. "Shit" he grunted after noticing blood stains all over him. "Fuckin dog done bled all over me." Killa aimed the rifle to the half dead animal. "Goodbye, you nasty fuckin mutt." He removed the rifle from the terrier's dome, then kicked it on top of the head as hard as he could. Sending him out of his misery, Killa glanced at his timer; 39 seconds left. He crept his way to the now unlocked door.

Tony Gangsta had sparked up a phony conversation with Rocca, who sat next to his left, a big baller from Blackwell. The kitchen was next to the bathroom, and he needed to keep an eye on it without drawing suspicion. While Rocca boasted of the crack and whip game Tony Gangsta pretended to be interested.

"I was thinking about switching over from heroin, ya know whaddum sayin?" Tony Gangsta shot back at Rocca, just to keep him talking. While Rocca rambled on, Tony Gangsta peeped out the kitchen. Tony Gangsta couldn't see the backdoor, nevertheless, he knew that the dogs were left out into the yard. He looked at his Movodo , three minutes to showtime for this talkin' muthafucka here, he thought, referring to Rocca. He'll be the first nigga I shoot. Adrenaline started to flow through his veins. Tony Gangsta threw 10 grand on the pool table, asking Rocca to hold the dice for him until he got back from the bathroom.

"Yo Porkchop, it don't cost to take a shit round' here, do it?" He asked , cracking a half smile. Porkchop stood over the pool table housing the dice game and looked Tony Gangsta in the eyes with a sarcastic smirk, yelling across the room "everything cost around here, nigga. Everything!" Then he catered to the next shooter up, moving his attention from Tony Gangsta. Tony Gangsta starred into the bathroom mirror, admiring his M.C. K.O. image. He pulled off his Cartier glasses and tucked them away inside his pocket. He put on his leather gloves and grabbed the Desert Eagles from their velcroed holster.

He stared in the mirror once more, crossing the two magnums over his chest just as MC K. O. did in his newest album cover. For the moment he pictured himself to be MC K.O., the hottest hard-core rapper on the planet. The reflection revealed MC K.O.'s thuggish smile, his gangsta pose and all the lyrics he represented. Tony Gangsta didn't exist at the moment. His whole persona was to live MC K. O.'s lyrical lifestyle and he did.

He couldn't help but think about his new image and how it destroyed his relationship with Nikki, his only baby momma'. He loved everything about her and his 9 month infant child even more. He knew Nikki was his only weakness, and he hated her for having that advantage over him.

Nikki never used the power of love against him. In fact , she avoided him and his chaos that came with it as much as she could. As he stood there in the backroom admiring himself in the mirror, he realized how much he wanted Nikki back. Tears started to build in his eyes.

He had no clue nor direction when it came to Nikki. He decided that he'd give her one more chance. Tony Gangsta wiped his eyes dry, made sure the magnums had one in the chamber, turned out the bathroom light, then exited the bathroom. He moved swiftly down the hallway toward the backroom. Nobody noticed the nickel plated rib cavers drawn by his side. Just as tony Gangsta scanned the room to make sure all eleven people were present, he saw Killa creep in through the back door.

Without warning, Tony Gangsta fired slugs into Big Ike, Rocca and two other big timers in the room. Killa fiercely split rounds striking Deena, the Southside Queenpin from Baltimore and Ike's irritating stereo system.

"By now I'm guessing you muthafucka's know what time it is" Killa yelled, aiming his rifle across the room. Tony Gangsta showed no remorse for killing Big Ike, he never did. "Why? Why you have to kill my baby? Why man" Porkchop cried out. Tony Gangsta pointed the tre pound down at the obese corpse "you mean this faggot here? Awh man! The gay bastard was cheating on you…with him, anyway." Pointing the pistol toward the blood soaked body of Rocca, Tony gangsta arrogantly turned his back to Porkchop, knowing he'd try him out of anger. Filled with rage Porkchop leaped on the pool table, diving in the air toward his lover's murderer. While he was in mid air, Killa squeezed off 6 rounds, striking and ripping Porkchop's chest to shreds. He died before he hit the floor. By this time Tony Gangsta had turned around. He stood over Chops body, aimed the 357 down at his head and calmly fired three slugs, sending a piece of skull and afro flying halfway across the room. "Just in case the nigga had nine lives" he said, smirking at Killa. "Alright you bitch ass muthafuckas, you gots 60 seconds to put all the money in this bag." He tossed a folded shopping bag from his back pocket onto the bullet riddled pool table. "Or you niggas will be joining them." Killa cold heartedly yelled. The panic stricken hustlers raced to gather all their money off the table and from the dead. Rico, one of the surviving ballers there, took off his Rolex, tossing it in the bag with the rest of the cash. Killa saw what the terrified hustler had done and approached him. "Yo nigga!" He screamed at Rico, showering his face with oral fluid, "Do it look like we need jewelry, bitch? Matter fact , nigga, did I ask you for your fuckin' watch, huh nigga? We look like petty thieves to you, huh? Get the fuckin' money! You throw anything else in that bag, I'm ma peel that wig back. We clear?" Rico nodded then went to the bag filled with cash to retrieve his watch.

"Yo!, yo what'chu think you doin'" Tony Gangsta calmly asked "um getting my watch out." Rico replied, looking confused. "Nawh playboy, hell nawh! You lost that joint, B. Jus' put no mo' jewelry in there".

In less than a minute, all the cash had been rounded up, along with seventeen pistols. Killa grabbed the cash and demanded the remaining ballers to lie on the floor, then headed to the kitchen, for the back door. Tony Gangsta grabbed the bag of weapons, looked around admiring the bloody scenery for a split moment, then at the ballers laying on the floor. "Feel lucky, you could've ended up like dem' K fuckin' O'd" he aggressively shouted as he backed into the kitchen, then out the back entrance. Killa had quick stepped through the back yard along side the house, up to the front yard.

He slowed his pace after realizing that Georgia avenue was quiet and clear of possible witnesses. "We did it, we really pulled this shit off" Killa said to himself as he made his way across the street toward the van. ""Ohhh shit".

Slim was taking a piss in a nearby bush when he heard gunshots coming from Big Ike's place. He tried calling Porkchop on the cellphone, but the screen read battery low so he dashed to the MPV, grabbed the streetsweeper and headed for the front yard, hiding behind a huge tree where a 600SL Benz was parked. Slim wondered if he should go inside or ring the door bell to see if everything was alright.

The thought of being shot once more crossed his mind "Fuck dat!"im'ma wait for 'em right here. Five hundred dollars ain't worth my dick in the dirt." He mumbled, nervously watching the front entrance of the house. He waited in the coldness for three agonizing minutes when he thought he heard footsteps cracking through the frozen grass. Slim's heart began pounding through his rib cage as the sounds grew closer and louder. He slowly and quietly maneuvered himself around the tree, being extra careful not to make any noise.

Killa walked past appearing to be in a hurry. Slim stared at him for a moment "Who's dat?" He asked himself "and how da hell he get past me?" He couldn't recall the tall, slim, dark skin brother at all. As Killa made his way toward the caravan, Slim stood slowly, then crept up behind him. "Chu-chilick' was the sound of the pump action in motion, filling the shot gun chamber with a 20 gauge slug.

"Oh shit" Killa recognized that unwelcome sound. When he turned around, Slim's barrel confronted his face. Killa knew Slim was going to shoot'em, he dropped the bag to the pavement, instinctively diving to the ground to reach under his trench coat for a 9mm. In mid air he fired three rounds at Slim before hitting the street. Slim fell to his knees, dropping his shotgun, after getting hit in the shoulder and leg.

Killa hadn't realized Slim fired his weapon, nor was he aware that one of the gauge's slugs had ripped through the right side of his neck. He uncoordinatedly aimed the AK-47 up at Slim, hoping to finish him off before he fired the pistol. His arm collapsed, falling from the sky down onto the ice cold streets. Slim reached down to pick up the streetsweeper. Just as his bloody fingertips touched the warm barrel, a shot rang out, sending Slim's body falling face first to the ground.

Tony Gangsta had witnessed the exchanged fire take place just as he reached the front yard. In seconds with guns drawn, he ran up for a closer analysis of his friend, wasting no time in spitting a round to the back of Slim's cranium. Killa was bleeding profusely and unconscious. Still, Tony Gangsta didn't panic. He slumped Killa's blood soaked body over his shoulder, carried him around to the other side of the van and opened the passenger door, positioning him in the front seat.

Quickly, he ran over to the driver's side, jumped in, slamming his foot on the gas pedal and shifting the gear to drive, all at once. Tony Gangsta sped up Georgia Ave, turning right on X st. in minutes he was on 9 mile road, accelerating up the interstate ramp. As he raced on the interstate, he noticed all the squad cars headed in the opposite direction. Tony Gangsta knew if Killa didn't get medical attention he'd die soon.

He exited off the highway and headed toward Virginia Medical College. He glanced over at Killa, giving him an examination of his own. "Killa, you gon make it baby. We at the hospital, you gon be a' right, yo'. Tony Gangsta didn't believe his own words. Somehow he figured if he spoke them out loud, hope would prevail. But Killa belched out his final breath, and Tony Gangsta knew that his long time friend was dead. He parked in front of the hospital's emergency entrance, and then grabbed the money and guns from the back seat.

Staring at Killa for the last time, he wiped the tears from his eye before they could build enough fluid to fall down his cheek. "Um sorry, man. Um sorry" he uttered as he exited the van, deciding to leave the door open so someone would discover Killa's body. Solemnly, he moped through the hospital parking lot toward Main Street. Just as he exited the premises, loud and horrifying screams echoed through the night. He dropped his bag to the side walk, stripping himself of the bloody trench coat. Tossing it in a nearby trash can, he picked up the goods and started running down Main st. Sirens grew closer and closer to the hospital. Tony Gangsta began to panic, ducking in between two buildings.

He felt that he may be finally caught. Then, a squad car crept by. Still, Tony Gangsta kept walking. The car stopped, shinning its spotlight on him. He ignored the brightness, never breaking stride in his step. It pulled up, never taking the light off Tony Gangsta. "Ayh you!" The officer yelled over his intercom. "Let me see some I.D., ma'man" Tony Gangsta stopped and looked toward the bright lights, then moved slowly toward the squad car "Godamn! Can you take that light outta' my face, officer?" he pleaded.

Just as the Spanish officer who sat in the driver's seat turned out the light the white one stepped out of the cruiser to run an identification check.

"Where ya headed this time uh' night?" The albino asked, glancing Tony Gangsta over "Home."I'm heading home." He replied looking away from the officer, giving him a clear view of the blood stains on his left cheek. Tony Gangsta realized the chubby officer noticed something out of place by the way he stepped back, suddenly grabbing hold of his service piece. "What'chu got in 'em bags, chief?"

Tony Gangsta ignored the question, looking up and down Main Street to see if there were back up police coming or witnesses nearby. He let out a long sigh, and then dropped the two bags in front of the officer's feet. When the officer put the flash light down on the bag, Tony Gangsta reached under his shirt, grabbing the Desert Eagle from his vlecroed vest. A second later, the chubby officer was dead. Tony Gangsta had fired one slug, striking him in the forehead. Before the Spanish cop could react, Tony Gangsta squeezed off on him, ripping two slugs through his arm. Fearing for his life, the officer sped off, crashing into Yo-Hung's deli restaurant. Assuming the Spanish officer was also dead; Tony Gangsta snatched up the bags and sprinted down the block to State Road, where the Yellow Cab Company was located. Luckily a vacant cab happen to be going his way. He flagged it down and jumped in. "Maryland Street. I'm in a hurry, "he demanded, throwing the cabbie a Benjamin. The driver put the hundred dollar bill up to the light to verify its authenticity, and then put the pedal to the metal, speeding down the highway toward the North side of Richmond.

CHAPTER 2
EARLIER THAT NIGHT.......

Nichole Wallace lived on the North side of Richmond in Holland Park, in a 3 bedroom house with her new 6'6" boyfriend Rodney, and Aunt Linda. Nichole's parents were killed in a car accident when she was 8 years old, and Aunt Linda moved into raise her niece. She used the life insurance money to keep the house up until Nichole turned eighteen years of age.

Nichole preferred to be called Nikki, because that's how her father used to address her. She was now twenty, tall and brown, with hazel eyes and shoulder length hair which she always wore in a ponytail. Nine months after she gave birth to Toniesha Oshea Wallace, her figure had shrunk back to normal size, slim and curvy. Nikki had just stepped out the shower when the phone rang. She reached up and grabbed a towel that lay over the curtain rod. Quickly drying her face and arms, Nikki reached down toward the toilet lid where the cordless receiver rested.

"Hello." She answered on the third ring, out of breath.

"What-is-up girl, you goin' or what?" Shawnte' asked energetically.

"Um getting' ready now." Nikki replied, wiping the fogged steam from the mirror so her hair wouldn't get wet. "What'chu wearing anyway?"

Shawnte' was a fashion diva and goldiggin' specialist, who took pride in dressing down like the stars did. High maintenance with big dreams, she always kept a baller in the bank and one on ice. Whatever Jay-Z rapped about or Lil' Kim modeled on the magazine covers, she had to have it in her closet to show off on special occasions.

"Girl you know me. I sucked Rocca dick 'til his ass couldn't move no mo', then I asked him for some money."

"How much you get?" Nikki asked curiously.

"I got two G's from him, went to the mall and bought that Fendi leather skirt I was talkin' about, and those Etu Evans stilettos."

"You dirty bitch." Nikki's tone was friendly. "Shawnte' you knew I wanted those shoes."

"Yeah I knew. But you can't afford them, remember?" Especially with that broke ass thug of a man you got over there. At least Tony Gangsta had some Luchi'ano."

Nikki tightened up her face, rolling her eyes. She hated the way Shawnte' pressed on about how she and Tony Gangsta should get back together. "You know, Shawnte', some things are more important than material come-ups."

"Yeah, like what? Love?"

"Yeah, love. What's wrong wit that? You act like love is a crime or something."

"It's no crime, Nikki, it jus don't ay."

"Well I love Rodney. He may be a broke ass thug, but I love 'em and my baby gon' get broke off a lil' something somethin'."

Shawnte' laughed at her girlfriend's wishful thinking. "While you dreamin' boo, um livin' it up."

Nikki knew she was hinting at Tony Gangsta. "Girl, you know Tony thinks he's MC K.O. and stuff. He dun' took that thug thing a little too far. He be calling here talkin' like MC Kayo all the time. I can't stand him or that bastard, MC K.O.'s music. Them niggas on the same planet will keep the crime rate up fa' sure." Bored with Nikki's ranting, Shawnte' cut the conversation short. "Well look, I'ma let 'chu get dressed. I'll be there in a little bit."

Just then the phone beeped.

"Hold on for a minute," Nikki interrupted, "my phone beepin'." She clicked the dial, switching over to the next line. "Hello." Nikki answered, smiling.

"Wuddup wuddup? You still thug lovin' me or what?" Tony Gangsta smoothly greeted.

Nikki began yelling in the receiver. "I thought I asked you not to call her talkin'' like some fuckin' rapper you not. What is wrong with you Tony? GOD!" She concluded, walking out of the bathroom to the bedroom wearing only her bra and panties.

"Um Tony fuckin' Gangsta, bitch, who's you? My momma or somethin'? Nikki, you ain't got to scream at me."

"Tony you right. I came off on you wrong. Sorry." She apologized after he argued that she went on him first.

"I need to see you right now." He demanded in a calm voice.

"I can't, I'm going to Club Secrets with Shawnte' and Princess, and wont be back "til after one. Anyway, what's this about?"

The line went silent, finally he replied. "Us. I wanna talk about us." Nikki let out a long sigh as she sat on the bed pulling her stocking up her left leg.

"Look, Tony, I gotta go. Call me tomorrow."

As soon as she hung the phone on the charger, it rang. She snatched it from the stand to cuss her ex-boyfriend out. "What now?"

"Godamn, bitch!" Shawnte' teased, sucking her teeth. "You forgot I was on hold, ya rude ass!"

"Shawnte', um sorry. That was Tony on the other line, talkin' crazy again. I forgot you were on the other line." Nikki explained.

"Uh, well, like I was saying before you rudely shitted on me. After I pick up Princess, which will be in the next twenty minutes, I'll be over there to get you. Rocca let me push the Escalade tonight."

"Damn girl, you really did a job on that dick, didn't 'cha? I gave Rodney a hit too, jus to keep him from whining like a girl. Why you comin' so early anyway?"

"Because."

"Cause what?"

"Damn Nikki, you fuck a surprise up."

"What surprise? What are you talking about?"

"I'll tell you when we get there."

"Shawnte", you know I don't like surprises."

"Oh yes you do, bitch! Stop fakin'."

"You right, but tell me anyway."

"Nikki, see you in a lil' bit."

"Don' hang up" it was too late, Shawnte' was gone. Nikki wondered if princess and Shawnte' had gained access to some VIP passes. The last thing she wanted was to be around some brothers with a little money, disrespecting her by patting her on the ass and spilling Cristal all over her outfit the whole night. She continued to get dressed, ignoring Rodney's ugly facial expressions he made as he lay on the bed.

Whenever Rodney wanted her to ask him what was wrong, he'd grimace his face ten different ways. Rodney hated Nikki's passive demeanor when it came to her baby's daddy. He flicked the remote at the television, changing from channel to channel, trying to break through Nikki's barrier. Sucking his teeth, he frisbees the remote control toward the edge of the bed. Rodney stared at his girl as she maneuvered herself in the mirror, wondering exactly what he was going to say. Frustrated, he sucked his teeth twice as loud, following up with an exaggerated long sigh.

"What?...What? Jus' go ahead and say it, God why you gotta pout like a lil' punk?"

You know what? Rodney calmly replied, pulling his boxer shorts away from his groin to regain blood circulation. "Tony Gangsta is what. You're my girl now, and if you gon be answering to any man, it's gonna be me. You're his babymomma, but you're still my heart. Rodney displayed seriousness.

Nikki cut him off "You don't understand Tony and me,"

"No!, You don't understand, I see what he's doing to you. Baby girl when you are upset, I'm upset, Nikki, I love you. I will never let Tony Gangsta or anyone else hurt you."

"I know, but"

"There is no buts". Rodney got up from the bed and stood behind her with his soft hands he began rubbing up and down her arms to emphasize his security. "There is no need to be afraid of him. He's jus' a wangsta."

Nikki didn't wanna go in depth with him , nor did she want to argue, so she sided with him just so he'd shut up. "Yeah, you right Rodney, he ain't nobody." She agreed knowing it would make him feel better about himself. Nikki turned around clutching her arms up under his shoulder blades, then kissed him from his chest up to his neck. She knew her soft lips would tame his anger. "Rod..Rod," she seductively whispered in his ear, "wait up for me tonight. Okay?" She let her arms fall down his back to his butt, giving it a firm squeeze and a pitty pat before letting go. "Let me hurry up and make those bottles for Toneisha before Shawnte" get here. "She reminded herself as she reached for some Chanel perfume on the dresser.

"Why you gotta put that shit on? You just goin' to the club. You already got a man remember?" He complained, as she left the bedroom for the kitchen.

"Shut up boy, you so crazy." She yelled back, brushing off his comment, Nikki didn't bother to explain that the perfume wasn't for another guy, but for her girlfriend and the quiet competition they pretended not to be in. She couldn't help but think about her and Rodney's future as she mixed the dry cereal with milk. She decided she would talk to him about possible marriage and having more kids, if things got better. If that nigga make it to the NBA then dump me for some blonde hair, pale skinned bitch, I'll kill his ass. The thought angered her.

Rodney was in the room hooking up the Playstation, aware that Nikki had kissed up to him in hopes of avoiding confrontation. " Fuck that bitch ass wangsta, " he mumbled to himself, switching the television over to channel four. The more he thought about Tony Gangsta the more riled up he became. Maybe if I whip his ass, he contemplated. My girl will recognize me as a man and not just some talented basketball player from the projects.

Aunt Linda was laying in the sofa watching the new Saprono's episode when the doorbell rang. "Nik-kayy, get the door" Shawnte' didn't hesitate to let herself in as she always did after ringing the bell. "Keep on lettin' yourself in here like you live here. Umm'a hand you one uhdese utility bills like you do...See what'cha freaky ass do then."

Shawnte" chuckled "Hey Aunt Linda, and I ain't no freak."

"Well you dress like one." Linda replied, grabbing a Newport from her cigarette case. She rolled her eyes from Shawnte" back to the television." Girl, you know I'm jus pickin'. Lend me ten dollars 'til I get paid." Shawnte" handed Linda a ten dollar bill as Nikki entered the front room.

Nikki squinched her eyes , sucking on her lips, "Aunt Linda can you please stop asking my friends for money? You know I hate dat." Linda gave her a hard stare, blowing the cigarette smoke in her direction before rolling her eyes back toward the television. "Girl you ten minutes early."

"I know, couldn't wait. Here, these are for you, "Shawnte" smiled, handing Nikki the shopping bag. When Nikki realized it contained the Etu Evan shoes she wanted, she couldn't hold back from screaming. "No you didn't." She said giving Shawnte' a hug. "You know I can't pay you back right now." "Girl please! I ain't trippin', Rocca is this week's sponsor.""Who's next week sponsor, freak?" Linda sarcastically giggled, never taking her eyes off the TV Nikki and Shawnte' shook their heads holding their tongues.

"Try the shoes on before we go, I just wanna see how they look on you." Shawnte' followed Nikki into the dining room ," Where's Princess?" Nikki asked, sitting in the chair, slipping a black leather shoe on her foot.

"Girl, she out in the truck pout'n." Shawnte' answered, raising her eyebrows waiting for Nikki to ask why. Nikki gave Shawnte' that look and slipped her foot into the second shoe, then paused, "What's the drama queen don' got herself into now?"

Shawnte' and Nikki labeled Princess the drama queen after the fight she got into at the Red Light Inn Strip Club. Princess had a nasty habit of breaking the rules by dating the customers. She previously got involved with two men, one of them married with three kids, the other was engaged to her second cousin from Hopewell. The two women confronted Princess on two different occasions, giving her the beat down of her life.

Princess had low self esteem, and was always insecure about her lips. She started dancing at the age of sixteen after a close decision over turning tricks. Nikki suspected Princess to be selling pussy at the Red Light Inn after Rodney informed her that his homies ran a train on her outside in the club's parking lot. But she never asked her because men were always lying on their dicks.

Really, she really didn't want to know the truth.

"Nik, don' say nothin', I know how you are." Shawnte' requested, lowering her voice.

"I ain't gonna say a word," Nikki replied. "Tell me, please."

"Girl, that bitch sittin in the truck looking stupid as hell. I asked her who her baby daddy was. She told me nuna my business, so I just let it go. Fo' real, I know she don't have a clue in hell."

Nikki let a quiet chuckle shaking her head. Shawnte' gave an admiring stare from head to toe. " You look real nice in them shoes, girl." Nikki assessed herself as well , gesturing a nod to Shawnte' to confirm she was in agreement. "C'mon, lets roll before the drama queen think we in here talkin about' er." Shawnte' exited the house while Nikki grabbed her coat out of the closet. " Aunt Linda, if Rodney doze off, please feed Toneisha for me." Linda didn't answer, she never did. Still, Nikki had to ask once more, "Aunt Linda, here me, huh, huh?"

"Yell a lil' louder , you'll be feed'n her ya damn self in uh minute."

Nikki ignored her aunt, "Rod, I'm leaving." She yelled from the foyer. He didn't reply, she put on her coat, zipped it up and looked the front room over for a moment before storming out the door. Right after the door shut, Linda leaped up from the sofa , tippy toeing to the door. She looked through the peephole, watching the SUV's lights disappear into the night, then turned the bolt lock and hooked the chains just in case her niece decided to make an unexpected U-turn back to the house. Rodney was playing Grand Theft Auto when the bedroom door opened.

"Is she gone?" He asked, keeping his eyes on the video game.

"Yeah," Linda whispered, cutting her eyes at the baby. "I got ten dollars, can you give me a twenty for dat?"

Stop playin' Lin, I don want'cha money. You know what I like," he said, sticking one hand under his boxer shorts. Turned on by Rodney's slim, long body, she climbed onto the bed, removing his hands from under his boxers, she skillfully slid two fingers through the release slot, pulling his trophy winner out. Slowly, she wrapped her warm and soothing lips around it as she always did.

With Linda it wasn't about the drugs. She loved licking Rodney all over his body. It started about four months ago when Rodney observed his girlfriend's aunt changing her clothes in the bathroom, leaving the door open on purpose. When Nikki wasn't around she'd talk about how she used to win a man's heart over by sucking the life out of his dick. No one had a clue that Rodney had a fetish for older women, he wanted her just as much as she wanted him. Nights later, Rodney was confident that Linda wanted his pleasures.

She boldly announced "I'm sucking n'at dick tonight. If you gon' tell Nikki, tell'er after I'm finished." From there on, twice and sometimes three times a week, Aunt Linda and Rodney would sex each other crazy. Linda, tall and curvy like Nikki, saddled herself over his knees, firmly gripping his penis as she stroked it into her mouth. Rodney slivered over the bed, knocking the comforter completely on the floor. She grabbed his nut sack, gently sucking one ball at a time.

You uh beast, Lin," Rodney began groaning. Linda didn't stop. In fact she stroked faster and faster. "uuhh, uhh I'm cumin' He yelled out as she placed his hand to the back of her head, pressing it down so his stiffness scrapped her tonsils. Seconds later he exploded in her mouth, and it turned him on to watch her swallow every single drop." Stop! stop just for a minute. Um s-sensitive right now," he stuttered out loudly, shaking from head to toe.

She popped his penis out of her mouth, then licked it clean of her saliva before planting a sweet peck on the tip. "I'll be on the couch, waitin'. Hurry, while my pussy wet." She moaned, wiping her mouth with the back of her hand. Linda then made her way out of the room up to the front.

Rodney took in a few deep breaths, trying to over come the sudden guilt he felt after every orgasm with Linda. Minutes later he had Auntie's legs up in the buck, slowly working his muscle through the narrow entrance of her vagina. Never before had he experienced coochie so tight. Every time he penetrated her, the sensuous feeling aroused him as if it were the first time. Gradually, he inched his entire package toward the back of her stomach. He knew if he thrust too fast, Linda would scream like a banshee, waking the baby. Still, he couldn't overcome the thrill of hearing her cry out his name.

With Linda's legs up in the air, he hunched over her midsection, clutching his arms over her shoulders to prevent her from avoiding his devastating pounds. In seconds he began pumping his hips and arching his back, penetrating her faster and faster. Soon Linda would scream, then her screams would turn to cries.....tears. The more she pleaded, the harder he rammed his balls against her ass. For almost two hours the pair took turns exploding orgasms on one another.

"Damn!" Linda cursed, pushing Rodney off her, "The baby cryin'. Get the bottle."

Rodney went into the kitchen to retrieve the bottle, then dashed toward the bedroom. In five minutes, Toniesha was fast asleep. He hurried back to the front room, hoping for another round. Linda was already in the bathroom, preparing for a shower. He went to the hall closet to retrieve a fresh cloth. Staggering back into the kitchen, he opened the refrigerator and grabbed the orange juice carton, took a few gulps, he reached over the sink and ran water until it was warm enough. Ringing the damp bath cloth , he began to wipe himself clean of dried fluids then tossed the cloth with the other dirty clothes as he entered the bedroom. Still feeling unclean, Rodney grabbed a baby wipe from under the bassinet and wiped himself once more, giving him that squeaky clean feeling he searched for. Minutes later, he dozed off into a deep sleep.

CHAPTER 3

"Where the hell is Te' at? Nikki ask herself while pretending to be entertained by some Jamaican promoter at the bar, who's name she'd already forgotten. But after the second drink he bought her, she became entertained by the charming accent he possessed and decided to give him small conversation. Not only did she find herself thinking of Rodney and his sexy body minutes into the club interview, she had fallen into a deep daze wondering what life would be like married with more children.

"Girl, me buy you drink, now ya ig me now!"

Nikki instantly snapped out of her elegant thought. "Nawh, I ain't ignoring you, Rasta man, uh,... whatever ya name mis. I'm just not feeling too well." She yelled over the music, glancing him in the eye briefly before scanning the VIP section over once more. "There's Princess goin' to the restroom. "Nikki mumbled under her breath. "What'ch say? Me can't hear you speak up !" the Rasta man requested after noticing she had spoken.

"I said, I have to use the bathroom, I'll be right back." Nikki screamed so he could understand her every word. She stood up, pulling the erosion of her skirt back down, grabbed her purse, then slowly made her way through the crowded VIP section toward the ladies room.

"Hello, it's me"

"What'ch doin' calling here Princess?"

"I had to call you. Um pregnant with your fuckin' baby, remember? And you act like you don't even care."

"Are you still at the club?"

"Yeah, I'm here in one of the restroom's private stalls, why?"

"I'm not avoiding you at all. I'm in the same boat you're in, Princess. I don't know what I wanna do at this moment. Anyway, how do I even know it's mine It ain't like you don't be get'na-round."

"Nigga, it's yours cause I SAID IT'S YOURS! You fucked me raw dog, and came up in my pussy ten days straight. Then you gon'come out'cho mouth like that ?"

"Nawh nigga, you stop trippin! I ain't started to trip out yet. It'll show you what tripping is, nigga, When I tell ya girl where her man been slangin his dick at the past three and a half months!"

Tomorrow, Tomorrow I will meet'chu in Henrico County, okay? I promise"

"If you don't, bitch, yo ass is....Hol'on for a second, gotta go, holla back." The line went dead.

"Princess you in here?" Nikki yelled over the closed stalls.

"Yeah! Hold on I'm on my way out" she replied, folding her cellular and tucking it in her jacket. She flushed the toilet as if she'd been using it, then exited the stall.

"You alright?" Nikki asked, "Your eyes look puffy and watery, girl." "Yeah, I'm good," Princess calmly replied, sucking her teeth, "Too much Belvedere I guess."

She walked past Nikki toward the restroom sink, checking out her eyeliner and lipstick in the mirror as she lathered her hands. Nikki stood behind her and observed, giving her a complete look over. She wanted to let Princess know she was aware of her pregnancy and there for her. Instead, she just stood there, feeling sorry for her girlfriend. I pray everything works out for her, Nikki thought to herself. "Where's Shawnte' she quickly asked after noticing Princess eyeing her though the mirror.

"Last time I seen her, she was sittin, on one of the Supa friends's lap, looking like she wanted to eat'im up." I should've known. Wherever there's a rapper, ya sure to find Te'."

Nikki added, checking herself out in the mirror as well.

"Wussup wit Mista Lord ah mercy? I saw you over there at the bar getting extremely acquainted."

"Girl, he sexy as hell, "Nikki replied, smiling.

"Sooooooo! Wussup? You hollerin' at him or what" Princess already knew what her longtime friend was going to say.

"I would, if his breath ain't smell like weed and ass, for one, secondly; I promised myself no more miscellaneous dicks. I'm a ask Rodney to marry me, I mean , ask him what he thinks about us getting' married, he supposed to ask me." Nikki corrected, emphasizing her point with hand movement. I'm ready to chill and settle down. I know y'all think I'm losing my mind, but I'm not. I'm in love. Fuckin' niggas for Gucci leathers was all good at first, long as I didn't get caught. But I'm putting all dat shit to rest from now on. If me and Rod can't afford it, we don't need it." Nikki added, leading the way out of the ladies room.

Princess couldn't believe what she had just heard. It conflicted with everything she'd dreamed of the past few months. The thought of not being with her baby's father made her nauseous. Even worse, she thought, If he marries Nikki, I'm doomed. As they squeezed their way through VIP, Princess contemplated the situation , Rodney said he was gonna leave her for me. Maybe the nigga jus' told me that to play with my head and get some pussy, or maybe he actually do wanna be with me. Rodney don't even have no idea about the two of them gettin' married. Damn! If I tell Nikki I'm pregnant by Rodney, she's sure to dump him. No that won't work, at least not right now. She might beat my ass and try to kick me in the stomach. I'll lose my baby. Shit! Angry, sad and disgusted, Princess detoured off into the crowd and headed downstairs to join the rest of Club Secret's fines guest.

"There go Deangelo and Madskillz, girl!" Nikki yelled only to turn around and find Princess gone. She quickly assumed she had been swallowed up in the crowd of party goers, and went her way. Her watch read 12:35. "Damn!, I gotta find Shawnte'. It's almost one o'clock." She mumbled to herself, ready to bounce. As soon as she started dashing past VIP'ers, a hand came from out of nowhere and gripped her arm. "Ya leavin' me so soon are ya now?" The Rasta man whispered in her ear, sliding his body close to hers.

"Baby girl, jus' cause me buya few drinks don' man ya obligated to take tis thing here, he smoothly continued, discreetly placing a phone number in the palm of her hand. "Me know you gotta' man, fine as you are. Don't matter, Ya break free, ya get at me aright?" Freeing her arm of his grip, Nikki couldn't help but shake her head. He's so fine. She knew whatever the circumstances , she wouldn't be chilling at the Waffle House with him later that night.

Shawnte' had reparked the Escalade in the back of the club where she and Hectic, the number one Hip-Hop producer from Virginia Beach, met up. From the outside, the Cadillac truck's windows were fogged, and it wobbled on it's struts from left to right. Inside, Shawnte' had swallowed and ecstasy tablet 30 minutes prior. She started out sucking Hectic's dick, warm up or pre-sex she often called it. Now the two of them were butt naked. Hectic had penetrated her on the passenger side, with the leather seat reclined as far back as possible. For ten heart-pounding minutes, he plowed deep into her. Soon afterward, Shawnte' rode the famous producer like a jack rabbit, exploding with multiple orgasms. The seats were dripping with sweat and warm fluid that had run from her coochie down her legs. The guilt from fucking in Rocca's truck had crossed her mind for the third time "Fuck it! This nigga famous, I gotta get mine." Were the words that silently ran across her lips, justifying her disrespectful actions as she always did. She exploded once more.

"Hol' up Boo, I think the rubba broke." Hectic whispered, still, she didn't want to stop. Instead she slowed down and commenced a slow, hard, grind, making sure her insides felt all of him. Shawnte' opened her eyes and immediately stopped, realizing Hectic was giving her a hard stare.

"What?" she blurted out, widening her eyes as if to say you disturbing my groove. Shawnte' leaned down, pressing her firm breasts against his hairy chest, then wrapped her arms around his neck and head. Slowly, she arched her back, gently rising to remove her warm vaginal lips from around their new found playmate. The producer reached around her leg toward his tool "Damn, it popped." He spazed out, pushing his one night stand up and away from his body. "Chill, nigga, I'm on the nora shot, " she responded, lifting his arms from under her armpits. "I can remove myself the same way I got up here."

Hectic sensed the tension, "Baby, it ain't like dat. A nigga tryn'a be on point. You know how broads be trying to trap a brother off' n shit." "That sound good and all, but uh, I'm the one who handed you the condom,remember?"

Hectic thought about her words for a moment. Then apologized, "My bad, shorty, you was indeed on point. I like that" Shawnte' rolled her eyes, reaching for the glove compartment, "yeah, right! Just a second ago I was trying to trap you off." She sarcastically mocked , drying herself with a handful of balled up Burger King napkins. "What, you wanna stop?" " I thought you wanted to stop, Mr. Gots'ta stay on point!" Hectic smirked, admiring her sassiness. He pulled her sweaty body down over his, then pecked both of her lips simultaneously until her mouth opened. The two touched tongue tips for a second they locked their lips together, breathing through their noses. Shawnte' reached toward the back of her ass, grabbing his prize possession and gently worming his limpness up inside her. Soon he was rock hard and full of energy all over again.

Nikki had covered every dark corner of the club looking for Shawnte' and Princess. "She always do this to me." She pouted, scanning over the club goers in an attempt to recognize a hair-do or outfit that looked familiar.

Frustrated, Nikki let out a long sigh, she began walking toward the restrooms to see if Shawnte' was getting her groove on in one of the bathroom stalls.

"Hey, Nikki," someone yelled across the lobby, "Nikki." Nikki turned around, hoping to find Shawnte' hey Cle," she replied giving the stripper a look as if to ask What you callin' me for?"

"Princess told me to let you know that she left with Alize' and Lexus to do a private party for some ballers outta Atlanta." I can't believe this trifling bitch ! She pregnant, and gonna sell some pussy? She already don't even know who her babydaddy is, Nikki thought to herself, disgusted. "Cle, you wouldn't happen to have seen Shawnte' in here, have you?"

'"Did she drive Rocca's Escalade to the club?"

"Yeah, why?

"I saw his truck parked in the back of the club about twenty minutes ago."

"Thanks," Nikki replied, already walking away from the bumpy face stripper. She reached in the corner of her purse to grab a handful of change, stopping at the pay phone. Inserting fifty cents, she dialed home. As the phone rang she checked her watch again 12:55 am.

"Hello?"

"Aunt Linda it's me, I'm on my way."

"If you on ya way why you callin' here telling me you on ya way instead'a bein on ya way?"

"Whatever," Nikki replied, rolling her eyes. "Soon as I find Shawnte' I'm on my way."

"Why you ain't say that at first?"

Nikki paused, her face tightened. "Look, can you tell Rodney I'm on my way, please?"

"Yeah, I gotcha, I think he still up."

"No! no, I don't wanna talk to him. I don't feel like hearing his cryin' ass. Just tell'm I'll be there in a few, okay?"

"Will do, Nikki" Linda spoke quickly, hoping Nikki hadn't yet hung up.

"I'm still here."

"Check the restroom. She prob'ly in there with a dick in her mouth."

She giggled then answered, "I already did," hanging up in her aunt's ear. Nikki confidently made her way outside the club. She knew Shawnte' was in the truck. With whom , doing what, was the million dollar question. She probably talkin' to one of Rocca's homeboys, and parked in the back so the gossiping skanks won't have nothing to report to Ghetto gossip.com. Nikki spotted the truck parked in the rear corner. "Somebody is in there, good I'm ready to go." She said out loud, trying not to stumble on the loose, uneven pavement. As she approached the truck, she noticed it rocking to and from. Nikki walked around to the front of the Escalade, which faced the side of a dry cleaners next to the club. She couldn't believe what she was seeing. "Uwwh! This bitch crazy." She whispered under her breath after witnessing her girlfriend's ass bounce up and down on some guys dick. "If Rocca only knew, he'd kill her ten times over." She mumbled as she walked toward the front of the club.

I ain't gonna bother to interrupt. Even if they do stop on account of me, I ain't sittin on those funky ass seats. Instead of reentering the club, Nikki decided to stand outside and wait for any face that looked halfway familiar. It was 1:15 when Big Dave, a kid from high school walked outside.

"Big David. " Nikki yelled "Big David, can I get a ride home?"

"My name ain't David anymore, it's Big Dave, you got that? "Big Dave."

"Sorry, Big Dave," Nikki replied, batting her eyelashes purposely.

"Man! You lucky I used to like you." He uttered, strolling across the street, "C'mon!" Nikki quick stepped behind him to his flamboyant Navigator.

"Nice," she said just to show her appreciation for the ride.

"I know" It was a decent ride, but she had seen better, Girl, um s'pose to be on my way to the Waffle House." Big Dave pouted.

"Don't worry, dem bitches will still be there, trust me."

"Somebody has to be the one to sponsor their free meals." They both laughed in unison.

The giggles faded into the speakers as Big Dave pumped up 'Body Blow', the latest single by MC K.O. Nikki closed her eyes hoping to avoid the hardcore rapper's lyrics, but she couldn't escape the inevitable. Fifteen minutes later they were in Holland Park, turning onto Maryland Street, then to Griffin Avenue. Nikki didn't bother to thank him. She was too tired and sleepy to think about her manners.

She slowly stumbled out of the truck and made her way toward the house. Big Dave didn't pull off until she reached the front porch. She waved him to go ahead, and the Navigator cruised up Griffin Street as Nikki made her way in the house.

CHAPTER 4

Tony Gangsta stashed the bag of guns and bloody cash in his walk-in closet, where he stored most of his out dated wardrobe. He stripped himself of the clothes he had on, and then placed them in a small plastic garbage bag, ready for disposal. With only his Joe Boxers on, he quietly eased into the bedroom, being extra careful not to wake Trish.

Patrisha was Tony Gangsta's current girlfriend; he didn't love her as much as he loved Nikki. Sometimes, he didn't even like her especially since she resembled Nikki from head to toe. Even though Trish reminded him of his ex, he knew she was just a fill- in-the-blank for his heart. He only let her move in because he appreciated the way she always sucked up to him, playing the role of his sex slave. He craved the control.

Tony Gangsta had been sitting on the edge of the bed contemplating in the dark for about five minutes, when Trish pretended to wake up. She knew he was there. Whenever the back door opened, she would awaken. While Tony Gangsta scrambled around the house, Trish lay in bed with her eyes closed, wondering what he was doing and why he was so sneaky about it. "Boo C'mon, lay down with me. I Miss you, baby. Whatever it is bothering you, we can talk about it tomorrow." Tony Gangsta momentary ignored her sincerity "Tony" Trish whispered, in her sleepy voice, elevating her upper body with her elbows. "C'mon, get in bed."

"Go back to sleep, bitch," he snapped "This my house, Tony Gangsta

"DO WHATEVA" Tony Gangsta please! Right now, Tony Gangsta ain't sleepy" he angerly announced, referring to himself in third person as he rose off the bed and stomped toward the closet. Trish plopped her head back down on the pillow, yanking the comforter over her head as if she were going back to sleep. Tony Gangsta rambled through the closet, and grabbed a pair of Phat Farm denims and Coogi sweater, impatiently throwing the clothes on his body.

From the sound of things, Trish knew he was ready to leave out again. Tony Gangsta slipped into a pair of Air Force Ones, snatched a Pelle' jacket off the hanger and marched out of the bedroom. Trish leaped from under the covers and dashed out the bedroom.

"Tony, Tony!" she yelled, merely out of breathe, "Where you goin'? You jus got home."Tony stopped at the backdoor upon hearing her plea. "I been here all day, waiting to spend some time wit' chu. Now you gon'up and leave? Tony, you know I do any and everything you want, but something gots to give. You gotta start showing me alil' respect."

Tony Gangsta gave her a devious stare then smirked sarcastically. "You do anything for me, huh?"

"Yea, you know that baby!" Trish answered sincerely, gazing into his eyes.

"Well Trish, you know what I want 'chu to do right now?" A stupid look on her face, Trish didn't bother to reply, already knowing what he was gonna say. "I want you to get the hell outta my face." He cursed, sending her to the kitchen floor with a lightening fast backhand across her face. "Bitch! Who's you, my momma?" he yelled, towering over her. "I toldju', this my crib. Don' nobody question me in my house. Talk about respect? You need to be showing me a little!" he finished, kicking her across the rib cage.

Bleeding from the mouth, Trish laid on the kitchen floor, balled up in the fetal position, holding her arm around her stomach. Tony Gangsta pulled out his pistol and pointed it down toward her body. "Um goin' to see my babymomma. You gotta problem with dat' shorty? I ain't think so, bitch." With that, he tucked the nine millimeter pistol by his side, gave her another wicked stare, then left out the door.

As soon as tony Gangsta jumped in his Jaguar, he shoved the K.O. CD into the disc played. He turned it to the "All Out" track, then sped out the driveway down Roosevelt Road. As he listened to the lyrics of his favorite song, he couldn't help but think about Killa , his body slumped over the passenger seat, in a river of blood. "Damn Killa," he mumbled, trying to hold back his tears. He needed to confide in someone he felt comfortable with, and that someone was Nikki. Nikki will understand how much I need her once I tell her about Killa, he thought to himself, lip syncing the lyrics of the song he'd subconsciously placed on repeat mode.

Slowly, Trish managed to make her way to the bathroom. As she wiped the blood from her mouth, her ears caught the harmonic chirp of her cellphone. With a cold washcloth pressed on her lip and an arm wrapped around her rib cage, she stumbled into the bedroom, wondering who might be calling after one o'clock in the morning. Maybe it's Tony calling me to apologize. "Hello?"

"Ay girl, it's me Angel. I got some bad news. Porkchop was jus' killed along with five other people at Big Ike's house 'bout forty-five minutes ago."

Trish's heart fell to her stomach. She couldn't believe the words Angel cries out to her. "My brother dead? You sure it's my brother? What happened" Trish screamed out.

"Look Trish, this crackhead named Londa said she saw Killa and Tony Gangsta make off in a dark colored van. Then I jus' found out through Mary-Anne that they jus' discovered Killa's body in the mini-van at the hospital. "

"D-Do my momma know?" Trish slowly stuttered out.

"Yeah, she know. She already in Churchhill. Is Tony there, girl? Do you think-"

Trish hung up, then burst into tears. She couldn't picture her boyfriend robbing and killing her only brother. "Get a grip, girl. Calm down, calm down." She whispered to herself, generating mental strength. Her mind was halfway at ease, but her body was trembling as if it were 20 degrees below. Quickly, she ran into the guest room walk-in closet to see what her man had hidden. In a matter of seconds, Trish was staring at a bag of guns and bloody money. She pictured the blood on the stacks of cash being her brother's, and pain instantly turned into anger. She grabbed one of the guns from the bag. With only her night gown and her body, she raced into the bedroom to retrieve her slippers, cell phone, and mink coat. "Um'ma kill that bastard myself!" She mumbled through tears that made their way down to the corners of her mouth. Trish marched out the front door. Slamming it locked she stormed through the freezing wind to her Honda. She leaped into the car, closing the door on a piece of her night gown and coat, then headed to the other side of Highland Park to the street she knew Nikki lived somewhere on. As she drove in silence, her mind raced at full speed. It was coming together for her. She realized that Tony Gangsta was no drug dealer, he was the Home Invader who'd been terrorizing the Carolina states. The thought of him using her to get close to her brother has crossed her mind a hundred times already. She couldn't believe how her life had fallen apart in an hour's time. I honestly thought he loved me...

Trish pulled over to the side, parking in front of a residential home, and broke down in tears. She didn't know how to be angry at the moment. "It's all my fault!" she cried out dropping her hands on the top of the steering wheel.

Resting her head in between, soon the tears swelled her eyes and clear mucus dripped from her nose. Trish couldn't help but blamed herself for introducing Tony Gangsta to Porkchop.

"I should've known. It's all my fault. Now he's dead!" she continued screaming, throwing a fit as she began pounding on the steering wheel with the bottom of her fists.

Trish reached down in her pocket, realizing her coat was caught in the door, then opened it to pull the damaged coat and gown inside. She grabbed the cellular from her pocket, dialed a few numbers, then wiped her tears, attempting to regain her composure. "Hello, 911." She said, adjusting the rough static in her throat. "I'd like to report a murder."

"Who's been murdered ma'am?" the dispatcher calmly asked as if she were taking a fast food order.

"My brother."

"Hello?"

"Yo this Tony Gangsta. Put Nikki on the phone."

"First of all, Nikki ain't here. Secondly, don' be callin' her 1:30 in the morning, disrespecting our family. And third, since we on the subject of respect, have some respect for ya self. Calling here pretending to wanna talk to your nine month old daughter ain't flyin'. To be frank, my brother, it's path-"

"Nigga!" Tony Gangsta snapped, cutting Rodney's lecture short. "Who the fuck you think you talking to, pussy! Don'chu know I'll kayo that ass to rest and ka-lick O's in that chest, you punk ass bi-"

Unimpressed by the MC K.O. lyrics Tony had recited word for word, Rodney hung up the telephone in his ear. "What a fuck'n clown! He really think's he a gangster. Rodney said, sarcastically laughing at the thought as he went into the bathroom to take a piss.

Tony Gangsta just parked his new X36 four houses down from Nikki's home. He couldn't fathom Rodney ever hanging up on him. He promised to kill the faggot on a later date. For now, he just wanted to talk to Nikki. There, on the dim lit street, he lit a cigarette, something he hasn't done in a long while. He was sitting in his car puffing smoke, when he noticed Big Dave's ride pull up in front of the house. "What's that all about?" he asked himself, watching Nikki make her way up to the front door.

Nikki quietly made her way toward the backroom. "Sure smell funky in here." She mumbled wondering what Linda had cooked after she departed. When she opened the bedroom door and noticed Rodney sitting up waiting for her. She ignored the angry look on his face and immediately kicked her shoes off onto the carpet. "I'm glad you up boo. I gotta talk to you about something. Was gonna wait 'til tomorrow," she let out a deep sigh, "but I can't wait. Its been on my mind all night long, and I gotta get it out in the open right now!" Nikki concluded for a moment, struggling to get out of her tight skirt.

"Well, that's kinda funny, cause I wanna talk to you too." Rodney's tone made Nikki uncomfortable. "Tony Gangsta called…I told'em how I felt, and I think you should do the same."

"What did you say to him Rodney?"

"I put that nigga in his place." He answered, scratching his testicles. "Now it's your turn."

Nikki shrugged, then sighed. "You jus' don't get it. Tony will kill you dead."

"No, you don't get it!" Rodney shot back at her. "I'm sick and tired of that punk muthafucka dictating you. All I'm trying to say is," Rodney paused, losing his train of thought as the phone rang.

"Hello." Nikki answered.

"Yo, I need to talk to you right now! It's important, Killa's dead." Before Nikki could respond, Rodney lunged forward, snatching the phone out her hand. He knew it was Tony by the look on her face.

"Look here nigga! What I just tell you?"

Nikki snatched the phone back from Rodney, halting him with the palm of her hand. 'I'm a handle this' her lips spoke silently. She put the receiver up to her ear, while taking a long sigh. "Tony, I'm sorry about Killa, but there's nothing I can do for you. I know you need someone to confide in, but I'm with Rodney now."

"Let me get this straight. In so many words, you sayin' fuck me, huh?"

"I really don't mean it like that, but uh-"

"But what?" Tony Gangsta snapped into his cellphone.

"I'm sayin', if you wanna take it like that, then so be it."Rodney was standing over Nikki, listening to the words Tony Gangsta barked at her. Out of frustration, he yelled at Nikki. "Fuck that wangster-wanna-be-gangster. Hang up on him." Silence. "I said hang up!" Toniesha was awakened by the aggressive tone in Rodney's voice. The last thing Tony heard was his little girl hollering at the top of her lungs before Nikki hung up. He looked outside, scanning the landscape of the rectangular-shaped brick home. Nikki's house was rather plain. From the outside, there was no driveway, just grass, with the exception of two bushes on each side of the porch.

"I changed my mind." he angrily snorted. "I think Rodney's ass will be dealt wit' right fuckin' now!" Puffing on the cigarette, he reached into the glove compartment to retrieve a pair of leather gloves. He pressed the mute button on his radio three times, shifted the manual gear into neutral, then tapped the cruise control button to engage his stash compartment. "Shit!" he barked. It didn't work the first time. In fact, it never worked the first try, and he hated that. All that did was make Tony Gangsta's blood boil over the top. He repeated the process a second time, and moments later, the armrest slowly rose up. It shifted forward until he could see a mini pit between the two seats. He placed the gun tucked in his wrist on the passenger seat, then reached inside the stash pit to retrieve two nickel-plated Smith&Wesson's with iced out grips. Each 9mm had $80,000 worth of diamonds in them, and he admired the beauty of the two pimped out burners for a moment.

Soon, the adrenaline began to rush through his body, and a feeling of tremendous power came over him. He gave one of the gleaming pistols a hard kiss. "It's a special occasion." He said, demonically, staring at the guns. "That's why I chose you two to dance with the devil ta'night." He hastily checked the chamber of each piece, then grabbed some additional clips. Placing the pistol in the stash pit, he closed it by hitting the seat warmer control. Tony Gangsta stared at the house once more, then looked up the street, firing up another cigarette. He then checked his rearview mirror, scratching his forehead, something he did when he was extremely angry. He let out a deep, smoke filled sigh, then opened the car door. Tony Gangsta didn't realize how hard he slammed the door and really didn't care. Slowly, he advanced toward the house. After he passed by the first home, he drew the bling stingers down to his side, hurrying in step. Once he reached Nikki's yard, his teeth gritted together and he grimaced from the anger and cold wind that smacked up against it. He didn't bother to look up and down the street again. With the warm air he breathed out into the night, he resembled a raging bull the way he took off running up the walkway. Both guns were now aimed forward. As he approached the steps of the porch, he overheard his daughter

Still crying. Tony Gangsta leaped up over the three steps, then plunged his foot in the door, nearly kicking it off its hinges.

Aside from the television, there was no other lighting in the front room. The loud boom alerted Linda, who was asleep on the couch. She jumped from the sofa, spitting curse words at Tony Gangsta, but he heard nothing she said. He was in the zone. Linda lunged at his body, hoping to force him back out the front door. With the pistol in his left hand he delivered a vicious backhand across her jaw, splashing sprinkles of blood on the carpet and across the television screen, and Linda crashing down into the coffee table. Before Tony Gangsta could make his way down the dark hallway, Rodney had run from the bedroom up the hallway to see what all the ruckus was about. When he reached the front room, Tony Gangsta welcomed him with two slugs to the abdomen and left side of his upper chest, ripping the panther tattoo clear off his arm. Rodney stumbled backwards into the wall, knocking a picture of Nikki's parents down to the floor, his body followed behind it.

Tony Gangsta towered over him with his arms crossed behind his back. A loud commotion resonated from down the hall in Nikki's bedroom. He glanced away from Rodney and down the hallway. "I'll be there in a minute to tuck you in too, Bitch!" he glanced back down, still admiring his work.

"Look, Rod, ya bleedin', Nik'ga!" Tony Gangsta huffed, sucking his teeth afterward. "Look like you jus' been fucked ma'mam. Real good too! I told you if my lil' girl tell me you been fucking with her again, I was gonna kill you. Didn't I tell you dat? Huh nigga?" he yelled, causing Rodney to flinch.

"You sick bastard," Rodney coughed out through his bloody mouth, "ya daughter can't even talk."

"Shut up!" Tony Gangsta roared, then began again in a calm tone. "Damn boy, you a tall mu'fucka! What'chu, bout six-six, six-seven?"

Dying slowly, Rodney didn't respond, his eyes simply followed Tony Gangsta's every word. "I bet'cha you be jammin' like T-Mac huh? How bout 'cha defense. How that defensive games these days?" He asked with a deep exaggerated laugh. "You blockin' niggas shots? Tall as you is, I bet'cha throw a nigga jumpshot into the cheap seats." Tony Gangsta uncrossed his arms from behind his back, pointing the nine millimeters down at Rodney's torso. The sarcastic smirk disappeared and he began digging his teeth into his bottom lip. "What I really wanna know is...can-you-block-this?" he began firing rounds into Rodney's upper both with both weapons.

Nikki knew that Tony Gangsta would kill her. She quickly grabbed Toniesha from the bassinet and tried to escape out of one of the windows. After realizing the first window was stuck from dried paint, she began to panic. Bumping into everything, she ran to the other window, blocked by her long dresser. Quickly, Nikki swung her arm over top of the dresser, knocking all of it's contents to the floor. She placed the baby on the bed, then climbed the dresser, knee first, trying to force the window open.

With every second that past by, Nikki began to panic more. Looking back towards the door to see if he had burst through, she prayed that Rodney had wrestled down her babydaddy and shot him. She knew the chances of that happening were slim to none, because Rodney would have informed her that he was alright. Once she realized that the second window could not be pried oped, gunshots rang out. Her nerves withered, jumping with every BOOM she heard.

Terrified of the worst, Nikki began sobbing, her cries graduated to screams. "Somebody help me! Please, please help me!" She screamed, looking outside the first window. She stopped hollering after noticing a squad car pull up in front of the house. For a second, a sense of relief came over her until she heard Aunt Linda scream.

While diamonds vibrated loose from the duel action of the guns, Linda regained consciousness. Slowly, she lifted her bloody figure from the shattered glass, and staggered over to the end table. Just as Tony Gangsta lifted his feet over his first victim, Linda swung a ceramic lamp at him, shattering it on the back of his head and sending blood misting through the air. Tony Gangsta was temporarily stunned, and fell to one knee, using the corner of the hall and front room wall to maintain balance.

Just as Linda started toward the kitchen to retrieve a butcher knife, Tony Gangsta reached backwards, snatching her legs from under her. She screamed out in terror after being caught off guard, thinking that she knocked him unconscious. Tony Gangsta stood up, now facing Linda, who was lying on a carpet full of broken glass and fresh blood. He reached toward the back of his head to assess the damage. Tony Gangsta's hand shot forward into view. With his thumb, he scratched his forehead raw.

"Fuck you! Punk ass pussy!" Linda shouted. "If you gon' kill me nigga, then do it!" Tony Gangsta didn't bother to entertain the small talk. He fired two slugs between her legs, ripping her pussy wide open, then fired a round straight through her heart.

"TONY GANGSTER! THE PLACE IS SURROUNDED! COME OUT WITH YOUR HANDS UP!" A police officer yelled through a bull horn.

He darted to the window, peeping through the mini blind's seams, only to have one of the police blind his view with a spotlight. Tony Gangsta ran down the hallway, forcing open the bedroom door with the weight of his shoulder. When he entered the bedroom, Nikki was standing near the window. Quickly, he chopped the wall, flicking the light switch, then pointed the pistol at Nikki as he hurried to the window to block any view the police had on him. He then walked towards Nikki, watching her body tremble from the sight of blood and sweat that ran down his face

Tony Gangsta sensed fear, but was in no mood to play. He picked her up by the hair after she folded herself down on the bed. Terror overwhelmed her face as Tony Gangsta gave her horrifying details of what had just transpired on the other side of her door. Tony Gangsta stared Nikki in the eyes for the last time, forcing her lips against his. She stood there with her arms down at her side, flinching at every peck of her ex-lover's lips. He worked his way down Nikki's chin, groping her all over her neck. But soon, the baby resumed crying from the deep and proper voices that sounded off outside.

The SWAT team surrounded the house, Tony Gangsta knew his reign of terror would soon come to an end. He released the grip of hair held firmly in hand, and brought it to the front of Nikki's face. Tony Gangsta octopused his leather glove around Nikki's jaw, covering her nose with his middle and index finger.

"The penalty for betrayal...is death!" He angrily whispered, looking away from her toward the window. "You my babymomma, bitch! You will always belong to me, even your soul!" He concluded, shoving her down to the bed with a forceful push of the face. Before Nikki could say a word, Tony Gangsta aimed, then fired, striking Nikki in the center of the forehead. After the back of her head exploded with a wave of thick blackish-reddish blood, he didn't bother to shoot again.

Slowly, he walked over to the other side of the bed to attend to his little girl. He began crying as he cradled her in his arms. Tony Gangsta couldn't believe he just killed Nikki, the love of his life. "There's no reason for you to go on living, Toniesha. Don' worry, mommy gon' take care of you in heaven. I'm sorry baby girl, but daddy won't be joining you. There's another place for me." He somberly cried. "Now go ta' sleep. It's gon' be ar'ight." He whispered to his daughter with his leather-covered hand wrapped tightly over her nose and mouth. "Go to sleep now."

By the time he made his way to the front room, Toniesha was at peace. Delicately, he plopped her body up on the sofa as if she were still alive, then released two empty clips before slapping a fresh twelve in each one.

"If um'ma die tonight," Tony Gangsta promised himself while staring at the ceiling, "I'm taking some mo people wit me." He grabbed his daughter from the sofa, walked over to the front door, opening it just enough to toss Toniesha's corpse outside onto the frozen lawn. The police quickly retrieved the little infant child's body.

"Did you see that, he just threw a baby out the door like it was garbage." The sarge said in disbelief.

"Sarge, the baby's dead. But there's no sign of gunshot wounds, sir."

"That's it!" the sergeant snapped. "We're going in."

Tony Gangsta knew once they realized his daughter was dead, they'd storm the house as he wanted them to. He unplugged the television, then dragged Linda's body against the wall, beside the TV, where he sat, using her lifeless body as a shield. For five minutes, he sat quietly in the car, the only light being the red and blue sirens that reflected from the window. He knew it was almost time. Just as he started to doze, windows shattered all over the house. The front door flew entirely from it frame to the floor. The first three SWAT team officers came through the door, and two more entered through the back. Another two came through the windows. Tony Gangsta shot all five SWAT members, killing four instantly. Before long, police swarmed from the kitchen, the bedroom, and the front entrance.

From outside, exchanged gunfire could be heard by Trish and other spectators, as the house illuminated with aggressive gunplay. Tony Gangsta had taken six slugs, while Linda's body absorbed over two hundred. He had run out of ammunition in the 30 seconds of gunfire, and pretended to be dead. When one of the cops got close enough, he snatched his machine gun, killing him and others.

Tony Gangsta was bleeding from the mouth as the slugs set fire to his inner torso. He felt himself weakening by the second. "I'm dying." He laughed, coughing up a mouthful of blood. Still firing with a jolt of strength, he stood to his feet after tossing aside his human vest and began charging the officers who'd taken cover. "Awhhhhh!" He screamed demonically, capping the machine gun off. In seconds, bullets pierced his body from every angle. Still he didn't fall, only spun in circles, spitting rounds into the ceiling. Tony Gangsta didn't descend until his weapon had run out of ammo. Once the gun double-clicked, he slumped to his knees, dropping the automatic. "All Out!" Were his last words before collapsing to the floor.

SWAT cautiously approached him with their guns drawn. One checked his neck for a pulse. "He's gone sir." The officer with the radio then relayed the message outside.

"Check the others."

"I don't think any of these people are alive, sir." Another said, shaking his head.

"Check anyway, Goddamnit!" the arriving lieutenant ordered, disgusted by the crime scene. He then headed out the front door, giving the signal that everyone inside the house was dead. Trish dropped to her knees, bursting into tears. "It's all my fault!"

"Wait Lieutenant," a police officer yelled, appearing in the doorway of the crime scene, "Lieutenant! We have a survivor!"

CHAPTER 5

Keith Osbourne had been in Rock Church for nearly two hours before temporarily dozing off into a light nap. He was awakened by the sound of an organ that chanted over the singing congregation. Keith quickly re-gained focus, careful not to draw attention to himself from the churchgoers who sat beside him. It was the fourth week he'd attended the well integrated congregation. It didn't matter that the pastor was an elderly white female, he was happy to be in the house of the Lord.

Rock was the sixth church he attended in Tidewater within the year. The pastors from the other five said he was no longer welcome because he was considered by many to be the Devil. Sitting there listening to Pastor McCoy give her sermon on greed, he felt someone watching him.

Keith glanced over his left shoulder , pretending to stretch his neck, to find a dark skinned female cutting at him. It's no way she could recognize me. Or has she already? He asked himself, turning back toward the front of the church. Keith bowed his head with the rest of the churchgoers as Pastor McCoy lead prayer through the podium's microphones.

Closing his eyes, lowering his head to his knees, Keith said a prayer of his own. "Dear heavenly Father, I come to you as humbly as I know how, and dear God, I wanna thank you, thank you for blessing me with another glorious day. And, Father, God I wanna thank you for blessing me with a nice home and lovely wife. I know Father, that without you nothing is possible, and Father please give me the strength to deal with those who view me as an outcast. You know my heart. I'm no devil, I'm just an entertainer." He paused, wiping his tears from his cheek, before concluding. "In his heavenly name, I pray….Amen."

Keith's head was still in the prayer position when his two-way vibrated. He slipped his hand into the breast pocket of his Armani blazer, pulling it out halfway in the open. Careful and quietly, he flipped the device open: 911-come- home -911. Keith folded the gadget, showing it back into his coat pocket. He glanced around to see if anyone had noticed his rude activity.

"Forgive me Father," he mumbled under his breath as he stood grazing past the churchgoers who's heads were still bent forward, ignoring a hard stare an old round woman dressed in a big multi colored hat had given him. Once he reached the aisle, Keith pulled the sleeves of his olive pinstripe suit and stealthly hurried out the corridors. He began trotting though the parking lot of cars to Dock road. He ran four blocks to Roger Avenue, where his new Bently was parked. While he ran, worst case scenarios passed through his mind. He hoped no one was dead or his newly purchased home hadn't burnt down. As his tie flapped over his shoulder from the wind, Keith Osbourne wished he had his cellular with him. On Sunday's he would turn the thing off and hide it away in the nightstand drawer. He didn't think about business, especially on his cellphone which rang constantly, 24 hours a day.

As Keith approached his ride he pulled the keys from his pocket. Pointing the car remote at his Rolls Royce he ignited the engine, and disarmed the twenty thousand dollar alarm system. He jumped in the car, jamming the key into the ignition so he could put the gear in drive.

"Please activate voice sensor, or I will alert the authorities." The female voice of the computerized alarm system repeated.

"Darnit, almost forgot." He whispered, snatching off his Gucci sunglasses and thick beard he often used as a disguise."Keith Osbourne!" he yelled into the security microphone.

"Welcome back, Mr. Osbourne." The female voice replied before shutting itself off.

"Whatever." Keith shifted gears then pulled off into traffic, racing towards Virginia Beach Boulevard. He contemplated on whether he should stop at a nearby payphone to call his wife or continue home. He convinced himself that he'd rather learn of the emergency when he arrived home.

Ten minutes later, Keith was entering Thurgood Estates, where his $4,000,000 mansion resided. It was almost the size of a grocery store, and rested on six acres of land by a calm lake. The front yard was decorated with marble statues, along with a dozen palm trees he had flown in from Miami. There was a huge driveway, two cars wide that formed a horseshoe. The front entrance was decorated in 30-foot high, gold-trimmed columns, which complimented a double door entrance, made from mahogany wood.

Keith leaped from the car, dashing up the platinum colored porch. Keys in hand. The door flew open before he could insert it in the lock.

"Hey baby!" Sheila said, greeting him with a light peck on his lips.

Confused and almost out of breath, he stared at his wife for a moment to make sure everything was okay. "Sheila, you did page me 911, right?"

"Oh! That's why you lookin' all crazy and stuff." She replied, grabbing his hand to lead him to the conference room. "Yeah! I wanted to let you know that me and Kayla were going down to Atlanta to see momma for a few days. I figured you was gon' be all tied up in the office with Hectic and Tim."

Keith Osbourne had met Sheila in Atlanta a year and a half ago during a promo tour. She worked at a local hip-hop station as Radio One's top promotional director. Sheila was a beautiful Hispanic female, with stunning curves and a smile that would make even the strongest-minded man fold in his hand. Her long, curly hair and hazel eyes easily captured the heart of Keith Osbourne, known to the rest of the world as MC K.O., aka Killa K, Kayo King, and his newest alias, The Devil, from the blazin' hot track, 'The Devil Going to Church'.

Sheila was thirty years old, three and a half years older that her newly wedded husband. Her five year old daughter Kayla was the daughter of Psycho, CEO of Psycho Records, the largest rap label in the south. She had been married to Psycho for two years before he was sent to prison from seven on conspiracy to bootleg his own artist's albums. Sheila divorced him only because Psycho advised her too. Three years later and two weeks ago, she wed and became Mrs. Osbourne.

"Beloved, I don' mind you spending time with ma dukes and 'em. I'm just wondering why in God's name you paged me 911, nearly scaring me half to death, to tell me that."

"If only yo' thug fans knew how sensitive you was, you wouldn't be selling albums like that white candy fellow." She quipped, rolling her eyes with a smile to let her husband know she was teasing. "I paged you because Alfred is here." She explained as they opened the door to the conference room where Alfred patiently waited. Keith gave Alfred the hawkeye. If anybody knew how seriously he treasured his Sunday afternoons, it was his goofy, Ivy League smiling road manager.

"I'm sorry to intrude Kayo."

"It's Keith. How many times I toldju?" he yelled across the long table as he sat down.

“Keith, I’m sorry to bother you, but I was just informed late last night that you reached the 15,000,000 mark in sales. That’s right baby, you’re 15 times platinum.”

Keith reclined in his chair, absorbing his road managers words. “Um the greatest rapper of all time, huh?”

“That’s right Kay- I mean Keith. Everybody is buying your album, even the people who don’t like you. Isn’t that just great?”

Keith didn’t reply. He thought about Alfred’s comment, and gave it instant evaluation. “Why do people who hate MC K.O. purchase his LP, Al?” he asked with a lack of concern.

“That’s easy,” Alfred countered, cracking a half-smile, “to hear what you’re going to rap about next. That shit about sacrificing the preacher in front of the whole church and drinking his blood of the lamb or however you said it, has everybody from East to West and in between listening to MC K.O. You’re an icon in the making, I promise ya.” Alfred said, emphasizing the extent of MC K.O.’s new stardom.

Not amused by his manager’s pep talk, he changed the subject. “Touring, when do we start touring? Matter fact, who’s touring wit me this summer?”

“I’m working on that, Keith.” He replied, unaware and caught off guard. “Uh, I was thinking R. Kelly, maybe your and him could tour together, but I didn’t know how to ask you, considering his dilemma in Chi-town.”

“Damn right! Ill tour with the R. His music is still off the heezy. People still copping his shit, and besides, I saw the tape. The girl rode dude like a pro.”

“Whether it’s him or not, it’s obvious that she’s been around a block or ten.” Alfred added, chuckling.

“Call ‘I’m up, and get back with me.” Alfred reached for the phone, only to be halted by MC K.O. “Whatchu doin’ goofy man?”

“I’m making the call.”

“Make the call! Just not from here. Today’s Sunday remember?”

“Oh! Almost forgot,” Alfred said raising up from the table, “no play on Sunday!”

“That’s right, Alfy. No play on Sundays.” The two of them exited the conference room for the front door.

“Man, this place is really beautiful.” Alfred whispered, admiring the huge statues and African paintings on the walls.

"Thanks." K.O. replied, walking proudly, locking his hands behind his back. "Sheila picked out and decorated all forty rooms here. Hell, a three bedroom would've done me just fine. To be honest, half'a these rooms I haven't even been in yet. Besides my bedroom, studio, Jacuzzi, and the indoor basketball court, I couldn't tell you what was in the others. This is what Sheila wanted so she got it."

"That's love." Alfred declared.

"No doubt, I love Sheila, for her, I'll go all out." Keith emphasized, opening the two front doors with a serious look on his face. "Al, I'll be recording over the next few days, so get at me Thursday." Alfred nodded walking to his car. "I am really slippin'" Keith mumbled to himself, closing the front entrance. He didn't recall seeing Alfred's Lexus parked on the other side of the horseshoe.

Keith brushed away the oversight to give thought to the 15 million mark he'd just been informed of. He had always viewed himself as the best pound for pound lyricist in the world, even before he went platinum. All the record sales had done was prove him right. He smiled to himself as he ascended the wide flight of steps.

Sheila had her designer luggage outside the bedroom, ready for departure. She peeked out of Kayla's room to make sure Keith was still in his study. Once she saw the coast was clear, she pulled out her Atlanta based wireless phone and called her mother, Betty Mae. "Hey Ma, I'll be stoppin' through there tonight."

"I know, I know, but you won't be staying for the night."

"Betty Mae, I ain't trying to hear it today. I'm dropping you off a grand. Just do what you do, when, and if he call. And I'll do me."

"Lil' girl, better get that sassiness off your tongue, fo' I reach through this here phone and pop you one good time. Sheila, one day, them games you play gon' catch up wit' chu."

"I gotta go ma. See you in a few hours." She concluded, hanging up the phone without saying good-bye.

Sheila pressed the power button until the fluorescent screen went blank, then dropped it in the side pouch of her Gucci purse. "Remember what I told you Kayla." She whispered, setting her daughter between her thighs as they sat on the little bed. "Make sure you say 'I love you daddy', okay?" Sheila coached, placing barrettes in her daughters hair.

"I don't like saying nat. Besides, Psycho's my daddy." Kayla pouted, folding her arms extra tight.

"Stop moving!" Sheila snapped, then toned her voice back down an octave before speaking again. "What did mommy tell you? It makes him feel good when you say nice things like that and-"

"I know mommy," Kayla interrupted, "it butters him soft, so I can get anything I want."

"That's my girl! You so smart and pretty. You gon' be a Diva one day, jus' like mommy." Sheila replied, placing the last of the barrettes in the child's hair before kissing her on the cheek. "Check your backpack, make sure your toothbrush and toothpaste are in there, and double check to see that you have five pairs of underclothes."

Before she could say she already had, Sheila advised her to check again. She had begun to straighten up Kayla's room when Keith appeared in the doorway. She didn't notice at first, because he hadn't made a sound. He simply stood there, admiring how beautiful his wife was. Often Keith asked himself how an average to near ugly guy like himself was lucky enough to marry a queen of such caliber.

"Hey baby, didn't see you standing there." Sheila said, wondering how long he'd been standing there.

"Sorry, I got caught up in the moment, admiring you and how lucky I am. I know I tell you ten times a day, but I love you Sheila. You make my day brighter and my heart smile. When I look into your eyes like I'm doing know, I feel the need to wrap you up in my arms."

Keith opened his arms, inviting his wife to come to him. Soon after, their tongues began fighting as if they were kissing for the first time, their arms locked around one another.

Kayla came running out the bathroom. "Yuck, das nastee!" she blurted out, covering her eyes with her hands only to peep through her little fingers. Slowly, they loosened the seal between their lips, gradually and reluctantly serenading. "So what time does your flight leave?"

"5:15"

"That's two hours from now."

"Yeah, that's why I'm hurrying up."

"I was hoping we could you know, Sundays is our day baby."

"Keith, don' worry, everyday will be our day." Sheila knew how to get Keith to smile.

He knew it too. For some odd reason,, he liked that part about her. "You know what to say, don' chu?" Sheila responded with a smile as she walked past him, out of Kayla's room and down the long hallway to their master suite. Kayla marched closely behind her. Keith couldn't resist giving his stepdaughter a long stare. Sheila always said that her child was also his child. He loved Kayla as his own. Still, he wanted to father his own child. The thought of becoming a daddy one day crossed his mind everyday of his life. Each year that passed by lessened his chances of fatherhood.

When he was 12 years old, Keith was accidentally shot during a gun battle at a corner store near the Washington Park Projects he stayed in. The bullet had struck him in the groin area, grazing his testicles, and doctors advised his mother that there was no chance of Keith ever having children.

Just three years ago, he decided to get a second opinion. The physician informed Keith that his chances had changed from impossible to about five percent, probable due to the fact that he'd nurtured his body with lots of Vitamin C over the years. After the doctors told him it was going to take a miracle, he began praying for one daily. Sometimes he wondered if the child he asked God for was indeed Kayla. His daze ended by the sound of the phone ringing.

"Get that baby. I'm in the tub!" Sheila's voice echoed from the bedroom-sized bathroom. "Keith, did you-"

"I heard you sweetie. I got it already." He yelled back as he reached toward the crystal phone in the hall. "Hello. Hi mom, of course I'm coming for dinner, just as soon as I drop Sheila and Kayla off at the airport. Okay, ma, I'll tell'er. Love you too." Keith made his way through the bedroom door.

"Tell her what?" Sheila asked, curiously.

"That was Arleen."

"I know." Sheila answered, standing in the two-man jet-stream marble hot tub. "What did she say?" Sheila asked again, looking impatient.

"She said, you should keep your behind home sometimes. And it won't kill you to come over for Sunday dinner."

Sheila rolled her eyes, unwrapping a towel from around her hair. Keith gently placed his hands around her petite waist, pulling her naked body close to his. Before she could respond, he placed his mouth against hers.

Instantly, she gave in. Keith gradually glided his tongue down her neck, nibbling on her shoulder. Soon, Sheila began to pant, a sensuous moan following every breath. From her shoulder he worked his warm mouth down to her breasts, catching steamed drops of water hanging from her inch long nipples on the tip of his tongue.

Keith took charge, bending Sheila over backwards. He lowered her to the floor with his arm wrapped around her waist. Sheila lay dripping wet, with her eyes closed and legs wide open. Keith hunched over her naked body, planting soft kissed across her navel area. He used one hand for support, the other to unzip his fly, unleashing his now stiff muscle. "C'mon baby." She cried out out impatiently, anxious to feel him inside her. "Uuuuungh!"

Just as Keith penetrated the hairy lips of Sheila's treasure, a knock came over the bathroom door. "Mom-meee. Are you ready to go yet?" Sheila quickly regained her composure. "I'm comin', I mean, uh, ill be right there. Go to your room, mommy coming out with no clothes on."

"I've seen you with no clothes on before." Kayla innocently replied.

"Go in your room and wait for me anyway!"

"Ohhkay, but hurry mommy. I'm hungwee!"

"I guess that's that." Sheila whispered in despair.

"Yeah! But I will tell you one thing, I will be here waiting to finish you off when you get back."

An hour later, Keith was pulling in the departure entrance of Norfolk international. He grabbed the luggage from the truck and checked the girls in at the luggage booth. "You sure you don't want me to walk you to the terminal?"

"I'm positive!!" Sheila blurted. "Last time you walked through the airport with us, this place turned into an autograph session." Just as her sentence ended, two white girls approached, interrupting their conversation.

"Uh, excuse me?" the taller one politely began. "I was wondering if me and my friend, Beasly, could have your autograph." Keith glances away from them, staring at his wife for a moment.

"See? I told'ju." Sheila sarcastically remarked before he returned his attention to the two females.

"No doubt, MC K.O. will go all out fa da fans." He answered, changing his tone of voice to the thuggish rapper that he was. Sheila grabbed Kayla's hand and helped her on the terminal ramp, then slammed the door to distract her husband for a moment.

Keith turned around, acknowledging her jealous gesture. "I love you babe!"

"I love you too." Sheila replied, cutting her eyes at the two horny white chicks. "Call you when I get to Betty Mae's house."

"Is that your wife, MC K.O.?" one of the females asked. "She's beautiful!"

"She is, isn't she?" he agreed, giving the ink pen back to the other girl.

"If you're ever interested in a foursome, call us." The taller woman offered with a giggle. "WE promise a good time."

Keith smirked at the ladies. "Thanks, but no thanks. Don't think the misses would be interested." He replied, walking from the truck to the driver's side of the car. He opened the door, then gave his fans another farewell wave.

"Damn it feels good to be appreciated!" he mumbled to himself as he exited the terminal. "I'm Em-Cee-Kayoo, the baddest rapper since Tupac and Biggie!" he shouted out, grabbing his clover sunshades from the armrest. He popped the Isley Brothers CD in the disc player and sang along the whole way back to Park Place, where his mother lived.

CHAPTER 6

It had been two weeks since the Tony Gangsta massacre had taken place. The last of the funerals had ended yesterday, but the city was still in mourning. Shawnte' hadn't been able to hold any food down on her stomach since learning of Rocca's death. After his funeral she'd barely slept, and heavy bags had built up under her eyes from constant tear shed.

She had just walked in her Henrico apartment when the phone rang. Setting some cranberry juice she'd purchased from a nearby convenience store on top of the coffee table, Shawnte' made her way to the kitchen to retrieve the cordless. She wasn't expecting any calls and didn't care to talk. Still, something told her to answer. "Hello." She drones, sounding half asleep.

"Ah, yes! Deese is Doctor Wang Tin from the medical center in Richmond. Is Shawnte' Battle in?" Shawnte's heart dropped, weakening her knees, as tears raced down her face. "Oh no, my girl has finally died." She thought.

Shawnte' paused for a second, wiping the tears off her cheek with the back of her wrist. "Yes, this is Shawnte' Battle speaking. How can I help you?" she finally replied, her voice cracking with every word. "I'm calling to inform you that Nichole Wallace has come out of her coma." Tears of joy sprang from her eyes, swallowing the once tears of sorrow. She tried to speak into the receiver, but her mouth would not allow any words to come out. "Mees Battle, are you still there?"

"Yes, yes I'm still here doctor!" she answered, full of excitement.

"She can now receive visitors too."

"Thank you doctor." Shawnte' replies, hanging up in his ear.

Shawnte' had been to the hospital everyday since Nikki entered her coma, only to be denied visitation. 'Only immediate family' is what the nurses told her. Shawnte', her best friend, was all the family she had now. Shawnte' had Aunt Linda and Toniesha cremated in 24 karat gold-trimmed urns, and saved all the newspaper articles the Richmond Times had published. She new one day Nikki would have a memorial of her own.

Shawnte' grabbed her juice and dashed out the front. Just as she opened the door to her Escalade, she vomited once more, decorating her driveway and part of her lawn with scrambled eggs she'd eaten earlier that morning. She grabbed a napkin from her purse, wiping her mouth, as she slowly climbed into the truck. Pulling out the driveway, she tossed the contaminated napkin in the street, just before heading down Perham Road.

On the dash rested the most recent picture of her and Rocca. "I'll see you one day." She said, smiling to herself as she maintained focus on the road. The Escalade, eighty grand or so, a few diamond necklaces and photos were all she had to remember him by.

As Shawnte' turned on the highway 95 ramp, she reflected back to the previous week's incident when Rocca's brother tried to rough off the Cadillac after the funeral. It was indeed Rocca's truck, and she was Rocca's girl. The black SUV was paid for. She pictured his face when she informed him who's name was on the title, and giggled louder. Shawnte' brushed the happy thought away, and concentrated on Nikki. Then, it suddenly occurred to her the temporary feeling of relief had vanished once more. She was overjoyed to learn that her girlfriend was out of the coma, but the fact that she had to be the one to tell Nikki that Rodney, Linda, and Toniesha didn't make it terrified her.

She thought about how Princess lost it at Rodney's funeral, falling out on the church's floor as if they used to be a couple. Everyone who attended assumed Princess was merely crushed by her girlfriend and the whole tragedy that had unfolded, but Shawnte' knew better.

She knew Princess, and the way she took Rodney's death made things quite evident. Princess's baby father-to-be was Rodney. Shawnte' didn't bother to question Princess about the matter. At the moment, she had considered it trivial compared to everything else. Now that Nikki is going to live, it's a whole new ball game, Shawnte' thought to herself.

Pulling up to the medical center, she decided not to tell Nikki about the two until the time was right. Shawnte' reasoned that once Nikki learned about Rodney fucking her aunt, it would bother her for years to come. Let alone the rest.

The third day after the Tony Gangsta massacre, the Richmond Times revealed through autopsy reports that Rodney and Linda were secret lovers, noting that Rodney's semen matched that found in Linda's vagina. Shawnte' contemplated on hiding that particular article from Nikki, but decided it was Nichole's duty to know. Shawnte' parked in one of the handicapped spaces, then reached in the glove compartment to remove a permit. She gave the hospital a long stare, took a deep sigh ad exited the truck. As she approached the entrance she noticed a young blonde being wheel chaired to a nearby car with a newborn on her lap.

Her eyes focused on the woman momentarily. "Could I be pregnant?" she asked herself. Nannnnnnnnh!" Walking past the lady into the hospital, Shawnte' thought once more. "Hel nawh, I ain't pregnant!" she whispered, trying to convince herself that mental trauma was the case for the vomiting and dizziness.

There, in the lobby, was a small gift store. Amused by all the baby blue and pink gifts in the window, she decided to pick out something for her girlfriend. "I know my girl will like dis." Shawnte' picked up a large, white teddy bear with 'Get Well Soon' logoed across its midsection, but quickly decided against it placing it back on the display rack. "Teddy bears might remind Nikki of kids, and we don't want that right now."

Minutes after Doctor Wang Tin called Nikki's next of kin, he had two orderlies move her from ICU to Critical Care on the fourth floor. Upon Nikki's arrival, two nurses changed the IVs in her and hooked an EKG monitor to her heart. The bigger of the two black nurses double checked the IV to make sure fluids were going into Nikki's body. After she confirmed her work, she quietly left the room. The smaller nurse was attempting to place the thermometer inside her armpit to get an accurate reading of her temperature when Nikki's eyes slowly cracked open.

For a moment, her vision was temporarily blurred. In seconds she gained focus and saw the nurse standing over her. Nikki instantly recalled Tony Gangsta's pistol flashing before her. "Tony shot me?" she slurred.

"Please, do not try to talk right now. Takes up too much energy." The nurse replied, not comprehending a word she said. "The doctor said to notify him once you've woken." She added, picking up the phone to dial a three-digit extension. "Doctor Wang Tin, Nichole Wallace is awake…yes…okay." She concluded, cradling the receiver. "The doctor is on his way." After conveying the message, the nurse exited, pushing a medical cart down the hall.

Nikki lay in the hospital bed staring at the ceiling, having no clue where she had been shot. Her head throbbed tremendously, bearing allowing her eyelids to remain open. She could move, but her entire body ached. Just as her eyelids began to close a voice sounded, causing her eyes to snap wide open.

"Hello Miss Wallace. I'm Doctor Wang Tin. I need to ask you a few questions. I'm going to place my fingers in your hand, and you will answer by gently squeezing my index finger." Wang Tin helped Nikki ball her hand in a fist, then place his finger inside. "Squeeze my finger once for no, twice for yes. Do you know where you are?" Nikki squeezed twice. "Okay, is your name Nichole Wallace? Okay. Do you know where you are right now? Good!" he answered to Nikki's response. "Are you aware that you were shot? Good! Do you know where?" Nikki squeezed one time. "I see." Wang Tin replied, removing his finger from her light grip before crossing his arms. Nikki fought to keep her eyes open. The sincere look that came over the doctor's face gave her good reason to believe something was terribly wrong with her. "Don't worry, Miss Wallace, you're not paralyzed, but you were shot in the head." He began explaining to her how the bullet pierced through her skin and traveled along her cranium, exiting through the back of her head. "A fragment of lead broke off, fracturing a small section of your skull. The good news is, you're not dead. The bad news is, your ability to stand up has been distorted and you will have to work on balancing yourself all over again. And, I… I had to cut all your pretty hair off." He finished, emphasizing how bad he felt in his tone of voice. "Don't worry. You hair will grow back very soon. Even where the staples were removed laser surgery will fix that." The doctor pointed down to her mummy wrapped forehead, where the bullet had entered. The smaller nurse entered the room, carrying a food tray with only a glass of water and two kid sized applesauce packs.

"Drink water slowly, your throat is sore, whether you know it or not. The warm water and applesauce will help you gain your voice back." He said, demonstrating with his fingers around his throat area where Nikki would experience the worst of pain over the next few days. "In two days you will start your physical therapy, so be careful not to exert too much energy." He concluded before exiting the room.

The nurse stepped forward soon after Doctor Wang's departure. "Looks like you gon' be alright after all Miss Wallace." She remarked with a natural smile. "My name is Mrs. Goodman, everyone calls me Lucille." Grabbing a wired remote, she adjusted the upper section of Nikki's bed to a half seated position. "I know that feels a lil' better for ya'."

Nikki watched as the nurse slid the tray over her lap, peeling the straw from its wrap and placing it in the glass of water. Just as the nurse lifted the glass of water up to Nikki's lips, Shawnte' entered the room looking as if she were lost. The nurse reacted to Nikki's eyes widening. She quietly looked over her shoulder, acknowledging Shawnte's presence, then tended back to Nikki.

"After you drink this down, we might jus' be able to understand you a little better." She said, attempting to be humorous. Nikki struggled to open her mouth. She could feel the pain in her jaw as her lips parted. The nurse gently guided the straw between Nikki's lips. Slowly she slipped, the more she drank, the stronger she felt. Before all the water was gone, Nikki managed to lift her head up to the glass and wrap her fingers around it.

With her eyes still on Nichole, Shawnte' walked to the other side of the bed then tied the 'Get Well Soon' balloons around a hospital vase.

As Nikki placed the empty glass down on the tray, the nurse inserted straws into the applesauce cups. Nikki, anxious to put anything with flavor on her tongue, scooped the applesauce to her mouth and began slurping. She began coughing once the appetizer reached the irritated part of her throat. After he caught her breath, she resumed swallowing until both cups were empty.

Shawnte' stood at the end of the bed, staring at Nikki with her arms folded. She was totally unaware of the sad expression that came over her face. While Nikki ate her food, she contemplated how to break the bad news to her. Soon the nurse exited the room, leaving the two of them alone.

"You look good girl." Shawnte' complimented, trying to hold back her tears.

A stiff smile appeared on Nikki's face. "Bitch! Stop lyin'." She countered in a hoarse voice. "I look worse than you, and you look ta' pieces."

Nikki's humor brought a smile to Shawnte's face. "Girl you stupid."

"I know I look like shit," Nikki coughed out, "because I feel like shit." She added, causing Shawnte' to laugh a little louder. Nikki placed both hands over her mouth, wiping the tears from her cheeks and covering her teeth at the same time.

Shawnte' stopped laughing and stared at Nikki for a moment. She tried to keep her composure, but the whole situation was too much for her. She suddenly burst into tears. "Everybody's gone Nikki." She cried out. "Tony Gangsta killed everybody." Shawnte' sat on the edge of the bed, placing one hand on Nikki's leg and the other to her face. "Nikki, he kil't Toniesha, he kil't his own daughter." Nikki's heart collapsed into her stomach, causing her own blood pressure to sky rocket, alerting the nurses at the front desk. It hadn't crossed her mind where her daughter was. In fact, it had slipped her mind that she even had a daughter. The events that took place that night she was shot flashed through her mind. "Rodney…aunt Linda?" slurred from her mouth.

Shawnte', who's eyes were now bloodshot red and puffy, understood just what Nikki was trying to ask. "Nikki, they are all dead. He even kil't Rocca too!"

Shocked and saddened about what happened, Nikki's eyes began filling with tears. Still staring at her girlfriend, who was on the verge of having a nervous breakdown, she blinked once more, and the build up raced down her cheeks.

Doctors and nurses came streaming into the room. After one doctor read the heart monitor, he instructed a nurse to check her vitals and temperature. "You'll have to leave now." Another informed Shawnte', wrapping her arm around her upon noticing she had been crying.

Nikki never saw the nurse inject the needle in her arm. She was blinded by her own inner thoughts and feelings. In seconds, her daze became a dream. The injected sedative put her fast asleep for the next eight hours.

Shawnte' had gone home to retrieve all the newspaper articles of the Tony Gangsta massacre, and returned to the hospital. Nikki awakened around nine o'clock that evening. The room was dim, the only source of light coming from the hallway. Her throat was itching, and the only soreness she felt came from her head, there, to the right of her bed, was a wired remote. As she reached for it, she realized that the wires connecting her heart monitor had been removed from from her upper body. She adjusted the bed until she was sitting in the upward position. Now she could see everything around her.

Nikki carefully scanned over the room. Someone was slumped over in a chair near the window. She focused her eyes for a moment before realizing it was Shawnte'. For hours, Nikki starred into the dark, reminiscing about Rodney, aunt Linda, and Toniesha. The more memorable the moments that flashed before her, the sadder she became. She wondered how Rocca had fallen victim to her ex when the police where already outside her home. She dismissed the thought, and began thinking about life and where she now fit in it. Without rationalizing, she convinced herself that it was not worth living.

God, why didn't you take me too? Why I had to be the lucky one? Toniesha was just a baby, God, just a baby. She never did anything to anyone! With her heart spilling to the Higher Power, she concluded. God, I know you want me to be strong. All I ask of you is to guide me, cause I can't make it without you. And if you really love your child, then deliver unto me another beautiful child and someone special to mend my wounded heart back together, and dear God, look over my family for me. I Miss them so much. Nikki never ended her prayer, nor said amen.

She dozed off to sleep, conversing with God, to be re-awakened with a leather glove pressed against her mouth. Terror flooded Nikki's eyes once she realized who the man was that towered over her. He snatched her from the bed, onto the floor. Blood flew through the air after the IVs separated from

Nikki's arms. She looked to the hallway, hoping someone would rescue her. She tried screaming, but her voice went mute. With all her might, she tried to move, but her body had lost all feeling.

The familiar face kicked her twice in the rib cage before drawing a shiny pistol from under his coat. She noticed Shawnte' still slumped over in the chair by the window. Why hasn't she woke up yet? Nikki thought as she focused through the darkness, her stomach knotted up after spotting a pool of blood forming under Shawnte's chair.

"That's right bitch! She dead! He yelled down at Nikki with the heat pointed at her torso. "Look at'chu, all terrified an' shit! He snapped with a deep laugh before cocking the hammer of his life-taker back. "Everybody wanna go to heaven, but don' no fuckin body wanna die. Where's your God now?" he asked, slowly pulling the trigger. Just as the gun fired, Nikki screamed at the top of her lungs, immediately awaking from her nightmare.

She looked around. No sign of Tony Gangsta. "It was only a dream." She mumbled, letting out a long sigh,

Nikki assumed she had dreamed everything. She adjusted the bed with the remote, only to notice that the heart monitor and IVs had been removed from her body. She looked toward the window, where she dreamed Shawnte' was sitting, only seeing a stack of newspapers in the chair. Weird, she thought as she scanned over the rest of the room. To the left of her was a small table where the telephone, a TV remote, and the vase with three silver and blue balloons wrapped around it rested. Just as Nikki noticed a walker near the table, Lucille walked in with a breakfast tray.

"Good morning, Miss Wallace. I took the liberty of removing the IVs from your arm, since you're able to eat on your own now." She explained, placing the tray over Nikki's lap. "Oh yeah, I apologize for making you jump in your sleep. I was having a hard time removing the tape from your arm, so I snatched It fast, taking a few hairs off with it. Sorry."

"It's quite alright" Nikki replied courteously, clearing her throat. Lucille exited the room, continuing down the hallway to finish her rounds. Nikki pushes the food over to the side, and slowly lifted one leg off the bed and down to the floor, placing one hand on the walker to pull it closer to the bed. Slowly, she lowered her second leg to the floor, then secured her other hand around the walker.

Before she could make her way toward the bathroom, Shawnte' entered the room with a cup of hot coffee and a new pair of bedroom shoes. She smiled when she saw Nikki up and trying to mobile herself around. "I thought you might be needing these." She offered, "Girl, you can't be walking around here barefooted."

Nikki returned the smile as Shawnte' placed the coffee on the food tray.

Shawnte' knelt down, slipping the shoes on her girlfriend's feet. When she stood up, Nikki pointed over to the chair, "last night?"

Shawnte' nodded, picking up the coffee up off the tray. "Girl I was knocked slam out." She answered with a weak chuckle." The nurse woke me up about twenty minutes ago, telling me I was snoring to loud. Shoot! I was tired."

Amused by Shawnte's newfound humor, she coughed out a short giggle. "Can you open the bathroom door for a handicapped sista?" Shawnte' shook her head as she made her way toward the tiny entrance. Same old Nikki, crazy as hell. Nikki stepped into the bathroom, walker first, maneuvering herself into position to sit on the toilet.

"Nikk'ay!" Shawnte' shouted through the door. "Im'ma go home and clean myself up."

"Okay." Nikki replied.

Shawnte' placed the newspaper on the end of Nikki's bed, then left. She decided not to be around when Nikki learned of the details the Richmond Times unveiled. After Nikki handled her business, she pulled a string that hung close beside the sink. Placing her hand around the walker, she pulled herself up off the toilet, then made way to the sink. Nikki hadn't bothered to look up at the mirror. When she did, she jumped in fear, not recognizing the reflection. Her skin was ashy and lips hard and dry, the bottom one peeling. She'd lost over twenty pounds and her caved-in jawbone revealed her weight loss.

Nikki stared at herself for a moment, trying to accept the reality of her present appearance. She looked up at the blood-stained bandages tightly wrapped around her skull, curious as to how she looked without any hair on her head. Emitting a deep sigh, she gently began to peel off the bandages. Placing them behind the sink knobs, careful to not let them fall into the basin, she gawked at the scar across her forehead. Instantly, Nikki recalled Tony Gangsta and her nightmare. 'I will not let you defeat me!' She grunted out at the mirror as if talking to Tony Gangsta himself. Disgusted with the thoughts, she erased him from her mind and began studying her funny shaped head. I could rock a Jada Pinkett hair-do, she thought, picturing herself in a particular haircut. Soon, a wave of comfort, relief, and hope came over her. Still staring in the mirror, she began smiling. "I'm gon' be alright. I will get past this. I know I will...my life is not over yet!"

TWO YEARS LATER

CHAPTER 7

Keith had arrived at Mom's house a few hours earlier than usual. He sat in the living room, pretending to be watching television, hoping his face could hide his stress and turmoil. Somehow Arlene knew when something was bothering her son.

Ever since Keith was a child, his pint-sized mother had been able to tell when he was troubled and depressed, and lately, the first cause that came to her mind was Sheila. She didn't want to sound as if she were being nosy, so she made small talk about the local news.

"I sho' hope they catch that serial rapist." Arlene said, awaiting some sort of a response. Keith was staring at the television, but he saw and heard nothing the anchor woman said. "That's the thirteenth woman in the past two years," she went on, pointing at the TV, "goin' 'round biting young black girls nipples off." Keith broke out of his daydream after his mothers words grew louder.

"Yeah ma, that's...that's just sick." He answered, trying to convince Arlene he'd been on point with the headline story from the beginning. "Its probably some crazy ass white boy who got a case of the fever."

Arlene snapped her neck toward Keith, shooting him the evil eye. Keith barely cussed offstage, and never in his mother's home. Her feeling were right, he was troubled over something. "Don't curse in my house boy! You may have fixed it up right nice around here, but this is still my house, and you will-"

"Sorry momma." Keith sincerely cut her off." "You know how I get when it comes to my beautiful black sisters."

“I don’t know why you pretendin’ there’s nothing wrong.” Arlene pouted out as she rose from her recliner. You think I don’ know that wife of yours is driving your nerves through the roof, ah-gain.” Arlene walked in the kitchen to check on the roast baking in the oven. Raising her voice so her son could still hear, she continued, “I’m sure you’re tired of hearing it, cause I’m tired of saying it, but it’s the truth. She-is-not-the-one for you! She never was, I tell ya.” Strolling back back into the living room, Arlene sank into her recliner, “She never comes ‘round, cause she know mu-in-law will see right through her.”

“Maybe you right,” Keith finally answered, “but how um supposed to know who’s right or wrong for me?”

Arlene looked him in the eye. “Trust me boy, you will know. Everything ain’t love at first sight.” Keith absorbed his mother’s words for a moment, reflecting back to the beautiful woman he’d encountered last night, and wondered how many other females hated MC K.O. after Arlene went back into the kitchen, he grabbed his jacket from the closet. He wanted to get some fresh air, and decided to sit on the front porch just long enough to gather up his thoughts.

* * *

Yesterday morning, Sheila had taken off to Atlanta as always, only she had raced out of the house at 6 a.m. after her mother called saying that Kayla was I’ll. Kayla had been staying with her grandmother for the past year so she could focus more on school, at least that’s what Sheila told Keith.

Around nine o’clock, Keith awakened and got dressed, then went for his morning jog through the neighborhood. Thirty-five minutes later he was back at his mansion, soaked in sweat. He peeled the wet shirt off his back and tossed it to the floor before making his way into the kitchen. He stood, debating on whether to cook breakfast or make a bowl of Raisin Bran cereal. Deciding to have neither, he settled for a glass of orange juice and a bagel.

Keith went to the bread box and retrieved two bagels, then walked over to the dishwasher for a plate. “Dirty, dirty, dirty.” He whispered, searching through the machine for a clean glass and plate. “Waste uh money.” After finding a semi-clean utensil, he sat them on the counter. Feeling a little dehydrated, Keith made his way over to the refrigerator, yanking it open to find an empty carton of orange juice sitting inside. He opened some apple juice, gulping it straight from the glass bottle until his thirst was temporarily quenched. The phone rang just as he’d started upstairs to the bedroom.

“Wassup Mont?” Keith energetically answered after looking at the caller ID box.

"Whussup Killa K, what's really good?"

"Sheila gone as usual. Um get'n ready to step out to the grocery store."

"I'm wit Timmy right now. We headed to Greenbrier to pick up the Dodge Viper he brought for Stacy."

"That's love. The boy is in love." Keith said with a fake chuckle. "Look, stop past here in about an hour."

"We already was, that's why I was callin' to make sure you were home."

Keith was in the bedroom when he ended the call with his younger cousin. He couldn't believe Timmy Tuff, his longtime friend and partner of the Salt Water Record Label they owned, would buy his baby's mother the same gift he'd given Sheila for their anniversary. Instead of angering himself, he took it as a compliment. I must have good taste, and Tim trust my judgment, he thought to himself as he searched for the keys to Sheila's electric blue viper.

Keith loved driving her car, and Sheila knew it. That's why she'd taken pleasure in hiding the keys from him. Only this time, he couldn't find them anywhere. Running out of places to look, he rambled through her drawer, where she kept an ample amount of flavored panties. Nested inside a pair of Peach Passion was a wireless telephone bill addressed to a Georgia phone company, along with a pack of morning after birth control tablets. He studied the tablets for a moment, easily coming to a harsh reality that Sheila was not only having an affair, but also having unprotected sex. It was evident, being that he was virtually infertile.

Keith's desire for orange juice vanished. The only thing he desired was answers. He removed the rest of his funky clothes and jumped in the shower, deciding not to confront his wife until he had concrete proof of her unadulterated activities. The thought of any man making love to his wife depressed him to no end. "Why?" he asked himself. Why do this to me? Wouldn't do anything to jeopardize our marriage." Keith exited the shower and threw on his Versace bathrobe, bypassing the towels on the rack. Barefooted, he walked through the game room and past his movie theatre for the indoor pool.

The water temperature read seventy-nine degrees. As Keith sat on the edge of the pool with his feet dangling his mind drifted back down memory lane. All the good times he and Sheila shared forced their way into his head. He guessed the fairytale story he'd had to come to an end sometime.

Keith was almost thirty, and hadn't been with four women his entire life. He thought about all the concerts and after parties, where groupies had constantly thrown themselves at him. Not once had he ever thought about sexing any of them. Because of Sheila, because of love. Keith believed in the principles of love and knowing more about his partner before he sexed her. That's how he'd fallen for Sheila. She led him to believe that she sought the same. Now he was feeling uncomfortably wrong.

He scanned the pool area, disgusted with everything in his sight. He tried fighting back the tears, the emotions ravaging his mind like a tornado. There was no way he could stop the tears from falling. Keith threw his hands in air. "Is this your way of punishing me?" he cried out gazing up at the forty foot ceiling. "I tried to please you, Lord. I even did right by Sheila. I didn't want this big house, she did. All I wanted was to be loved, have a family. Now, you tell me I'm not worthy of that."

Keith was convinced that God was punishing him for his lack of faith thirteen months ago. After a young girl at Rock Church discovered that the bearded man was MC K.O., the congregation chanted 'Devil Worshiper' to the rapper, chasing him off the premises. Never before had Keith been so hurt, so humiliated. He decided to give up on the house of fellowship.

Sitting by the pool, the rapper wondered what his next step would be. His world tour was coming up in just three months. If Sheila was cheating in him, he knew it would take more than three months to reconcile their differences.

Keith jumped at the sound of the doorbell, and hurried to the other side of the house. He'd forgotten that Mont and Timmy Tuff were on their way. Hearing the two of them snickering as he approached the front door, he took in a deep breath and wiped the tears from the corners of his eyes.

"Wuzzup K-baby?" Tim greeted. "What'chu in here doin', takin' a shit or jackin' off?"

Timmy Tuff was a chubby white kid who looked to be of Cuban or Italian descent. His father, Henry was the senator of Maryland from 1990-92. His parents divorced shortly before Henry died in a tragic car accident. Tim was the only child, and by law inherited all his father's assets.

He and Keith met at Old Dominion University around the time his father passed. A big fan of rap music with a knack for aggressive hip hop beats, he and Keith started Salt Water Record Label. Timmy Tuff was the ladies man, a big spender with the gift of gab. He loved to party and always traveled with an entourage.

"I see you went and copped your baby mom's the Vipe." Keith replied, ignoring Timmy's remark.

"She's not my baby mom's, Stacy is wifey."

Mont interrupted, "Nigga, any female with some half decent coochie is wifey to you!" the two laughed at Mont's comical remark.

Mont and Timmy constantly joked on each other, and MC K.O. always laughed, whether it was half-funny or not. The two of them sensed something was wrong when he didn't even bother to crack up a smile. He glanced over at the platinum-colored viper parked on the far side of the horseshoe, than back at Mont and Timmy. ""That's nice man, I hope Stacy likes it."

Tim quickly assumed that K.O. was upset about him buying the same gift for his girl. But he was confused, when Mont had called K.O., he said that Keith sounded all hyped up about the purchase.

"What's wrong, K?" Timmy asked. "You ain't mad about the Viper is'ju?" Keith gestured them in the house, closing the doors, "Nawh man, it ain't that at all. You know we better than that, it's Sheila." Nodding his head, scratching his forehead with his thumb, he broke the news. "Sheila's cheating on me. I don't know with who, when, or where. I'm guessing Atlanta, but I don't have any proof."

"Beat that ass, that's what I would do!"

"Shut up Mont, this shit is serious!" Timmy yelled back.

"Nawh this ain't serious. He just took her serious, when in all actuality she was nothing more then a hoe."

Keith was in no mood for jokes, but his cousin's humor had brought a smirk to his face. Despite the fact that Mont was talking about him and his relationship, Keith admired him for lifting his spirits up all the times he was feeling nervous, insecure and upset. Mont was dark skinned, six foot tall and paper thin. He was MC Kayo's, hype man, who bounced around on stage yelling into the microphone, amping the crowd up and backing K.O.'s words wherever fatigue set in. Off stage, all he did was party, smile, and crack jokes.

"You know what?" Mont said, scratching his chin as if he had just thought of the most brilliant idea. "We got to party tonight

Keith and Tim stared, giving him a look as if to say 'tell us something we don't know.'

"'Nawh man," Mont whined after reading the look on their faces, "we gon' have Stacy's party right here, tonight."

Timmy Tuff was feeling the idea, but he knew Keith's crib was party repellent. Hell, Keith don't even attend his own parties, he thought. "C'mon kid, you know K-love ain't havin-"

"It's on." Keith interrupted, surprising them both. "Yo, the party is goin' down here! God knows I could use one."

Mont knew his cousin would fold in his hand. He always did when he got depressed. Timmy Tuff looked at him as if he had gone crazy. Mont was already on the phone informing the Salt Water Boys where the party was going own.

“That’s right.” Keith yelled as he made his way up the wide steps.

“Y’all plan everything, y’all clean up everything, and I don’t need to mention that you two brothers are responsible for everything. I don’t care if a nigga get drunk and shit on my lawn. I want it scooped up.”

“We got ‘chu man!” Mont yelled up to his cousin with his hand over the phone.

11:13 THAT NIGHT

The party was jam packed with local celebrities and wanna-be VIP’s. Virginia’s finest groupies were associating themselves with anyone who looked like they were doing halfway good, male or female. It didn’t matter, as long as a dollar was involved. Most of the partygoers occupied the back section of the mansion. DJ Stroke mixed records from the ballroom, while the concert-sized speakers vibrated the house.

Some were playing basketball in the gym. Others occupied the indoor pool, while the majority barbecued near Keith’s Olympic pool. There, in the backyard, was Stacy’s Dodge Viper, wrapped in a huge red ribbon and bow. Leaning against the exotic car was a seven foot envelope.

* * *

Keith had walked the back section of the mansion ten times over. Determined not to reveal his depression to his guests, he strolled from one room to another, playing the ideal host for the evening.

11:35

A female friend of Stacy’s made an announcement over the DJ’s microphone, “Attention, can I have you alls attention? Everyone, please come outside near the pool. We are about to sing happy birthday to the birthday girl. Thank you.”

While everyone gathered around the pool to celebrate Stacy’s special day, Timmy Tuff stood on top of a picnic table and began speaking into the cordless mic.” One two, one two. How’s everybody doin’ out there?” the crowd gave different responses all at once.

“As you all know, it’s my baby’s birthday, and I just wanna wish her a very happy birthday. Love you baby.”

Stacy was standing around her girlfriends. As Tim gave his speech, she squeezed her way through the crowd to where her man was standing high.

"Since my boo is over here, we gon' open up the thirty pound envelope first, then, we gonna sing happy birthday."

The five foot redbone ripped the huge envelope from the side, then made her way around it. While she peeled off the pink paper, everyone curiously and quietly watched. Stacy stared at the huge birthday card, admiring her boyfriend's humor.

"Open it!" a girl yelled from the gathering.

"Yeah baby, open it!" Timmy Tuff added in a sexy baritone voice.

Stacy tilted the colossal greeting card against her new car, impatiently pulling it apart. She burst into tears after her eyes read the billboard-sized words that read 'I love you, will you marry me?'

Timmy Tuff leaped down from the table and greeted his fiancé with open arms, giving her a warm hug and a kiss on the top of her head. People clapped and cheered for the couple of the hour. Then Timmy gestured his hand to the crowd to stop the applause. He unwrapped his arm from around his girl, pushing her away from his body. Stacy had no idea what he was doing until he knelt on one knee.

"Timmy, not right here. You gonna get your Sean John's dirty."

Timmy looked into her eyes, trying to get his words together. "Baby," he said with a static in his voice, "baby, I...I don't care about this sweat suit, its replaceable. You, my love, are not. I wanna be with you for life, Stacy. You are and will always be forever...in my heart."

With that said, Timmy Tuff pulled out a ten-carat diamond ring and slid it over her delicate finger, sending the partygoers into a frenzy. Mont came over to the table and looked on with everyone else. People outside stood in complete silence, waiting for Timmy Tuff to crack the final question.

"God damn man," Mont blurted out for everyone to hear, "that big ass diamond sittin' on twenty-fo's!" Everyone broke out in laughter, even Tim and Stacy let a chuckle or two slip.

Soon, it was quiet again, and Timmy Tuff regained composure, staring Stacy in the eyes once more. "My lady of beauty, will you marry me?"

Stacy smiled as wide as her cheeks would allow. Looking Timmy Tuff straight in the eyes, she screamed out yes. "Yes baby, I will marry you!" as the two tongues intertwined, everyone celebrated.

Keith stood behind the crowd, happy for his friend, but he didn't bother to join in singing happy birthday. Once half of the party goers had made had made their way back into the house, he slowly followed. He told himself he wasn't cleaning up earlier, yet he found himself tossing empty bottles of Crystal, Alize', and Moet into the many trash bags. As Keith walked into the ballroom, six or seven Salt Water Boys spat lyrics into a small cipher. Unamused by the kid's rhymes, K.O. simply stood back, leaning against the wall. Keith noticed about thirty charms, just like his. All these people here represent the Salt Water Clique, and I have no idea who half of these people are, he thought to himself as he made his way toward the game room.

"What up Kayo?" a voice yelled over the music as he felt a tap on his shoulder.

"What's up Hectic?" he answered , realizing who it was.

"I just wanted to let 'chu know, your new album is like dat! Them beats are somethin' else man."

Keith detected a little animosity, but wasn't in the mood to check him, so he played along, shaking his head, smiling and throwing a few thank you's and I try's. Just as the conversation ended a girl walked up under Hectic's arm.

"OH, I'd like you to meet my wife, Shawnte'. This is the famous MC K.O."

"Keith, my name is Keith." He corrected.

"This is the famous Keith, known to the rap world as MC K.O." Hectic reintroduced, pointing his finger back and forth as he talked. "And Keith, this is Shawnte', my lovely, beautiful, and stunning wife." He concluded, kissing his woman on the cheek.

Keith complimented her, then went on his way, making rounds through the house. In the game room, a few kids were laid up with some locals. He didn't bother to disturb them. Tonight, I'm just not in the mood, he told himself as he walked through. But he stopped after noticing a jacket hung over one of his favorite statues. He glanced over the game room, witnessing the mini orgy in progress, then went over to the statue, grabbing the designer leather and tossing it over the pool table.

"Yo stickman," a drunk brother slurred, "that's a five thousand dollar jacket, baby boy."

Keith gave the wasted baller a sarcastic smirk. "Yo stickman," he yelled back, "that's a fifty thousand dollar statue!" He concluded before making his way towards the front of the house. The drunk baller watched K.O. exit the room, then stared at the couples who had stopped making out to stare at him. Feeling stupid, he turned toward the chickenhead he was hugged up with. "My bad." He apologized, then resumed kissing as if nothing had happened.

Shelia was running through the back of Keith's mind as he headed for the conference room. I wonder what she's doing right now. Maybe I should call up…No…No I can't, won't. I wonder does her mom know. Hell, she's probably covering for her. I wouldn't be surprised. A commotion from the back section of the house disrupted his thoughts. He didn't even bother to go see who had started scrapping. "As long as no one gets shot or kilt, I gives a fuck, "he whispered under his breath.

Just as Keith put his hand around the doorknob to enter the room, he paused for a moment. Chills flashed through his spine. Slowly, he raised his head and looked to his right to find an incredibly attractive woman with eyes of the devil staring him down. He could tell the long-legged sista resting her head on the palm of her hand had been sitting there for quite a while. Her facial expression revealed that she was tired, angry and ready to leave. He wanted to say something to the woman, but the intimidating look she displayed told Keith to leave her be. Keith strolled into the conference room and sat down at the long table. He turned on the security monitor and watched the woman on the screen, then zoomed the camera in for a closer look. Keith didn't want to admit it, but he couldn't deny what he saw. The girl is a twelve, even with that ugly grit on her face, he thought.

Keith turned the monitors off and focused on Sheila, the upcoming tour and how his life was going to be after he retired the microphone. He sat there in a daze, contemplating on whether to rejoin the party or retire to his room for the night. He wasn't sleepy or in the mood to be in anyone's presence.

Beside an 8 foot aquarium sat his answer. Once Keith noticed the black case leaning up against the Fish tank, he leaped from the recliner toward the instrument, deciding to spend the remainder of the night playing the saxophone in his room. Keith Osbourne had been blowing the tenor sax since junior high school. As a child, he constantly tried to emulate his older brother, Dorseey, a jazz musician. But every year, Keith's dreams changed as he matured.

Turning out the lights, Keith left the conference room. The girl was still alone, looking as if she hated the world. Since he had to walk past her to the stairwell, he decided to say something hospitable. The woman's eyes followed him all the way up the hall as he approached her. Keith stopped, slowly turning towards her, careful not to hit her legs with the black case.

"Is everything okay Miss?" he asked in a sincere voice. The girl didn't respond. "Well, I wouldn't let him get to you. I'd try to enjoy myself anyhow." He suggested, assuming a male friend had pissed her off. The girl maintained her angry stare, not reacting to his advice.

"Um sorry,"…Keith apologized, " I was jus….just trying to help, that's all." " I didn't come here with no guy, Mr. K.O.! " she snapped, catching

Keith off guard with her aggressive tone. " The only problem I got …is you, and if you wanna help, you can leave." Startled by the woman's remark, Keith stood speechless for a moment. "I do not care for you at all ! So please take you and your gun case elsewhere, thank you."

He turned to face the lady once more, "Look lady, do you know me? he snapped back, pointing his finger to his chest. " Have you seen me before? Have you?" the female looked at the famous rapper as if he'd just asked the dumbest question in the world. "Oh! That's right, dumb question,huh? I'm MC K. O., everybody knows me right? Wrong, my name is Keith Osbourne, and I never did anything to hurt or disrespect you. Let me give you a piece of advice, Miss Lady…..know more of me before you decide to disrespect me in my own home." With that, Keith stormed away, then stopped without turning around. "Oh! And this ……this ain't no gun case, it's a saxophone……But you probably knew that already." The woman kept her eyes on him until he disappeared. I know you a'right, you ruined my life.

1:49 A.M.

While Keith harmoniously blew every sad song he could think of, the size of the party tripled. The back section of his mansion hazed with the weed and cigarette smoke. Beer cans and wine bottles began to pile up in the corners of every room. Just outside the ballroom was a huge closet where partygoers rested their clothes while they splashed in the pool. No one noticed a guy slip into the closet.

The man squeezed the pockets on a pair of Versace denims hanging across a cushioned hanger, then stuck his hand inside, pulling out a thick stack of hundred dollar bills and the keys to a Ducati Motorcycle. He shoved the money back into the denims and dropped the keys into his back pocket, then slipped out of the closet.

Someone spotted him as he exited. "Yo dawg, put a nigga on!

"I'll holla at my man'n nem. He the boss." The man told the local rapper as he walked past the indoor pool and through the glass door, outside to where the majority of the crowd was bouncing to the sounds of Frankie Beverly. He lit up a Black and Mild cigar and began walking around the far side of the mansion, where it was dark. Once he was out of view, he tossed the cigar and began running to the front of the estate. He stopped and hid behind an end column of the porch, scanning the front yard. The coast was clear, so he ran to a Range Rover, opened the door and grabbed a small duffle bag before closing it quickly.

A motorcycle was parked next to a Jaguar. The man spotted the exotic bike, and quickly made his way toward it. Placing the keys in the ignition, he cranked up the bike, then glanced at his iced out Jacob & C.O. It read 1:52 a.m. Fifteen minutes should be more than enough time, the man thought as he sped off from MC K. O.'s mansion. The bike raced three miles down Virginia Beach Boulevard to the Long Point Condominiums. He parked it under a tree, dashing toward the targeted condo. By the time he reached the door, he'd put on a black ski mask, gloves and a hoody. The keys to the condo wasn't the one on the keychain, but that didn't matter. He reached in his bag and pulled out a small tool kit. In seconds, gained entry .

He eased up the steps into the living room, grabbed the telephone from the table and took it off the receiver, he checked his watch, 1:56am., quickly changing to 1:57, as he made his way to the large bedroom. There lay a black woman, under the covers. The lights were out, and her face was buried in the pillow.

"Baby, you home already?" assuming it was her boyfriend. "Maybe we can go another round." By then, the man had pulled his pants down. He gently climbed on top of the bed, removing the blanket. He kissed the lady on her thigh, then on her ass. "That tickles!" she giggled , still lying on her stomach. "C'mon put it in."

The man spread her legs apart, then climbed in between her, kissing the woman sensually over her back. Slowly , he entered her. "Damn baby!" The woman cried out as the dick penetrated her vagina, then lost her voice as the rapist forced all of himself inside. She knew there was no way her boyfriend's dick had grown that many inches in an hour's time.

"S-stop Please, you're hurting me!" the girl pleaded in agony. She tried to turn around, only to be greeted with a knife to her throat. "Listen here, baby doll, you take this big long dick like a champ, or die like a tramp. " The man covered her mouth as he fucked her as hard and fast as he could. The girl's body trembled from the pounding to her vagina. "Turn over, Bitch, so I can cum," he commanded.

The terrified woman obeyed, flipping on her back before timidly spreading her legs. He wrapped his arms around her thighs and began taking her once more. The more she moaned and cried, the wider he split her pussy. "I'm cum'min, so you know what that means." He said sarcastically, looking down at her chest, then bent over to pin her arms. He licked the woman's left titty. Seconds later, the tip of her breast disappeared inside his mouth.

Just as the woman let out a deep sigh, the man clamped down with all 32's, ripping the nipple clear off her chest. The woman screamed at the top of her lungs, only to have her attacker smother her cry for help with his hand. Blood gushed from the woman's chest, down the side of her torso to the satin sheets.

“I’m leaving. Not a word or sound.” The man ordered as he raised off her. The woman, bleeding profusely wondered if the rapist was going to kill her. As he hurried out of the bedroom, she spotted his iced out diamond necklace and charm that favored the Salt Water Boys emblem in all of the music videos.

2:02 A.M.

The man pulled up to K.O.’s estate after tossing his bloody clothes in a McDonald’s dumpster on the way, undected.

2:03 A.M.

He was back mingling with the rest of the partygoers as if he’d never left.

……………….back to the following day at Arlene’s house…………………………………………………

As soon as Keith stepped out onto the porch, he noticed an unmarked police car parked close to the bumper of his Bently. He was used to being harassed by the locals, who always mistook him for a big time drug dealer. Keith approached the unmarked vehicle to inform the officers that ridin’ on twenty fo’s was the law for guys like him and Juvee.

“Hello officers, this is my vehicle. How can I be of assistance to you today?” Keith politely greeted the officer on the passenger side. “Hello to you, Mr.Rape’r-Oops I meant Rapper. I get it all mixed up sometimes, especially being that you rape woman on the low low.” Keith looked at the officer, baffled and confused. “I think you’ve mistaken me for some-“

“No, Keith Osbourne, I think we haven’t!” The officer cut him off with attitude in his voice. “We’re from the Virginia Beach Police Department, and we’d like to take you back to the precinct for questioning.”

“Question me for what?” Keith snapped, instantly offended.

“ For…rape…..what else?”

CHAPTER 8

Nikki was relaxing at her Suffolk townhouse when she thought she heard the front door slam shut. She leaped from under the covers toward the night stand, where her loaded Smith & Wesson rested. Just as she opened the mini-drawer, she paused after noticing the familiar silhouette out of her peripheral, standing in her bedroom doorway. "Shawnte", " Nikki squealed, taking a deep breath, "You scared the hell outta me!"

"Girl, whatever" she responded, rolling her eyes. "You know I'm the only one with a key to your place, so stop trippin'." Shawnte" sat on the bed as Nikki climbed back under the covers, pretending to go back to sleep. She knew Nikki was upset with her, so she contemplated the best way to approach her best friend without striking up an argument. Nikki, Nikki..." Shawnte' called out awaiting a response, only to have Nikki pull the blanket completely over her head. She knew making up wasn't going to be easy, so she didn't try. " How you get home last night?"

"Why?" Nikki sarcastically replied, refusing to remove the blanket, "Did you take me home last night?"

"No."

"But'chu bought me there, didn't you?" Nikki finally resurfaced from under the covers and sat up on the bed, facing Shawnte'. "Look Nikki, I swear I didn't know they were gonna move Stacy's party to MC K.O.'s crib. Damn Nik, I didn't know it was his spot until we arrived there. Nobody knew where K.O. lived. He never had functions at his place." Nikki could see how bad Shawnte' was feeling, but she wasn't ready to let her off the hook just yet. "Well, if you knew how I felt about Keith"

"Who's Keith?" Shawnte' quickly interjected in.

"I-I mean K.O. anyways, why didn't you just take me home?" Shawnte' nodded, letting out a long sigh. "You got a point there, to give you an excuse would be just that, an excuse. I was thinking about myself, I guess." Shawnte's sincerity always melted Nikki's heart. Still, she kept her angry face on.

"You know Hectic's babymomma was there last night, and I didn't wanna leave him around her for one second. That bitch'll suck his dick every chance she gets. Which is one of the reasons I ain't take you home. You know me and her got to rumblin' last night." Nikki's eyes widened as Shawnte' captured her undivided attention. "Girl, I beat that skank down. I had her by the throat first, then I started wailing' on that pretty face of hers." For the moment, Nikki had forgotten she was supposed to be angry. The only thing her expression revealed was excitement as she took the details of the brawl. "Once I slammed her over the pool table, it was ova! You hear me? I decorated the entire room with her dry ass weave. I was hoping you came out from where ever you were hiding….Hold up! "Shawnte' stopped in mid sentence as curiosity flooded her mind. "Nikki, how did you know Kayo's name is Keith? Nobody knows that."

"He told me after we got into an argument, "Nikki replied hesitantly. "Ooooowwhh girl, you got into a fight with your nemesis?"

"Not a fight, an argument" Nikki corrected.

"So, how did the devil's name go from MC K.O. to Keith?" Shawnte' propped herself over Nikki's bed with her elbows on the mattress, chin resting in her hand. " I'm dying to hear the answer, Miss I'll kill his ass if he ever looks at me funny." Even though they were Nikki's exact words she wasn't amused by her friends comment. "Look, I ain't trying to talk about it fa'real, we argued, that's that. We ain't cool, and we damn sure ain't friends. I jus' don't like him, even if I don't know him. So let's get off the subject Please!"She concluded, raising her voice as she climbed out of bed and stomped her way into the bathroom.

"Well, excuuuuuse me," Shawnte' whispered to herself as Nikki slammed the door. "You need some dick…..and bad."

"I heard that!" Nikki yelled through the bathroom door.

"Good, I wanted you to."

Shawnte' is right….., Nikki thought. Maybe I could use a nice warm dick in my life. I deserve to be loved, she convinced herself, staring at her perfectly curved reflection in a four foot long mirror attached to the back of the bathroom door. After therapy, Nikki had continued to work out. Her tall, slim figure filled out, and once averaged sized booty blossomed. Nikki's hair do was the epitome of her natural beauty. The only thing she had left of the tragic night were a barely visible scar over her forehead, a few pictures of her parents, Linda, her daughter and memories. She kept pictures of Rodney for a while, but threw them away, realizing she had been in love with a lie. Nikki often thought about him, though.

Sometimes she smiled, most of the time she cried. The nightmares were the only demons left to conquer. Sometimes she'd dream Tony Gangsta to be MC K.O. himself. The legendary rapper became her possessed baby's father, trying to kill her.

Nikki relocated to Suffolk, Virginia after leaving Richmond 18 months ago. Upon regaining her health, she sold her parents home, donated what was left of the furniture to the Salvation Army and collected just over $200,000 in life insurance money. At first she wasn't sure where to begin her new life, until Shawnte' revealed that she was pregnant and there was a possibility the father was a big time producer from Virginia Beach.

When Hectic learned of the little girl Shawnte' was carrying, he broke the relationship with his gold-diggin' babymomma. He and Shawnte' moved into a beach condo together in Buckroe, Virginia, and got married soon after. Shawnte', being Nikki's dearest friend thought it was a great idea to move down to the Tidewater area so they could be close.

Nikki cleaned herself up then exited the bathroom to find Shawnte' flicking through the cable channels. " Why Princess can baby sit for you, but don't ever stop past to see me?" "Nikki you act like you stay down the block. Let's be real, you live in the country. I'm forty minutes from Richmond, but'chu fifty minutes from my place and a hour and a half from Richmond."

Nikki pondered her reasoning for a second. She felt that if Princess was a true friend, she'd make the drive down to see her anyway. It bothered her that Princess had chosen not to be apart of her life. Princess never said so, but that's the way she was carrying it. She decided not to press the issue, because the last thing she wanted to do was come off as being selfish. "Where's the baby anyway? Hectic's keeping her?" Nikki asked, knowing it would get Shawnte' started.

"And you know it. He loves his daughter to death."

But she ain't even his daughter, Shawnte', it's Rocca's."

"For one, Rocca is dead and gone, god Bless him. Secondly, Hectic don' know that. Shidddddd, he even think Daisha looks like him."

"That's because he never saw a photo of Rocca,"

"And he never will!" Shawnte' assured her.

"Didn't he even question the possibility of someone else being Daisha's father?"

"Yeah."

"And?" Nikki anxiously awaited an answer.

"And, I told him that according to the doctors, I got pregnant the night of the Escalade escapade. There was no chance of it being Rocca's because….. because Rocca had been in Texas for the past ten days, taking care of some business. And, I wasn't with anyone else but him." Nikki could not stop herself from laughing . " Girl, I can't believe he ate that shit. You ain't no damn good, Te' Someone is going to stop you one day, "she added, still giggling.

"I know you think its fucked up but, look at it from my perspective. Daisha's father is dead. Hectic is the only father she will ever know, and he loves her. Isn't that what counts?" Nikki didn't bother to comment. She knew Shawnte' would not like what she had to say. "Whatever works for you." Nikki didn't mean that at all, but did not know what else to say. " You never told me how you got home anyway. "Shawnte' said, changing topics. "Stacy woke me up around six that morning. I wasn't aware that I fell asleep on the stairwell."

"You mean the steps heading up to the bedrooms?" "girl, shut up!"

"I'm just sayin', first you despise the man that haunts you in your dreams, now you referring to him by his first name and falling asleep in his mansion an shit. Jus' don't add up to me, Shawnte' teased. Anyway, before I was rudely cut off, Stacy and Tiny, I mean Timmy Tuff or whatever his name is, gave me a ride home." "I know she can't wait to talk about that at Glamour Girls."

" I ain't thinkin' bout Stacy or any of them other gossiping hoochies. Besides, they yo' beauty parlor Barbie friends, not mine, "Nikki said with a tight smirk on her face. "Those are not my friends, they're nothing more that associates, thank you very much, Miss slick ass. "Shawnte' replied, squinting her eyes. She hated how Nikki made her feel bad for having other friends and wanted to say something to Nikki about the situation, but decided better against it. She understood that Nikki valued their friendship to the utmost, and that the majority of her girlfriend's time was spent passing out cold lunch trays and counting inmates four times a day. "What time you gotta be at work?" "Why?" Nikki asked, sensing that it had something to do with her presence. "What'chu wanna use my crib again?" "Yeah, I'm trying to see Big Daddy." " I thought you said you weren't going to mess around with Portsmouth brothers anymore." "I know, but my coochie needs a good poundin' right now." "Damn, Shawnte', I thought Hectic had that bomb ass dick." " He do, I ain't lie about that. But Big Daddy lives up to his name." "I don't know why you even bothered to say I do,"Nikki said, slipping into her uniform. "Just clean up after ya'self, okay?" "Oh yeah, there's one more thing, "Shawnte' said, looking away from Nikki knowing she would flip out. "I need to use your Cherokee to go pick him up." "What's wrong with your Jeep?" "C'mon Nik, you know how suspicious it looks driving in P-Town in a new Range Rover. Besides, someone might recognize me. Hectic thinks I'm over here puttin' micro braids in one of your girlfriends head." "That's crazy, you're my only friend." " I know that , but he don't!" "Girl, you, somebody gon stop you one day!" Nikki reiterated, laughing. " Long as they ain't try'na stop me tonight, cause I gotta get mines." Still chuckling, Nikki tucked in her shirt, checking herself over in the mirror. " I gotta be at work in a little over an hour. I was gonna do some grocery shopping first, but it can wait. What I'll do is drive you to Portsmouth, pick'im up and bring the two of you back here. "Amazed by her friend's willingness to compromise Shawnte' began smiling. "What'chu smiling for?" " I'm only doing it because I wanna see this Big Daddy fellow. He must be something special, got'chu sneaking around like a crackhead. If he is all you say he is, maybe I'll get broke off a lil' somethin' proper too." Nikki scurried out of the bedroom after realizing Shawnte' was looking for something to throw at her. " You better run, bitch!" Nikki returned once she heard Shawnte's laugh. "Let's go now so I won't be late for work." Shawnte's happy face disappeared once she saw what her friend had on. "Unh unh, you ain't going dress like dat, are you?" She asked, frowning. "Yeah! Why?" "Why? Because you dressed like a cop!" "But I'm not a police, I'm a Correctional Officer. As long as you know, nothing else should matter." Shawnte' shrugged. Nikki had a point, but she still disapproved of it. She let out a deep sigh, staring at her stubborn girlfriend's face, "Well, let's go then," Nikki grabbed her keys, then turned on the living room lamp as she and Shawnte' left out the door. Ten minutes into the drive down Highway 58, neither one of them said anything to the other. Nikki was in a comfort zone from the local radio station. Slow jams and R&B music had become her favorite. It reminded her of Aunt Linda and how she would clean up around the house with Phillip Bailey pumping through the speakers. Luther, Patty and Stevie's soothing voice often sent Nikki into a musical high.

Shawnte' professed to feel the music as well as she stared at the many trees turn into silhouettes as the skies grew darker. She thought about her future with Hectic, and how she felt about Big Daddy. I wonder if Nikki thinks I'm a slut. If she does, she probably won't tell me. Maybe I should tell her the truth about how I feel about Big Daddy, she thought. " Hol'up, girl, that's my song! Nikki blurted after Shawnte' disrupted her flow, pressing the volume button. " Look , I gotta ask you somethin' . But first, I ain't been totally, honest with you. "Nikki could sense something was bothering her friend, so she gave her full attention, glancing back and forth at the road to let her know that she was listening. " It's about Reece....Big Daddy. His real name is Reece. I kinda lied to you when I said I stopped seeing Reece, because I didn't want you to think I was playing myself. Shawnte's voice started to crack, and her emotions began to spread over her face. " Nikki, I love Big Daddy. I love him so much I don't know what else to do." :What about Hectic?" Nikki asked, curious to her friends response. "I still care about him, of course, but I don't wanna be with him like I want to be with Reece." "Well, why don't you tell Hectic how you feel, and move on?" Nikki suggested, glancing at her , then back at the highway. "Shawnte', if you love Big Daddy, I mean Reece, then follow your heart. Whatever you do, just be a woman about it. Playing games will get'chu hurt, girl. And , I ain't talkin' about your feelings either." " I know , but "Shawnte' paused for a moment to gather the right words. " I just can't up and leave Hectic. I need him. Nikki vexed, "Need him for what?" "You know." "No, I don't know. Tell me!" Shawnte' knew Nikki wasn't going to make things easy for her, but she needed to say what she felt." I'm jus sayin' Nik, I truly love and wanna be with Reece, but he can't take care of me like Hectic can." Nikki switched over to the next lane while fighting the urge to bite her tongue. "I don't mean no harm, but there's a fine line between the two, girl." Shawnte felt chastised by the comment. "I'm sorry , I didn't mean it like that. "Nikki apologized, she sensed her best friend's feelings were hurt. "I just don't wanna see you end up with the short end of the stick. I love you Shawnte'. If anything happen to you , I don't know what I will do with myself. " Shawnte'smiled, Nikki's sincerity touched her. Nikki was turning into the Washington Park Projects when she spotted the smile, "You still a slut!" They both burst out in laughter. Shawnte' whipped out her cellular and called Big Daddy to inform him she was outside, while Nikki checked herself over. "Heeyyyyy Daddy , I'm outside your Aunt Peaches." "Four minutes, okay?" "I'm inside a black Cherokee." Big Daddy was a small time hustler and big time womanizer in the streets of the ghetto. Aunt Peaches and Reece's only relation was that he sold coke and she smoked it. At night Aunt Peaches kept a full house, mainly hustlers and friends. Her daughter and two nieces sold hot dinners and warm pussy to whomever was buying. Big Daddy was in the middle of a quickie when Shawnte' called. After he hung up , he began thrusting the twenty dollar freak twice as hard.

Nikki turned up her radio, while Shawnte' admired the many people who loitered around the neighborhood. Out of the corner of her eye, she thought she saw a familiar face quick stepping out of one of the houses. "Nikki!"Shawnte' yelled, causing Nikki to jump. "Look, you see that?" "See what?" Nikki asked, looking uncomfortably alert. "Nikki, I'm not trying to be funny , but I could have sworn I just saw Curls slip into that apartment over there, "Shawnte' pointed her finger in the direction of a guy who resembled Nikki's current boyfriend. Curls was the second man Nikki dated since she moved down to Suffolk. The relationship was going well until Nelson smacked her across the face one night. Half drunk, Nikki grabbed her service piece and pistol whipped Nelson until he fell unconscious, then called the police. When they arrived , she told them he was an ex-boyfriend who had used a spare key to gain entry in her home and assaulted her. Curls was nothing like Nelson, and his passive demeanor and energetic smile were enough to attract her attention. The light skinned brother with greenish-brown eyes had been in the Navy for over five years, according to Nikki. She loved neither him or Nelson. She tried, but her heart just wouldn't oblige. Curls was always gone to sea. Sometimes he'd write, most of the time he didn't . He had been at sea for over four months, and she knew the U.S.S. Kennedy Aircraft Carrier had two months of ocean drifting left before it reached the Norfolk Naval base. "Girl, Curls is in the middle of nowhere, getting seasick! "Nikki assured her. Still, Shawnte' wasn't convinced, sure of what she'd seen. "Te', boat boys like Curls couldn't survive in the projects, especially this one. Besides he's from the Beach, the suburbs I might add. What would it look like for him to be here....in the hood? Don make sense" Shawnte' started laughing at the thought of Curls strolling through the hood dressed in some blue bell –bottom denims. "Nik, you right. That dude had on a Rocawear sweatsuit and a platinum necklace." " I know damn well you ain't see no Curls, with his preppy dressin ass!" The two of them flinched as someone knocked on the back window of the jeep. Shawnte' and Nikki quickly turned to find Big Daddy waiting to hop in. "Dammmnn girl , he is cute with his big nose, Nikki said without moving her lips. "It isn't the biggest thing on 'im, Shawnte' mumbled back while Nikki unlocked the door. : It's open! Hey baby, what took you so long? "Shawnte' whined out like a spoil little girl. " I had to make sure Aunt Peaches took her medicine before I left." " That's why I love him, he's so considerate and caring of others, "she said looking at Nikki, waiting on her smile of approval. Nikki didn't show any emotion as she shifted the manual gear in reverse, backing out into the street. "Oh,Nikki, this is Reese. Reese, this is my best friend in the whole world, Nikki." "Hey Reese." "Hello there Nikki. I love that hairstyle on you, it really fits your face perfectly." "Thank you." All Nikki could do was blush. She knew this Reese fellow was a smooth talker and a seasoned charmer, she just didn't know to what degree. As Nikki ascended the ramp to I-264, Shawnte' turned around. While Reese leaned up toward the passenger seat, the two of them began whispering and laughing as if they were a longtime couple madly in love. Nikki tried to ignore the love pecks and snickering , but couldn't. She began pondering if she would ever find that special someone to share kisses of love and hugs of hope for a promising future. I'm tired of drifting. She got two lovers, and all I got is inmates, writing immature poems and drawing me crooked ass flowers, she thought. Nikki decided to turn the radio up after the fifth I love you, too. She checked her watch, ignoring the radio clock because it was 15 minutes fast. I got plenty of time, she thought. Just as she reached the Suffolk city limits, a special report came over the radio. Just in ....controversial rapper MC K.O. was picked up for questioning at his mother's home in Norfolk hours ago....for the rape of a woman who's name is being withheld at this time. The offense occurred around one this morning. According to Virginia Beach investigators, witnesses say the rapper disappeared around 12:30 from a birthday party he hosted at his Thorgood Mansion, and hadn't been seen the remainder of the party…

Sources say the rapper was identified by the victim, by his personalized diamond engraved charm. Authorities say the Grammy Award winning artist may be charged with rape if the evidence mounts….This is Lady Silk, stay tuned to 103 Jamz for further updates and any new developments. Shawnte' and Big Daddy had stopped the lovey dovey to focus on the special report. "Lucky you," Shawnte' said after turning the volume back down, "Looks like they got' cha boy." Nikki didn't reply, her emotions raced through her body. She didn't care for MC K.O. at all, yet felt as if she had to do something. There's no way he could have raped anyone last night, she assured herself. "That isn't right." Nikki said, shaking her head.

"What ain't right?" Shawnte' asked, eying her friend as if she were crazy.

"Te', we were at the party last night. He did not rape nobody last night."

"And how do you know that?"

"Cause, I know." Nikki sensed Shawnte' wanted more specific answers by the way she was looking. "Listen Shawnte'," she said, taking in a deep breath while looking into her rearview mirror to see if Reese was attentive to their conversation. "I know he didn't rape that girl last night because –"

"No you didn't girl!" Shawnte' shouted, excited, assuming that Nikki was gonna say that she had slept with the famous rapper or something of that nature.

"Hell no, I didn't sleep with him, if that's what 'chu thinkin'. After we argued, he walked upstairs while I sat in the hallway near the front room. He had a saxophone in his hand. Minutes later, I heard him blowing Earth, Wind, and Fire's 'Reasons'. He sounded so good, I tippy toed up the steps and followed the tunes down a long hall to his bedroom. I peeped inside, and there he was, playing the instrument as if he were making love to me. I mean it… I'm not sure how long I stood there listening to him, but I do know it was quite a while. When my legs got tired, I walked back down the hall and sat on the steps. I listened to the harmony until I fell asleep. The last time I checked my watch it read 2:40 a.m. and I was jus' getting sleepy."

"Damn Nikki, you was cold stalkin' a brother wont 'chu?"

"Stop playin', this is serious. Rape is a terrible allegation, especially when a man is innocent."

"You sure all you did was stand in the doorway of his bedroom, cause you soundin' like y'all long time acquaintances, not some bitch who wanna kill 'em."

"I don' like him, and as sure as hell don't want 'em, I told you that before. So don't even go there!" Nikki emphasized defensively.

"If he didn't rape her, trust me Nikki, he won't be charged."

"That's right," Big Daddy chimed in from the back seat.

"Fo'real, I could care less what they do to him. I'm just saying I know he didn't do it, that's all."

Nothing else was said the rest of the ride. Once they reached Nikki's townhouse, she ran inside, leaving the driver's side door of the SUV open. She darted to the bedroom and grabbed her pistol and holster belt. By the time she exited the room, Shawnte' and Reese were already getting comfortable in the living room.

"Nice to meet 'chu again, Big Daddy." Nikki said, making toward the front door, aiming to catch Shawnte's attention so she could give that 'don't forget what I told you about my bedroom. Look.'

"I got 'chu covered girl." Shawnte' assured, noticing Nikki's eyes cutting at her.

As soon as the engine started, Shawnte' reached down Big Daddy's pants, pulling out his prized possession. Like a mad woman, she grabbed him tightly, then gave Reese a hard, aggressive jerk. Shawnte' looked her lover in the eyes and started to purr. Whenever she did this it was Big Daddy's cue to tear it up. Shawnte' occupied her other hand with Reese's balls. In seconds, her saliva ran along the long neck of Big Daddy's dick as her tongue slithered around the thick, warm head.

Nikki was in deep thought as she headed for work, having mixed emotions about Keith Osbourne. I can't believe I took up for him the way I did. What's wrong with me? The sensuous melodies Keith played on his sax slow danced through her mind, and was evident that the rapper had left an impression. Momentary, her thoughts wandered to a quiet place in the woods, under a stern cherry tree. There, on a quilt, Keith Osbourne sat beside her, playing his instrument. Just as the rapper attempted to kiss her, the gloomy vision disappeared after a commuter sounded his horn. "What's wrong with me?" she asked herself. "I can't believe I'm thinking of him like this." Moments later, she felt a tingle between her legs, along with a cold draft. All Nikki could do was shake her head after realizing she'd become wet. She quickly picked up the cellular and pressed star-3.

"Is Seargent Crawford in yet?"

"Yes he is, as a matter of fact."

Silence.

“Sergeant Crawford speaking.”

“Yes sergeant, this is Nicole Wallace, I’m gonna be a little late. I have to stop at the Virginia Beach police department. I’m a possible witness to a crime.”

….. “I think”……….

CHAPTER 9

Keith had been questioned for nearly three hours before the interrogation got ugly. After a scuffle with detectives, other officers witnessing behind a mirrored glass rushed into the interview room, aggressively wrestling Keith down to the floor. They handcuffed the rapper, then escorted him to a central booking where he was placed in a holding cell with three other gentlemen.

"Am I under arrest?" Keith yelled through the bars as an officer locked the iron gate. Out of anger, he wrapped his fingers around the bars to the entrance and began shaking them with all his might. "Damn it! Can I at least make a phone call?" he pleaded.

"Ayh kid," a calm voice spoke from behind, "that'll get you nowhere. Come sit down over here. You're getting yourself all worked up buddy."

Keith turned around to find that the voice belonged to a middle-aged white man with a kangaroo pouch for a belly. "I got money. Um'ma millionaire, I ain't gotta put up with dis!" he declared.

The saggy faced gentleman shrugged at the statement. "This Virginia Beach kid. Everybody has money 'round here. That doesn't stop the MAN from locking us up, now does it?" he replied, extending out a half-roll of tissue to Keith. "Here, clean yourself up."

Keith grabbed the tissue, sitting down beside the silver-haired gentleman making an attempt to be hospitable. "Thanks." He said, trying to calm himself down.

"Mitch-Mitch Holley." He introduced himself as they shook hands. "I already know who you are. We all do." He assured, gesturing toward the white kid talking to his hands and a drunk brother laying on the cement floor, sobering up. “You are the famous rapper K.O. Regardless of what people say bout ‘chu, my daughter digs your ste-lo fa’ sheezy ma’ neezy.”

Keith couldn’t help breaking out in a cheesy smile. The street slang the old man spoke easily caught him off guard. “Where you from, what you do?” he said, trying to disguise the smoldering giggle in his voice.

“I work for people like you.” Mitch replied. Keith looked confused for a moment, as he pondered Mitch’s words. Maybe he’s an accountant. He’s too old to do house cleaning, and he damn sure ain’t security. Maybe he cleans pools or something, he thought. Mitch read the rappers expression and decided to let him in on the mystery profession. “I’m a Private Investigator.”

“You a police officer too?”

Mitch threw up his fist like a boxer. “Who you callin’ one time man?” he said in a joking manner.

“I thought private inve-”

“You thought wrong babe,” Mitch corrected. “I’m an ex-con, that’s what I am. No need to be sorry, jus’ be careful, slick.”

“I like you Mitch, you al’right man.”

“Man you ain’t been locked up a whole day, and tryin’ to shack up already!”

They both laughed in unison.

Soon, Keith’s mind wandered off. Recently things hadn’t been going so well for him.

Now he couldn’t believe he was locked up in a holding cell with an ex-con-median. For the first time in two days, he was feeling high spirited and sure of himself. “Everything is gonna be all right.” Keith mumbled to himself unconsciously.

“What’s that kid? Didn’t quite catch that,”

“I said, what ‘chu in for, and are you gonna be a’right?” the rapper countered, snapping out of his daydream.

“Trespassing,” Mitch blurted out. “I was working for this rich lawyer a few months back. He hired me to find out who his wife was screwing. She, too, was a lawyer. I tracked her down in six days. I could’ve done it in one, but I wanted to milk the rich bastard for all I could.” Keith sat there on the hard floor iron bench, giving Mitch all his attention, while the drunk on the floor raised his head from under his coat to hear the story.

"Anyway, I tracked her down to this secluded condo on the beach. I ran the license plates to find a woman lived in the house alone. I stake out the beach house until it was dark enough for me to snoop around a little. I knew his wife was fucking this broad, all I had to do was take some pictures of them hugging or even sitting extra close."

"Who was the lawyer?" The drunk interrupted, only to get a harsh stare from Mitch.

"Like I was saying before somebody rudely fumed the room with Budweiser breath. I made my way to the back of the condo before realizing I wasn't going to get anything good from the front or side windows. I eased up onto the deck...and there they were, in plain view."

"What do you mean, plain view?" Keith asked.

"There on the deck was a huge glass sliding. Not only were the curtains made of sheer material, but they were wide open. The two of them were butt naked, making love on a Persian rug near the fireplace. I took so many pictures," he said chuckling," of course I kept some for my uh, uh, portfolio if you will." Once Keith and the drunk's laughter subsided, he continued. "I gave the lawyer the pictures to use as exhibitions in divorce court. He won the house and all that shit. She turns around a few weeks later and fucks his nephew, not for revenge, but for my name and number so her dyke girlfriend could bring up charges against me. And here I am."

Not only was Keith enticed by the story, he had an idea. If Sheila is living in adultery, I'm gonna know for sure, he thought.

An officer walked passes the cell, breaking his thought. "Is that MC K.O.?" the officer practically screamed. "Yo ma' man, I'm a big fan of yours. Can I trouble you for an autograph?"

Keith studied the young brother as he walked over to the bars. "Who's this going to?"

"Sign it to 'my main man Chuck', if you don't mind." The police officer said enthusiastically.

"Yo check it out." Keith whispered, surveying the walkway. "I need to get on that jack. They got me locked up, and I ain't even made a phone call yet. Think you can look out?"

"Sure man, anything you need." The police officer looked around, then unlocked the gate, letting the rapper out. "The phone's over there. Take your time, and thank you for your autograph."

Keith ignored the officer hawking him from behind the main control and walked towards the phone. He started dialing Alfred's number then hung up.

No I should call Timmy Tuff, he has a good attorney, he contemplated as he commenced dialing. But just as Keith heard the first ring, he hung up again. I need to call Arlene before she catches another heart attack. Once again, he dialed. "Hello? Momma it's me. I just called to let you know I'm alright."

"These people on the news sayin' my boys a rapist. Why are they saying these things about you Keith?"

"Momma listen to me for jus' one moment. Don't pay the reporters no mind. If anyone knows me, it's you, and I'm telling you, I didn't rape anyone. Once I clear this matter up, I'll call you back momma, okay?"

"One more thing, Keith, they went over to your place and searched it."

"Thanks ma, I figured they'd do that. Hope nothing disappears."

"Osbourne-Keith!" a police officer yelled in his direction.

"Love you, momma, gotta go." Keith hung up the phone. His eyes scanned the room for the voice that echoed his name.

"Are you Keith Osbourne?" The police officer asked in his most professional voice. Keith nodded, confirming his identity. "Come with me, you're wanted upstairs for questioning."

'How many times they gon' question me? Nawh, they don't wanna ask any questions, they probably wanna harass me and beat my ass some more.' Keith thought as the officer escorted him to the elevator up to the 2nd floor, where a tall black detective met him at the entrance of the interrogation room."Hello Mr. Osbourne, I'm Detective Fish. I went over to your home, lovely place."

"I know, my mother saw it on the news."

"Sorry 'bout that, just doing my job." He said, placing his hand around Keith's arm. They started down the end of the hall. "I want to apologize about the incident earlier today. You're welcome to file a complaint with Internal Affairs if you like."

"It wasn't all their fault, and no, I'm not interested in filing any complaints. Where are they taking me anyway?"

"Right here to the Forensics Lab."

Keith looked at the lab technician through the square glass window, and for the moment his mind recalled the times he'd watched Forensic Detective on the Discovery Channel. The door opened and the droopy shaded lady with the red hair gestured him to come in. Fish and Keith entered the lab, where the woman greeted Keith in a friendly introduction.

"Mr. Osbourne, I'm going to take your fingerprints. Then I'll need a DNA hair sample from your head, even though you're hairless. Last but not least, I will need to take a few snapshots of your genitals."

Keith couldn't believe what had just been asked of him. He turned towards Fish, shaking his head, "This is degrading. I can't let this woman take pictures of my-"

"Dick?"

"No. I wasn't going to say that!" Keith replied, offended.

"Look, this is a rape investigation. A picture of your dick ...is necessary and crucial to this ongoing case."

I'm in a no-win situation.

As soon as Keith exited the room, the woman began chuckling under her breath. "This is your rape suspect?" she asked the Detective. "His dick is the size of a premature mushroom. There's no way it will erect to past half a foot. Thirteen to fourteen inches is out of the question."

Fish's grin widened. "I happened to glance down too, and if that thing he calls a penis erects past five inches I'd be surprised.

The technician snickered once more, "He's definitely not our man.'

"I know, but I'm confident he'll lead us to the serial rapist."

"So you think he knows who is raping these women?"

"He hasn't a clue," Fish answered deviously, "but I wouldn't tell him that, as long as he's our prime suspect, the real offender won't be alarmed by the media."

The lab technician looked at the detective with concern on her face. "What about Mr. Osbourne's reputation?" Fish gave the chubby woman a cold-hearted stare.

"He's a rapper for Christ's sake, he has no good reputation." Ignoring her disappointed stare, Fish continued, "If using him to get our man is what it takes, then so be it."

"Still it's wrong, Fish."

"So is rape!" he countered, "Besides, this kinda thing might even help with his record sales or something." He added with a dumbfounded countenance.

"If it makes you sleep better at night. I have work to do, chat with you later." Fish turned around and headed for the door. Just before it closed, the lab technician and yelled, "Call me when you're ready to do real police work!"

Fish stood motionless, absorbing the words of his co-worker without turning around. That bothered him a little, but neither his face nor attitude would show it.

"Look son," Fish said as he assessed her comment, "let me ask you a question. How do you feel about rape?"

Keith looked at the detective as he escorted him down the hall by the arm

"What is this, game you playin'? What now, I'm supposed to say something incriminating, right?"

"No, you're supposed to give me a simple answer." Keith didn't say anything else as they walked toward the line-up room. Fish stopped, and squared shoulders with the rapper, staring him directly in the face.

"You got somethin' to say, then say it." Keith demanded.

"I'm level with you Mr. Osbourne. I don't think you raped anyone."

"Well, if that's the case, then why am I still being treated like a criminal?"

"Because witnesses says you disappeared at 12:30. She claims the voice she heard resembled one of your rap videos, and you have been known to rap about maiming people. That makes you a suspect."

"Now you gonna go in there," Fish pointed to the line-up room, "and this girl who's titty just got bitten halfway off is going to identify you."

"Why?"

"Why? Because you are a famous entertainer, that's why. And her boyfriend, Roach, you know. Roach Gotti don't cha?" Keith nodded. "Well, Roach was at your party, says he saw you jump in your Bentley around 12:45 last night, but don't worry son." He concluded, lighting up a cigarette. "Here, you might need this before going in there."

"I don't smoke, and why in the hell should I not worry about some kid lying on me and a rape victim pointing me out? It don't take a genius to know if someone picks you out of a lineup, your ass is in trouble."

"Calm down, calm down man, you making my blood pressure go up. I say don't worry because I'm the Fish. I find the worms without getting hooked on bullshit police theories and silly investigation procedures. Of course she's gonna pick you, but it won't matter because the statement she conveyed to the police at the hospital said the assailant had a mask on. Plenty of witnesses said you disappeared around 12:30, but the only witness who saw you drive off in your car is the boyfriend of the victim. I'm not convinced right now, but let me tell you this, Mr. Osbourne, Keith, or whatever you go by, if it turns out that you are the man I'm looking for, you will go down for the rest of your natural life, but not before I square these Stacy Adams off in yo' punk ass.

Unfazed by the detective's John Shaft impersonation, Keith rolled his eyes and began stroking his temple with his thumb. "What we waiting for of-fi-cer Fish?" The detective didn't respond, he simply stood quietly, puffing the cigarette. Minutes later, an officer stepped into the hallway.

"Fish you're on!" he yelled before re-entering the room. Fish ushered Keith into the lineup room. An elderly black police officer with droopy cheeks then walked over to them and instructed Keith to jump anywhere in the line. Keith obliged, standing second to last toward the right side of the lineup.

"Listen up!" the officer shouted, looking up at the eight men standing on the platform under the radiant lights. "When I call your number , step forward. I will ask you to turn sideways, then forward again. You will all read these words out loud." He pointed to the small sign in his hand, "If you do not understand, please raise your hands now." Nobody raised their hands.

The woman and her boyfriend stepped inside the identification room. Fish entered moments later. "Alright Chuck, we're ready!" The mini blinds rose, and the young woman immediately scanned over the men until she recognized a familiar face. Fish read her expression all the way. Surprisingly, the woman didn't react when she saw MC K.O. As they went through the procedures, the woman nodded. "That's him right there!" Roach belted out, only to have Fish grab him by his long cornrolled ponytail and toss him out the small room. "Okay, I think we are ready now." One by one the men stepped forward, reading the lines from the small sign the officer held in between his arms. When Keith's turn came, he stepped forward just as the blue coat had instructed. "Now, turn sideways." Keith obliged. "Now, face the window. Read the words on the sign in front of you." Keith sighed deeply, "Turn over bitch, I'm about to cum." The girl studied the rapper over for a few seconds. Fish continued to analyze her face as she shook her head. " Does he talk like that all the time?" she asked without taking her eyes off Keith. "What do you mean?" Fish asked, already having a good idea where she was going. "I mean , is that his normal voice, the one he uses outside his entertainment life?"

Impressed by the young woman's ability to see past the rapper's fame and concentrate on the profile she witnessed the previous night, Fish replied "Yes, that's the way he speaks off stage." That's what I figured, she thought to herself, still staring him over through the glass. "Detective Fish is it?.... That's not him. He's too small, and the guy that raped me , his voice seemed to be tryin to imitate MC K.O.'s in a way." "Are you sure?" "No, I'm not, and right now what matters is being positively sure, right?"

"Well. Miss Swinson, thanks for coming down. I'll be over to see you tomorrow with more questions. For now, get some rest and if you think of anything that could help solve this case, please call me." Fish nodded, gesturing to Chuck to drop the blinds over the window. "Hold Mr. Osbourne for a moment while I find Miss Swinson an escort." Fish stepped out of the room behind the victim. He ignored the hostile look Roach was beaming at him as he stood against the wall with his arms folded. Words mumbling under his breath. "Cuse me, did you say something?" The detective barked with a mean mug of his own. " I said, he gon' pay for raping my girl, one way or the other!"

"I don't think he did it baby, "Miss Swinson chimed in. "Shut up, you don' went groupie on me that fast, huh? I know he did it." Fish looked at the young woman then shook his head, "Miss Swinson, talk to him before he finds himself in some shit he can't get out of." A deputy heading toward the main lobby with donuts and coffee in his hand was making his way past the small crowd when Fish stopped him. " Hey bud, You going up front?" The officer, who'd taken a mouthful of chocolate custard, nodded his head, "Good, escort these two up front, will ya?" The detective watched them until they disappeared behind the door. He began to wonder. If she was smart enough not to pick Mr. Osbourne out of a line-up, there must be something else she hasn't told us. The detective started to go after her, but decided better against it. She just been raped, Fish contemplated, God knows what she's going through right now. Roach soon came to mind, something tells me this Roach Gotti fellow will bring the pain to Mr. Osbourne any chance he gets. Fish walked to the line –up room, then opened the door. The old man had Keith by the arm, already waiting for Fish. Chuck yelled over the intercom, "The sergeant just called for you. There's a woman up front who says she's a witness to your investigation or something. You might want to hold Osbourne until you've interviewed her, his name was mentioned." Fish nodded firmly, turned to the rapper, looking him in the eyes, " I wonder what this witness will tell me?" he said as he led Keith down the hall toward the elevator. "Yeaahhh, I wonder too." Nothing else was said the rest of the way to the holding cell. Keith could not phantom any kind of witness to a crime he hadn't committed. First he thought setup, then conspiracy, a plot to eliminate the biggest money maker in the rap world from the industry.

As he sat quietly in the cell rationalizing his theory, he came to the conclusion that he was thinking as a fool would. Mitch stared at his new acquaintance, wondering if he should say something. "They tryin' to fuck ya, huh?" Keith's eyes cut at Mitch, his head slowly followed, I'll know in a few minutes." Mitch didn't have a clue as to what Keith meant , so he said nothing. "What about you?" the rapper continued, "You gon' be alright?" "Yeah, this ain't nothing, I told ju. I got the magistrate scratching my back, between me and you- “The P.I. interrupted himself, “ Oh, that means I got the juice, pull, clout, back-“ I know what chu’ mean, Keith replied, cutting him off. “Look Mitch, I may have a job for you if you’re interested.” Mitch smirked sarcastically, “If I’m interested? If it pays, I’m interested, believe that!” The P.I. produced a business card from his back pocket then handed it to the famous entertainer, “Here, call me.” “I will, jus don’t milk a bastard like myself too bad, okay?” They began to laughing in unison, only to be distracted by the shadow of two people standing in front of the holding cell. Keith’s jaw practically fell to the floor when he looked up and saw the beautiful woman dressed in a deputy sheriff’s uniform, standing beside Detective Fish. It took him a split second to recognize the face, it was the same woman he’d gotten into a small dispute with last night at his home. This is a set up, he thought. This police bitch is surely going to say I left out the front door. Keith’s eyes widened, as his heart began pounding through his chest. I’m going down! “Is this the man? “ Fish demanded to know, “Is this the man you saw playing a saxophone in his bedroom during Stacy’s party?” The woman did not respond right away. Once her eyes met Keith’s, she was in a temporary trance. “Miss Wallace, Fish whispered, his stare still on Keith. “Yes that’s him.” Keith’s expression changed to a surprised one. He couldn’t believe that the same lady who wanted to cut his head off last night had just cleared him of rape. Standing slowly, he walked toward the bars and gazed into her eyes. They don’t look the same, Keith analyzed, her eyes are breath taking, she’s beautiful! Keith looked over at Fish, who was informing an officer behind the desk that he wasn’t going to be charged, then back at the police lady in front of him. “ I’m confused,” he said to the woman as he read her name tag. “I thought you didn’t like me.” The female officer gave him a non chalant stare, up and down before responding, “ You thought right…… because I don’t!” Keith wasn’t sure what had just transpired. All he knew was that he wasn’t going to ever forget the name Nichole Wallace. His eyes followed her all the way out of view. “She’s a cutie, and she likes you, man!” Mitch declared, reading Keith’s sudden daydream. “ I think I like her as well. Just one problem, I don’t know her or why she was in my bedroom watching me….It just doesn’t make sense!”

CHAPTER 10

It had been three months since she had seen Keith Osbourne at the Virginia Beach Police department, yet 3 seconds since he'd last crossed her mind. Whether she wanted to or not, Nichole Wallace thought about the rapper every day since their last encounter. Sometimes she smiled from the pleasant images she pictured. At other moments she cried, hating him for everything he stood for in the streets.

It was Nikki's day off, and she sat on the living room loveseat, cuddled up with one of her small pillows used for decoration. In one hand was a remote control, in the other, a celery stick drenched in sour cream spread. Her mind touched on Curls as she flicked through the channels and nibbled on her midnight snack, unable to phantom why he had not yet called. The Navy Carrier had docked in Norfolk two days ago. "Fuck 'em, I ain't feeling him like that anymore, anyways, she reasoned, trying to convince herself she wasn't pressed. But I sure wouldn't mind a booty call from him right now, from anybody. It had been over six months since Nikki last sexed a man, and it was at the point where every time she saw two people making love in a movie or two females kissing each other on MTV, her hormones would surge through her body, causing her to dash to the bedroom closet to retrieve Big Willie. Big Willie was her savior, an eight inch chocolate vibrator that delivered explosive, earth shattering orgasms. Sometimes she'd conquer a pair of D-sized Energizer batteries in one late night session, turning the big vibrator into a baby's rattler toy. Now Nikki was tired of her reliable companion. It was good, but her body needed the touch of a warm sensuous dick, stroking her insides to putty. She desired the feel of a man's firm, hairy chest friction up against her breasts. She needed to sweat a river, like she used to do with Rodney.

Nikki mute the television once the phone rang. The cordless was tucked in the seam of the cushion behind her. By the second ring she was screening the call, hoping it would be Curls calling to let her know he was coming over to rescue her body from the plastic man. So much for hope. "Hey Te', what'chu want?" Nikki answered disappointedly. " Damn girl, whats' wrong with you? I ain't seen you in almost three weeks, and you sounding like I'm worrying you!" "Naw, it isn't that, I'm just bored as hell I guess." "Well, that's why I'm calling. Hectic is having an album release party for Novocaine." "The Novocaine from Churchill?" Nikki blurted. "Yeah that's him. And Hectic said his album is definitely going platinum, because the West Coast Doctor did a few tracks and everything the Doc touches turns platinum," Shawnte' said as if she were going platinum herself. "So, you wanna go or what?" "Girl, you must be crazy if you think I'm leaving up outta here in the rain." "Chill, Miss Premenstrual Cycle, the party ain't til tomorrow night." "Oh, Nikki replied, "my bad, and I'm not on my period, thank you very much." "Well, I gotta go, I'm meeting Big Daddy at the Marriot." Nikki hung up without saying goodbye. The last thing she wanted to hear about was somebody else getting their groove on.

Thunder and lightning was in full throttle, and rain drops could be heard dancing a tune on Nikki's living room window frame. She was watching the Soul Food mini-series on television when a loud, thunderous knock came over the door. She leaped from the sofa, ran into her bedroom and grabbed her pistols from the nightstand, then hurried toward the front door. She didn't get many visits at all, and just finished conversing with Shawnte'. It has to be Curls, she thought ecstatically. Still, Nikki took no chances. "Who is it?" "It's me", a calm proper and intelligent voice replied. There was only one person she knew that spoke like a proper European from Harvard, and that was Curls. She quickly opened the door with one hand, hiding the gun behind her back in the other. A sudden shock rushed her body. Nikki's eyes opened wide as she drew the gun toward the person in front of her. Standing in the doorway, soaked down in a pair of pinstriped slacks and thin button down Armani shirt that clung to his body like shiny skin, accenting his chest and stomach muscles, was Keith Osbourne.

"What are you doing here?" Nikki asked with the gun pointed into his chest, "And what –do-you-want?" Keith was too sexy, with the rain dribbling down the side of his smooth, bald head. "I think you know why I'm here." Nikki's heart began rattling in her rib cage. Her arm began shaking, as well as the weapon in her hand, "Are you gonna," assuming what she was going to ask, Keith calmly chimed in, "that's right Nichole, I'm gonna make love to you." Keith grabbed the gun from his chest, slowly pulling Nikki close to his wet body. Her mind told her to resist, but her body quickly gave into his touch. Just as she started to tell Keith to stop, he tossed the gun to the carpet behind her and began pressing his lips against hers. Nikki opened her mouth to invite his kiss, her body on fire. Goose bumps ravaged her skin as she interlocked tongues with his. She grabbed hold, pulling him into her house and closing the door behind him. Nikki wasted little time peeling the wet shirt off his body. Her hands rubbed his chiseled frame up and down, studying every inch. Nikki's head fell back as Keith's lips explored the side of her neck. Her body was defenseless to his hypnotic foreplay, and right then and there shc yearned to share a hot explosive orgasm with him.

Like a delicate rose, Keith gently laid Nikki down on the sofa. Her nipples began to erect as Keith's drenched slacks hit the carpet. Kicking his feet free of his pants, he climbed in between Nikki and began to slow grind his tool against her jewel. Soon, she felt him inside her. Nikki closed her eyes, taking in every breath slow, cherishing each methodical stroke inside her body. Keith began thrusting her fast, then faster. Nikki proceeded to tremble and shiver. She could feel an enormous orgasm ready to erupt inside. Her eyes were still closed when she heard a voice call out her name. "Nikki!" "Huh, baby?" she moaned out. "Nikki…Nikki!" Nikki opened her eyes to see why her new lover was calling out her name so unattractively. When she did, disappointment flooded her body. It was Curls, towering over her. He had been trying to awaken her for nearly five minutes. Nikki elevated from the sofa to catch a sunray beaming on the right side of her face. Damn, that was the best dream I had in a long time, and I'm wet, Nikki thought as she tried to regain her composure and focus on the situation at hand.

Before she could ask Curls how he'd gotten in the apartment, he said, "I knocked on the door but it was open, so I let myself in. It's unlike you to leave your door open, Nikki!" Nikki thought about the statement and quickly came to the conclusion that she'd forgotten to lock the door when she returned from the local 7-eleven with the sour cream she purchased earlier last night. Curls sat on the love seat and gave his girl a warm hug. "Nikki, I really missed you. All I've been thinking 'bout the last six months…was you." Nikki looked him over as he perched beside her, "Why did it take you three days to stop past here?" Caught off guard by Nikki's demanding question, Curls brows rose to the center of his fore head. Although he looked to be of Latin decent, Curls, who stood 6 feet 3 inches, was half German and half African American with greenish brown eyes. The heart throbber adopted the name by the way his hair grew wild. His thick, black eyebrows emphasized his every facial expression. "Oh…uh, yeah. I was...well ,I got into a little scuffle with one of the flight deck crewman while we were in the middle of a training exercise," he explained with his brows arched and eyes wide open. "I've been locked down in the Navy Brig over 90 days. I wasn't sure what day we arrived here, and assumed they let me out of the brig once our carrier docked." Nikki gave him a kiss on the cheek which led to a wet juicy one on the mouth. Minutes later they lay naked in the bedroom, bumping bodies between the sheets, leaving a clothing trail from the living room to the bedroom. Afterwards, Nikki and Curls lay cuddled up next to each other in silence. She wanted to ask him when he got the huge diamond studded earring, but it was not the time. Instead, she analyzed the sex she had just experienced. It was good, but not six months good. I thought we'd be cumming all over the place simultaneously. Hope he don't think the 25 minutes he gave me done the trick. Maybe I should play with his bat and balls, see if he wants to try and hit a home run. Nikki began rubbing his leg, and then gently grabbed the wet and slimy muscle that stuck to his inner thigh. She could feel the blood rushing through it. Her coochie proceeded to tingle; aware that round two was near. Curls rolled over, looking Nikki in the eyes, giving her that energetic smile of innocence.

"You ready, because I am," Curls whispered, pecking Nikki on the neck and lips, "but first I have to take a time out in the john."

"He so damn nerdy." Nikki mumbled under her breath as she watched his firmness scurry into the bathroom.

While she waited for his return, she jumped from the bed and grabbed a towel that hung from the back of the door. She quickly wiped herself dry of excess fluids, retrieved another condom from the top drawer, then climbed back into the bed. Curls exited the bathroom with both hands between his legs covering his private as if he was a shy little boy.

Nikki couldn't help but smile at his wholesomeness. Curls is definitely loveable, I see him as husband material, she thought to herself as he climbed under the covers, grabbing hold of her. He gently massaged Nikki's titties with his soft wet tongue, then he eased his hand between her thighs and gently began rubbing the lips of her already moistened poon-tang. Soon, they were back at it. 15 minutes into their session, the lovebirds were dripping in sticky, wet sweat.

Nikki commanded Curls to stop and lay belly up so she could get on top and take control of their episode. As she started to place the limpness of what was left of curls inside her, he unconsciously spoke. "Oh yeah, Nikki, babe," he muttered, "I picked up your gun off the carpet and tucked it under the sofa cushion after I let myself in. you must've dropped it somehow."

Nikki's heart fell to the pit of her stomach. "You found my pistol where?"

"On the floor, near the front door." Curls sensed something was wrong by the horrified look on her face. "What's wrong? Is everything alright Nikki?" he asked, full of concern.

Nikki didn't reply until she unsaddled herself from Curls, laying beside him. "Yeah, Curls, everything is fine, I just can't believe I was that careless, that's all."

It was a lie, but she was in no mood for questions. She needed to think to herself for a moment, her own questions requiring immediate answers.

Was Keith Osbourne really here last night, or was I dreaming? And if he wasn't here, then how did my .38 find its way to the living room carpet? For a second, she forgot about Curls, focus switching to MC K.O.

Curls tried to wrap his arms around her, but Nikki rudely declined. "Not now Curls, I'm not feeling up to it." He responded with a facial gesture, letting his girlfriend know that he understood.

The next twelve minutes, they silently lay in bed. All of a sudden, a burst of energy came over Curls, and he leaped off the bed. "You hungry? Matter of fact, today I'm cooking breakfast for you."

"I don't have breakfast food to cook."

"No problem!" Curls hummed, smiling. "You stay right here and I'll run to the store, get what you need, come back in a jif and fix you a nice hot breakfast in bed."

"I could really use that." Nikki replied as Curls walked out of the bedroom to gather his clothes off the floor.

Minutes later the front door shut, informing Nikki that he was on his way.

As Shawnte's Range Rover pulled up in the front of the townhouse, a white Dodge rental car cruised up the street. Big Daddy was certain he had just witnessed his rival enemy and first cousin leave Nikki's place. "what the hell is he doing here?" Big Daddy asked himself. "I hope Nikki ain't fall for Sonny's navy boy act, because she damn sure isn't the street hustler type."

Big Daddy leaped from the Rover and darted to Nikki's front door, knocking as hard as he could. Nikki jumped out of the bed, wrapping her bathrobe around her sticky body. Keith flashed across her mind as the thumping knocks resembled those she thought she heard last night. She quickly dismissed the thought as foolish and partly wishful thinking, and hurried to the door anticipating Curls. When she opened the door, Big Daddy was standing with a stern face.

"Hey Big Daddy, where's Shawnte'?" she asked curiously after noticing her girlfriends Jeep parked out front.

Looking confused and worried, Big Daddy said, "I was hoping you could tell me."

Nikki instantly sensed trouble.

"And did Sonny just leave from here?"

"Who the hell is Sonny?" Nikki snapped, frustrated, still wondering where her best friend was and if she was okay.

"The light skinned brother with the good hair."

"The who?"

The two were suddenly distracted by the chilling sound of the telephone.

CHAPTER 11

Keith awakened to the sound of ringing, "Get the phone, Sheila." He slurred out with the satin pillow smothering his mouth. After the eight ring, he jumped up only to find Sheila gone, as usual. Ever since he had found evidence of his wife's infidelity, their marriage had begun to slide. Sheila's reason for not trying to make the relationship work was the rape allegations her husband dealt with every other day.

After the first two weeks of pleading his case about the false accusations, he stopped trying and used it as a reason not to sex her, at least until he found out she was indeed committing adultery. Sheila not only knew her husband wasn't a rapist, but she knew exactly who the perpetrator was. She encountered him a few years back at a hotel party in Atlanta, where she was attacked and forced into her hotel room. In seconds, the rapist ripped off the little clothes she had on, thrown her down on the bed and forced himself inside her.

He began pumping her harder and harder, but Sheila didn't fight. Although the attacker had on a mask, she knew exactly who he was. She studied that familiar stride over and over. She started moving her body in motion, throwing the pussy back at him. Soon Sheila had her legs up in the air, then behind her head.

"Fuck this pussy harder! Nigga!" she commanded him. "I- oooh! I know who you are," she began to groan, "and I'm glad you want this as much as me." When she revealed his name, the man took off the mask, and rape became consensual. "It's our little secret." Were Sheila's last words to the unmasked man before leaving her room.

Keith answered the phone sounding hoarse and half awake. "Yo! Who's dis callin' here this early?" he asked with a sudden attitude.

"It's me kiddo…I'm on the job, baby, holla back."

"Okay man." Keith's tone lowered to calm after recognizing the caller. "Ring my wireless when you hear something. I won't be here in Virginia. I'm leaving for Chi-town in two days. My spring tour starts on Monday."

"Okay." The caller replied, then hung up. The phone rung immediately after the rapper answered, sounding irritated.

"Calm down K.O., it's just me, man."

"What's up Alfred, everything in tact?"

"Of course. Am I the best road manager in the world or not? Huh, huh?"

"Yeah, yeah." Keith shot back quickly just to cut off his irritating voice.

"What's going on for the day, because Mont. Timmy Tuff and the rest of the Salt Water Boys going up to Buckroe Beach?"

"What's happening in Buckroe?" Keith asked, yawning.

"You don' know? Hectic is throwing a huge album release party for his new artist. Word is, this Novocaine kid spits it raw and hardcore."

Alfred's tone sparked a sudden interest in Keith. He wants me to check out my new competition, and if he's bringin' the fire like that. Maybe I will, Keith pondered.

"Look here. Uh, alfy, if you think that I'm going up there, you can forget it."

Alfred heard the dial tone soon after. Keith laid back down on his bed contemplating what he should wear to the party. He marveled at the thought of popping up there and surprising everyone.

As he lay across his spread trying to gather enough energy to get up and take a leak, his thoughts drifted back to the woman he'd seen in the holding cell three months ago. Every day since, Nicole Wallace was all he'd been thinking of. In fact, he dreamed of her body, wishing it was the one he made love to nightly. The few times he did have sex with his wife, he'd close his eyes tight, pretending he was sexing Nichole crazy. Thanks to Mitch, he not only knew where Nichole Wallace lived, but he knew she wasn't seeing anyone.

Yesterday after Sheila disappeared into the stormy night to a local club, Keith built up the courage to go over to Nikki's house. Now, he was sitting on the edge of the bed, smiling to himself. I knew she'd been thinking of me. He rose from the bed and walked into his wardrobe closet, putting his bladder on hold. When he returned home, he brought a souvenir with him, a wallet sized photo of Nichole from off the crease of her bedroom mirror. He wondered who all the other people in the pictures she had hanging up were, but didn't spend time thinking about it.

Keith stood in his closet dazed momentary. He stepped out, never taking his eyes off the photo, deciding to call her right then and there. "Damn, it's busy." He hung up and tried again, still busy. "Haven't heard of an answering machine or voice mailbox?" Keith retired the phone, placed the photo on the nightstand, then went to the bathroom to run the shower.

Outside his estate, across the street in a white van that read 'Jake's Plumbing' sat Detective Fish and his sidekick, Pataki. Pataki was a short white fellow with a thin build, who'd recently transferred from Kansas City to be close to his ailing sister, who was suffering from breast cancer.

"Sure wish he'd go to that damn party." Fish said out loud, removing the large headphones from his ear so he could hear himself talk.

Pataki looked on, confused, as he sat in the back of the van.

"What's that, sir?"

"How long you say you was a Detective in Kansas City?" Fish's tone was sarcastic.

"Why you ask?"

"Because, he may lead us to our man if it turns out he's not our guy, in which my instincts tell me."

"He's calling someone." Pataki stated, ignoring Fish's theory

Fish scanned the screen to see where Keith Osbourne had placed his last call.

"Strange." he muttered, massaging his bottom lip, something the detective did when his instincts were at work. "Never has he ever called this number here." He said, pointing to the screen. Fish sought out a warrant to wire tap the Rapper's phone through the Circuit Court Judge. Keith's line had been tapped ever since the day of his questioning.

Maybe it's that Wallace girl's number. 555 is the Suffolk County area isn't it?"

"That's right Pataki, it is. Tell me about the incident last night once more." Pataki looked at Fish as if he'd gone crazy. He'd told him what transpired last night seven times already.

"Like I said, Fish, it was so bizarre-"

“Like something outta a movie right?”

“That’s right, like a movie. Jenkins and I watched Mr. Osbourne storm outta his mansion like a madman. He, he looked to be on a mission. The rain was pouring down, it was thundering and-”

Fish cut him off. “Get to the part I want to hear about.” He commanded.

“The Suffolk part?”

Fish nodded.

He pulled up to these upscale townhouses then leaped from his car. By then, the rain, the rain was coming down twice as hard. He just stood there as if he were in no hurry. He knocked on the door only to be greeted by a .38 pointed at his dome. We thought it was a rape in progress but-”

“But he wore no mask as our prime suspect did right?” Fish chimed in.

“Anyway, he takes the pistol away from the woman then plants a kiss on her lips, weird huh?”

Fish gazed out the back window, “Now why would she first want to shoot him, then end up making out?” Pataki shrugged, lost in his own thoughts.

“Don’t make any sense.” Fish concluded, frustrated.

“Maybe he just wanted to thank her for speaking out for him.” Pataki shot back, sure of his theory.

“Yeah that makes perfect good sense to wait three months to show his gratitude…and he show it by sexing her. You’re a genius partner! Case fucking solved!”

Pataki despised Fish’s sarcasm. He sucked his teeth, calling his partner an asshole under his breath. Fish overheard Pataki mumble something but couldn’t figured out the words he uttered.

“Say something there?” Fish asked, hoping his partner would boldly repeat himself like a man so he could pop him in the mouth one good time.

“I said stake outs suck.” Pataki muttered. He almost revealed to Fish what he really said but decided better against it. Besides jeopardizing the assignment, he didn’t wanna get his ass kicked, Fish sensed it as well.

As Pataki maneuvered around the front seat of the van he spotted a blue Hummer with dark tinted windows pull up just pass the Rapper’s estate.

“Aye Fish, check this out.” Fish maneuvered around the wires, he almost tangled himself to get a clear view of the jeep that was parked suspiciously in the upscale neighborhood.

"How long has it been there?"

"Just pulled up."

For the moment they watched the SUV waiting to see who'd exit from it. Fish advised Pataki to get the number of the license plate. As Fish made his way back to the monitor, Pataki reached behind the driver's seat for the binoculars.

In seconds, the I.D. tags were in clear view.

"The plates read Virginia tag number Bravo…Golf…Echo…7-1-9 'er."

Fish relayed BGE-719. Data from the Department of Motor Vehicles files appeared moments later.

"The Hummer belongs to a William P. Wallnut." Fish paused, recalling where he had heard that particular name. Just as it occurred to him, two men exited the Jeep with machine guns.

"Call for backup! Its Roach Gotti and company, and he's packing heavy.

"No! There's another. Maybe we can take 'em Fish."

"What kind of gun are you holdin'?"

"A .40 cal, why?"

"And what kind of weapon you say they got?" Fish gave Pataki that look as if to say 'Damn! You so stupid!'

"Officer needs assistance at the Osbourne Estate. This is a Code 7-red."

As the water splashed against Keith's face, his mind struggled to picture something else but couldn't help himself.

Last night was the best love making I experienced in a long, long time." He convinced himself. "If and when Mitch finds what I know he'll find, I'm going to leave that no good wife of mine with the quickness." Keith turned off the shower, a beeping sound alerted him immediately. After realizing he motion security alarm had been triggered, he darted butt naked dripping water on the Iraqi rug. There on the chest drawer lay the pocket size security monitor. He snatched it up and quickly turned it on. After tapping a few buttons all the camera angles popped up on the mini-screen.

"What the fuuuu-" Keith spotted two unfamiliar faces with guns on the monitor. Home Invaders! Nigga's try'na stick me for my paper? A devious look came over the Rapper's face as he stared down, watching their every move. He picked up the phone and dialed 911.

"911, what's your emergency?" the dispatcher asked calmly.

"Yeah, this is MC K.O., I got two dead people in my house."

"Are you sure they're dead sir?"

"Yeah because I'm about to kill 'em. So send the fuckin' coroner!"

'Click!' He slammed the phone down.

"It's on muthafuckas! I'll show these punks what all out really means."

Keith punched in a code on the monitor. In seconds, the huge mirror with the African print that hung beside the bed opened, revealing the arsenal Keith Osbourne collected. He scurried past the large assault weapons and grabbed the .357 Desert Eagles. "Don't worry niggas, I'm coming for ya'."

Keith put on a bullet proof vest, then checked the clips for rounds. After double checking his ammo he slapped the clips into a semi-automatic. With the targets location pinpointed he dashed into the hallway naked with only the vest on.

'What am I doing? I'm naked.' He reminded himself, turning around re-entering the bedroom. Keith retrieved a pair of orange valour Phat Farm sweats. With no time to wrestle socks on his semi-dry feet, he stuck his toes in the Air Force Ones, then sprinted toward the intruders. "Oh shit! They're in my home. Eeewwwwhhhhhh! These cats 'bout to get more than they bargained for." He chimed dashing downstairs with the loaded Desert Eagles in both hands. One of the gunmen was at the front door; he was attempting to break the windows with the butt of his M16 when he heard footsteps growing closer and closer. Just as Keith aimed his party spoilers at the window, the intruder eased away from the pane and drew his machine gun at the double doors. As he knelt on one knee, Keith silhouetted the man's frame out. He flicked both safetys' off in unison, ready to take on the first intruder. The other had already gained entry through the rear. If Keith didn't take him out now, he'd be at a disadvantage sooner or later.

Holes decorated the front doors in seconds as Keith fired, striking the home invader with every slug. The gunman staggered backward into the driveway with his finger still on the trigger, the M16 continued spitting rounds everywhere. Hotballs pierced the windows, ricocheted off the marble and spit through the doors, striking the rapper in the chest numerous times, which the vest intercepted. Keith noticed his attacker still moving. He kicked the door, forcing it open. Bleeding by the pint, the gunman tried taking aim at the man's cranium. Instant peace! He darted back into the house and headed towards the back of the mansion.

As Roach Gotti made his way through the back door, he checked the chamber slot to make sure there was a slug on tap. As he crept along the side of the pool, he quickly ducked once gunshots erupted. At the moment he thought they were flying his way. 'What am I doing?' he asked himself, regaining his composure. Remembering his way around the back section of the mansion from Stacy's birthday party he stealthily made his way towards the ballroom.

"Holy Mary, Mother of Jesus," Pataki muttered in disbelief, "did you just see that?"

"That shit was like something outta Blockbuster action flick. Fuckin' unbelievable!" Fish explained, shaking his head in disbelief.

"Fish, we gotta go do something before someone else dies." Fish did not comment, Pataki didn't wait for one. They leaped from the van and dashed across the street towards the rapper's estate.

"How we gonna get past the gate?" Pataki asked, "There's no damn way we could shoot through the main entrance."

"Even if we had fire power that could blast through it, we'd still go that route." Fish answered, pointing toward the ten foot iron gate they were about to ascend.

Keith pulled the remote from his pocket then tossed it on the floor, realizing it was no good for the moment. Slowly, he crept through each room with his .375's leading the way. "I know you're here playa. Your partner is dead! I really messed dude up." Keith said, knowing the intruder was listening. "After I kill ya ass I bet 'chu no other niggas will attempt to rob VA's baddest again." He exited the basketball court into the game room. He paused, then drew his guns toward the pool table, after hearing a noise.

"Uh oh! Looks like you 'bout to be kay fuckin' yo'ed." Keith sarcastically taunted.

He inched toward the pool table anticipating someone behind it. Roach Gotti eases out of the closet. Now he stood behind MC K.O.

"Don't even think about it baby boy," Roach said invitingly, forcing his weapon against the back of Keith's dome, "This ain't no robbery bitch! Its revenge! Revenge for raping my girl." Roach's tone grew with every word. "I just found out my girl's pregnant and guess what? Mr. K.O., she's 12 weeks into her pregnancy, which means I gotta kill you because I don't know if I'm the father."

"I didn't rape your woman."

"Shut up!" Roach Gotti growled. "I'm talking here already. I didn't rape your woman." Roach repeated, mocking MC K.O.'s sudden feminine tone. "You raped her, I know you did it! Now imma rape you as blood flow leaks from your head nigga."

Roach Gotti squeezed the trigger hoping to send Keith Osbourne to hell. 'Click.' Nothing! His assault rifle jammed. Instinctively Keith spun around aiming his Nevada Birds at Roach.

'Click click click!'

"Damnit man, they're empty." Keith said with an exaggerated sigh. Roach Gotti shoved the rifle up at Keith face. Keith eluded the incoming blow, then wind milled the .357 magnum across Roach's jaw all in one motion, striking him with a fierce backhand. Blackish red blood misted off Roach's lips as he fell to one knee. Keith dropped the useless weapons to the floor then dove on top of his prey, only to meet the butt of Roach's M16. Keith fell on the floor, gasping for air after being struck in the abdomen. Roach stood to his feet staggering, he wiped the blood from his mouth then kicked the rapper across the ribs. Keith laid beside the pool table aching in pain. Roach Gotti towered over him admiring his handy work for a moment. "Looks like MC K.O. needs an 8-count." Roach then plunged the heel of his Timberland toward the face of his foe. Keith clutched both hands together intercepting the incoming boot inches from his nose. He twisted the leg with all his might causing Roach to spin through the air towards the floor. Suddenly energized, the rapper scissor kicked into a spin and landed on his feet. Before Roach could stand up, Keith delivered a fury of punches as if he were a top contender. Roach stumble backwards until the wall caught him. Keith went into demolition mode realizing Roach was out on his feet. He dashed into the game room to retrieve the M16, he gave the chamber a few jigs sending the jammed caliber flying onto the pool table. A fresh round filled the chamber. He walked up to the battered man, aiming the rifle.

"Like I said playa, I didn't rape your girl."

"Kill me now because I'll kill you later, you can bet on that." Roach slurred.

Keith shrugged as if to say 'fuck it, I think I'll pull the trigger.'

"You don't wanna do that son! Trust me."

Once Keith Osbourne realized it was the detective he tossed his weapon to the floor.

"I really need a break right now." He told himself as his hands elevated. Once police secured all the weapons in view, Keith's adrenaline began to simmer, then it hit him like Arlene's backhand 'I just killed a man!'

CHAPTER 12

Shawnte' and Hectic lay close together in bed after awaking to a sensuous episode of love making. As they cuddled, Hectic's mind still wandered in circles about the incident. The events that took place weren't adding up, and Shawnte' sensed it in him. Shawnte' had to do something. The last thing she needed was for her husband to be suspicious.

"Let me call Nikki, see when she's bringing the Jeep back."

Shawnte'' reached toward the nightstand for the cordless. Hectic turned away, closing his eyes as if he were going back to sleep. She grabbed his arm then settled it around her waist as the phone started ringing. She wanted Hectic close to her, knowing he would be listening.

"Wake me up in 'bout an hour so I can get an early start on the party tonight." Hectic asked of his wife just as Nikki picked up.

Shawnte' smirked devilishly, rolling her eyes, he so phony! "Hey Nikki, wassup? When you bringing the Jeep back?"

"Are you alright?" Nikki replies with a question of her own.

"Yeah girl- uh huh- not really."

"Are you talking to me?" Nikki hadn't quite caught on to Te's game. Shawnte' overheard another familiar voice on the other end.

"Is that Shawnte'? Let me speak with her." Big Daddy yelled over Nikki's shoulder.

Shawnte' instantly recognized the man in the background. It was her lover.

“Don do that.” Shawnte’ grunted into the receiver, causing Hectic to jump.

“Wus wrong?” Hectic whispered, concerned, only to be waved off by Shawnte’s hand.

“Do not put Big Daddy on the phone. No I wasn’t going to, stupid.”

“Thanks, because I need me Jeep before then.” Shawnte’’ said loud enough to throw her husband off.

“Let me guess! Hectic is laying up under you and you’re giving him the 52 fake out.”

“That’s right!” Hectic said loud enough for Nikki.

“I don’t know what you’re talking about but I can’t wait to hear the story and soon.”

Suddenly feeling secure of his wife, Hectic jumped from the bed for the bathroom with a jolly attitude.

“Hol’ on Nik.” Shawnte’ covered the phone with her hand. Her eyes followed Hectic across the bedroom. “I thought you were gonna rest another hour. I wanted to do it before you got cleaned up.” she whined in her spoiled tone, which always turned on her husband.

“I need the early start baby. This party is going to be bombdigidy.”

“Okay. I love you.” Shawnte’ concluded giving him the puppy eyes.

He smiled then disappeared behind the bathroom door. Shawnte’ quickly uncovered the phone. “I can talk now,” she let out a sigh, “Hectic’s taking a shower. First I want you to take Big Daddy home.”

Hectic stormed out of the bathroom in a flash when he over heard that name come out of his wife’s mouth.

“Who’s Big Daddy?”

“A friend of Nikki’s. I was telling her that she should bring him, Big Daddy, to the party tonight, so she won’t be looking stupid or getting bored as she usually does. She knows I gotta watch my man, bitches go be all over you and I ain’t having it.”

“Relax love, my heart belongs to you and only you. Oh yeah, tell Nikki to do that, he’s surely welcome to come.” Hectic concluded, grabbing his shower cap. Moments later, he was gone.

“Girl, you are playing with fire, “Nikki whispered into the receiver so Big Daddy couldn’t hear.

"Let me speak to him real quick." "Who Big Daddy?"

"Duh! Who you think."

Nikki handed the phone over to him then crossed her arms with attitude. Ain't nothing ignorant about me! Nikki promised herself to straighten her later on face to face. While they conversed Nikki went into the bedroom to get dressed. The bathrobe was making her sweat and she felt uncomfortable not having any clothes on around Mr. Long Dong Silver.

When she returned Big Daddy relayed the phone undressing her with his eyes at the same time. The gesture made Nikki even more uneasy. If this brother say anything that sounds funny imma busta' cap off in that ass. "Where's the bathroom?" Big Daddy asked. Nikki pointed toward the hall, cutting her eyes at him. She couldn't wait for Curls to return. She pondered telling Shawnte" about her other man. The truth was he done nothing wrong. I could be paranoid. She squatted on the loveseat, placing the phone to her face. "Yeah."

"Look, Big Daddy gonna hold my jeep for the day. He's going to pick you up later on tonight and come up here with you. Please make sure that you are behind the wheel." "Uhn-unh, "Nikki said, "You gotta tell me what happened last night. And how this boy wind up with your Range.

"Okay but I gotta hurry up," Shawnte" glanced at the bathroom door. "Remember after I met Big Daddy at the Marriot. I pulled up at the front entrance of the hotel then ran inside to check if Reece was there waiting on me. He was." "Hurry up and get to the good part, "Nikki demanded. "Damn girl! Hol'up, anyway I went upstairs to tell Reece I was going to park the jeep across the street at Waterside. Girl, I didn't know Novocaine and his manager was staying in the same hotel. Homeboy spotted me strolling through the lobby and immediately called Hectic. All the parking spaces at the Waterside were occupied so I parked a few blocks down the street near McAuthor Center. Me and Big Daddy had sexed each other and err'thing. After we took a shower and stuff I convinced him to experiment with some sex gadgets and creams. I got dressed while he laid across the waterbed naked, looking good and"

"Te', I ain't try'na hear all dat. Just stick to the interesting part, o.k." "Okay." I headed downstairs towards the front lobby. Girl, I was too weak when I saw my husband and four of his flunkies asking the front desk clerk questions. I almost pissed on myself, girl you hear me."

"No, not the female extraordinaire, "Nikki teased ready for the conclusion. " I jumped back into the elevator, at the time, I wasn't sure what I was gonna do. My first instincts were to go back up to Big Daddy's room and hide out there. When the elevator opened up on the 3rd floor a hotel keeper stepped in. And that's when I knew everything would work out." "What did you do next?" Nikki asked, extremely curious. "I gave the house keeper $1,100 dollars and my diamond earrings for her uniform. Plus she had to press up a name tag which took a few minutes to process."

"He fell for it didn't he?"

"Damn bitch," Shawnte" whispered with a giggle, "Is u gonna let me finish or what? The house keeper was working for that money. She found out what floor Hectic was combing over and called me from the laundry room. He was on the 5th floor while his peeps searched the others. So I hurried to his location with the laundry cart knowing he would be there snooping around. Girl, I was pushing that cart to the rooms I knew where empty. That's when I saw Hectic but I pretended not to notice. I really looked like a tired out employee. He yelled out my name after spotting me. He was sprinting toward me when I turned around."

"Shawnte', what are you doing here" he asked me. That's when I put on my sad face explaining to him that I wanted to get a job so he would appreciate me more. He told me "that's foolish, I do appreciate you. What da hell you talkin' bout, Shawnte' ?"

"I don't feel like you do, so I got a job here." I shot back at him. "I figured if I worked here for a few years I could be the manager or something. Maybe, then, I could take care of you, years down the line" Hectic wrapped his arms around me like I was a lost puppy. " I love you so much, girl," he whispered in my ear. Tears ran down his face and everything. He was like ca'mon boo we goin' home. You don't need to work at all. You my wifey and I got'cha back love. He wiped his tears then pulled out his cellular, calling his boys to explain the situation.

He asked me where the jeep was parked once we arrived in the lobby. I couldn't tell him that I parked at the mall, it didn't sound right, so I told him that I let you borrow it. Why I say that? Girl, I don't know because that just made Hectic even more suspicious. I never lent my jeep out, you never asked, so that's why I called you to throw his ass off. He was pouting at first, now he straight." You tough, girl, I can't believe you pulled that off."

"Me either. I can't be—I gotta go. He's coming out the bathroom, bye." Soon after Shawnte' hung up Big Daddy exited the restroom, at the same time Curls walked through the front door holding a bag of groceries. Nikki hadn't noticed the hard stares between the two. Her attention was diverted by the breaking news story that flashed over the television. I hope nothing happened to Keith. Nikki was suddenly distracted by Big Daddy and Curls.

"Nikki!" Big Daddy barked as if were her man. "This is Sonny, Anthony Sonny Sanderson. A.K. A. Curls the Navy cadet."

Nikki leaped from the couch with her arms tightly crossed. "Curls, is that true? Is that really your name. And how does someone like him know you.?"

Big Daddy looked Nikki up and down resenting her undertone. "Nikki, I don't know this gentleman, he has me confused with someone else, I'm sure. I mean its obvious!" Curls pleaded, innocently.

"Bullshit!" Reece lashed out, "C'mon with the Navy boy act Sonny." Big Daddy looked Nikki in the eyes with his finger pointed at Curls. "This is my cousin. Ths nigga been frontin like this forever. He got two kids by my child's mother."

"What the hell is he talkin' about?" Nikki snapped.

"I….I….uh,uh,"Curls voice changed from night to day. "Damn cuz!" He shouted, shaking his head in disbelief. "You'sa hatin' ass nigga, man."

"Yeah! Whateva Sonny, you'sa lying ass Nigga and."

"Look negro," Nikki chimed in, "Let me talk to you for a second." Her eyes filled with tears. "I just got one question and I expect the truth. Are you not in the Navy or are you?" Curls looked at her as if she just asked the most dumbest question. With his cousin there another lie was moot. "No. I ain't in the Navy, I had a crackhead write you those letters from the ship." "You what?" Nikki barked, crying. "I can't believe this shit, even your nerdy voice is fake."

The situation at hand suddenly seemed funny to Nikki. She began laughing as if someone had cracked a joke. Sonny and Big Daddy stared, apparently confused. Soon Curls began laughing along. Big Daddy continued staring, wondering what was going on. "I'm'ma put these groceries in the kitchen and get breakfast started, "Curls laughed out assuming everything between him and Nikki was okay.

"No..no you not, you gon getcho' ass outta here. That's what you gon do."

"You dumping me for him?"

"Who Big Daddy, boy please! He practically my brother-in-law. Can't you tell." Nikki pointed to the front door, "Curls, Sonny, whatever your name is, get out of my house please." Curls gritted on Big Daddy, I'll catch yo hatin' ass out on the block." "Hol-hold up." Nikki insisted, "what do you mean by on the block?"

"You heard me bitch! I'm a drug dealer and um' grindin, gettin paid. And if this pussy ass nigga come out Washington Park again imma put sizzle to him, cousin or not." Big Daddy launched himself at Curls tackling him into the wall. Curls tried to maneuver his way loose but found himself being overpowered so he bit Reece on the shoulder sending him screaming in agony. Nikki yelled frantically, hoping damage would be minimal. Her cry was mute to them as they grappled on to each other. Big Daddy landed on his back , Curls now saddled him.

He grabbed a brass ornament from the broken table nearby, cocked the object back ready to bash his cousin's face in. "Yeah cuz, catch this with ya face. Willya?"He motioned the descending object towards Reese's skull. "You don wanna doooooooo-that," Nikki suggested, "You got three seconds to get up and bounce or I'm gunning. And you almost out-of-time." Curls cautiously placed the ornament to the floor then slowly elevated from his foe.

Just as Curls was ready to exit the front door, he stopped with his back turned toward Nikki. "Tell me you don't love me, tell me" he asked in a charming tone. "Nigga! I don't even know you" she replied matter of factly.

"One thing for sure, I made you bitch! Without me , you's just a motherless slut." His words echoed through her spine sending a wave of chills. Nikki quickly drew her pistol towards her lover and forced him out the door with a slug to his left butt cheek.

"Whoa! Nikki you dangerous to a brother's health." Big Daddy blurted, shocked. Nikki turned, staring at the bloody face of Reese. She cracked a sarcastic smirk, "Looks like Sonny is bad for yours."

CHAPTER 13

Authorities questioned Keith all morning while the TV cameras posted outside his estate hoping and waiting to gather any details. Forensic Investigators snapped photos of the scene, including the profile of Roach Gotti after his arrest.

As Keith leaned against his wife's car his eyes gazed about. He spotted the media circus on the other side of the gate. His gaze continued on the many police officers that occupied his front lawn his stare locked on Fish. He wondered if he had been staking him out all this time. "Bastards probably got my phone bugged." He mumbled under his breath as he watched Fish's partner depart from the scene.

Fish had just gave Pataki specific details of their next stake out.

"Look Pataki, I'm going to question him some more. When I'm finished I'm gonna question him again."

"For what? We're not going to bring any charges against him." Pataki asked, throwing his hands shoulder high, unsure what Fish was up to.

"Who are you looking at like that?" Fish demanded to know. "I'll question him as much as I see fit, jus' because I can partna!" the Detective had his finger pointing directly to Pataki's nose.

Pataki turned away, "Don't...don't fuckin' swear at me, man." he grunted, "and get your finger out-of-my-face."

"You know what? If I didn't know any better, I'd swear you think you could whip me boy." Fish barked, finally removing his finger, then planting both hands around his waist.

"Whatever man."

"It ain't whatever. It's get that stake out set up at Buckroe, that's what is is partner!"

"You got issues Fish."

"Yeah! And you got one coming'. I see it now." Pataki cut his eyes at Fish as he quick stepped to the van.

Fish looked over at Keith who was already staring his way. "I love this job." The detective told himself as he walked over to him.

"Look detective! Enough with the questions already. I gotta headache."

"Damn Killa! How you figure that I was gonna ask more questions?"

Keith gave Fish an angry glare. "Don't call me Killa! And because you're a cop, asking questions over and over is what cops do.'

Fish wanted to apologize for his comment, it was inappropriate at a time like this. I'm sorry wasn't in his vocabulary, instead a sly grin appeared on his face. "Yeah you right," Fish said huffing afterwards. "I was gonna ask more questions. I tell you what, we'll resume this tomorrow. Meanwhile, get somebody to clean this place up for ya."

"I got twenty Molly Maids over there waiting to make my crib look like new." Keith pointed to a group of women huddled up beside the Channel 10 News van.

"Whatever you do…try and get out for some fresh air tonight. No need sitting 'round here feeling sorry for yourself, ya know."

"Getting out is a must. I definitely need to be around some vibrant people."

"Yeah, I know what you mean." Fish concluded, then walked off. 'I know exactly what you mean. You're going to Hectic's party where all the vibrant people are. And we'll be there waiting, anticipating your homie's every move.' The detective assured himself smirking devilishly. "I can feel it, some poor girl will get sexually assaulted tonight."

It was close to 6p.m. when the house cleaning crew and emergency carpenter departed. Keith walked into the bedroom where he realized that Nichole Wallace's photo was parked on the nightstand where he left it. He picked it up and studied every inch of her. If it's God's will, I'll love you forever and ever. He picked up the phone with the picture up to his face. He needed to hear her voice badly. The phone rang a few times then went to voicemail. That's funny Keith thought, earlier this morning I kept getting the busy signal. He shrugged the thought away assuming she was probably on a three way like women usually are.

Should I leave a message? It wouldn't help if I did. He hung up then walked into the closet to retrieve something for the party. Keith jumped to the sound of the telephone. "What's wrong with me?" Keith asked himself as he hurried to the bed where the cordless receiver lay. He took a deep breath then pressed the power button.

"Hello?"

"hey it's me, they got you on CNN, so I called to see if you were okay."

As Keith digested her every word he wished it was his newfound love on the other end. "Yeah, I'm good Sheila. Wasn't too bad. The insurance man will be here tomorrow to access the damage."

"Well I just called to check up on you. Me and Momma getting' ready to go out see one of those gospel comedy plays, so I'll talk to you later."

"She-" Too late! She was gone. He contemplated on calling her back, but just as he decided better against it, the phone chirped again. He quickly answered.

"Yo Kay baby, dis you? Yo son, what happened? You all over the news."

"It's a long story Timmy, I'll give you the details a lil' later. Tell Mont I'm good."

"He said that bout 'chu from the jump.'"

"That's my cousin. Well, I'll get with you in a few alright."

"A'ight."

"Ar'ight, peace." Suddenly feeling depressed Keith turned off the ringer. After he returned to the wardrobe closet he realized how dumb it was to turn the volume off knowingly he had over thirty phones through out his mansion that would ring. He sighed deeply, "Kenneth Cole or Burberry?" he asked himself out loud hoping to energize his spirits. I think I'll Kenneth Cole it tonight. He removed the egg shell white two-piece from the hanger. Sportscoats always made the Rapper smile and smile is just what he needed.

Keith arrived at Buckroe Beach around 10:20pm. He cruised the 5mph limit in his convertible Bently until he came to this huge three story condo facing the Atlantic Ocean. The condominium was structured in fine oak, the blue beach sand that decorated the mini mansions in the night looked eloquent and extraordinary. He was certain that it was Hectic's crib by the many cars he recognized parked along the sandy road. Keith parked then converted the Gucci top over his ride. Someone tapped him on the shoulder, startling the rapper, "Hey bud, hi ya doin'? Nice car!" Keith looked at the security guard unflattered by his compliment saying nothing in return. "I'm with Buckroe Security, I need you to pull your vehicle up just a little. The neighbors are complaining about people parking in front of their driveway." The officer turned and walked away before he could say anything.

"What am I doing here?" he asked himself out loud. Keith reparked two condo's down then checked himself over in the mirror. He reached in the glove compartment and produced his Jacob & Co wrist watch, his iced out necklace and Salt Water Boys emblem he had specially made to be different. Mr. Jacob had taken out some stones and replaced them with rare black diamonds that no other crew member possessed. No one would ever mistake him for a rapist if he had anything to do with it.

He placed the necklace around his knolls realizing that he was extremely over dressed for that particular jewelry. Keith removed it from his neck and tossed it back into the glove compartment. Gently, he slid his wrist into the watch before climbing out of his ride. He checked himself over, scanning his suit from top to bottom then back up. "No doubt MC K.O. is the one neck turner," he told himself as he started to stroll down the sandy road toward the party.

MINUTES EARLIER

Pataki had set up surveillance cameras all over Hectic's neighborhood. He'd been waiting on the rapper's arrival for nearly two hours. When Keith finally showed, he parked directly in front of a hidden camera.

Watson was a Buckroe Detective who was elected to assist in the stake out. The last thing Fish wanted was to work with another department. It was Watson's jurisdiction so Fish had no other choice. Officer Watson arranged for Buckroe security to take the night off with pay while he posed as the happy-go-lucky security guard.

"Watson!" Pataki yelled from the back of the Buckroe Security van. "Keith, I mean K.O. bourne, hell I mean Keith Osbourne is blocking one of the cameras. Have him park elsewhere, will ya?"

"No problem," Watson replied will a serious tone. He jumped from the van and darted over to the rapper's Bently. As the detective informed Keith to repark Fish arrived to the stake out. "What's up? What we got so far?"

"What we got is Mr. Osbourne blocking the cameras pointing down toward the side of the condo." Pataki updated him. "It's no problem. Watson's taking care of it. See, he moving already." he said pointing at the monitor. Fish nodded then clamped the headphones around his head, eavesdropping on conversations that weren't too distorted by the DJ's thumping sound system.

That's how Fish would spend his next hour or so. As Pataki monitored the partly goers coming and going, Watson maintained an close eye on those sitting in cars too long or suspicious persons walking off onto the beach's darkness.

Impressed, Keith nodded as he scanned around. Hectic's place was decorated under the Hawaiian Island theme. Out of nowhere Mont and Timmy Tuff appeared from the crowd.

"Yo, what's up Killa K?" Mont shouted, giving his cousin a dapper handshake. "Shit is crazy yo!" Keith replied, leading Tim and Mont away from the ear hustlers. "I killed Roach Gotti's right hand man. He and Roach broke into my crib lookin' to kill me over that girl that was raped that night." "Dammmnnn! You a'ight though, right?" Timmy Tuff chimed in, pulling his pants up after he felt the wind creeping down his butt. "I didn't wanna do it man. To be honest, I thought niggas was tryin' stick me up. You know that nigga Long neck Junie from across the river is known for hittin' up celeb's spots." Mont nodded, "Yo, before the scuffle me and Roach had, he tells me that his girlfriend is pregnant."

"The girl that got raped?" Mont asked, surprised.

"I don't mean no harm K-baby, but if my girl was pregnant I'd be flipping out too." Timmy added, relating to Roach's gripe. The next thirty minutes Keith gave the Killa Kayo version of his story of what transpired.

"Yo Shawty! Churchill in the place to be, punk!," someone barked from the crowd. MC K.O. and company were still conversing amongst themselves when Novocaine rudely interrupted, "Wus really good nig'ka? I appreciate you stopping past to check a brother out an shit." By then Novocaine was up in Keith's face looking around to make sure he had an audience, "But if I catch you writing my lyrics down nigga umma bustshu' in yo soft ass." Giggles echoed over the music that suddenly lowered. MC K.O. gazed over the mini-crowd that accumulated around them. Timmy Tuff stepped inbetween the two rappers "Ma'man, we didn't come here for this."

"Shut the fuck up! White boy!" Novocaine snapped, smacking Timmy Tuff's hand from his chest, I'm jus sayin'," Novocaine yelled into the crowd as if he were conducting a townhall meeting, "This the only hardcore rapper in the world that doesn't even have a misdemeanor in his rap sheet. Hell, Felonious Elliot got some kind of charge in her record. She ain't even hardcore."

Everyone laughed in unison. "Only thing you got in yo jacket is a rape beef." One of Novocaine's homies emerged from the crowd, stepping up behind him then whispered something in his ear. Moments later the man disappeared behind the DJ booth.

Novocaine's stare cut at MC K.O. momentary. He waited for the giggles to simmer, I'm jus joking, everybody give it up for V.A.'s finest. On the real… this nigga's a beast, he represents to the fullest." The party goers applauded, entertained by Novocaine's humor. "Quiet down, quiet down, I ain't finished, he demanded, "and if my record sales don't do so good…I'm'a be knocking on your door for a job." He concluded giving MC K.O. a shoulder tap hug. During the exchange, Novocaine whispered in Keith's ear, "Sorry 'bout that, jus puttin' on a show for Vivo Magazine. The reporter's over there. No disrespect!"

"None taken, Novocaine." Keith shot back as they released each other's arm, "Excuse me pimpin', I gotta holla at my mans an nem'." As the music elevated Novocaine disappeared. He darted inside the condo to speak with his homie that put the bug in his ear. "Yo Shawty praya!" Novocaine barked, "Why in the fuck nobody told me this nigga MC K.O. just killed a muthafucka dis morning. Man, I gots to get my ass back up to Richmond before one yall niggas run me up on a snag."

It was close to midnight when the multitudes began to thin out. The remainder of the party goers moved to the first floor on the condo. Inside, the DJ played slippets of Novocaine's album. Keith perched on the cajon sofa, chillin', taking in a cold sip of spring water. His mind wandered from Sheila to the tour, the tour to the dead guy that lay in front of his home earlier. At the moment Keith decided to call it a night. Just as the rapper finished the beverage off, his eyes gazed over the party goers. That's when he spotted her. Her stare immediately locked onto his…….

CHAPTER 14
EARLIER THAT DAY

By the time authorities arrived at Nikki's place Big Daddy was long gone. She had explained herself to Investigators over and over again how Anthony Sanderson refused to leave her home and became hostile with her guest. "I'm confused," the officer said, scratching the tip of his nose. "Usually when someone is acting in a hostile manner they're usually facing their victims. In this case, he uh…attacked you-excuse me, I mean showed hostility with his back turned toward you." The Investigator began stroking his shadow beard. "Miss Wallace, if I didn't know better I'd say you were indeed the aggressor here." Nikki sat on the arm of her couch with her face tightened. "But this is my house. He wouldn't't"

The officer cut her off, "but it seems as if he were trying to leave Miss Wallace. After all, he was shot in your doorway." The officer's undertone was getting to her. She rose from the sofa never breaking eye contact with the bluecoat. "Look, are you gonna charge me or what? If not, you all will be leaving now." Nikki pointed toward the door emphasizing her frustration.

"Not a problem Miss Wallace, but I will be calling your boss. With any luck you'll lose that shield as well as that arrogant look on your face." "shield! What the fuck am I, A cop? I –am-a-correctional officer. DIFFERENCE! Nikki snapped, "And go ahead and call my supervisors. I was thinking about a job change any damn way." She ended the conversation with the door slamming in the officer's face. Nikki plopped down on the couch then let out a long sigh. "Gotta calm my nerves, gotta calm down." She mumbled to herself. For over a half hour she lay quietly in silence, staring up into the ceiling. Her eyes closed briefly as she reflected on old memories of her child hood. A single tear rolled down her face as her eyes opened. Her gaze followed the ceiling to the far side of the living room where pictures of her mother, father, Aunt Linda and Toniesha hung. For hours her stare held position, recalling buried memories. Good and the bad.

"I miss y'all so much." Nikki began sobbing. "Why God? Why'd you have to take them away from me so soon." Instantly thoughts of Tony Gangsta forced their way inside her head. Then Keith Osbourne chased him out placing a wide smile across her face. If what happened was real last night, and I know Curls. Immediately she snatched the sheets and comforter from the mattress and slammed them to the floor, retrieving a fresh set from the closet. Nikki shook the sheet loose then parachuted it over the bed. Once she conquered all four corners of the mattress, she unfolded the other. The cotton linen fell from corners of the mattress, she unfolded the other. The cotton linen fell from her hands as she darted into the bathroom once again. This time she arrived at the toilet's rim before puking once more. Her mind instantly recalled everything she'd eaten. That's funny. I haven't took in anything today. All I had last night was sour cream and celery sticks. It occurred to her that Curls used protection so pregnancy had been ruled out. But wait… What about Keith? Last night , oh my God. I'm pregnant by MC K.O. He didn't wear any protection. Oh my God. Nikki cleaned herself up and laid across the bed in awe. Before long, she was fast asleep.

Around 8 o'clock the phone rung. Nikki's eyes cracked, she lay there hoping the caller would give up. Reluctantly she answered. As she slurred into the receiver repeated knocks echoed off the front door. "Hey girl, you ready yet?"

"hol'on Te', somebody's bangin on my door." Nikki muttered, revealing to Shawnte' that she was asleep. "Who is it?" Nikki yelled, elevating from the bed.

"It's me Curls" a voice replied.

Nikki cautiously opened the door, "You ain't funny, Big Daddy. You don't sound nothing like Curls." Nikki returned to her room. "Lock the door behind you. And the remote is on top of the entertainment center. Relax, you gon' be here for a while. As Nikki entered the hallway she noticed one of her photos missing off the wall. She quickly assumed it had fallen behind the television.

Nikki grabbed the receiver, plunging down on her bed, back first. "Te' don't be mad at me. that was Reese a the door……I ain't ready." "you was sleep wont'chu?" Nikki sighed, "pretty much. My bad girl, its just that a lot of wild shit happened today." "With who, you?" Shawnte' asked, curious.

"Yeah, who the hell else? You ain't talked to Big daddy yet?" Nikki knew she hadn't. "Well, Curls got to whippin up on your man's ass earlier today and I wind up shooting Curls in the ass," Nikki explained, giggling afterward. "What happened girl?" Nikki marveled at the excitement in Shawnte' s voice but had no time for details. " Look Te', I'm get myself together, I'll holla atchu' when I get there." Nikki rudely hung up. She walked to the closet and stood there wondering what she would wear to the beach house event. Picking out an outfit was the worst part about going places with Nikki because figuring out what to wear often gave her headaches. She liked Dolce' & Garbana outfit but had no bra to match. The Sergio Valente' denim shaped her butt in a funny manner. Nikki recently purchased a $800 Gucci dress but disliked the panty line it revealed. And, there was no way she was going anywhere pantyless.

Just as frustration set in she noticed a velour sweat suit hanging in the rear. She pulled the sky blue and white Baby Phat garment from the hanger then looked it up and down for approval. All I need now is a halter top. Nikki quick stepped to the dresser drawer, retrieving a matching piece to her sweat suit. "Shawnte' is going to hate me for showing off my abs." Nikki whispered to herself, admiring her six pack in the mirror. "She'll live I guess."

Nikki and Big Daddy arrived at the beach house in Shawnte''s Range Rover. Shawnte' greeted them upon arrival, introducing herself to Big Daddy as if they never met. She looked over her shoulder before blowing a kiss at him. "Damn, Nik, Yo man look so edible on this gorgeous night." Nikki inched toward Shawnte', "Well, he's not really my man , he's yours." She whispered, giggling.

Big Daddy strolled past them and into the hip-hop scenery after noticing some Spanish mommies checking him out. Shawnte' cut her eyes at him then folded her arms. "What didju expect, no really?" Nikki asked, not expecting an answer. Shawnte' sighed, her face revealing disappointment, c'mon girl, let's go up to my room for some girlfriend chit chat."

"Girl , this is nice. I had no idea bedrooms were made this big." "girl please, you seen bigger." Before Nikki could respond Shawnte' reminded her of the huge bedroom MC K.O. played his saxophone in. "But that's different, he has a mansion, this is a condo." Realizing Shawnte' didn't take the comment well, she spiced it up a little. "Damn Te', I never saw a condominium this large. Hectic must own acres of sand. That's got to cost a fortune in a neighborhood like this?" Instant smile over Shawnte' s face just as Nikki had planned. She began explaining to Nikki the real estate value in the area as if she were a property surveyor. Nikki cut the conversation short minutes later. "Girl, let me tell you what happened before I forget," She suggested with an exaggerated smile on her mug, hoping to gain Shawnte' s attention and off the current subject.

Big Daddy squeezed through the party goers toward the rear entrance of the condo. After observing all of Hectic's wealth he questioned why a woman like Shawnte' would mess around with a bad boy like him. He has so much money, and it shows. His ego soon took over, He must be lacking else where. Hectic broke his contemplation when he strolled by with two women under his arm. Big Daddy's eyes followed Shawnte' s husband until he disappeared into the crowd. He began feeling uneasy and out of place. "What the hell am I doing?" he asked himself, "Playin the disrespect game was never my style." Big Daddy turned and made way back into the condo and out the front door. He decided not to advise his lover of the departure. There was no doubt she'd protest against it. Reese stood outside staring down the huge condos that faced the long chain of fly automobiles for the moment as he contemplated. "Now," he whispered to himself after slamming his champagne glass in the side of the condo. "All I need is a ride back to P-town, "He let out another sigh as he started walking down the road. During the stroll he peeped in any car that looked familiar to him with hopes that he'd bump into someone he knew.

Just as Nikki and Shawnte' headed for the bedroom door Princess came storming through it. "Shawnte' ! Some girl"she paused after Nikki's presence caught her off guard. Uneasiness covered her face instantly. "Oh, hey Nikki."

"Hey? Girl please!" Nikki rushed over to give her a warm hug. "I been thinkin' aboutchu' Princess." At that very moment Princess rather had been in the middle of the Atlantic, drowning than to be in the presence of her old friend. Drenched in guilt, her reflexes took over. Princess's arms slowly elevated around Nikki giving her a fake there you go. Now get off me, Bitch! Kinda hug. Nikki felt the tenseness in her. She assumed that she was feeling guilty for not visiting her when she were in Tidewater. Her eyes locked onto Princess's. I ain't mad atchu' for not coming to see me. I understand that its' a long tiresome journey to Suffolk. I'm happy to be seeing you now. Princess, I love you no matter what."

"Enough of that shit, Nik," Shawnte' cut in after noticing Princess was feeling gutterish with each second that past by. "Oh yeah, I almost forgot. Some chick is all over your husband outside. I think its' his babymomma." "oh no he didn't invite that bitch into my home. That's straight disrespect." "and what do you call Big Daddy's presence here tonight?" Seriousness covered Nikki's face. Shawnte' cut her eyes at her before darting out of the bed room for the party. Desperate to get away from Nikki, Princess followed close behind.

"Let me get this girl before she gets to actin stupid."

"Too late for that, Nikki mumbled, following suit.

As Nikki made her way for the back door she sensed that someone was eyeing her. Intuition told her to turn around. Her gaze surveyed the room in a I'm looking for someone kinda way. Nikki's heart dropped to her stomach as her eyes fixed on Keith Osbourne. He was parked on the sofa looking her way. She professed not to notice his stare and continued to gaze about. Nikki's mind spun like a F5 tornado. Butterflies flapped by the dozens inside her. She began breathing heavily. Her body heated up instantly. The humid air had begun to settle on her.

"Get outside, you'll be okay, girl." Nikki repeating to herself.

Once she reached the back deck she searched over the party goers for Shawnte' or Princess, too many people in the dimness to recognize either of them. Nikki gave up and headed for an empty chair. As she started to sit down a hand landed on her shoulder. She flinched ready scream. "Get a grip, Nik, it's jus'me," Shawnte' said, looking at Nikki as if she'd lost her mind. " Anyway, that way a false alarm."

"What's a false alarm?" Nikki asked, still gathering her thoughts. "The girl…The one with Hectic. It was some groupie chick looking to get hooked up with Novocaine." Shawnte' let out a long sigh, staring over Nikki's shoulder. "Speaking of rapper…There's one coming your way." Before Nikki could respond MC K.O. eased up behind her, gently placing his hand over hers. He slowly spun around until she faced him. Without any regrets, he pulled Nikki close to him then kissed he like he'd never smouch any other. She wanted to protest but her body would not comply. It felt so unreal, almost like a dream, a dream she hoped that would never end. Nikki began feeling weak, her body went numb. She couldn't feel nothing, nor had realized that she'd fallen toward the stand until she opened her eyes. Nikki stared into his eyes as he elevated her wholesomeness from the earth.

By then, party goers gathered around Shawnte' to see if Nikki was okay. "MC K.O. almost kissed her into a coma, "someone shouted from the crowd.

"Nichole, are you alright?" Keith whispered to her, his suit sparkling under the moon. Nikki regained balance then answered the rapper's question with a jolting open hand slap across his jaw. "Eeeeewwwhhhh!"The party goers hummed in unison.

Nikki dust herself off then marched away from the fiesta. MC K.O. stood there stroking his chin as he watched Nikki head toward the beach's pier. We just made love last night and she greets me by rocking my jaw. What's that all about? As speculation started to mount Keith Osbourne took off behind Nikki. He needed answers and aimed to get them. Nichole!....Nichole!" Keith yelled over the clapping waves. Nichole Wallace, I want to talk to you." Nikki continued down the beach ignoring his plea. Keith took off his shoes then trotted behind her. He quickly gained ground, catching up to her in seconds. Now he stood in front of her, blocking her path. Nikki gave him an angry stare momentary.

Before Keith could get out a single word Nikki grabbed him by the waist with one hand and pulled his head down with the other. She planted her lips against his then kissed him with all her heart and soul. Confused, Keith tried reasoning under the pecks, but Nikki would not allow him to get a word out. She forced Keith down to the sand, locking her tongue with his until they could no longer breathe. Nikki's gaze settled on Keith after their lips unlocked. Now I know the reason for the butterflies, Nikki told herself, It's because I'm in love with him. As Keith stare into Nikki's eyes, admiring the sparkle in it, he noticed how his lover was in deep thought. "Nichole, what are you thinking about right now?"

"I can't tell you at this very moment, but I can share this with you"

"Share what?" Keith asked, eager to hear her sensuous voice. "Well, its like this, you have sand all over your goatee." Nikki smiled then laughed. Keith chuckled along. As Nikki continued to hide her true emotions behind her laugh she contemplated on sharing the words her heart spoke for her new love. For some reason her conscious was telling her to say "I Love You" but the words would not allow themselves to form off her tongue. "Nichole," Keith whispered, unconsciously mimicking Barry White, elevating from the shores and resting on his elbows.

Nikki unsaddled him, yet found herself a victim of his hypnotic stare. No matter how hard she tried, she couldn't break eye contact with him. Sensing the next words out of Keith's mouth she tried looking away. With all her strength, Nikki forced her lips to move. "Yes Keith," she finally answered. "Why did you pop me like that in front of all those people?"

Nikki shrugged, "I'on know." She sighed, giving the question more thought. "Seemed appropriate at the moment I guess," she added, "Oh! I know why I smacked you now. Because of what you did last night." An uncomfortable look appeared on the rapper's face which made her nervous. The way Keith kissed her back at the party assured Nikki that she had not been dreaming. Now she wasn't so sure if it were or not. "Nichole.......I don't understand. Last night ...was beautiful. I've been thinking of you every minute since. I tried calling you but your line was busy so I came here hoping to take a load off.

Nikki's eyes widened Its real, I wasn't dreaming, she concluded. "Yes Keith, it was beautiful. I'm just upset with you because you didn't use protection and I don't go that way." Nikki's head slowly dropped, "now I'm pregnant, I think. I've thrown up three times today already." Shocked by the revelation , Keith was speechless. The chances of him fathering a child was one in a trillion he imagined. Still the possibility was there. Doubt clouded his mind momentary as thoughts of Nikki being with another haunted him. Keith shirked off the negative thoughts and forced a smile on his face. For the past 90 days the rapper had his private investigator follow her every move. According to Mitch Holley, she hadn't encountered a man the duration of that time period.

"Are you sure?" he asked instead.

"No, I'm not," Nikki replied, "but I'm not sick either."

Keith threw his arms around his new love letting her know he would be there for her. As they silently held each other Keith stared into the darkness of the ocean, watching the black waves form then clap in front of them. Should I say what I feel? He pondered. "I love you"Keith spoke silently. "Whatchu say baby?"

Keith began stuttering unaware that something came out of his mouth. He took a deep breath then loosened his arms to plant a wet kiss on the softness of her lips. Slowly he guided her down to the sand after taking his blazer off and laying it down underneath her. Keith eased between her velour thighs then locked his eyes on hers once more. "Nichole Wallce, I-I love you" the rapper was suddenly distracted by someone running toward them with a shiny object in hand. Nikki read the look of concern in his face an turned in the direction Keith stared in. Instantly she recognized a white man with a gun drawn by his side.

"Oh shit!" Keith blurted, "they got me." He assumed it was more of Roaches homeboys looking to finish the beef. He sighed in relief after realizing it was the security guard for Buckroe Beach.

"Freeze!" the bluecoat yelled out drawing his service piece. Upon further analysis, the officer holstered his gun. "I'm sorry. I truly do…apologize Mr. Osbourne. Got a call that someone was being mugged out here." The security guard apologized once more then quick stepped up the beach in between two condos.

"Lets go Nichole, something fishy is going on."

"It was just an honest mistake."

"Not exactly" Keith replied, his eyes cutting in the direction of the officer.

"We are being watched" his tone lowered.

"How do you know such a thing?"

"Because I do. Now lets get outta here."

"You're just paranoid, most famous people are like that I hear."

"Nichole, he called me Mister Osbourne. I don't recall giving my name, that's' how I know."

Nikki didn't waste any more time, she and Keith wiped the sand from their clothes and hurried back to Hectic's place. As they held hands they conversed about the dramatic day they had. Keith was quite amused that Nichole had shot someone on the same day as he. She trusted Keith enough to talk about her traumatic past but decided better against it. Just as they reached the party she pulled on Keith's arm, stopping the rapper in his tracks. Nikki looked into his eyes then cracked a smile. "What were you about to say after you said what you said back on the beach before we were interrupted?" Keith returned a smile of his own briefly. Seriousness soon erased the expression away. He took in a deep sigh, hoping to disguise his watery eyes, "I said, was about to say, I think you are my soul mate Nichole Wallace."

CHAPTER 15

"Watson, how we lookin' out there?" Fish conveyed over the radio.

"That's a negative on the beach. Headed your way now."

"Roger that." Fish hoisted his radio then fixed his gaze on Pataki. "I'm curious.," he said, scratching his chin. Pataki's mug began to tighten as he braced for another verbal assault. Fish instantly spotted the Detective's uncomfortable expression and turned on the monitors. "How in the hell did you manage to bug the inside of the condo?"

Unsure if he were being critiqued or complimented Pataki didn't answer.

"Proud of you Pataki. That's good police work there."

Pataki managed a half smile on his face. Just as he started to ask his partner the question that had been haunting him since the day the met, fish snapped, putting the thought on hold.

"I think we got one!" Fish's eyes were locked on the screen.

On the monitor, a man strolled slowly down the street with no sense of direction. His eyes darted left to right to see if anyone were watching him.

Afterward he'd peep inside every other parked car.

"Watson!" Fish grunted into the Motorola. "Get back to the fort. I need you here with Pataki." The detective snatched the Sony's from his ears and tossed the headphones over the monitors then checked his .40 caliber. "This one's mine." Fish mumbled to himself as he scrambled to the rear of the van.

"Have a squad car nearby."

"Already on it." Pataki shot back, shuffling some wires under his foot.

As mystery man strode toward the main highway fish discreetly followed, squatting alongside the automobiles. Fish stood frozen after mystery man stopped to converse with a woman who'd just pulled up. The Detective tried to decipher the exchanged words. The screaming winds over the roaring ocean made it impossible to move. The driver let out what appeared to be a muffled scream. "Pataki, I need a squad car, now!" he barked into the Motorola as the car sped off. Moments later a Buckroe police cruiser pulled up and fish leapt in. "Follow that maroon Lexus." He commanded the patrolman.

Fish snatched the radio once inside. "Officer needs assistance. In pursuit of a maroon Lexus, LX 400 model...heading west bound toward the Phoebus city limits. Possible serial rapist."

Pataki and Watson had their receivers tuned in awaiting the outcome of Fish's new lead when one of the surveillance cameras displayed a man chasing down a woman on the beach near the pier.

"Look!" Watson said in a baffled tone. "Something is definitely unfolding with these two on the beach."

Pataki maneuvered towards the back of the van. He analyzed the screen Watson's eyes were glued on. The man on the beach looked quite familiar to him. He quickly zoomed the night vision lens in on the two. "That's Keith Osbourne!" he blurted, fearing the worst. "He's going to rape that woman under the pier."

Watson leapt out the backdoors leaving them swinging. Pataki scrambled to the front, retrieving his pistol from the glove compartment. The detective jumped out the driver's side door closing the rear doors Watson left ajar. As he started for the beach he climbed back into the van for a radio. Then he made his way through the condo's alleyway. "Fish! come in detective Fish."

"Detective Fish, what's good?"

"Keith Osbourne just chased a woman on the beach near the pier. I'm in pursuit now...over!"

Fish and ten other bluecoats had cornered the Lexus at an intersection just as it started to ascend I-64. With guns drawn all around the sedan, Fish cautiously rushed the passenger side door. He yanked open the door and forced mystery man to the pavement.

"What did I do?" mystery man demanded to know.

"Shut up punk! I'm asking the questions here." Fish countered as he slapped the handcuffs on his suspect.

“Mam, please step out of the vehicle, slow man.” Another officer instructed the driver.

“Take him to the squad car while I have a chat with this young lady.” Fish side-stepped to the other side of the Lexus as the blue and whites asked routine questions. “I’ll take it from here officer.” Fish commanded, wrapping his arms around the nervous woman. Only to have his hospitality rejected. The detective proceeded to escort the young lady away from the others hoping to gain some privacy. “I’m sorry…for all the confusion but I think you were almost a victim of rape. Are you okay? Did that man hurt you in any way?”

The female stared at the detective in total disbelief. “What do you mean victim of rape? Just what the hell are you talking ‘bout?” the woman snapped.

Fish fixed his stare on her, “I’m talking about the gentleman in your car.”

“Who, Big Daddy? Negro please! My baby’s father ain’t no damn rapist, trust me.”

You mean you know that man?”

The woman wondered if Fish had some sort of learning disability. “Know ‘em? This is his ride, not mines, he let me borrow it tonight for a party I wanted to go to. Didn’t expect to bump into him up here.”

Fish reflected on the wiretap conversation in Shawnte’s bedroom. It had occurred to him that the man in custody was indeed Shawnte’s secret lover. The detective turned and darted to the patrol car that Big Daddy sat uncomfortably in.

“Look young playa, I don’t apologize very often, but uh, tonight is different.” Fish’s undertone was far from sincere. “I-am-sorry for the inconvenience.”

Unmoved by the detective’s words Big Daddy cut his eyes in the opposite direction. “I have to ask you a few questions before I release you. First off, who’s car is that?”

“Mine.” Big Daddy replied nonchalantly.

“How do you know that woman?”

“She’s the mother of my children and my girlfriend.”

“What’s your full name?”

“Maurice Fashun, spelled with a u-n.”

Fish typed his name in on the screen and relayed the information to headquarters for a warrant check. “Look young brother, Shawnte” isn’t for you.”

Big Daddy's eyes widened in disbelief, "How did you-"

"Don't worry about all that just stick with your baby moms. I can tell she's a pleasant woman, hard to come by these days."

Big Daddy wondered what he meant by it but didn't ask. He silently pondered detective's surprise revelation.

Fish let out a deep sigh as the warrants crawled across the monitor. "Damn!"

Immediately he drew Big Daddy's attention. "You from P-town huh?"

"Yeah …that's right why?"

"Why…because…" he interrupted himself after a call from Pataki came over his radio. "Detective Fish here, what's good?" Once Pataki revealed to him the situation on the rapper Fish turned to his suspect. "Tonight's your lucky night playa."

"What's that supposed to mean?" Big Daddy asked, already feeling violated. "Because I'm working on a major rape case right now. Since you got three outstanding drug indictments in Portsmouth on you I won't worry about it. "

Big Daddy couldn't believe the detective was releasing him. He leaned forward over the front seat and focused on the monitor. In plain view Big Daddy confirmed what Fish had conveyed. "So you gonna let me go?"

"That's right ma man. I'll let Portsmouth worry about you." Fish commanded the officers to vacate the scene after informing them that this wasn't his guy. He uncuffed Big Daddy and released him. The patrolman peeled off toward Buckroe beach immediately after.

"Pataki where are you?" Watson yelled into the Motorola as he struggled to build momentum through the thick sand. Watson holstered his radio soon after. He spotted the silhouette of a body blanketing another. 'Oh my God' he thought, 'he's raping her at this very moment.' Watson's chest began pounding as he approached Keith Osbourne and his latest victim. Maimed titties flashed in his head. Thoughts of blood was the motivating factor in the detective's increase in speed.

"Come in Watson." A voice relayed across the radio.

Watson hit the receiver. He was nearly out of breath when he responded. "he's assaulting her now!"

Tiny images of the two in the sand grew larger and larger by the second. Which meant the detective was getting closer and closer. Just as the rapper noticed him, Watson drew his weapon. It occurred to the officer that Keith

Osbourne and his acquaintances were sharing a moment on the shoreline. The look on their faces told Watson they were just as frightened as he.

"I apologize Mr. Osbourne." The officer turned, then hurried away. He discreetly whispered in this radio. "False alarm! I repea-"

"Roger that." Pataki replied.

As Watson headed back to his van he began laughing to himself, reflecting the terrifying expression on the hardcore rapper's mug. "Sure didn't look like a killer a few moments ago."

While Pataki, Fish, and Watson sat in the van in silence contemplating their next move, Keith and Nikki cuddled up on a sofa in the section of the condo as if to be longtime lovers. The rapper was explaining why he suspected his wife of adultery when Nikki felt an uncomfortable chill creep down her spine. Her stare gazed away and into the eyes of a familiar face returning the stare. Nikki quickly fixed her eyes back on Keith. She waited a few moments then glanced over his shoulder once more to find the creepy eyes gone.

The rapist was checking out Nikki as she and MC K.O. conversed on the sofa. He scanned the room looking for a victim soon after. Once creepy eyes spotted Shawnte' ascending the stairwell his focus shifted to Hectic momentarily. He studied the producer as he entertained a group of party goers. Stealthily, creepy eyes climbed the step to the third floor. He peeped into the master bedroom too find Shawnte' repeatedly dialing a number. Creepy eyes jolted past the open door into the next bedroom. There in the dark, he began massaging his tool until it stiffened. The rapist then placed a magnum over the tip then pulled out his ski-mask. The leather gloves followed…

Pulsating, ready to breakdown his next victim, creepy eyes inched out of the bedroom and into the master room.

Shawnte' began weeping once she realized her Big Daddy had departed. "He's gone. I know he is." She continued crying in her palms. As Shawnte's head elevated, a firm grip wrapped around her wrist. Instinctively she recoiled, her teary eyes climbing the female in front of her. Princess!

"Shawnte', I'm out. And I just wanted you to know in case you didn't, that Hectic's baby momma is here. That's the story he wanted me to pass on. Oh, one more thing, tell Nikki I'll see her later."

Shawnte' let out a deep sigh. "You know where she is. Go tell 'er ya' self"

"I can't look her in the face, you know that. Please do that for me." Princess begged. Shawnte' looked into Princess's eyes revealing her recent tears. "Check this out." She said shrugging. "I'm tired of playing your game. You need to be a woman about yours."

Princess's head fell. She turned around and left. "Fuck 'er! The bitch should've never opened her legs to him." She grabbed her cellular from her purse and began dialing Big Daddy's number repeatedly. All she wanted to know was "why"? Why had he disappeared without informing her? The answer to the question had begun to eat away at her. Tears began to roll down her face once more. She was in no mood to wipe the descending pain. Instead, she hung her head and perched on the edge of the bed hoping that her message would get a response. Shawnte's head quickly shot up after a huge shadow towered over her. Before her eyes could ascend the figure in front of her, a daisy bomb of a punch bombarded into her jaw. The blow sent Shawnte' tumbling backward across the bed and down to the floor. Stunned momentarily, she tried regaining her vision only to catch a vicious knee to her rib cage. The mask man yanked her up by the throat and body slammed her back over the bed. Like a madman, creepy eyes forced Shawnte's thighs apart causing her miniskirt to rise. He snatched the thong from her crotch as if it were threadless.

Shawnte' lay there gulping in the air, hoping to build enough energy to fight off her attacker. Creepy eyes pulled out his monster size penetration and forced himself deep inside Shawnte's walls. She screamed instantly. No one could hear her cries. In seconds the pain increased. Her walls continued to stretch beyond imagination. Just as the rapist leaned down to take a bite of her shirt, Shawnte' head butted him on the bridge of his nose. His firm grip instantly loosened from her wrists. Still pinned by his weight, Shawnte' reached up towards her attacker's face and snatched his mask off.

"Oh my God!" she screamed in disbelief. The familiar face octopused his fingers around his victim's throat and proceeded to squeeze the life out her. Like a wounded animal trapped in the corner, Shawnte' was prepared to fight for her life. She delivered a lightning fast overhand to his leaking nostrils. Pressure of his weight lightened up a little.

As creepy eyes nursed his injury Shawnte' flipped over off the bed and made a dash for the door. The rapist grabbed one leg executing a fixed grip around her ankle.

"Where you think you goin' bitch?" he barked, laughing wickedly afterward. "Only way you leavin' here is in a body bag." Off balance, struggling to break free from her exposed attacker, Shawnte' grabbed her Gucci stiletto laying near the bed and hammered it across his forehead. Still creepy refused to release his fist. Instinctively, Shawnte' struck the desperate man with all the strength she could muster. Finally his fingers released her ankle. She stumbled out of the bedroom with the little energy she possessed.

None of the party goers noticed her staggering down the stairs. Shawnte' tried screaming for help but her voice was gone. She extended her arm out with all her might and placed it on the shoulder of a nearby woman hoping to gain her attention.

"Please! Please help me." Her mumbling words were barely audible over the thumping sound system. Tha female turned around acknowledging Shawnte's cry for help. Shawnte's eyes flooded with tears of horror after she realized who the woman was. She tried back stepping away; Too late!

Hectic's baby mama forced a six inch blade to Shawnte's abdomen collapsing her abused frame on the makeshift dance floor. The girl disappeared in the crowd of party goers as screams echoed across the room. Keith and Nikki arrived in a hurry.

"Nooooo!" Nikki cried out, "Someone dial 911!....Please somebody help her."

Shawnte' s lips quivered as her mouth opened, her arm slowly began to ascend. She attempted to utter something. Her voice died over the somber crowd. Keith gazed up hoping to put a face with the voice he just heard. It didn't surprise him when he spotted Detective Fish and Pataki. The rapper shot to his feet then eased away from Shawnte'. His eyes were fixed on the detective. I knew it!

The Buckroe security guard came storming through the front door moments later. "Fish, the suspect that fled is now in custody."

Fish nodded as he applied pressure to Shawnte's stomach. Carefully he studied every inch of her for additional injuries. Hectic appeared drunk but conscious to what had just transpired. Fish's head shot up to survey the crowd. Something's terribly wrong here, Fish thought, fixing his stare back on Shawnte'. As he examined her over his heart began pounding through his chest. "Holy Mary of God!" he whispered out after raising her mini-skirt to confirm his evidential theory. "Pataki, Watson, secure the area around the house, immediately!"

Confused Watson asked"what for?"

Fish's eyes hardened, "look at'er. She's been raped!"

CHAPTER 16

Kayla peeped through the bedroom door of the room that once belong to her mother then eased the door open. The little girl moved swiftly across the room to the bed with the cordless clutched under her pits. "Mommy," Kayla whispered over Sheila as she slept, careful not to waken the gentleman laying beside her. The toddler settled her eyes on the firm buff chest of the dark skinned man wondering if he were really related to her. If that's my uncle why is he naked? She asked herself. Finally Kayla's eyes fixed on her mother once again. "Mommy, wake up. Daddy's on the phone." Sheila's eyes instantly snapped open. She was half conscious and her voice was barely audible when she grabbed the phone from her stomach after Kayla placed it there.

"Hun-lo?" she cleared her throat, waving Kayla out of the room. "Baby, I'm get'n up right now."

"What time you think you'll be arriving here?"

Sheila let a long tiresome sigh, emphasizing her position. "Ten,"she finally answered, yarning afterward. "I should be there by 10 o'clock." Her eyes focused in on the alarm clock that perched over the television.

"Well, I'll see you in a minute. I love you."

"And I love you, Psycho." The line went dead. She hung up.

She turned over until her morning gaze met Psycho's brother. "Get up!" Sheila began rattling his sculpted shoulder blades. Thunder's eyes blinked open. He rested on both elbows now. Thunder was a male exotic dancer in Atlanta and abroad. Sheila never crept with brothers before. Once her eyes fixed on the stripper her appetite for him would not settle until she had his chocolate bar between her thighs. She propositioned her brother-in-law $7,500 for an hour of pleasure. He accepted.

"What time is it?"

"A little past seven. You gotta hurry up and get dressed before Betty Mae finds you here. Thunder leapt from the covers gathering his belongings off the floor. "You going to visit my brother again?"

"Yepp." She replied, climbing from the bed.

"Look Sheila, don't even mention that you saw me, okay." She shrugged then rolled her eyes, "What makes you think I was gonna do that?"

"I didn't, just assumed."

"You know what they say about assumers, playa."

Thunder cut at her as he fastened his gator buckle. He reached into his pocket pulling out the wad of cash she'd given him last night."Thanks, but no thanks! I enjoyed myself just as much as you did." He turned and walked out the bedroom without saying goodbye. As he quick stepped down the stairwell Kayla met him at the bottom. "Excuse me, sir." She said, halting him with her palm. "Are you really my uncle?" A curious look covered her innocent stare.

"Yeah, my name is uncle Thunder."

"Are uncles supposed to be sleeping with mommies?"

"Nawh baby girl, it ain't like that at all." The dancer began to explain, squatting until his eyes met hers. "Uncle /thunder got drunk last night and mommy brought me here so nothing would happen to me. You wouldn't want anything to happen to Uncle Thunder would you?"

Kayla shook her head satisfied with his reply. "Ohhhhhh! That makes sense. Thunder smiled, admiring his niece's wit. Moments later he was gone. Sheila was in the shower when Kayla arrived upstairs. She looked around for Betty Mae before sneaking in her mother's room to investigate. She hurried over to the king size and snatched the blanket to the floor. There on the odorous sheets the little girl noticed a large stain embedded on them. She looked at the door making sure no one was coming. Slowly, Kayla bent over the bed. She then took in a deep sniff. Her face tightened immediately after. That's a funky smell! She concluded. "Um telling my daddy!" she told herself, running out of the room and into the bathroom.

Kayla knocked on the door then let herself in. Sheila was in the tub cleaning her jewels with one leg elevated. "Yes, Kayla" she answered instantly spotting her frown.

"Isju' goin to see my daddy?"

"You know I am sweetie."

"Can I go?"

Sheila snapped, "How many times do we have to go through this?" A deep sigh. "I took you to see him yesterday. You should know how this works by now, Kayla. We've been doing this for five years now. Saturday is Kayla day. Sunday's belong to mommy." Kayla's frown arched even more. "Girl, don't even try it."

"You don't love me!" Kayla pouted as she stormed out the bathroom. "And I'm telling my daddy what you did too!"

Sheila marveled at her daughter's threat. "That's my girl" she reached outside the tub, dripping water onto the pink tile. She grabbed a long narrow box. Inside was the vinegar scented vaginal cleanser she used for post sex. Sheila's legs flew up and the cleaning process took place. "Good, right, nice and tight."

FORTY MINUTES LATER

Sheila cruised North east on I-75 in the red convertible red SL55 Mercedes Benz Psycho recently purchased for her. Her destination, Georgia Federal Prison.

After Psycho hung up the phone he gestured to the next man waiting in line. With two hours to spare, he decided to stop past his boyfriend's cell to make sure the tickets were ready for distribution in the chow hall and across the rec yard. The millionaire had been running numbers since the beginning of his bid. He partnered with this slim white kid who called himself Jelly. Together they dictated the cash flow that came in and out of the joint.

When it came to money, Psycho trusted no one, not even Sheila. Over time he learned to trust and believe in Jelly. That's how the two became close. It started with handshakes which made Psycho extremely uncomfortable. Next, were the friendly hugs. Then came the back massages. Jelly had enticed and manipulated another vulnerable inmate. Only he , who preferred to be called' she' liked her new man. Psycho struggled with himself mentally. Temptation overwhelmed him. The millionaire's mental wall of manhood had been infiltrated. Before long, Psycho was sneaking in and out of mop closets getting his dick sucked. He was determined not to let another learn of his sexual appetite for boys.(fags) Unfortunately his cover didn't last too long. Jelly had Psycho on a two a day throat massage. One Friday night while everyone was posted in the TV room watching Kobe shoot the Lakers out the playoffs, Psycho slipped into Jelly's cell only to be denied his usual fix. Jelly explained to him that the only way he'd get her pleasures ever again was if Psycho declared Jelly his number one Bitch. Of course Psycho agreed, and then Jelly demanded that he fuck him in the ass. Psycho instantly snapped on Jelly. “I can’t do it.” He told her, “I just cannot do that.” “You do want your dick in my mouth don’t you?” Jelly shot back moaning afterward.

The Millionaire began shaking and sweating like an addict going through withdrawals. He needed his dick sucked; he desired the gratification his body so badly craved. Psycho needed to close his eyes and pretend the female of his choice were on her knees taking care of the big time CEO that he once were. He agreed to Jelly’s terms as long as it stayed on the down low. And if someone approached Jelly about their relationship he was to deny everything. Jelly agreed! That’s been the story of Psycho’s prison life ever since.

“Yo Jelly, how that money looking?” he asked, kissing his lover on the neck. “Ole Tyrone and Hammerhead haven’t paid up yet, but it’s no biggie.” Psycho nodded, his eyes fixed on the stack of cash. “I hollered at the C.O. He’s suppose to move you back to my cell on Tuesday. He laid across her bunk,” He also said that if we get caught fucking again, I’m going to the hole and you’re gettin’ transferred to Cali somewhere.”

Jelly giggled, “How much?”

A confused look surfaced on his face, “How much for what?”

“How much did we pay the C.O.?”

“Oooh, “he hummed, “I paid I’m three gees.”

“Three grand hunh? Jelly smiled elevating from the small iron desk, turning off the lights afterwards. “You must really love me.”

“And you know it. You my boo!”

Jelly sasheed toward the small bed and began massaging Psycho’s khakis. “Not now, Jelly. I got a visit coming in a few.” He forced his lover off him. Only to have Jelly come on stronger.

“Who’s your number one bitch?” he purred, trying her best to sound femine. Psycho didn’t respond. He were in no mood to be arguing early in the morning. The millionaire sucked his teeth , placing his forearm over his eyes while Jelly proceeded to give his boyfriend the satisfaction he did not want.

Thirty minutes later he was cleaning himself up. Just as he started to exit the 6x9 Jelly called out for him, stopping Psycho in his tracks. “When you gonna tell her about us,Psycho?”

Without turning, he replied in a firm tone. “Soon.”

“Soon was two years ago.” Jelly barked, frustrated.

“As long as Sheila is bringing my little girl up here to see me…..the answer to your question is ….soon!” Psycho departed immediately after. That bitch must be out of her mind if she thinks I'ma tell my ex-wife that I am gay. He pondered. The CEO of Psycho records strode down the tier to his cell. "One more year of this shit then I'll be free, start over fresh. Never ever will I let another man touch or even look at me wrong. All I wanna see is big ole tits and teardrop shaped booties" he promised himself. Thoughts of Sheila's curves bought a smile to his face. "What'chu all jolly about?" Ironhead Eddie interjected. Hey, ma'main man Ironhead Eddie. You know what time it is." Psycho greeted, dapping him up.

"Nigga, call me Ironhead again, it's gon' be trouble. I just look seventy." Eddie shot back, throwing super slow punches in the CEO's direction. "Eddie you crazy as hell, man." Once the laughter simmered Psycho asked Ironhead Eddie into his cell. "You know what Eddie? You've been ironing my clothes for what, six years almost?"

"That's right nigga. That's what I do. I'm Ironhead Eddie muthafucka. What's really good nigga?" Psycho cut him off."Yo, check it! Fa'real, I just wanted to let you know I appreciate you taking care of me every single weekend."

"Nigga, you don't have to appreciate, just pay me." Eddie snickered afterward. "I heard that ole man." Psycho handed Ironhead Eddie his khaki uniform and five thousand dollars in cash. Eddie's eyes settled on the swollen knot of dough. "Godt Damn, Boy!" His lips began shaking," I ain't seen this much since I heisted that bank in 82." "Well, its yours, all yours." Ironhead Eddie's eyes cut up at Psycho. His brows rose to the top of his forehead. Ima take this here money cause you gave it to me, but I'm letting you know right muthafuck'n know, nigga. I do not go that way. Sooooo, don't be lookin at my old wrinkle ass n' shit when I ain't lookin" his fist flew up again. A smile came soon after.

Psycho burst into laughs. He wondered if his old friend were really joking or being truthful in a humorous manner. Psycho's thought instantly reflected on the words Sheila used to quote back when they were married. A lot of truth and honest feelings are expressed through jokes. He dismissed the proverb realizing Sheila was no college professor nor could she be regarded as wise. Hell, she barely graduated from high school!

Psycho removed the photo of his ex-wife from his mirror, admiring the handmade frame his amigo friend crafted together. His eyes settled on the center of the picture, "It's gon be me and you, Sheila. One more year to go. One more."

Sheila Osbourne calculated in her mind just how much a divorce lawyer would cost her and how much cheese she'd walk away with as she cruised the highway. "Keith is loaded." She kept telling herself. As long as she walked away from it with something she'd be her own millionaire. Sheila began smiling as visions of her lonely husband flashed before her. He's probably home lookin stupid and pitiful, not wanting to speak with anyone or go anywhere besides his fake ass mammie's house. What a loser! Boring ass nigga! The coupe slowed then turned into the Federal Institution's parking lot. The facility had plenty of available parking spaces, especially up front. After Sheila spotted a black 1997 SL500 Mercedes Benz at the far end of the lot she didn't hesitate parking beside it. "Once the owner of that played out shit gets a wift of this new 5 series he'll know to get that garbage upgraded into the millennium years." She snickered proudly. The engine continued running as Sheila adjusted the rearview mirror down toward her. She grabbed the cherry red lip gloss from her purse and gently applied it. Sheila rarely wore make-up. In fact, she hated it. Her love for her ex was so strong she honored his obsession every Sunday. Sheila leaned forward for a closer peep in the mirror. She puckered her lips, hoping to even out the application. Sheila surveyed the parking lot then killed the engine as another vehicle turned onto the premises. The seat discreetly reclined as far back as it could. Sheila's skirt eroded to her waist. Her panties slid down to her ankles. She kicked Victoria's secret under the seat. I could put them back on once we're done, she pondered, yeah; I think I'd better bring them along. Psycho's fluids will be racing down my legs again. She cuffed the undies from under the seat and tucked them in between her breast.

The car door swung open. Sheila gave her lips the final inspection then she repositioned her curly hair over the shoulders. Moments later, the Diva was halfway across the parking lot. "Chirp, chirp" "Lady Diva, your Benz is now secure." The computerized system announced. Sheila smiled to herself. I love it when it does that.

As she passed by a grey van filtered with tinted windows, a camera was recording every radiant step of her million dollar stride.

CHAPTER 17

After Fish declared Shawnte' had been a victim of rape. The party goers stampeded to their rides. Detective Watson tried to slow them down. He was no match for the thundering herd of vehicles that sped off from the estate.

Pataki searched the bedrooms. He discovered the mattress hanging off the box spring with fresh blood stains in view. The broken glass was evident that their suspect had leapt three stories down through the window. He damned himself for not monitoring the bedroom a while longer but was confident they'd catch up with their guy sooner or later.

THE FOLLOWING MORNING

Keith and Nikki slumped in the chair of the emergency room at Hampton general, the nearest trauma center. An infant crying through the wee hours would not allow Nikki to get much sleep. Every fifteen minutes she'd awaken. Nikki hadn't noticed the woman and her child missing until they re-entered the waiting room. As they headed for the exit the baby began crying once more after the gleaming sun rays covered her face. Uncoordinately, Nikki sprung up from the chair, focusing her eyes across the room to learn it were midmorning and the sleep killer was finally departing.

"What time is it?" she asked herself, gazing up at the clock hanging over the clerk's station. It read 9:21 am. Her stare settled on Keith momentary. Nikki marveled at the way he slept so peacefully. "He must've been very tired." She concluded, making way to the front desk. She instantly noticed there were a different clerk perched in the chair this time. "Good morning. My name is Nichole Wallace and"

"Yes, I know," the receptionist cut her off, "the clerk from the last shift informed me that you and your husband are waiting for Shawnte" Battles-Howard, is it?" "Battle is her maiden name." Nikki offered so the clerk would kill the suspicious stare.

"I see."

Nikki's eyes cut at the receptionist ready to check her undertone. "Is my friend going to be okay?"

"It appears so. In fact, she's in surgery now. It's just a matter of how long she'll be unconscious." The clerk, offered darting her pupils back and forth. "Could be days, could be weeks. It is all up to Miss Howard, right?" another fake smile.

"Well, when can I see her?"

"I'll page the doctor. When I know, you'll know, alrighty."

Reluctantly, Nikki forced herself away from the counter with a disgusted look on her face. "that bitch don't know me. I'll beat her ass up in here." She mumbled. Nikki snatched up her purse and marched to the vending section. As she made change she replayed the clerk's words in her mind. 'you and your husband' a wide smile surfaced immediately after she purchased her first coffee. Her gaze fixed on Keith once more as he shifted in his chair. As Nikki watched him sleep she began fantasizing that they were actually married happily ever after.

"Darnit! No more coffee" Nikki surveyed her other choices then purchased a cup of hot cocoa from the next vending machine. She scooped up a handful of napkins and tucked them in her Fendi leather. As Nikki made her way past the clerk she shot a wicked grin in her direction hoping to spoil her day. When she sat down she had already decided to keep the coffee for herself.

"Keith." She whispered in his ear, nudging him lightly afterward. "Keith, wake up." Unalert, eyes blood shot red, the rapper's lids slowly opened. "How is she?" he mumbled, stretching his arms. "She's okay I guess. I'll know for sure in a moment. "Nikki placed the larger cup in his palms. It's hot cocoa. I hope you don't—

"How did you know?" Keith asked, cutting her off.

"Know what?"

The rapper downed a few gulps before answering. "How did you know I didn't drink coffee?"

Nikki would surely lose some points if she revealed the truth. Instead, she shrugged, smiling innocently.

"I love hot cocoa." He offered, taking another sip. For the next couple of minutes the two buried their faces in the cups of their morning starters.

"Excuse me Miss Wallace." The receptionist announced across the lounge. She then gestured her hand for Nikki to come up to her station.

Nikki placed her cup in the chair then darted to the front desk. "I was hoping you could answer a few questions for…uh… Miss Howard she isn't available to at this moment." The clerk's eyes shot down to the papers in front of her. "First question, does Miss Howard have any medical insurance?"

"Medical insurance?" Nikki's teeth clinched together in anger. "My homegirl is fighting for her life and you wanna question me about some damn medical bill?"

Her tone elevated with every word. The receptionist had struck another cord.

"Nawh, she doesn't have health insurance because she doesn't need any."

The clerk gave Nikki a look as to say 'you a fool to believe such a thing."

Keith Osbourne arrived at the front desk after Nikki's tone caught attention. Gently he wrapped his arm around her pulling his lover away and stepping in front.

"What she means is her husband is a multi-millionaire, which unquestionably makes her a millionaire as well." The rapper glanced over his shoulder momentary, feeling Nikki's heavy breathing. "I'm almost certain that Mrs. Howard is covered by Blue Cross Platinum.

"How could you possibly know that?" the clerk asked in a skeptical tone, without taking her eyes off the angry woman standing behind him.

"You wanna know how I know such a thing huh?"

"Well yeah." The receptionist's fake smile widened for the third time.

"Stand up!" the rapper demanded the clerk, changing his subtle tone to an aggressive one.

"Look outside that window into the parking lot. You see that shiny ass automobile. That's a Bentley, I'm sure your thick neck father wished your husband drove one of them." The clerk stood there baffled by his tone.

"Dig this lady, Mrs. Howard is a millionaire. Her husband is a millionaire. I-am-a-millionaire. We all millionaires up in this piece!"

The receptionist eyes darted back to Nikki, she waited for her to claim her status as well. ""Nawh, I ain't no millionaire, just a Deputy Corrections Officer lookin' to beat a snobbish white bitch's ass on a fine Sunday morning."

The rapper quickly took over, "I apologize for her remarks. What she means to convey is don't assume that every person of color that comes through these doors is ignorant, poor, and uneducated. Because when you do, you a insulting not just her and I, but our entire race as a whole." Keith Osbourne concluded with a phony smile of his own. "Now can you tell us rich negros when-we-will be able to see our rich negro friend?"

The receptionist snatched up the receiver and dialed to the Hospital Director. A brief moment passed by before she hung up. "Awh yes. Mr. Wallace, you and your wife can see Mrs. Howard up on the third floor. She's in I.C.U."

In unison, Nikki and Keith turned to each other marveling at the thought of being a couple. Their gaze shifted back to the clerk. "Thank you." Keith gestured, then walked away with Nikki's hand in his.

INTENSIVE CARE UNIT

The doctor was explaining Shawnte's condition to Keith and Nikki when Hectic arrived from an elevator. Nikki sprung to her feet and wrapped her arms around him.

"This is her husband, Mr. Howard." Nikki introduced.

"As you aware Mrs. Howard was indeed sexually assaulted and suffered a deep puncture wound," the doctor said, "she also suffered a concussion to her cranium." A deep sigh. "She is definitely going to live. How long she remains in a coma is not yet determined." The doctor turned to MC K.O. who appeared to be much calmer. "Mrs. Howard can now receive visits, but only from one person at a time." The surgeon nodded the started down the hall. "Oh yes, Mr. Howard, I am sorry to say, your wife was seven weeks pregnant. She lost her unborn."

The doctor's head hung as he continued for the elevator.

Hectic's eyes instantly flooded with tears. Keith Osbourne gave the producer a encouraging hug after noticing the misty eyes. "Hectic! Go in there." The rapper's arm extended out towards the I.C.U. doors. "Go and be strong for your wife man. You can do it."

Hectic nodded and slowly walked through the double doors. Nikki sat down tightly clutching her waist.

"Baby are you all right?" Keith asked after noticing her wince.

"It's those symptoms again."

The rapper's face lit up instantly. "The pregnant ones?"

Nikki hesitantly nodded emphasizing her pain.

"What uh…can I do anything? Want me to get somebody?"

Through the agony, Nikki managed to cough out a laugh. Keith's eagerness to help was humorous to her. "I'm not in labor." She said, forcing out a light giggle.

"I wanna help but I don't know how."

"You can start by calming down before I laugh cramps in my side."

"Okay okay." The rapper shot back, taking deep breaths as if he were in labor.

"What are you doing man?"

Keith Osbourne fixed his eyes on her. "I'm trying to simmer all this excitement built up inside me."

Nikki suddenly marveled at the thought of having a famous rapper's child. In fact was impressed that he hadn't mentioned the 'A' word. "Keith don't breathe so hard, you'll make someone go in labor around here." Tickled by Nikki's humor, Keith began laughing. It had just occurred to him that he'd just made a fool of himself. "All I need you to do is wait while I get myself cleaned up." Keith managed to her feet. Her gaze locked in Keith Osbourne's momentary.

"I love you Nichole Wallace."

"I love you Keith sensitive Osbourne." A million thoughts clouded her mind all at once. "oh my God, I can't believe I just uttered that. Why did I say that? Why did he say those words to me? Does he really mean it is what I want to know.

The elevator slid open. Nikki stepped in, her mind somewhere else. A young black nurse with two platinum teeth and matching weave waited patiently in the rear.

"Excuse me Miss?" Nikki said politely.

"Wussup baby girl, you okay?" the nurse shot back noticing Nikki was holding her stomach.

"I'm good. I was wondering If you sold pregnancy test here?"

"Ohhh, you pregnant huh? Well at least think you are." The woman's platinum smile eased Nikki's pain a little. "Sorry sister, they don't sell 'em here but…they do administer them."

"They do?"

“Of course. Not in a clinic kind of way, but they do test some folks. Depends on the circumstance I guess. Platinum grill moved closer and started whispering as if someone else was in the shaft with them. “For fiddy dollars, I can get my girl upstairs to hook you all the way up. Tell how many weeks you are, even down to the exact day and position. I’m kiddin’ bout dat part, but you get what I’m sayin.’

Nikki rumbled through her purse producing a fifty dollar bill almost in an instant. The elevator suddenly opened. “Sorry, medical emergency, catch the next one please.” The nurse instructed the small gathering in her professional tone. Moments later the shaft arrived at the ninth floor where the medical lab resided.

The rapper sat alone in the hallway contemplating when Hectic staggered out. The producer looked like he had just seen a ghost. Before Keith Osbourne could ask, Hectic cried out, “She look so bad.”

Keith sprung up helping the teary eyed man sit in a nearby chair. “Relax, everything is gonna be fine.” He assured Hectic, silently praying he did not utter those heart crushing words. Keith stood back up and glazed toward the I.C.U. corridor. “I’ma go inside and give my get well wishes to her if you don’t mind.”

Hectic’s face lay buried in his palms, he just waved him off, refusing to let MC K.O. witness the downpour of tears. The rapper hardly knew Shawnte’ yet was anxious to speak with her. Soon as he stepped into the Intensive Care Unit a R.N. escorted him to Shawnte’s gurney then disappeared from his side. Keith settled his eyes on the tubes that germinated from her mouth.

“Damn! She is in bad shape.” He whispered to himself. Shawnte’s eyes instantly snapped open as if she were programmed to react to the rapper’s voice. The fear in her eyes startled him momentarily. Keith’s eyes darted left and right to see if anyone was watching. He then inched closer to Shawnte’ and prepared himself to ask the one question that had been eating away at him all night long.

“Shawnte’.” He whispered, his face only inches away from hers. “Were you trying to tell me who raped you?” Shawnte’ began to tremble. “Was it Mont that assaulted you?” No response. “Is it someone I know?” Shawnte’s pupils widened. She tried moving her lips but soon realized that it were gagged by tubes. All she could manage to utter was “WHU…Whu?”

Keith began shaking his head. “I don’t understand you, Shawnte’.” His thoughts quilted to his crew members. Who’s name in the Salt Water Boys Camp sounds like a ‘Whu?’ he asked himself. “Maybe Timmy Tuff can help me with the names of my team.” Shawnte’ reacted with a sudden jolt of energy. Medical personnel soon stormed in and asked the rapper to leave.

Keith ignored them momentarily. He fixed his stare on Shawnte's falling tears. He now understood what she had been trying to tell him last night and moments ago.

She was trying to say white. White man! Timmy Tuff raped her? He pondered the thought as he headed for the exit. My longtime friend a serial rapist? But why? Keith decided not to share his new intel until he knew for sure that the perpetrator was indeed white. She could have easily been trying to tell me that Timmy Tuff was the guy who raped her. After all, the suspect had a black profile. He was convince his partner was most likely an acquaintance of the vicious criminal.

Moments later the nurse returned with the test results. "Girlfriend, I don't know whether you takin' it as a good or bad thing, but either way you're pregnant! You're ultra sound isn't showing much, which means you're just a few days." The nurse didn't wait for a response, she started back toward her station as if they never met.

Nikki stepped into the elevator wondering how she was going to break the factual news to her lover. Should I get calm, happy, play and look tired? She pondered. I'm just gonna tell him. However it comes out is how it's going to sound.

The shaft arrived at the third floor. When the doors opened Keith appeared in front of her with his head hung. Just as he stepped in, Nikki's arms extended open for him to meet her warm embrace. "I took the test. I'm two days pregnant." She announced, gently placing a kiss on his lips afterward.

No reaction.

"What's wrong?" she asked, instantly regretting her statement. "I thought you would be happy about having your first child."

"I am." Keith whispered. "It's not about the baby, it's about Shawnte'."

Keith's tone made Nikki's neck hairs erect. She swallowed hard as Keith pressed the lobby button.

"Is she?"

"Shawnte" is going to be fine." He cut her off, sensing he'd given the wrong impression. "I visited Shawnte' only moments ago. She tried to tell me who raped her."

"What did she say to you?"

"I couldn't make out her words and that's what bothers me. I feel I must at least investigate." Keith had a decent idea but felt uncomfortable about sharing his hunch with Nikki.

The elevator opened. They stepped into the lobby and headed toward the emergency room section of where his car was parked. “Look Nichole, this is what we’re going to do. First I’m going to my house to get some clothes then I’m going to your place so you can do the same. From there we are gonna go down and check ourselves into Norfolk’s most comfortable hotel.”

“First of all, you ain’t running nothing. Secondly, I like the way that sounds. And third, I will be driving my car behind you because I gotta be to work by nine o’ clock tonight.”

They jumped into the Bentley smiling at each other.

Five minutes into their journey Keith turned to Nikki then settled his stare onto the road. “I was thinking…maybe you could not go to work tonight. After all, I am a millionaire.” His tone emphasized his proudness. “Matter of fact, you never have to work again if that’s your desire.”

Nikki’s eyes cut sharply in his direction. “Now doesn’t that sound just nice.” She said, unmoved by the offer. “Unfortunately for you, I like feeling independent. Which incidentally, stems from actually, independence! Sooooo thanks, but no thanks.”

“If you gon’ be my woman-”

Nikki cut him off, “Who said I was your girl? You still married, remember?”

“Not for long…not for long, trust me!” Keith’s tone was serious.

“And when I do become your woman,” her tone stressing every word, “you-will-not-run-shit-over-her. Ain’t going through that again.”

“I feel you love. I’m feeling you and the strong head on your shoulders.”

Nikki’s arms folded tightly, her lips poked out, confident she’d just won that argument. She fixed her gaze back on Keith to find a huge smirk perched in the corner of her mouth. “Look Keith Osbourne, if we are going to be together, there is no boss between us. We compromise and find common ground in whatever we have a disagreement on.”

“Who said we were going to be together. I have a wife, remember?” A sarcastic smile appeared on his face.

“Okay, you got me. I’m being serious now.”

“Nichole, I’m not like that. I never use my assets or manhood to sway or dictate a relationship. In fact, the only thing I’m ever excited about is love.” He said. “I care for nothing about this car, the house, or the money. Those materialistic items do not define just who I am. All I want is to be loved just as equally as I love, that’s it.”

Nikki didn't respond. She closed her eyes and soaked in the rapper's sincerity.

"We'll see Mr. Loverboy, we'll see!"

"Nichole Wallace, you're the one. The one I've been waiting for my entire life. You are the very one Arleen, my mother, told me would come with time and patience. I will love you even when you do not love yourself. Never will I leave you lonesome, or break your heart. I know I haven't known you that long, love. Still, I feel as if the soul of me had known you all my life. You are my soul mate!" His voice lowered to a whisper, "I know you do not see it, nor do you feel it yet. In time you come to understand and know that my love for you and our unborn is genuine. I love you."

Nikki was fast asleep. Somehow his words found her in dreamland. Keith was aware that his lover had dozed off moments ago. That did not prevent his dire need to express what his heart desired to say.

"Keith." Nikki whispered, her lids still shuttered.

"Yes beloved?"

"I love you more."

CHAPTER 18

Mitch Holley had been tailing Sheila Osbourne since she departed early yesterday morning. Thanks to Keith, his flight was purchased in advance. Soon after the private investigator arrived at the O'Hara Airport. He followed Sheila onto the shuttle train. It stopped at the departure section. As they waited for their luggage he noticed the subject had ventured off to a nearby locker. He discretely followed. From where Mitch stood he could make not out what she had retrieved from the small box. Sheila moved swiftly toward the baggage claim area afterward. The P.I. eased over to the locker and jotted down the number and location of it. He moved through the crowd with his eyes darting in every direction. As Mitch Holley arrived at the moving luggage he spotted Keith's wife heaving a suitcase from the conveyer belt and scurry to the exit.

Mitch's eyes surfed the wave of bags and cases hoping to see his luggage. He didn't, which startled the P.I. with every passing second. His stare fixed on the exit. Sheila Osbourne was nowhere in sight. I gotta do something!

Mitch Holley leaped onto the moving train of luggage and moved steadily in the opposite direction, ignoring the travelers that pointed and whispersed amongst themselves. He spotted Airport Security out of the corner of his eye. They were quickly closing in on his location. Too late! Mitch's Louis Vuitton glided from under the chute. The P.I. scooped it up and jumped down, forcing his way through the crowd. Once Mitch Holley arrived at the baggage ramp he instantly recognized his subject cruising by in a red convertible Mercedez Benz. Before he could get a cabbie's attention he was distracted by a hand that wrapped around his wrist. The P.I. spun instinctively forcing his arm free of the airport police.

"I need to check your bag sir!"

Mitch responded by whipping out a phony government badge. "FBI, chief! Now beat it. I'm on a very important case, domestic terrorism." He turned and darted to the back seat of a yellow cab, laughing to himself afterward. Can't believe that FBI shit still works. Mitch instructed the driver to follow Mrs. Osbourne after the cabbie turned around.

He checked his watch soon after Sheila arrived at her mother's home. It read 8:59 a.m. The P.I. then directed the driver to the nearest car rental. Twenty minutes later Mitch arrived back at Betty Mae's in a gray passenger van. He parked across the street and set up his 35 mm digital camera. He snapped shots of the house, the car, and the license plates.

Before long, MC K.O.'s wife appeared in the doorway holding a little girl's hand. They descended the brick steps and climbed into the Benz and merked off. Mitch Holley cautiously followed. His watch read 11:14 a.m. when the red coupe turned into the parking lot of the Federal Institution. He killed the engine into the parking lot and flicked pictures of Sheila and Kayla as they marched into the main entrance.

For hours he sat in the van trying to figure out just how he could gain access inside the visiting room. It suddenly occurred to him as he spotted the Federal Correctional Officers storm the staff parking lot after completing their 12-hour shift. He pulled the binoculars up to his face and focused on the officers that climb inside their vehicles. Almost instantly Mitch Holley spotted a mark. A young European kid with streaks of blond dye blended into his hair. A punk rocker or skateboarder perhaps! He considered. The binoculars fell to the seat. The P.I. cranked the engine and sped off behind the Ford truck the slinky white kid drove. For nearly 15 minutes Mitch Holley tailed the pick-up. The Ford signaled to the other commuters that it were about to exit the freeway.

Mitch reached into the back seat scrambling through his suit case without taking his eyes off the road. He pulled out a blue and red strobe light. And plugged it into the cigarette adapter. As the C.O. descended the ramp, Mitch flicked on the siren. The skateboarder quickly veered onto the shoulder lane. The P.I. followed. Mitch had to move swiftly. Time was critical, if a Georgia trooper passed by, there was no doubt in the investigator's mind that he'd land back in prison. Mitch whipped out the FBI badge as he arrived to the driver's side. "FBI! I need to ask you a few questions."

The young man trembled instantly. "I…I didn't do it…IT was…it was Chad." Mitch observed the sweat forming over the C.O.'s forehead and decided to work him for the time being. "Yes, the Bureau is aware of Chad. You could lose your job as well go to prison." The kid's face shook like a bobble head. “The good thing is, if you help me get into the visiting room, I’ll forget all about you and Chad’s activities.” Mitch’s stare tightened, he couldn’t help but wonder what kind of activities they were into. “Look kid, help me, and I’ll even pay you a few grand.”

A curious stare formed on the officer’s face. Mitch Holley advised the punk rocker to follow him. The P.I. quickly killed the strobe lights then sped down the ramp. The pick-up followed the passenger van to a nearby Denny’s. The two walked inside and took a seat at the first available table. After the waiter took their orders the P.I. pulled out his camera and showed the kid a photo image of Sheila Osbourne and her daughter.

“Do you recognize this woman?” Mitch didn’t wait for an answer. “I’m investigating her and whomever she’s visiting.”

“Yeah, but what’s that got to do with me?”

“Let me finish, okay.” The C.O. nodded, massaging his temple. “This is the deal, son. I need your assistance in helping me gain access into the visiting room. I suspect her smuggling potent narcotics in from off the street to an inmate.”

“We can phone the warden, he’ll take care of your problem.”

“No!” Mitch snapped, lowering his tone back to a whisper. “The Director of the Bureau does not want anyone in the Bureau of Prisons to know ‘bout our covert operation.” The P.I.’s tone was firm as his eyes. He said, “We at the Bureau cannot risk the warden taking measures into his own hands.”

“So…what exactly do you want me to do?”

“I need someone I can visit tomorrow. Someone with no family ties and receives no visits. And of course, has to be over sixty.” Mitch Holley produced two-thousand dollars from his breast pocket. “All I need is my name processed in the B.O.P.’s mainframe computer.”

“That’s it, that’s all?” the C.O. asked, suddenly feeling relieved. “And I get to keep this money?” His eyes locked on the envelope that lay beside the shaker.

“Yepp! That’s it.” Mitch slid his number across the table with his information scribbled under it. “Call this number. Text or leave me a message with the info on the inmate plus a detailed profile of him.” The Private Investigator didn’t wait for the punk rocker to ask anything else. He sprung from the table and walked away.

“Will you be eating alone?” the waiter asked the Correctional Officer.

“I guess so….I guess so.”

Mitch Holley settled in at the Holiday Inn just off of Route 40. Upon a nice warm shower the P.I. decided to stake out Betty Mae's two story home until Sheila arrived. As he parked a few blocks down the street from her mother's, the P.I. came up with a brilliant idea. Mitch wrapped some of the gadgets he brought along around his waist in the form of a tool belt. He approached the phone pole that towered across the street. "I thought she would." He mumbled to himself as he pressed the doorbell.

Moments later, the front door swung open. Sheila's mother greeted the, middle aged European in front of her. "Yes, how can I help you?"

Mitch's fingers folded around his makeshift tool belt looking as though he were a real handyman. "Yes mam! How do you do? I'm with the cable company and we've located signals of an electrical surge through the lines around her."

"But my cable is just fine." Betty Mae offered.

Mitch sucked in his lips then shook his head. "That's a good thing. The bad part about that is that it's sending jammed signals to the main satellites. All I need is to test all of your outlets if the E-Ser." the P.I. interrupted himself to explain, "That's what they call the electrical surge in the cable world, mamm." Mitch's arm slid across his forehead emphasizing the perspiration that formed over it. . "Soon as I check for the E-Ser, I'll be on my way."

Betty Mae didn't hesitate to let him in. She escorted him to the den where the outlet connected to the cable box. The P.I. pulled out a tracking transmitter and placed it near the socket, blocking the view of Betty Mae who anxiously stared.

"Just as I thought!" Mitch blurted out with a long sigh behind it. "The E-Ser, it's getting weaker. Have to check your other outlets to make sure."

"I have two more cable outlets upstairs but there's no cable line running through them."

"Good. The test will go even faster." Betty Mae led the gentleman upstairs to her bedroom. Instantly he spotted two additional rooms occupied with furniture once he reached the top. That must be Sheila's bedroom. And that's where her daughter sleeps.

"There is another socket." Betty Mae said, pointing to the wall near the window. Mitch placed the transmitter over the outlet then pressed a button forcing the rhythmic beep once again. "Why is it beeping?" she asked, just as the P.I. had hoped she would.

"That means the surge is strong." Mitch raised up hinting to the woman that he was ready to inspect the next room.

Betty Mae escorted him into Sheila's room. "This is my daughter's room when ever she's in town. She's married to this famous rapper nam-"

"I don't mean to be rude ma'am, but I do not listen to rap music." Mitch smiled pleasantly.

"Oh yes, of course. What was I thinkin?"

She countered, embarrassed. "The last outlet is somewhere behind this dresser." She grunted out as she attempted to heave the large chest.

"Ma'am please let me handle that for you." Mitch offered, smiling warmly. "If it's not too much trouble, can I have a glass of water? I'm probably going to need it."

"Why no, it's no trouble at all." Betty Mae excused herself in almost an instant. Once the P.I. heard the sound of footsteps fade he reached into his gadget box and pulled out his newly purchased Roach. The Roach was a small spy camera that favored the pesky cock roach. He scanned across the bedroom for a place to disguise his set-up. Perched in the corner was a Korean made straw chair with Teddy Bears decorating the cushion. The P.I. moved swiftly across the room to the old, raggly animal. Betty Mae's footsteps were growing louder and louder. Mitch had to hurry, she was only moments away. His fingernails dug into the face of the stuffed animal and ripped the left eye completely off. Quickly, the P.I. positioned the roach in the teddy bear's socket. Betty Mae now stood at the top of the stairwell. Mitch Holley repositioned the bear so it would face the entire room. When he spun around Betty Mae was towering over him.

"Is everything okay?"

"Ah yes, I was just admiring this Asian craft. Made in Korea, real nice."

"I didn't even know it was Korean." She replied, dumbfounded.

"Well I'm all finished up here. I'll have to report back to my supervisor and inform him of the E-Ser, ASAP!"

"What about your water?"

"Sorry to take you through the troubles, mamm, but I really must be going."

Betty Mae escorted him downstairs to the front door. The P.I. nodded then started toward the next block. "Damn. I am good." Mitch said out loud, whistling Earth, Wind, and Fire tunes to himself afterward.

Soon after Mitch Holley jumped into the van, the red Mercadez Benz pulled up to the corner. He quickly climbed into the back seat and assembled the recording monitors. Within moments the P.I. had at live footage of Sheila's room. Mitch climbed back into the front seat and drove off hoping the signal would remain strong. As soon as he reached the main road static and snow appeared on the screen. "No problem! Once I get myself something to nibble on, me and you are going to get very much acquainted. Whether you know it or not!" the Private investigator said under his breath. His eyes cut into the rearview mirror and locked on the Mercedez Benz.

Later that evening, Mitch Holley followed Mrs. Osbourne to a male strip club just outside of Buckhead. He didn't want to frequent it, but the $250,000 Keith Osbourne had paid him said he had to go inside. As the P.I. stepped in line of the male exotic strip joint he mumbled every curse word in the French language. After an hour of professing to be homosexual, intrigued by hung black dudes dressed in silly costumes, Mitch finally caught a break. He spotted Sheila leaving. She escorted one of the dancers outside to her car. The P.I. stealthy followed behind, while snapping shots from his belt buckle camera. He followed the red Benz back to her mother's place. After witnessing the two enter the house he checked his watch. It read 2:01 a.m. With the press of a button the screen blinked on, the recording began. "Right on time baby." The P.I. calmly whispered to himself as he watched Sheila Osbourne and the unknown stripper undress each other. "This may be better than a triple X rental." Mitch clamped his fingers over his stomach and set back.

By morning, Mitch Holley was sure he had all the evidence he needed. Still he had to go on Keith's gut instinct and hidden phone bill he discovered.

At 7:30 a.m., the P.I. received a text. It read: 'Call Randy Wright at 555-9726.'

For a moment he'd forgotten who Randy was. Before long it occurred to the P.I. that it was indeed the C.O. Mitch whipped out his cellular and dialed him up. "Hello. Special Agent Holley speaking. Who's this?"

"It's me Randy…Randy Wright."

"Is everything a go Mr. Wright?"

"Almost."

"What do you mean, almost?"

"I took care of everything you asked of me. In the process, I found out that you aren't FBI. Sooo, who are you?" the C.O.'s tone was more curious than upset.

Mitch Holley had a pretty good idea of where the surfer was going with this. Why else would he still call knowing I was a fake, he pondered. "Look kid, I'ma level wit 'chu! I'm a Private Investigator."

Randy shouted into the receiver, almost in celebration. "I knew it man. I knew it. I was right on the money!" his voice lowered to a calm. "Speaking of money, I'm gonna need two more G's, bro."

"Come on kid, we had a deal!"

"Unh unh! I had a deal with an FBI agent, not a Private Investigator."

"Alright kid, you win. Let's do business."

"Okay listen up, I'll be working the front desk. When you arrive in the lobby come over to me and ask for inmate Simon Alexander. He's an elderly white guy from Canada. He's also in a wheelchair, has no family, and doesn't get any visits, just like you requested."

"What about the girl?"

"Figured you might ask." The C.O. said. "So I took the liberty to do some investigating myself. Sheila Johnson is married to Harvey 'Psycho' Johnson. According to our records, she has visited Mr. Johnson faithfully every single weekend for the past five years." Randy Wright paused momentarily.

"I'm curious about something."

"Don't be!" Mitch suggested. "Just know she's no longer married to Psycho but to the rapper MC K.O."

"Thee MC K.O.?"

"That's right and thanks to you, Slut Barbie is going down in divorce court."

"Think you could get me an autograph?"

"Of course kiddo. Now where do I meet you for the other two grand you demanded?"

"Upon presenting me your I.D., slide the money, that will be placed in envelope, to me."

"Gotcha!" the line went dead. Mitch hung up, extended his arms, yawning soon after. The engine turned over, a few miles later, the P.I. pulled up to his hotel room.

Once inside, he called Keith Osbourne only to get his voice mail. Mitch didn't hesitate to leave a message. "Yooo! Keith, this is your main man Mitch. I just wanted to let you know that I have obtained the evidence you paid me for." Mitch sighed. "Your wife's a slut G! She's sleeping around with her ex's brother. I'm going to visit my uncle in Federal prison. I'll hit you back up afterward with the damage." The message ended.

A few hours later, Mitch Holley was pulling into the Institution's parking lot. He fixed his camera on the sidewalk. From the backseat of the van, he armed himself with micro-cameras. One was disguised as a charm, the other in his belt buckle. The P.I. scanned the lot where Sheila was parked, wondering why she hadn't exited her car. Mitch flicked on the monitors then hopped out of the rental, discretely waving into the camera. Once Mitch Holley arrived inside Randy Wright was at the front door as planned. He slid the envelope across the counter along with his identification card. Moments later the P.I. was escorted down the hall through a iron mobile gate where the visiting room resided. Mitch had been waiting on his visit for almost five minutes when Sheila pranced through the gate quickly finding a seat near the vending machine. Mitch positioned his back to the wall which gave him visual of the entire area. As Sheila waited for her visit, the P.I. surveyed his surroundings. Kids running wildly. Couples were aggressively making out as if they were in there alone. The C.O.'s conversed amongst themselves, ignoring the inmate who vigorously finger fucked his ole' lady right beside them.

Before long, a man appeared from the shake down room. His wheelchair cruised in the P.I.'s direction. Mitch stood up to meet the elderly gentleman. "Hello Simon." He said, extending his arm. Only for the two wheeler to sail past him and be welcomed by another visitor. "Ooohps! Wrong guy." He pretended to be stretching afterward. As he sat down he noticed Sheila Osbourne greet a heavy set gentleman. That must be Psycho? He guessed to be true, aiming his charm in their direction while staring blankly in the other.

Moments later, another wheelchair surfaced from the back. The inmate was being escorted by a Correctional Officer. 'This has to be my guy?' Mitch declared. This guy looks half dead.

The C.O. pushed the inmate to Mitch's table. For the next 40 minutes the P.I. played the long lost nephew role while his camera recorded Sheila's presence. Simon Alexander had fell into a light nap. Mitch sat back in his chair observing his surroundings. At a quarter to twelve the shift change had commenced.

At 12:19 pm a officer arrived at Sheila's table. The expression on the C.O.'s face told the P.I. that he was pissed about something and probably scolding Psycho for wrong doing. Will you look at that! The entire scene was well rehearsed. The C.O.'s hand moved swiftly as he scooped up a wad of cash that Sheila sat on the table. Mitch captured it all on tape. Now all I want to know is, what's the payoff for?

Soon after the C.O. departed, Sheila Osbourne and her ex-husband stood and headed between the vending machines. The P.I. couldn't help but smile to himself. This is too good to be true. Mitch waited a few minutes then made his way to the snack machines. In plain view, Sheila Osbourne was on her knees…deep throating Psycho's prize possession. Psycho mean mugged the P.I. as if to say 'you're interrupting my groove, dirty'.

Mitch put on his Italian Mafioso impression, shrugging, as if to say 'Hey, no big deal. I get head all the time.'

It worked. Psycho Johnson continued his business, ignoring the P.I.'s presence. Mitch moved swiftly from the vending area as if he saw nothing.

He placed the two chip bags on the table.

"Damn almost forgot." He cursed loud enough to draw some stares, snapping his fingers afterward. "Definitely need a coke with this." Mitch returned to the snack machines. This time Psycho's back faced him upon arrival. He had Sheila Osbourne pinned against the wall. He skirt was raised around her hips.

Psycho had one leg clutched around him while he thrust deep inside her. Mitch didn't bother to purchase anything, he stood there in shock as his camera caught the whole degrading event.

Just as psycho showed signs of climax the P.I. turned around and started for his table. He was met by a tall, buff Correctional Officer.

"Enjoying yourself?"

"Very much." Mitch Holley replied, smiling. :In fact, I think I need to go rent a movie. My nuts are starting to ache."

The C.O. cracked a hard smirk, finally stepping aside and letting the P.I. pass by. Mitch wasted no time informing the other officer that his visit was over with Simon Alexander. The P.I. stormed out of the visiting room. After he exited the building Mitch quick-stepped down the sidewalk. He was nearly out of breath when he arrived at the rental van. Once inside, the P.I. whipped out his cellular and called Keith Osbourne.

CHAPTER 19

While Nikki slept in the passenger seat, Keith's grip tightened on the steering wheel. Tears fell without consent. The information Mitch Holley relayed angered the rapper.

"Call me once your flight lands."

"Sure thing kiddo. You okay?" Mitch sensed his sniffles.

"No doubt, I'm good. Holla back." Keith hung up then wiped his face dry. A wave of sadness suddenly overcame him as he pulled into his neighborhood. Moments later Keith arrived at his estate to discover the entrance was blocked off by a silver Z3 BMW. Detective Fish leaned against the coupe with his legs and arms folded, looking as if he'd been waiting for hours. The rapper stepped out of the car careful not to awaken Nikki. Tired and looking a day old in yesterday's clothes, Keith approached the detective.

"Jesus, man. Every time I turn around I see you." Keith snapped, extending his finger up to the officer's face. "And right about now, I'm sick and tired of seeing your ugly ass mug."

"Ugly?" Fish repeated, smirking sarcastically. "Negro please! If I had half your dough id be mackin' all these hoes too." The detective's stare cut at the woman in the passenger seat, instantly noticing her as Nichole Wallace.

The rapper's sharp stare cut like a Ginsui. Fish sensed his anger and got straight to the point. "Look Mr. Osbourne, I know one of our homeboys raped that girl last night, but that's not why I'm here. The district attorney is taking your case before a Grand jury. You may be soon charged with first degree manslaughter of Chavis Payton, the young kid you killed yesterday.

I'm doing everything in my power to prevent the D.A. from bringin charges against you. In the meantime you won't be able to leave Virginia, much less the Tidewater Area."

The rapper exploded. "That's crazy! I go on tour tomorrow.

"For the next seven days you will not be able to go anywhere. Not until we sort everything out."

Keith huffed, "Guess I should be thanking you, huh?"

Fish's cheeks shrugged. He turned and climbed inside the Beamer then glided off.

Nikki continued napping as Keith walked through the front door. Chills crept down his spine as thoughts of a dead man laying on the front step flooded his mind. The rapper was instantly spooked as images of Chavis Payton haunted his mansion popped in his head. MC K.O. nervously packed his belongings. He flinched to every little sound he heard. Keith's eyes shot up at the ceiling after swearing to hear footsteps. The rapper grabbed his suitcases and slowly eased backward out of the bedroom with his eye fixed on the wall. A loud squeak echoed through the walls once more. His pupils swelled like a crackhead. Keith Osbourne spun around and darted out of the bedroom and into Nikki. The two crashed to the hallway floor.

"Um, I'm sorry. Nikki…your stomach…the baby, you okay?"

"I'm fine, calm down." Nikki offered, climbing to her feet. "What's wrong and why were you running?" she asked.

Keith Osbourne forced a deep chuckle, "Baby, I was trying to hurry back to you. A brother was missing you already."

Nikki figured him to be lying but didn't trip at all. In fact, she appreciated his flattery. Probably trying to bounce with the quickness before his wife shows up. He didn't even bother to wake me, she guessed, as they ascended the stairwell. "Oh yeah, I wont be going to work later on."

"What, you forgot your days off?"

"No crazy!" Nikki giggled, "I used your cellular to check my messages to learn that Sergeant Crawford found out about the incident with Curls."

"Who's Sergeant Crawford, your boss?"

"Yeah, something like that. He put me on suspend leave. So I will not be going to work anytime soon."

Keith now had pleasant thoughts of spending quality time with Nikki. "Well looks like we're in the same boat. As you know, I was supposed to start the Final Chapter Tour tomorrow night," his gaze drifted from the disappointed look on Nikki's face momentary, "but while you were sleeping, I had a run-in with Detective Fish. He was at my entrance gate. He advised me not to leave the state because I'm under investigation by the D.A.'s office. So, it looks like we will be spending a lot of time together. If that's alright with you."

Instant smiles!

Nikki wrapped her arms around his and rested her head on his shoulder. "I can't believe this is really happening." Keith desired to know what she meant by that but he kept quiet. He turned up the radio. Together they cruised the highway while their minds journeyed down separate roads.

Keith was massaging his temple as he reflected on the event that had transpired over the past 24 hours. I can't...there's just too much drama in my life right now. People think I'ma rapist, can't go to church...just killed a man. And now, Sheila. Even though the rapper had strong desires for Nikki, letting go of past love wasn't going to be easy. He'd spent the last 3 and a half years with Sheila. Despite Nikki's pregnancy, it bothered him to know that his wife was sharing herself with other men. Keith's insecurity settled in. Negative thoughts followed closely behind. Her unborn could actually be someone else's. After all, I hardly know her. Keith dismissed the foolish thought after gazing at Nikki's golden brown skin for the third time. Everything will be alright, I can feel it.

"Nikki's thoughts shifted from the job to making love to Keith Osbourne under a hot steamy rain forest. The exotic dream escape was overshadowed by thoughts of her best friend laying half dead in the hospital. Girl, you gotta slow you roll. Try being faithful for once. Too many games, too much unnecessary drama. Think I'll stop pass there early tomorrow morning and check on her condition. Maybe, just maybe she'll be out of her coma. God, I hope so. Nikki's thoughts shifted once again. She pondered her future with Keith and her unborn. God, is this true? Is this your work? My prayers are finally being answered. If this is your work Lord...thank you. Thoughts of Curls forced their way into Nikki's head. A disappointing thought occurred to her. What if the condom broke? And...and my unborn child is really curl's. How do I tell Keith that I had sex soon after he left my place. He'd surely frown upon me-"

"Who's this fool standing in the middle of the road?" Keith blurted, breaking to an emergency stop.

Nikki's eyes snapped open. The hooded stranger moved swiftly to the passenger side door and snatched it open. Nikki's pupils widened with fear.

"WHAT BITCH! YOU THOUGHT I WASN'T COMIN' BACK?!" the stranger barked, pulling the hoodie from his head. The stranger's arms extended out. Two 357 Desert Eagles Magnums stared at Keith Osbourne and Nikki. 'BOOM BOOM BOOM BOOM'

The rapper's brains splattered over the window and steering column. Nikki shook her head in disbelief.

"I thought you were dead."

A wicked laugh. "Guess who's next, bitch? I will always own you!" his weapons tilted sideways.

"Noooo Tony Gangsta! Please...please don't kill me" Tears sprinted down Nikki's cheeks as she pleaded for her life.

Too late! Gunshots cannoned from the stranger's barrel.

Nikki's torso trembled until she woke up.

"You alright, baby?" Keith demanded to know after witnessing his girl experience a nightmare. "Love, its okay. You were just having a bad dream."

Nikki sat up straight to regain her composure. It took a few moments to realize she was parked in front of her apartment. "Damn damn damn." Nikki burst into tears, confirming the rapper's hunch. Nikki turned to him, her tears already drying.

"Can I ask you a question?" she nodded hesitately, fighting back the new wave of tears. "Who is Tony gangster?"

Nikki's stare shied away from his, "you really want to know?" Keith nodded. She let a deep sigh as she grabbed her purse. "Well, lets go inside. "Nikki climbed out of the Bently. Keith Osbourne followed her inside her apt. Nikki flicked on the living room lamp and tossed her pocketbook on the sofa on the way to her bedroom. Before the rapper could get comfortable she asked him to follow. Nikki scooped up the remote, the television blinked on soon after. Keith perched on the edge of the bed. His gaze wondered across the room until it settled on the tube. The controller landed on his lap after Nikki tossed it.

She disappeared into the closet momentarily. As the rapper flicked through the channels Nikki dropped a stack of newspaper articles beside him.

"MC K.O. meet your number one fan,.....Tony Gangsta."

Keith gazed ascended her then fell down on the clippings before picking them up. His stare shot back up after Nikki's clothes fell to the floor. The rapper swallowed hard as he studied every inch of Nikki's flawlessness move seductively behind the bathroom door. Once the door closed Keith Osbourne broke free of the daze realizing the news articles in his palms.

Nikki had been soaking in the tub for over 20 minutes when she decided to let the water drain. She stood up and peeled back the shower curtain to retrieve the Oil of Olay cream over the top of the sink's cabinet. She was surprisingly met with her lover's presence. "Jesus. You scared me." she said, placing her palm across her breast. Oh my God ran through her mind once more after fixing her eyes on his naked body. His chiseled frame moistened her tongue with sweet thoughts of tasting him.

"Got room for one more?"

"It's a small tub but I think we can manage." The bathtub was nearly empty when Nikki turned on the shower.

Keith Osbourne climbed in, gently locking lips with her under the warm mist. Despite the shower head's heavy spring rush Nikki could see the rapper's tears flowing from the wears of his eyes. She recoiled until her lips parted from his and fixed her gaze on him. There was no doubt the Nikki's lover had tried disguising his sudden flow of tears. But why? Her finger tips glided across his cheeks. The tears continued, his head hung, his arms hang lifeless by his side. Like a child abandoned by his mother, the rapper began crying harder.

"There's no need to cry. I'm okay now. "Nikki offered, sensing the news clippings of her past had saddeded him. As the warm mist bounced from their shoulders, Nikki picked up the sponge and soap. In a circular motion, she began caressing his chest until suds formed. One by one she gently began wiping his arms.

It occurred to the rapper as Nikki scrubbed his back that he'd never been bathed by a woman before. For the moment, the rapper wished that the soothing feeling would never end. Before long, Nikki was on her knees holding a handful of Keith's chocolate bar in one hand and delicately scrubbing his testicles with the other.

"Whoa! She's cleaning me better than I cleanse myself."

In a surprise move, Nikki licked the tip of his prize possession just to arouse him. Keith gazed down at his lover until their eyes locked on one another. Without taking her seductive stare from his, Nikki's soft lips pecked the rapper's tip once more. The warmness of her mouth gently wrapped around his chocolate stick. She delicately massaged the tip of his jewel with her erect tongue. The rapper squirmed side to side in a pleasurous manner. His body movement turned Nikki on even more. She stretched her jaw and took in a few more inches of his carmel candy which sent Keith Osbourne climbing up the checker tile.

As Nikki stroked his stiffness to the back of her throat she wondered if he would kiss her afterward. Soon after she finished she slowly elevated until her stare leveled his. Keith didn't hesitate to reel her close to him. The rapper kissed Nikki as if it had been years since their last encounter. Nikki despised how Rodney used to reject her kiss after his needs were satisfied. Joyous tears formed under her eyelids. Nikki was convinced that Keith's sincere words of love, hope and happiness were from the heart. She turned off the shower, their tongues continued to tangle.

Before long, they were laying each other across the bed. Keith began nibbling on Nikki's earlobe. Slowly, the rapper worked his tongue down her neck. The instant sensation took her breath away. By then, Keith Osbourne catwalked over top his prey. Nikki submissively spread her thighs for the lion to feast on her goodies. Keith then slid his mouth to the front of her shoulder blade. Their bodies began to intensify with burning passion. Nikki locked her fingers around Keith's neck, holding him tightly as he thrusted pass her juicy walls. Nikki's moan echoed off the walls. Soon her moans turned to sensuous cries of pleasure.

For the first time in 2 and a half years she felt the spiritual feeling of love and felt as though she were actually making love.

As Keith Osbourne stroked her in a circular motion, Nikki worked her hips hoping to return the pleasure. She wanted to give all of herself to him. And she did. Nikki held nothing back. Every emotion, every feeling and every moment of pain that had built up in her over the years was finally released in love. Nikki slid her palms down his firm backside and squeezed as he grinded deeper. The way Keith stretched the back of her walls made her want to scream in ecstasy. Keith elevated himself then arched his back as another orgasm exploded. Yet the rapper refuse to let up. Nikki raised up and settled her gaze on Keith as he broke her something proper. Before long, her eyes climbed his body until stares reconnected. At that very moment of sizzling passion, Nikki was for certain that Keith Osbourne had given all of himself to her.

Keith leaned then glided over her until his lips landed on the softness of her chin. Nikki's clutch tightened even more after another orgasm erupted. For hours the rapper caressed her most delicate spots. Nikki's 7th orgasm was so strong and hard she fell asleep almost instantly afterward. Keith carefully recoiled from her moistness. Moments later they cuddled in the fetal position and dozed into a deep sleep.

Nikki's eyes cracked open on the second chirp of the telephone. Her pupils focused in at the clock on the wall. It read 7:30am. As her hand extended out for the receiver she noticed Keith reading through the last of the 'Tony Gangsta massacre clippings.'

"Hello?" she yarned afterward, her stare fixed on Keith's masculine shoulders.

"Good morning Miss Wallace. Keith Osbourne around?"

Sounds like a white guy? "It's for you. Sounds like a white guy!"

White dude? Wonder if Detective Fish followed me out here and is now looking to give a brother a hard time? An idea suddenly occurred to him as he put the receiver to his face. "Yo, who's this and why are you calling me at this number?"

"Relax, its me pimp'n Mitch Holley." The P.I. said I'm over at Arleen's place."

"Hey Mitch." The rapper was overwhelmed with relief. "How'd you know I'd be here?"

"C'mon kiddo, you should know me by now. That's what I do, homie. Besides, I was for certain you loved that woman from the very first moment you laid eyes on the P.Y.T."

"On who?" Keith asked, unfamiliar with the initials.

"P.Y.T. Pretty young thang! You know, Michael Jackson."

"Oh, okay, but I think it's pretty young thing."

"Look kiddo, forget it already. Everybody's looking for you."

"Everybody like who?"

"Everybody as in your mother, your cousin Mont and some goofy white named Alfred is getting to my nerves with his 20 questions."

"Damn it. I forgot."

"Forgot what, man?"

"Forgot to inform them that our first tour dates have been rescheduled because I can't leave the state at the moment?"

"I see. You're under investigation at the moment?"

The rapper sighed "yeah man."

"Well hurry up and get over here. I'm going back inside for a nice breakfast and some kick-it. Arleen's kinda fly and I'm single so hurry because I might end up being your step daddy." Laughs.

"Yeah right, I'll be there in 30 minutes. Later" the line went dead. Keith rose up, instantly falling in deep thought momentary.

"Keith, did you take one of my photos from the living room wall?" Nikki finally interjected.

Keith Osbourne nodded as he shot to his feet. He placed the articles on the dresser and turned to Nikki. "Do you trust me?" his tone was firm.

"You know I do." Their gazes locked once again. "Why do you ask?"

Keith planted both hands around his waist and moved briskly to the bed. "I think I know who raped Shawnte', and is quite possibly the serial rapist." Nikki's face lit up in suspense. Her voice cracked with every word uttered.

"Who do you think it is?"

"I can't share that with you until I know for sure. But trust me love, come tomorrow, we'll know for certain once he's in custody."

"That doesn't make any sense to me , Keith."

"It's not supposed to. So, for now, just trust me."

The rapper perched on the bed after Nikki peeled the sheets back. "I know your past is long gone but I, I just wanted to say…I'm sorry….Sorry that that Tony Gangsta character was trying to live out my lyrics and videos. And I'm sorry that you suffered the way you did, mentally and physically. Your daughter, ex-boyfriend and Aunty were not victims of my music. That kind of evil was instilled in Tony Gangsta all long. All my lyrics did was give his wickedness on outlet to express his built in aggression."

Tears race quickly down Nikki's face. The rapper was so absolutely correct. Not only was he precise, he had enlightened Nikki with a different perspective that she hadn't been able to see before. I was wrong for blaming MC K.O. for another grown ass man's actions she told herself.

Keith's warm embrace overwhelmed his woman. Finally, his hold loosened. He placed Nikki's hand in his. Their stares gazing upon each other. Keith Osbourne began explaining to his lover what she had to do to overcome her nightmares of your past is to…..go back to Richmond….back to your old house and leave everything inside you right there on the front steps. The fears that burden you will be gone , forever. I promise."

"How do you know all of this?"

"Lets just say I had some fears of my own to face. We all do at some point in our lives."

Nikki vowed to never travel up I-64 again. Somehow , she believed it was some thing she needed to do, alone. "Your right, Keith. I'ma drive up to Richmond tomorrow after I stop pass the hospital." She planted a kiss on his cheeks before cracking a wide smile. " I never thought that I, Nichole Wallace, would be saying this but I'm glad you're in my life."

"Couldn't have said it any better myself, love." Keith stood up and walked into the bathroom. He turned around just before entering. "When this is over I want to introduce you to a very special person in my life."

An half hour later, the rapper kissed his woman and exited the front door. Butterflies twisted his stomach. Heartburn flared in his chest like a premature heart attack. Thoughts of the evidence Mitch Holley was going to present once he arrived at Arleen's made him worse.

CHAPTER 20

Keith Osbourne was explaining to Mont and Alfred how they could make up for the canceled tour dates when Timmy Tuff walked through the front door. His bandages and noticeable ankle bracelet he sported without a tennis shoe caught everyone's attention.

"Whoa! Playa." Mont shouted across the room "Where you been and what happened to you?"

"I got trampled over last night at the party." Timmy Tuff replied, frowning.

"Everytime I tried to get up tennis shoes and hi heels kept stomping me."

"You poor baby. What did the doctor say?" Arleen asked, walking up for a closer observation.

Mitch sat on the couch sipping a glass of tea. As he stared upon the producer his investigative instincts kicked in. Why is he wearing a long sleeve in the middle of May?

"Consider yourself lucky. People get killed in stampedes all the time." Alfred offered, looking around for someone to agree with him. Keith didn't say much nor did he give his longtime partner any clue of his suspicion. The rapper pat his friend on the back. "Glad you're okay man. Don't know what we'd do without you."

Everyone had departed with the exception of Mitch Holley. He and Keith Osbourne leaned against the Ford van jawing about nothing. The rapper could not prolong the inevitable yet refused to rush into the footage the P.I. had gathered for him.

Mitch Holley turned to the Millionaire. His eyes were firm and serious. “I’m gonna level with ya kiddo. The footage I have is very explicit.”

“Isn’t that why I paid you ah quarter mill?”

The P.I. forced a smile on his face. “That’s right, that’s why you paid me the big bucks. To get.....the goods. “His arms extended out, ‘okay kiddo, get in the van.” The two climbed in the astro van’s side door and squatted in the first row of seats. “Before I show you this you gotta promise me that you’re not gonna go and do something stupid.”

“Stupid like what?”

“Stupid as in murder.”

The rapper’s eyes darted to the corners, “yeah right.” The lights faded. Mitch Holley flicked on the rear bulb and handed Keith Osbourne a manila envelope. Inside contained twenty five photos. The first pictures revealed his wife behind the wheel of a cherry red Mercedes Benz he knew nothing about. “I had the tags run. Your wife owns that Benzo complements of Psycho Entertainment.

Her ex-husband? Keith began to feel uneasy as a lump developed in the back of his throat. He began flipping through the photos, freezing momentary after recognizing the image of the Georgia Federal Bureau of prison billboard. “She visits her ex on the regular.” The P.I. ‘s head hung. “Your wife has been to see Psycho every weekend for the past five years.”

The rapper’s nervousness instantly vanished. A Tsunami of rage overcame him.

“That Bitch!”

“You cool, man?”

I’m good. Sheila did not have to lie about visiting her child’s father. I would’ve understood. He has a right to see his kid.” Mitch Holley didn’t respond. Once Keith Osbourne laid eyes on the next 8 or so photos his emotions would bubble through the roof for certain. “What....what is this?” The rapper’s stare transfixed on the obscenity.

“That is your wife, Sheila, in the vending section of the visitation room.” Keith Osbourne’s stomach flipped into a whirlwind. He yanked the side open and leapt out of the van. Mitch quickly followed suit. He found the rapper slumped over a nearby curb throwing up.

“You gon’ be alright kiddo?” The P.I. spoke in a whisper. Keith Osbourne fanned him away as he attempted to re-gain control over his sudden emotional breakdown. Mitch obliged, back stepping into the van.

"When your' ready…..I got more. It gets worse!" The P.I. left the door ajar so he could keep a close eye on the rapper. He wouldn't understand how Keith's heartbreaking moment ended up in a loud obnoxious laugh. "He's gone crazy."Mitch whispered to himself.

Keith wiped his eyes as he gazed upon his mother's porch praying she hadn't witnessed his trying moment. The rapper's stare shifted to the neighbor's yard to find any eyes beamed on him. Finally, he stepped back into the van.

"What's so funny, cry baby?" Mitch asked, smiling.

"Everything!" the millionaire's tone emphasized his seriousness. "I was thinking that that was the worst thing Sheila could ever do to me….but then you say that I have not seen the worst. I had to laugh because I couldn't think she could possibly do anything more degrading."

"I could just tell you what's on this tape and throw it in the trash." The P.I. offered, placing the VHS tape on his lap.

" I think I can handle it."

Mitch hesitated as he inserted the footage into the mobile VCR. "Excuse me. Let an old man pass will you? Need to light up a smoke." The P.I. hurdled Keith's kneecaps.

"Didn't know you smoke?"

"I didn't, just started." Mitch lied. The rapper realized it were an innocent fib to give him some privacy. For hours Keith Osbourne viewed footage of his wife getting busy with a cock diesel brother whose skin was so dark that his features didn't show up on camera. Mitch dozed off in the front seat and woke up around the time Keith Osbourne ejected the tape. Mitch was amused how well the rapper handled the viewing. "Now this is what I suspected of her."

The P.I. shrugged, "I don't follow you."

"I mean, I expected to see her in this adulterated form. But never in a million years did I think she'd disgrace herself in public the way she did."

"Prison isn't exactly public and …"

Keith Osbourne cut him off. "But you know what I mean, right?"

"I suppose I do. Your kinda saying the she cold disrespected the both of you."

"Exactly!" Keith said. "That man….in Sheila's bed, that's Psycho's brother right?"

Mitch nodded, "he's one of the hottest male stripper's in Atlanta."

"Woww! That's a hell of a title to proclaim. It all makes sense to me now. It's all coming together." The rapper suddenly snapped.

"Calm down, kiddo. Remember, you have Nichole now. That wife of yours is history, right?"

The millionaire's tone had lowered to a calm, "Right." For the past few hours Keith had forgotten all about Nikki. And how good he felt when she were near.

"You love'er don'tchu?"

"Who?" The rapper asked, assuring the P.I. were referring to Nichole Wallace.

"I know you're madly in love with the Wallace girl, but you still love Sheila as well, don't you?"

Keith let out a long sigh, "Yes....yes I do as of right now, G....I'm moving on. Just seems so bizarre how this love thing works. I mean, I wanted a reason to justify my relationship with Nichole and I wanted you to dig up the dirt on my wife. Now that I have it.....I'm having a hard time dealing with it."

"You'll be fine, kiddo. Trust yourself. That Wallace girl and you make the perfect item."

"Think so?"

"I know so." The P.I. shot back, hoping to cheer the rapper up. "Whatever you do, make sure you handle business first before shacking up with Miss Wallace. Last thing you want is Sheila learning of your new relationship. Definitely leverage for her in divorce court."

Keith nodded, "Your right. I'ma call it a night. Gotta get home and take care of some business." He scooped up the goods and exited the van. "Call me first thing tomorrow morning, Mitch. I'm going to need your help with something."

"Sure kid. Anything you need."

The rapper arrived at his mansion just after midnight. His gaze wondered over the plush furniture that suffered damage. For the first time in Keith Osbourne's life he felt that the property he stood on was no longer a home. His stare shifted and settled on the arcrlic phone. He cuffed the jack's receiver and dialed Nikki's home. Two rings then an answer. "Hello."

"Hey love, I just walked in a few seconds ago. Just wanted to let you know that I love you and Miss you dearly."

Nikki let out a long yarn, "why didn't you come back over here tonight? I wanted to give you a nice oil massage."

"That sounds quenching baby but I have to handle some serious business first thing tomorrow. I was hoping to catch you later on tomorrow."

"I planned on taking a trip to Richmond. Maybe I'll see you when I return?"

"Cool baby, I'm wit that. I can't wait to see you."

"Same here."

Silence as they listen to each other breath into the receiver.

"Goodnight." The line went dead. Keith hung up hoping Nikki would utter something else. She didn't. He picked up his saxophone and headed for his bedroom. The rapper had been blowing into his instrument for only a couple of minutes when the phone rang. "Hello?" His tone was charming for the late hour.

"Hope I didn't wake you. I was missing you." A feminine tone spoke softly in his ear.

"I Miss you too." Keith's face tightened instantly. The utterance of his wife's tone brought a bitter taste to his mouth. "Look Sheila, baby, when do you think you'll be headed back home? I need to know because daddy got a special something for you."

" You do?" Sheila's voice flooded with excitement.

"Yepp baby, I sure do." The millionaire forced his tone to her level. "So when you coming home?"

"I'll be there around 2 o'clock tomorrow afternoon."

"Beautiful! See you then"

"Keith, I love…" Keith killed the connection before his wife could finish her deceptive lie.

For the remainder of the night, the rapper rambled through his photo albums of their wedding reminiscing of the brighter days of his past.

The doorbell had been ringing for nearly 15 minutes when the rapper finally woke up. His wrist flew up to his face as his pupils adjusted. "Damn! It's almost noon." Keith Osbourne launched himself from the recliner and sprinted downstairs. "I'm coming I'm coming. Please , just stop pressing the bell." He shouted as he arrived to the front entrance of his home. The double doors swung open. Standing in front of him was Mitch Holley and a claims investigator from the insurance company.

"Man, we rich folks sure sleep late round here don't we?" Mitch said, walking past the rapper. Once the I.I. introduced himself Keith invited him inside.

"Holy, Mary, mother of God!" The insurance investigator blurted upon noticing the bullet holes riddled everywhere. "Looks like the bombing of the Republican Guard in here." The I.I. whipped out a digital camera and surveyed the walls and furniture ruins.

"It's more damages in the back." Keith Osbourne's arm extended down the long hallway. "Go that way and once you arrive at the indoor backetball court, walk through the gym. You'll find more damages to be assessed in the gameroom." The Investigator moved briskly down the long Asian carpet. His stare darted left to right, then up and down to make certain he didn't Miss anything. "This is going to cost a fortune to repair." He offered, "All these bullet holes and only one man was killed." The I.I. turned to them, halfway down the hall, sucking his teeth rhythmically.

Keith managed a smile as the Insurance Investigator continued to the back. He turned to Mitch Holley and invited him upstairs to his room for a private chat. Mitch, I need a box."

"I don't do boxes, kiddo."

"I mean a box in the form or likeness of a gift."

"Present for who?"

"My lovely wife of course." A devilish grin appeared on the millionaire's face.

"What's the celebration for on this afternoon?" Mitch asked, mocking an English accented butler.

Keith Osbourne complemented the P.I. with an European impression of his own.

"Meeetch we'air cairla brat-tang air der vorce por-tay."

"Howw spleeendid, sir."

Laughs.

Once the chuckles simmered, the rapper excused himself. He stepped in the closet and pulled the door closed. Keith walked to the back of his closet, shifted 2 hangers from the rack at the same time then flicked the lights on and off 4 times straight. Moments later an iron vault glided from under the wall. The rapper placed his ear to the door assuring himself the P.I. wasn't snooping. It took the millionaire just a few moments to gain entry into the safe and in a few more seconds to reverse the process.

Keith Osbourne stepped out of the closet with a pair of Mauri Gators in hand. "Yeah right," Mitch burst into laughs. "All that time in there for a pair of shoes? Man, you ain't fooling nobody." The rapper's hands flew up.

"You right, G. I don't know what I was thinking trying to fool you. Had to try anyway." Keith pulled out clean stacks of cash and tossed it in the P.I.'s direction.

"What's this forty..fifty grand?" Mitch estimated after the presidents landed between his fingers.

"Close! It's sixty grand."

"The real question is what's it for?"

"It's a gift of appreciation." Keith now stood inches from Mitch Holley. His arm extended around him. "Mitch, I appreciate you not milking a rich bastard like myself."

More laughs. The two were suddenly distracted by a male's figure standing under the doorway. The rapper's instincts kicked in before his reflexes. Before he could dive for his weapon's cache he realized the figure belonged to the Insurance Investigator. "Scared me for a second."

"I'm finished here. The Insurance Company will notify you in the near future. You'll be receiving a check minus the deductible of course." "Mitch Holley turned to Keith, "I'll show him out. And I'll be back with that huge present box or whatever you call it."

2:39 P.M.

Keith Osbourne was chilling in his lazy boy puffing on a Cuban cigar when Sheila sashayed through the bedroom door. A warm smile surfaced on her face as her stare settled on the huge metallic box wrapped in thick red velvet ribbon. The millionaire returned the gesture with a smile of his own, shifting his attention on the present that sat on the bed momentarily. It wasn't her birthday or their anniversary, so what was the occasion? Sheila gazed in her husbands direction "hello honey." Her energetic tone reminded Keith of a woman who was proudly married to him. The rapper played along, "Hey love, how was the flight from ATL?" he asked, forcing another smile, hoping to disguise the sudden disgust that formed in the pit of his belly.

"Is that a cigar? When did you start smoking?" Sheila asked, holding her perfect smile in place. He must really want this marriage to continue growing. If that fool only knew I filed for divorce the other day he wouldn't be smiling at all! She pondered, oh well, no need to spoil a perfect moment. I'll tell him afterwards....

Keith Osbourne sprung up from the recliner and hurried across the room to greet his wife along with a warm hug. She had no idea it would be her last.

"Got something for you, baby. Go over and open it while the mood is set." The rapper suggested, "and the cigar, it's a one time thing. I'm only puffing this because it is indeed a special celebration. "The millionaire ushered his wife to the edge of their bed. "In this box is our future.......and represents our past."

Overwhelmed with joy, Sheila Osbourne began ripping away. As the ribbon flew to the carpet, Keith flicked his remote at the plasma screen then puffed on the Cuban cigar, inhaling thick smoke afterward. His eyes instantly darkened. His loving smile was replaced with a wicked smirk. The rapper moved swiftly to the opposite side of the bed. He wanted to be staring his wife in the eye once she unveiled her surprise. Sheila saucered the top of the gift box to the far side of the room. The millionaire's devious smile began to flare with anticipation. His teeth clutched tighter as his wife's fingers descended through the fragile protectant. She felt something in the bottom. Her fingertips wrapped around it and reeled the item into view.

"OH MY GOD!"

CHAPTER 21
EARLIER THAT MORNING 9:30A.M.

Nikki was only minutes away from Hampton General Hospital when she decided to call Keith Osbourne. Thoughts of Sheila answering the phone made her dial even faster. "Shoot!" No answer. Nikki dialed the rapper again. As she listened to the ringing she fell into daydreams of her unborn. If it's a boy I'ma name him Nicholas. Nannnhh! Too corny. I like Keshawn better. Besides it represents the two people I love the most. Her thoughts drifted. Nikki pictured herself giving birth to another Toneisha. She forced the image from her mind as a tidal wave of depression struck her. Tears soon followed. What was I thinking about? Toneisha could never be replaced..not ever!

Nikki sat in the hospital's parking lot for a few moments hoping to regain herself. She took in a deep breath as her gaze met the hospital's entrance. Nikki cuffed her purse and stepped down from the SUV. As she started across the street she spotted Timmy Tuff moving gingerly out the Hospital's entrance.

"Hey Timmy" Nikki called out, flagging him down.

His eyes cut in her direction as he sped his pace. Timmy Tuff gave a disgusted look to her as if she were a groupie looking for an autograph. "Damn! Wus his problem? She mumbled, suddenly feeling embarrassed. Nikki fanned the Producer off as the revolving door swallowed her in.

Hectic sat in the waiting room seriously contemplating if he should push the issue at hand. Moments before his wife under went her second surgery Hectic stood at Shawnte's bedside at his daughter's request. The two year old begged her father to take her to see her mommy. So the Producer complemented Daisha's wish. As Hectic held his daughter on his hip he gazed down at his wife's medical chart that hung from the foot of her gurney. Curious to Shawnte's condition, he picked it up and skimmed through it. Most of what he read was unreadable and made no sense to him. As the medical chart descended from his face he noticed his wife's blood type read; A-negative. My blood type is B-negative. I ain't no DNA specialist but I know A+B doesn't produce O-positive. Which is Daisha's blood type? Hmm?

Now the faithful, loving husband sat in the chair with his daughter cradled in his arm. He gazed upon the infant he'd come to love as his own. "I love you Daisha. You are my little girl no matter what your blood type says." He whispered in the child's sleeping ear. Gently, the producer planted a kiss on her forehead. Hectic promised himself he'd mention it to Shawnte' once she were well. He planned on letting his wife know that he knew the truth about his daughter and would remain her daddy forever.

Once the truth got out people would criticize him for letting his wife play him for a fool. I'ma real man. And for love, I'm willing to deal with the embarrassment. I love my wife and I love my daughter even more. God willing, I'll continue to do so. His promising thought was put on hold momentarily. Hectic gazed up to find Nikki standing over him.

"How is she doing?"

"Not good, the doctors say she has a slight case of pneumonia, which is critical at this point because she had to undergo surgery to stop the fluid build up from behind her intestine." His stare settled back on Daisha.

"She's so pretty isn't she?"

"She is adorable." Nikki replied, squatting beside him. "So when do you think anyone will be able to see her?"

Hectic sighed, "I don't know. Couple of hours I guess."

"What's wrong?" Nikki sensed the Producer was troubled over something else. "You seem distant today." She said, "was it because Timmy Tuff paid Shawnte' a visit?"

Silence.

Hectic's eyes shot up to Nikki momentarily. Finally he spoke, "What are you talkin' bout,Nikki? Timmy Tuff hasn't been here." The Producer's tone emphasized his suspicions. "Why you ask? What , she fucking around with him or something?"

"No, of course not." Nikki shot back, "It's just that he was leaving as I was coming in." She shrugged, "Maybe he came to visit someone else. Hectic looked unconvinced. This boy thinks I'm lying for Te'. Nikki could sense it in his expression. "Well, I'll be going." Nikki raised from the chair. Hectic ignored her farewell, placing his eyes on Daisha. "Nikki, do you think Daisha looks like me or Shawnte' ?"

For some reason that question sent chills through her. Nikki's stare locked on Hectic's. She got the feeling that Shawnte' husband had somehow discovered the truth about his daughter. Perhaps it is my guilt eating away at me she guessed, "I think she looks more like Shawnte's mother to me." A sarcastic smirk perched in the corner of Hectic's mouth, "Yeah, I think so too." His eyes seemed to darken all of a sudden, "I think so too." Nikki said her good-byes and left in a hurry. "What was that all about?" she whispered to herself, stepping into the elevator.

Soon after the shaft's door closed the next elevator door slid open. Big daddy stepped out with a female on his hip. After the party Big Daddy had come to realize that his place was with Shirley, his baby's momma. Yesterday evening the police raided Shirley's apartment looking to serve Reece an indictment. As he waited to make bond, the hustler pondered his relationship between Shawnte' and Shirley. He loved Shawnte' but he also loved his child's mother. The truth of the matter stared him in the face. And that was the married woman he'd come to love was not guaranteed to him. More importantly, Shirley always had his back no matter what. So the Hustler came to the conclusion that he and Shirley should get married like the responsible man he wanted to be. Big Daddy explained his secret relationship to his baby momma. They agreed that the best way to say his good-byes was to stop to the hospital and say it with some flowers and a card. Since Big Daddy had nothing to hide, he invited his fiance' along.

Hectic hadn't noticed the two of them until Big Daddy 's arms extended out to him. "Hello there, my name is Reece and this," his head tilted to the tall woman standing at his side, "this is my fiance'." Careful not to waken Daisha, the producer maneuvered his hand to greet the stranger towering over him. "Yo, do I know you?"

"Of course not. Shawnte' and I are old friends."

Hectic's eyes glided down to his daughter then climbed back up to Reese, hoping not to appear obvious. Nannnnhhh! Don't look nothing like him. He assured himself.

"Me and my woman just wanted to drop these gifts to you for Shawnte'." Shirley placed the gift bag in the chair beside them. "Unfortunately she doesn't have a room as of yet." His voice cracked with each word uttered,"She's undergoing surgery as we speak." Tears formed in the Producer's eyes.

A ton of guilt came tumbling on Big Daddy. He could feel Hectic's love for his wife because he felt it as well. It tore the Hustler apart that he couldn't express his true feelings. Without hesitation, he leaned down and gave the producer a comforting embrace. "Be strong brother, no matter what." Reese whispered to him, standing erect afterwards. His stare met the I.C.U. doors as if they were Shawnte' herself. Big Daddy's lips didn't speak but the words from his heart said it all. It was the hustler's final goodbye. He broke out of his daze, placed Shirley's palm in his hand and quietly walked away.

Nikki glanced at her watch as she drove up I-64 to Richmond. It read; 10:02. She was certain Keith was probably asleep. Forty minutes had passed by since she last called. She hoped he'd be awake by now, since the rapper turned in late it were highly unlikely. Nikki pressed redial, more ringing. She sucked her teeth as the cellular landed in the passenger's seat. As the Cherokee swallowed road, she couldn't help but wonder if her lover actually knew who was raping all those women. If he does , why wouldn't he want me to know? Maybe he's trying to protect whomever it is. Her lips tightened at the dreadful thought. It's probably his cousin Mont. 'his sneaky lookin' ass.'

Nikki's fist crashed into the steering wheel. Her teeth grinded in sudden rage as the horn sounded. She instantly caught the attention of the commuter that recklessly pulled in front of her. The driver ahead of her responded with a middle finger.

"Calm down, girl, you can do this." Nikki took in a deep breath. Before long, the super charged mustang had sped out of view. The incident moments ago had become a memory. As the Richmond city limit sign glide closer and closer thoughts of her parents came knocking. Nikki began reflecting on how her father and she used to watch Nickelodeon and Nic at Nite. The memories brought a wide smile to her grill. Jolts of unmeasurable confidence and an undetermined courage took over her. The once terrifying thoughts that troubled Nikki whenever she envisioned home was no more.

As sudden calmness moved beside her. I'm going to church from now on. Nikki always told herself that whatever the mood called for it. Her intentions were always good. But when Sunday morning rolled around like everyone else, Nikki would find some ridiculous reason not to attend.

20 MINUTES LATER

Nikki fell in deep thought as the Cherokee parked a few houses down from her old home. A couple of children were outside playing amongst themselves. Asiatic lilies and spring plants decorated the single story's foundation. The entire scenery seemed perfect for her. It was exactly how Nikki had fairytaled her life with Rodney. She knew nothing about the residing family yet felt happy for them. Misty tears of joy formed as she rubbed the bottom of her stomach. One day…that'll be you with your sisters and brothers. Her gaze settled back on the brick structure. It was foolish of me to think that old house would always be haunted by Tony Gangsta. Richmond isn't such a bad memory after all. Looks like everyone around here has moved on. Maybe it's time to do the same.

With that thought Nikki shifted gears and pulled off down Maryland Avenue. Once she arrived at Parham Road she decided to pay Princess a surprise visit. I'm sure she'll be pleased to see me. With all the emotional tension soaring, she hadn't noticed that her jeep was low on fuel until the icon lit up. Wa-Wa gas station was just moments up the road. The Cherokee turned into the convenient store's lot. Nikki's eyes fixed on the prices towering on the billboard as the suv glided to a stop. Might as well be Exxon high as these prices are. She hopped from the jeep, observing the pump's number. Pump 8. She could not help herself from being distracted from every little thing around her. It feels good to be back home. She told herself as she entered the store. Nikki immediately recognized the familiar face stooped behind the register. She started to speak to the clerk but decided better against it since she couldn't recall her name. The woman continued her stare as Nikki waited in line. She pretended not to notice the clerks attentive gaze by fixing her attention on the Novocaine posters that decorated the store's windows. The woman ignored the two patrons standing in line. "Nichole, Nichole Wallace?"

Nikki's gaze shot back to the clerk in an instant. "How you doin' girl?" Nikki's stare was curious, "I know I know you from somewhere, "she began to brainstorm.

"Stop playing! You know I used to date Tony Gangsta."

In an instant, the familiar face had a name. "Ooooh hey Patrisha. Girl, you look so different. How you doing?"

"I'm doing okay. And yourself?" she replied, taking a customer's money.

"Just taking it one day at a time. This is my first day back in Richmond since I left the hospital. Can you believe it?"

Patrisha didn't know what to say at the moment. Instead she responded with an overwhelming smile.

"Look Partrisha, I didn't know about your brother or anyone else for that matter until I read the newspaper articles."

"Excuse me Miss." A customer chimed from the back of the aisle. "How much are these heartburn tablets?"

Partrisha quoted a price then fixed her stare back on Nikki.

"Like I was saying, I just wanna thank you for sending the police over to my place."

A sudden sadness flooded the clerk as memories of Tony Gangsta flashed in her mind. Why is she thanking me? Everyone in her house died, she lost everything.

"I did what was right. I'm just glad you made it through."

Nikki shrugged, "I guess I did, didn't I? A smile formed over her face.

"So how long you been working here?"

"Bought this place a while back. I work in here most of the day so I won't get bored."

"That's really great."

"It's alright. I ain't rich but it pays me and my mother's bills."

"Good for you." Nikki handed the clerk a twenty dollar bill. ""'pump8." Patrisha inserted the money into the register. "So what brings you back to Richmond?" she asked curious. Nikki's personal business was nobody else's. And , the last thing she wanted was to embarrass herself, so she lied. "Thought I'd visit Princess. We hardly see each other any more, you know?"

"Now that is true friendship." Patrisha appeared to be shocked. Nikki quickly picked up on it. "Personally, its no fuckin' way I could have forgiven her for what she did." Nikki was lost in the clerk's comment, so she responded indirectly. "Well ain't nobody perfect." Patrisha shrugged half heartedly, "to each it's own."

Nikki said her goodbyes after exchanging numbers. She exited the coinvent store and moved swiftly to the gas pumps. She began contemplating Patrisha's statement "to each its own." Before long, it occurred to Nikki what the clerk had been referring to. All this time? Princess has been neglecting me because she still feels guilty about not visiting me in the hospital. The gas nozzle clicked ending the fueling. Nikki hopped in her jeep and peeled off toward Blackwell Apartments. As the Cherokee pulled into the ailing apartment complex she couldn't help noticing how the neighborhood had badly depleted since the last time she were there. Air conditions dangled from every other window. The once perfect landscape was decorated with dirt patches and liquor bottles. Windows were sporadically boarded up. Insect screens hung off their frames, including Princess's. Nikki sat behind the wheel of her SUV. Momentarily, her gaze continued over the eye soaring project.

In front of her friend's apartment , a group of adolescents were having a slap boxing match. Excitement struck her as thoughts of one of the little kids belonging to Princess crawled in her head. She dismissed the foolish assumption. Those kids are way too old to be hers. How old is Princess's little boy anyway? Nikki began calculating the months in her head. Almost two if he wasn't born prematurely. She guessed. "Enough procrastinating." Nikki stepped out of her Jeep then locked her doors upon noticing the small gathering of hustlers posted a couple of units down. She shot them the hawk eye. In which they paid her no mind. As Nikki arrived to the front door a strong odor met her."Yuck!" She spotted the air condition hanging from the window's frame. It's dripping had formed an odorous puddle underneath the window. Carefully she recoiled the screen door, hoping the depleted siding wouldn't fall off its hinges. It didn't. She knocked on the door.

Moments later the front door swung open. A man stood before her. Nikki immediately recognized him. Rasta man from Club Secrets? His chinky eyes told her Rasta man hadn't remembered her. Nikki couldn't help but wonder if Princess knew this was indeed the same Jamaican she conversed with at Club Secrets. Who cares? That was over two years ago. And besides, all he did was buy me a few drinks. "Is princess home?" Nikki asked.

"She sleep, Mon, me wake her up. Hol' on." Rasta man disappeared behind the door leaving Nikki standing outside.

A small figure appeared at the door catching Nikki's attention. She knelt down until her stare leveled with his. "He's so cute…Yes he is." She teased, admiring his huge radiant eyes. Wonder if she knows who the father is yet?

The Jamaican reappeared, stepping in front of the young toddler. "Rodenaly, go upstairs so me give you bath. Den, we go to playground." The little boy's face lit up with a smile. He took off running out of Nikki's view. Nikki's heart felt like it crashed into a wall the moment Rasta man referred to the child as Rodney. It took everything less than a split second to piece itself together in her head. How could I have been so naïve? She scolded herself. That boy looks just like Rodney…even got is eyes. "She wants to know who you be becasue she tired, she say?"

Nikki swallowed hard as she fought back the tears. "Tell her its Nichole." The Jamaican stepped away once again. This time Nikki let herself in. Her stare glided over the living room she noticed high school and college photos of her ex-boyfriend hanging on the wall. Princess's son's baby pictures were neatly positioned under his. Tears trail blazed her cheeks.

Rodney Jr.'s head peeped into the living room. He ran up to her afterwards. "Lay-dee why you quiy'n?" There was no right way to respond even if she wanted to.

Nikki was caught by Princess's presence. "Rodney! Rodney, get cho' ass up them stairs" his mother barked. The child darted out of view.

Nikki and princess now stood face to face. "How could you do that to me?" Nikki cried out, "You were my friend. I trusted you…I loved you as a sister."

Her cries began to smother her words.

A school of guilt swarmed princess. She shrugged, unsure what to say. “Nikki…Nikki I’m sorry. It just happened.”

Sudden rage filled Nikki’s eyes. “It just happened huh? You jus’ happened to spread your legs and fuck my boyfriend? Just like you happen to hook up with Rasta man too?”

“Girl, you trippin’! Paully don’ even remember you.” Princess’s undertone was as defensive as her response.

Nikki managed to giggle behind her tears. I shouldn’t be upset that my man was fucking every damn body. After all, he was screwing Linda too. Can’t get any worse than that. She wiped her eyes and forced a smile. “Your son is a handsome little boy.”

Nikki spun around and walked out.

Princess’s pupils started to water as she watched her childhood friend storm down the sidewalk. She quickly ran behind her. “Wait! Nikki wait a minute please.” Nikki stood frozen, the tears continued down her face. “Can you turn around and talk to me?”

Nikki complemented her request. Their misty eyes locked on each other momentarily. “What’s there to talk about?”

“I was hoping we could still be friends like we used to? I Miss you like hell. Nikki…I…I just don’t know what to do.” Princess confessed, shying her stare away from Nikki’s.”So…how bout’ it?” Her arms slowly extended out to Nikki. Nikki’s gazed climbed to the clouds as she pondered the idea. Her stare floated down from the blue sky unit their eyes leveled. Nikki settled them just over Princess’s shoulder to make sure her son wasn’t standing in the doorway.

Curious as to what caught Nikki’s attention, Princess peeped over her shoulder. When she turned back around, Nikki met her face with a lightening right hand. The thumping blow sent Princess and her weave crashing into the patchy lawn. Nikki towered over her as she lay in the grass nursing her mouth.

“I think we can be friends again. Just not today. Next week maybe…but definitely not today.”

Nikki’s arm extended down, helping princess to her feet. She walked off without saying good-bye. She paused before climbing behind the wheel.

“Hey princess, how about you bring lil’ Rodney down for the weekend?

I'm sure I'll be home…oh yeah, almost forgot! Shawnte' got raped and stabbed after you bounced from that party last night. Don't worry. She's going to be fine." Nikki's tone lowered with each word. "We all are!"

Despite Princess's pulsating lips, Nikki's promising words brought peace to her heart.

CHAPTER 22

The element of surprise marveled Keith Osbourne as he studied the reaction on his wife's mug as she shuffled through photos the P.I. snapped. The bitch probably wants to beg for my forgiveness, he guessed. A cloud of smoke blew from the millionaire. It floated across the bed in Sheila's direction.

Sheila smirked sarcastically as she stared upon the last of the photos. "Very clever of you." She said, tossing the flicks over the bed. Didn't know you had it in you?"

"How ironic, didn't know you was having-it-in-you?....Way up in you!" The rapper moved briskly to the other side of the bed without breaking eye contact. Sheila Osbourne could sense the anger brewing in his eyes. But she was not intimidated at all. "So, this is your idea of a celebration huh?" Keith's face was now just inches from hers,"No doubt, bitch!"He barked, calmly lowering his tone afterward. "This is a divorce party. And, best believe this shit is just the beginning." The millionaire dug his fingers in her arm and tugged her across the room until they stood facing the plasma screen. "Hey sweetie, recognize that place?" The rapper laughed hard, "Let me guess, that's ya bedroom at Betty Mae's crib, isn't it?" His arm extended out with the remote in hand. He fast forward the tape to the explicit action. Sheila knew what was to come. She tried turning away. Keith's fingers octupused her neck forcing Sheila's face back on the porno flick. "Look darling, another devilish laugh, "You' a fuck'n porn star!" His tone roared like a lion. The volume elevated, "Who's he? Ya other boyfriend?" The rapper's grip loosened, he forced his wife to look into his eyes. "C'mon, tell me. Is-he-your other man?"

"You tell me, nigga. You the one who hired a Private Investigator" Amused by his wife's sassyness, the millionaire cracked a half smile. "That's cute! And you're right. I do know who he is. Thunder is a stripper. Atlanta's finest I hear."

"Well you know it wasn't anything serious. If so, I would've have offered him money, now would I?"

"Seems like you're trying to down play all this." Sheila rolled her eyes, "But the truth of the matter is, you're a nasty ass whore who likes doing brothers." His wife snapped, definitively. "All of a sudden you better than me? What…you can't do no wrong, Mister Fuck'n perfect? Mista Pope John fuck'n Paul!"

"No Sheila, I'm none of those things." The rapper's voice lowered to a whisper. "I'm just a man who fell in love, got married to the woman of my dreams. I trusted and believed I'd spend my entire life with you." Tears formed in the millionaire's heart, yet his eyes remained dry. "No one's perfect, but it evident that you had evil intentions from the jump." His gaze shifted and settled on the wide screen. "I can't believe I married that." Keith's finger sharply aimed on the woman being plowed in the doggy-style position. "Instead of trying to believe it, you should be trying to take some notes from a nigga who knows how to fuck a real woman like myself. Because you damn sure wasn't laying pipe like you should'a!"

The unthinkable transpired, the rapper struck Sheila with a sudden fury. His pimp smack sent her curly hair flying haphazard as she tumbled backwards to the bed. "BITCH!" blood rushed through his glassy pupils. "You can disrespect me anywhere you chose to. But I'll be damned if you gonna disrespect me in my own home."

"FUCK YOU NIGGA!" Sheila fired back, holding her jaw. "Yeah I said it…you little dick bastard! If you had a bigger dick to match them deep pockets like Timmy does, we wouldn't be going through this shit." A look of satisfaction filled her. She indeed struck a nerve.

She must've slept with him? How else would she know what he's working with? He thought. "I know what 'chu think'n." she chimed, forcing a hard laugh of her own. "Yeah, I fucked 'I'm! And his shit is twice the size of yours and then some."

Keith Osbourne was a split second from his wife's throat, but decided better against it. "You ain't worth it!"

"Just as I thought, you's a soft ass punk. I would've fucked ya cousin Mont, but that silly ass lil' boy's dick is smaller then yours." She said. "Go figure. Must run in the family."

Keith grabbed Sheila by the ankle and yanked her from the bed. Sheila's backside flared in pain after it smacked the floor. She refuse to wince in front of him. Instead she giggled even louder. Watching the millionaire explode was far more satisfying.

Mitch and two other gentlemen walked into the bedroom instantly distracting the two. The P.I. pointed to his watch and shrugged.

Keith Osbourne nodded then turned to his wife. "Sheila, meet Mr. Wise Guy and his two sons." He killed the amateur porn and backed away from her. "These men are the movers." Instant satisfaction overtook him. "First of all, you gets nothing as far as cash. Secondly, the divorce papers will arrived to you very soon."

"Don't bother." Sheila smirked devilishly. "I already filed them last week."

"Good, looks like we're on the same page." The rapper looked shocked by the news. "Where was I? Oh yeah, you will take all your belongings out of here today. Since I don't give a damn about this house and the crap in it, you can take whatever you desire. If you be a good little whore that you are, I might give you the house and let 'chu keep the Viper."

"Negro please!" Sheila sprung from the bed. "Fuck that car, you seen the photos, I own a SL55. Think I give a damn about a corny ass ride that Ronald McDonald be driving? You drive it, you the clown! And this house… I'ma get this house any damn way!"

"Think so?" her boldness riled him up. "I'd love to sit here and continue this verbal sparring match with you. But I gotta bounce, my soul mate awaits yours truly."

"News flash! You're nothing but a dreamer. Nobody wants your ugly ass for you. They want your money. You're useless for anything else. Can't fuck…can't make no babies, your useless."

"It's okay to be a dreamer. And yes, I do have someone…you definitely had MC K.O. fucked up if you thought I was just going to sit around and let life pass me by. And unlike you, money means nothing to her. About me being infertile…"

Mitch's face tightened, his eyes said to Keith 'Don't say it!'. "Being a father one day remains to be seen. I believe that if I keep praying on it…one day fatherhood will happen for me. The rapper turned and walked out of the bedroom.

Mitch stepped forward, "Alright lady," his deep voice shook the walls, "I gotta truck outside with your name on it. So start pointing so we can start moving." Sheila ignored the P.I. momentarily. She began contemplating her next move.

"Pardon me, Miss Thang," Mitch had no time for patience, "you gettin' up outta here whether we move anything or not. So be a good little bitch and start pointing to the items that you're taking away from this divorce party."

Sheila's stare shot on him, "Who are you?" she demanded to know.

"I'm the Wise Guy." The P.I. cracked a sly grin.

Sheila marched across the room for the VHS tape. Mitch Holley met her at the VCR. "That stays but the photos are yours to keep. There's plenty of them, isn't that right fellows?"

The P.I. turned to the two gentlemen that waited for his instructions. The movers nodded sensing Mitch had wanted them to.

Keith entered the conference room and cuffed his cellular from the table. He stared upon it, momentarily falling into a daze. The rapper pictured his wife having passionate sex with Timmy Tuff all the times he left the two alone. And how they probably exchanged secret winks when he was in their presence. How could I have been such a fool? He scolded himself, as the cell phone arrived at his ear. Keith Osbourne began feeling down even though he stunted on Sheila just as he planned. In the rapper's heart, he felt that his wife had undoubtedly flipped the script, getting the best of him. Hearing Nikki's pleasant voice would surely elevate his spirits.

"Hello?"

"Hello to you love. It's me, Keith. I was just thinking about you."

"That's crazy because I was just thinking about you as well. I wanted to talk to you about Shawnte's perpetrator. But first, I wanna hold you in my arms for a little while."

The rapper sensed her tension. "What's wrong, Nichole, is everything okay?"

"I'm alright I guess. Just having a bad day."

"You too, huh? Must be a bad day virus going around today."

Nikki chuckled, "Must be." Silence. "I saw ya boy at the hospital this morning. He was really upset too."

"My boy who…Hectic?"

"Nope! Your main man Timmy Tuff."

"He was at the same hospital as Shawnte'?" the millionaire's tone elevated, his eyes widened. "You sure it was him?"

"Course I a.m. is everything okay?"

"Everything's fine baby."

"Why are you talking like that? You're starting to scare me."

"Uh, Nichole baby, I'm good." More silence. "Yo, check this out, I'ma hit you back in ten minutes."

"Why? What's going on?" Nikki demanded to know.

"I'll explain later...I love you." The rapper hung up and dialed the Virginia Beach Police Department.

Fish was on his way out to lunch when a female bluecoat informed him that he had a call on line 5. Before the detective could consider taking the caller, the officer told him the caller claimed to be Mister Keith Osbourne. That's strange? Fish thought, massaging his temple. He re-routed back to his desk, the detective's stare met Pataki's as the phone shot up to his ear. "Hello, this is Detective Fish. With whom am I speaking with? And what's it in reference to?"

"It's me, Keith Osbourne."

"Well well well! What do I owe the pleasure?" Fish's tone elevated loud enough to confirm the caller to his partner. "So what can I do for you on this fine day?" Probably wants to beg permission to leave the state......

"About the serial rapist you've been investigating."

"What, you know who's biting off these young girl's nipples, do you?:

The rapper paused, "I know but I don't know." He replied, sounding confused.

"Well Mr. Osbourne, that makes perfectly good sense, now doesn't it?"

The millionaire growled back, "Look man! This is hard enough as it is! I don't need any B.S. from you right now!"

"My bad playa." The detective's tone smoothed down.

"Its between A or B. I'm certain it's A, but I wanna be positively sure." The rapper explained his plan to Fish five or six times over until the Detective was convinced it would work.

"I gotta give it to you Mister Osbourne, that's one hell of a plan." Pataki complimented. "It takes a lot of balls to do what you're doing."

Fish chimed in, "Hell, I could round them up, run DNA tests on the two based on the info provided to us."

"You heard what Mr. Osbourne said. Besides, the suspect is quite evasive. Catching him with his pants down makes this a open and shut case for the District Attorney."

Fish's stare settled on Pataki. "You're absolutely right."

Pataki cracked a half smile. That was the first compliment Fish gestured to him since they partnered up.

"Pataki get Hectic on the horn. Inform him of what's going down. Better yet, get security over to Hampton General just in case he or the other returns."

The rapper chimed, "Call me once everything's in place."

"Sure thing Mr. Osbourne. Good-bye. One more thing Keith-"

"I'm still here, wussup?"

"Just thought I'd say thanks for your help. You're a noble man."

The millionaire didn't respond. He hung up the phone and dialed Nikki's number. There was a lot of explaining to do. Keith Osbourne decided now was as good as any to tell his lover just what he knew.

CHAPTER 23

By mid-evening the scorching heat simmered, everything was in place and Sheila was long gone. Incidentally, the rapper couldn't help but think of her. I'm supposed to be happy, Keith told himself as Mitch cruised down Portsmouth boulevard. The millionaire turned to the P.I.. "You know Mitch," Keith said, keeping his eyes cut ahead. "You know I trust you more than anyone else?"

"Whadda coincidence, I trust me too, so?" Mitch replied, gazing upon a Bayliner fishing boat that was parked in a yard with a 'for sale' sign.

"I'm serious Mitch."

"So was I." Giggles. "I'm just curious as to where this is going?"

"I'll tell ya if you gimme a chance." The rapper was trying not to laugh at the P.I.'s animated facial expression. "I'm moving Arlene into the Thurgood Mansion. And… I was hoping you'd move in with her." A seriousness slapped Mitch Holley across the face. Silence as he contemplated the idea. "Momma ain't gonna be able to keep the place up on her own. Besides, she digs your company."

"She does, doesn't she?"

Keith admired his boastful humor. "So, you'll do it?"

"If Arlene's cool with it then I guess I could give it a try. And when the neighbors ask where's you move to, I'ma tell 'em all that you moved back to the ghetto, man."

The two burst into laughs as a Bentley turned into the Chesapeake square shopping plaza.

Nikki sat at the bar sipping a lemonade and nibbling on a plate of Ruby Tuesday's grilled chicken strips. Her swollen eyes told the waitress she'd been crying recently. Princess's deceptiveness struck her deep. Reminiscing thoughts of Rodney and herself planning on having a little boy one day crawled across her mind. She asked herself was it wrong to feel the way she did. After all, she was over Rodney and now in love with her baby daddy's role model. Maybe I'm in shock or something? She pondered. 'Who am I fooling?' Little Rodney's face popped in Nikki's head.

Instant rage!

"I should'a stomped a mud hole in that bitch's ass for GP." Nikki mumbled under her breath, gazing around the bar top hoping that no one noticed her sudden grit. I don't understand, if I'm so happy about my present situation, then why am I allowing the past to torment me like this. Her thoughts continued as she massaged her belly. It just doesn't make any sense to me. Nikki's thoughts were interrupted by the special news story that flashed over the television her stare settled on the wide screen that hung up behind the bar.

"This is Langley James…Just in…the serial rapist's only possible witness has died this evening during surgery. Authorities believe she was an eye witness to her own assault."

As the anchor woman continued, Nikki continued to cry. The thought of it being true brought a flood of tears to her eyes. Nikki darted to the restroom to gather herself. She stood over the sink staring at the woman in the mirror. Is it me, she asked herself, or is my face starting to get fat. Her fingertips glided over the scar on her hairline. Nikki's stare shifted to her new growth. Its time for a perm, my new growth is looking something terrible. Her eyes followed the tall, slim blonde as she hurriedly moved into a vacant stall.

"Oh no she didn't?" Nikki snapped loud enough for the woman to hear. Upon entering the lady's room, she noticed the blonde was strutting barefooted with her high heels in each hand. By the second flush Nikki had forgotten about her. She turned on the faucet and let the cold water spill over her palms. When Nikki stood up she spotted the barefooted woman's legs though the mirror. She zoomed in on the pale ankles. Her jaw fell on the floor. She scooped up her belongings and darted out into the restaurant. When she arrived to the bar Keith Osbourne and Mitch Holley were waiting there for her.

"What's wrong, baby. You alright?"

Keith asked, noticing she'd been spooked by something. "Look like you just seen a ghost."

“Close!” Nikki shot back, “I just saw a white chick taking a piss.”

The P.I. stared at Nikki as if she’d gone crazy. “What’s so scary about that?” he asked.

“She was standing up!”

“Ooohhhh!” the rapper chimed.

Moments later the drag queen appeared from the restroom. She sashayed to a nearby table where a short Asian gentleman greeted her. The three laughed in unison.

“Damn! Ugly as she is, I’d be in shock too.” Mitch blurted giggles. “He funny as hell.” Nikki pulled Keith Osbourne close to her and planted a kiss on his chin. “Who is he, your manager or something?”

“Nawh, just a friend. My best friend, next to you.”

“Let’s take care of this,” Mitch interrupted, “We’re running out of time.”

The three found a table on the other side of the bar. For the next thirty minutes Keith instructed his lover what to do after she went home.

“Of course it’s going to work.” The rapper assured her. “Mitch is going to be close by just in case you need something.”

Nikki nodded, ending all discussion. They stood from the table. Mitch departed first so the rapper and his girl could get their smooches on.

“Woman, you are so beautiful.” Nikki blushed as the millionaire held her waist in his palms. He reeled Nikki close to him. Their lips gently locked soon after. Their kiss was so passionate that they hadn’t noticed the busboy standing beside them. The employee cleared his throat in an exaggerating manner. Momentarily interrupting the couple’s moment. “Sorry mam and sir, but this is not a Waffle House.” His undertone emphasized his sarcasm. The busboy’s face instantly lit up upon recognizing the rapper. “Hol’ up! You’re, you’re MC K.O.?” he started jumping around, excited. “Can I get an autograph? No…no, a picture?” The busboy was nearly out of wind. “Let me go get my camera. I gotta get a picture, dude.” The employee made a beeline pass the bar. He disappeared through the kitchen door. Keith and Nikki walked to the hostess with the bill in hand. There beside the register was an ink pen and a stack of complimentary napkins. The rapper jotted down something on one of them.

“Do me a favor?” he asked the hostess. “Give this to the busboy when he returns.”

As they exited the restaurant, the busboy stormed from the back with his digital camera in hand. He looked left. Then right. No MC K.O. he quick-stepped to the hostess's station. "Where'd they go?" his loud tone instantly drew attention from the other patrons.

"SShhhh!" the female slid the personal note the rapper left for him.

He unfolded the napkin which read 'If you really want an autograph and a picture with me, I'll be at the Waffle House.'

"Where you going?"

"To the Waffle House. MC K.O. is signing autographs there." Just as he started out the door, the kid stopped in his tracks. He shot the napkin up to his face and read it once more. Then it hit him. "Fuck!" he snapped, "This is a screw you message!"

10:49 P.M.

Keith called Alfred, Mont, and Timmy Tuff for a meeting at his place. He gathered them after the road manager had logged in the new tour dates. Once the rescheduling was complete, the sat around listening and laughing at Keith's story of Sheila. Mont laughed cramps in his waist side once the rapper explained the way his wife looked upon opening her gift. After a while, the chuckles simmered down. Mont, Alfred, and Timmy Tuff jawed amongst themselves.

"It's hot in this mutha." Mont shouted after noticing his cousin's Versace shirt float to the sofa.

"Yeah I know, and it's making me sleepy." Keith Osbourne let out a exaggerated yawn. His gaze climbed to the clock on the desk. The millionaire's eyes shifted on the Fish tank as his S. Carter's plopped on the table.

"Those sneakers are going to damage your table." Alfred advise as if he purchased the Red Oak himself.

The rapper's stare cut in his manager direction, "I think MC K.O. can afford to mess up Red Wood dining tables, don't 'chu?"

Alfred's face turned red. "You're getting more and more like-"

Keith stopped his manager in mid-sentence with the erection of his index finger.

As the phone rang, the rapper's stare darted to the clock once more. It read 11 o'clock. Right on the money! He told himself. "Probably Sheila lookin' to suck her way back up in this piece."

Laughs.

His gaze surfed the room as his fingers constricted the receiver. "My balls aren't small enough for her mouth right now." Mont and Timmy

Tuff's chuckles simmered as the phone glided up to Keith's face. "Yo! MC Millionaire here, fucking up Red Oak tables as he pleases, wus gud?" he greeted the caller, shooting Alfred a sarcastic smirk afterward. "How can I help you? Oh, it's you?" he smothered the phone with his palm." Damn, he whispered, apparently upset. "This broad is worrisome as hell. I'm not in the mood to hear her voice right now." The millionaire uncovered the receiver. "Yeah, Nichole, I'm here...sorry about that, had to change phones."

As Keith Osbourne talked nonchalantly on the phone, his team sat quietly pretending not to be listening to the loud conversation the rapper was having, Keith Osbourne suddenly fell silent. Horror covered his face. He tried to speak but lost his breath. The millionaire's eyes fell to his lap. "Well...I am concerned about your friend and your feelings too."......Silence. "Yeah yeah...I'll be over there in the morning. No! Don't talk to the authorities until I get over there to see you." Curiosity grew stronger and stronger as the conversation continued. Everyone in the room wanted to know just how the police were involved. And what it was in reference to.

"I'm too tired to go anywhere tonight...yes, I promise I'll be there in the morning." The rapper hung up without saying good-bye.

"What was that all about?" Alfred asked, sounding concerned.

Keith Osbourne yawned, looking unconcerned. "You know that chick that got raped and stabbed?"

"Hectic's wife?" Mont answered.

"Yeah her. Well...she died earlier this evening." Keith noticed a sudden relief that came over his producer. There was no doubt in his mind that his college roommate and long time friend was the perpetrator.

"Sorry to hear that," Timmy Tuff said, his tone appeared somber.

"So what's that got to do with her calling the police or something?" Alfred asked, trying to piece the puzzle together.

"Oh yeah, she was there at the hospital today and that girl Shawnte' told her who'd raped her before she passed."

"Who'd she say it was?" Timmy Tuff asked nonchalantly.

"She didn't!" Keith said, shrugging, "What she did say was...she wanted to tell me in person because what she found out...obviously she's having a hard time believing it. Whatever that means?"

Alfred stood to his feet, "Keith, I know you're tired but this is important. I could drive you if you want?"

"Alfred I appreciate that, but her friend is dead. So talking to her tonight ain't gonna bring her back." The road manager threw his hands up in disgust. "Well gentlemen, I think I'm going to call it a night. A brother feeling drowsy than a mutha."

Timmy Tuff nodded, "Do that, K-baby, them eyes are red as hell."

Keith Osbourne escorted the three to the door. Timmy and Mont gave the rapper dap and bounced to their rides. Alfred stared the rapper up and down, obviously upset.

"Why you lookin' at me like dat?"

"Because…I'm so disappointed in you man."

About that girl Nichole? Man, she'll be fine, I'm tired. She can wait til' tomorrow."

His voice carried loud enough for Timmy Tuff and Mont to hear.

Alfred shook his head in grief. "And shave your head! You look terrible." He snapped out of frustration before walking off toward his car.

Keith Osbourne stood in the door grinning to himself as Timmy Tuff and Alfred's sports cars peeled off. Guess I don't feel so sleepy after all. The phone began to ring. The millionaire shut the door and darted to the nearest jack.

"Hello?"

"They still there?"

"No, everyone's gone."

"So, what do you think, Keith?"

"I don't know Mitch. I don't know. The best thing we can do is sit back and wait until I receive the call from Mont."

A few hours earlier, Keith Osbourne met up with his cousin at Arlene's place. He didn't feel right leaving his cousin out on his plan. So he explained to Mont what he knew and what he suspected. The rapper's only concern was that Mont would flip the script and alert Timmy Tuff. Just in case that transpired, Keith Osbourne decided to keep the major details to himself.

12:02 A.M.

The millionaire's phone finally rung. Keith cuffed it to his ear on the first chirp. "Hello?"

"Yo cuz, it's me Mont. Timmy Tuff bit on it. I think he could be the serial rapist. Because he was acting kinda funny and shit."

“Is he headed to Suffolk or what?” the rapper was anxious to know.

“Nawh man, Stacy called him. Said she needed him at the crib, ASAP!”

“Alright! I’ll call Nichole and tell her to cut the camcorder off.” Keith Osbourne sounded as if his idea was a failure.

“A’ight cuz, holla at ‘chu tomorrow.”

“A’ight Mont, I’m out.” The rapper slammed the phone down so hard it cracked in two. “That little mutha…he flipped the script on me.” he growled out loud.“I can’t believe he told Timmy Tuff.” The millionaire whipped out his cellular and punches some numbers. Someone picked up on the first ring. “This is Keith. It’s on baby!” The rapper hung up, snatched his Versace shirt from the couch, scooped his car keys and made a dash for the front door.

CHAPTER 24

12:23 A.M.

There was only one thing on Timmy Tuff's mind as he raced down highway-58. Murder…death…kill…no witnesses! I can't be caught! The premeditated thoughts kept circling through his head. He switched into the exit lane and descended the exit ramp. The producer stopped at the yield sign, recalling the night he and his girl gave Nikki a ride home. The range rover proceeded straight ahead. He turned left at the traffic signal. Once Timmy Tuff arrived on east Washington Street, he hoped to spot anything familiar. The rover sailed a mile or so before it passed by the old fire station and Thelma's steakhouse. "Yeah, this is the right way." He whispered to himself after recognizing the antique fire truck on display on main street.

Timmy Tuff made another left at the traffic signal landing on Main Street.

"Here we go. I know where I'm at now." The producer said, as if he'd just solved a Wheel of Fortune puzzle. Positively certain of his destination, the SUV accelerated pass the Shady Lane Townhouse billboard.

"Eeeeeerrrrr!" the rover skidded 40 feet into the opposite lane after Timmy Tuff floored the brakes. His sunken eyes shot up to the rear view mirror. No incoming commuters were on the road. The rover made a U-turn in the middle of the road and killed his headlamps before cruising into the Shady Lane apartment complex.

As the producer sailed over speed bumps his dark stare met every make and model of parked cars. Nikki's Cherokee was parked out in front of her apartment. Timmy Tuff spotted it in between a Honda and a Kia sedan. His eyes darted to the front door of her home, then to the window. He noticed the silhouette of a tall female walking from one side of the window to the other. The Range Rover sped to the end of Shady Lane and made a left onto Cedar Grove. After circling Nikki's place for the third time Timmy Tuff was convinced Cedar Grove was the best location for a clean getaway. The producer parked six units away from Main Street in between a Chevy Blazer and an old Maxima. He killed the engine and sat in the dark surveying the premises. Before long, his eyes closed, instant meditation. The producer's mind took him back a few nights when he uninvitingly entered Shawnte'. Timmy Tuff decide he should rape Nikki after her long sexy legs sashayed across his mind. Why not? His eyes snapped open. He scanned the neighboring cars looking to see if anyone were out and about, walking dogs, chilling in their rides or making out. After I ram this submarine into her kidney, I'ma slit her throat. Once she's dead…I'ma fuck 'er again. Erotic thoughts of penetrating Nikki in every position caused Timmy Tuff's nature to rise. His eyes darted left then right as he whipped out his 16 inch trophy. Creepy eyes began fondling the tip. Gently he commenced to stroking his muscle to a stiff erection with one hand, holding his nut sack in the other. In minutes time the producer's eyes were rolled back in his head. The steering wheel column, arm rest, and center console were victimized by his organic eruption. It usually took Timmy Tuff five minutes or more to get off, thoughts of skeeting off on Nikki's lifeless tongue made him more anxious and excited. He reached into the glove compartment and pulled out a handful of fast food napkins. The producer wiped his hands dry, then his denims, finally tossing the contaminated toiletries out the window. Timmy Tuff didn't think twice about wiping his prized possession, considering it was about to get wet in Nikki's juices. He cuffed the leather gloves and a jig tooth hunting knife from the compartment and forced the remaining napkins inside. The producer slid out of the Jeep, his creepy eyes shot up and down Cedar Grove. Everything remained calm. He reached over the steering wheel and cranked the engine then guided the door close. Creepy eyes checked his watch as he moved briskly to the rear of the Range Rover. His dark sunken stare shot over at the parked cars across the parking lot after hearing a commotion in the darkness. "I'm trippin'." Timmy Tuff continued on upon spotting two kittens chase each other under the street lamp. Just two fuckin' cats. The back door of his Jeep swung open. Destined for his next victim, Timmy Tuff reached under the seat and pulled out his tote bag. The producer trotted up the sidewalk then cut right towards Shady Lane.

Moments after Timmy Tuff took off into the darkness a man dressed in all black attire moved swiftly to the producer's Range Rover. He opened the door and jumped behind the steering wheel.

Once Timmy Tuff arrived on Nikki's street he squatted behind a plumbing van that was parked a few units from the corner. His creepy eyes surfed the many vehicles until he spotted the tail of her SUV once more. Coast clear… Oh shit! The producer repositioned himself after a pair of head lamps faded out of view. Creepy eyes stealthily moved towards the Cherokee. It took Timmy Tuff under a minute to reach Nikki's ride. He posted up against the rear tire and fixed his stare on her apartment door and placed his ear to it. The lights in the front room were now off. He listened intently, hoping to detect any noises on the other side. There were none. Timmy Tuff's bag dropped down to the dirty home sweet home mat. The zipper of the bag peeled back, in seconds he produced a locksmith kit. Picking the bolt lock in record time. His leather glove octupused the door knob. Never did Timmy Tuff completely shut the door. He didn't want to chance alerting his victims. The only source of lighting bounced off the hallway's walls.

His pupils quickly adjusted to the dim setting. This joint is much smaller than I thought. Timmy Tuff whipped the ski mask from his bag, then changed his mind, shoving it back in. What do I need to cover my face for? I'ma kill 'er anyhow! Creepy eyes drew his blade as he stalked down the hall to Nikki's bedroom. Her bedroom door was partially cracked. The lamps let off a dullness. The producer inched closer and closer. His grip intensified on the knife's handle. Timmy Tuff's creepy stare had finally arrived to the cracked door. He could see the bed and his victim laying haphazardly under the comforter.

As the bedroom door floated open the producer spotted the camcorder's lens facing the ceiling, a sure sign that it was not in use. Got 'chu now bitch! The producer moved stealthily to the edge of her bed and glided his leather fingers over the long sexy legs with hopes of awaking his victim.

No response.

Timmy Tuff's hormones were jumping through his denims as thought of Nikki's skinless body flashed in his head. The serial rapist grew tired of stalking his prey. It was time to get down to business. Creepy eyes held a fistful of the comforter in his leather grip. Like the mad man that he was, Timmy Tuff yanked the blanket from over top of his victim… "WHAT… THE FUUUUUUU?"

10 MINUTES EARLIER

Nikki had just woken from another gruesome nightmare. For the moment she lay under covers wondering how Shawnte's child would respond to all that would transpire in the future. She raised from the bed and gazed through the darkness. She flicked the lights after realizing Mitch Holley was no longer propped in the chair. He wasn't supposed to leave me alone. Nikki shrugged, walking into the bathroom. "I don't like this." She muttered, wishing her pistol was on hand.

The toilet flushed. Nikki exited the bathroom and went to make sure the P.I. had locked the door. Once she secured it, she climbed back under the sheets. Her eyes closed with Keith Osbourne on her mind. Before long, the two were kissing under a cherry tree by the lake. Nikki had fallen asleep.

The front door opened instantly, awakening her. Nikki felt a sudden breeze creep under the seam of the blanket. Footsteps squeaked towards the bed. Someone now stood over her. Nikki's eyes widened, fully alert. She started to move but froze after hearing heavy breathing. Her heart began thumping faster and faster. The presence of the stalker's body heat sent chills through her. Nikki foolishly thought if she pretended to sleep that whoever towered above would go away. The presence remained in the room. I ain't going out like this. She told herself. Her fingers slowly curled into a tight fist. If someone is gonna try and take me and my unborn away from here then they gots to put in some work…I can go all out too.

In a split second, everything that ever meant something to Nikki flashed before her just on the other side of the comforter. As Nikki readied to launch herself from under the covers a hand snatched the blanket from over her. Instinctively, Nikki rolled backward and sent a flurry of bicycle kicks to her perpetrator. Screams followed after he foot struck the man across his nose. Nikki leapt from the bed once her attacker hit the floor and snatched the hotel lap from the dresser.

"Hey…Hol' up! Stop…put that down!" Mitch pleaded, catching the blood from his nose. "It's just me, Mitch Holley. You-do-remember me, don't 'chu? Your temporary bodyguard." He said sarcastically after Nikki lowered the lamp to the dresser. "Geeez! You are a demon child."

After Nikki collected herself she hurried into the bathroom to get a cold towel for the private investigator. "I'm sorry Mitch! I truly am, I got spooked. Thought you were-"

"Timmy Tuff." Mitch Holley answered for her.

Nikki sighed, "Yeah…I…I did."

"Nope, it's just me, easy nose bleeding Mitch Holley."

Nikki burst into laughs. She couldn't help it.

"Get dressed" the P.I. demanded, ignoring her giggles. "Timmy Tuff just pulled into Shady Lane Townhouses. He's under surveillance as we speak. Everyone's in place. Only one missing from the party is us."

Moments later, the two were leaving Super 8 hotel for the apartment complex.

After Keith Osbourne and Detective Fish agreed on a plan, Pataki and Suffolk SWAT team placed the entire complex under surveillance. All the rapper had to do was lure the guilty one to their fate. Stacy was accompanied by the detective since earlier that evening. That's how Keith Osbourne figured his cousin had tipped off the producer.

Upon hanging up with Mitch Holley, the millionaire jumped behind the wheel of Sheila's Viper and headed out to Suffolk. As he torpedoed down I-58 he spotted Timmy Tuff's SUV. Keith hoped the producer hadn't recognized him. He fell back then called up Fish to advise him Timmy Tuff was minutes away from Shady Lane Townhouses and in bird's eye view of him.

Upon arrival to the apartment complex, the rapper climbed in the car of an undercover. He and the officer parked on Cedar Grove in the darkness at Fish's direction.

The rapper had been sitting in the squad car for a few minutes when a voice whispered across the radio.

"We have a visual of the subject."

"Confirm." Pataki shot back.

"Black Discovery Range Rover." The officer then relayed the tag number.

"That's our man." Another officer chimed.

"Okay, I have visual Fish. His headlights are off and cruising our way real slow."

"Get the girl ready!"

"I'm ready." The female officer relayed over the radio.

"Okay…" Pataki said, "you're on in 3-2-1."

As Timmy Tuff sailed past Nikki's apartment the female office sashay past the window in her most seductive strut.

"He's looking…I think." Keith sat in the dark listening to the undercover operation unravel. He couldn't help but replay all the good memories with his old friend. Guilt swarmed him soon after. What else was I suppose to do? He asked to himself. His thoughts were put on hold.

"Duck down! He's cruising by again."

"Fish, come in!"

"This is Fish, talk."

"I think he knows something's up." Pataki suggested.

"He hasn't a clue. He's just combing the area, checking for wondering eyes and securing a getaway route."

"Think you're right. He's parking now…over!"

"Good. Very good!" Fish's whisper sent chills through MC K.O. as he continued to listen. "Now stay off the air til' he makes a move."

The millionaire and the undercover spotted the Range Rover as it glided into a vacant parking space. They wondered why Timmy Tuff hadn't exited the Jeep. "Wassup? What's going on?" Keith asked the officer, suddenly feeling uncomfortable.

"We have visual." An officer relayed over the air.

"What's going on?" Pataki demanded to know.

"Is Mister Tuff's girlfriend presently with you?" Another undercover asked.

"Of course she is why?"

"Because I don't want to say exactly what he's up to it."

"C'mon spill it out. What is he jackin' off for christsakes?"

"Uh…well, actually he is…..Detective, sir."

Stacy perched beside a SWAT member soaking in everything she heard about her fiancé', her face revealed no emotion.

Keith Osbourne couldn't believe that the man he knew for so long was the same guy beating himself off in his Jeep. "Damn, can't believe this." The rapper mumbled, shaking his head in grief. The officer's stare cut sharply on the Millionaire as if he were a jerk off as well.

When Timmy Tuff opened the driver side door, the undercover cracked open his. He squatted and moved to the rear of the car and popped the trunk open just enough to stick his hand inside. His fingers bounced around until it constricted a spare clip to his service pistol. As the officer pulled it out he fumbled the magazine. It tumbled down to the bumper and landed onto the driveway, after he tried to ease the trunk closed. The noise instantly caught the Producer's attention. Keith Osbourne slid back down into the seat after Timmy Tuff's eyes shot his way.

"What the hell is he doing back there?" The Rapper growled as his head lay beside the manual shift gear.

"What's going on out there?" Pataki growled into his radio.

No response!

The officer now lay on the ground. Whipped out his pepper spray spotting two kittens curl on a nearby porch, the undercover fumed the mace in the animal's direction. The kittens jolted away from the apartment door across the street. Once the producer saw the kittens fleeing under the street lamp he continued his activity.

"He's heading your way." A whisper came across the air wave.

"Roger that."

Keith Osbourne ascended until his stare leveled the dashboard. He could see Timmy Tuff moving swiftly to the end of the apartment unit over to the Shady Lane Drive. From the corner of his eye the rapper spotted a SWAT team officer moving stealthily. He erected in the seat and focused on the person quick-stepping towards Timmy Tuff's Jeep. The man, presumably an officer of the law, jumped inside and drove off.

The undercover slid back into the driver's seat once the suspect disappeared onto the next street.

"We seized his vehicle."

"I don't have any visual." Pataki chimed.

"You guys, stay on your toes out there." Fish's tone was matter of factly.

"Ssshhhhhh!" the SWAT team's sergeant pointed to the walls of the plumbing van. "He right there, ducking down."

Pataki's pupils gazed over the rear of the truck as silence swept through.

"I need visual God Damnit!" his whisper carried over the radio.

Seconds later, an undercover's car glided past the van pretending not to notice Timmy Tuff posted in between the cars. "Detective Pataki."

"Pataki talk!"

"He's three cars away from your location, squatting down in between the maroon Camry and dark colored Taurus."

"Roger that. We now have visual."

For the next sixty seconds everyone waited until Timmy Tuff gained entry to the apartment. "The subject is in the house. I repeat, the subject is in." all at once police stormed from tree branches, from under parked cars. Vacant apartment unit, and near the plumbing van. 30 seconds flat is what it took for 45 or so blue and whites to set up a blockade outside of Nikki's front door.

As authorities waited, Mitch Holley and Nikki pulled up joining Keith and Stacy behind the perimeter line. "Should we go in?" One of the SWAT members asked.

"Nannnhhh!" Pataki shot back. "Trust me, that Timmy Tuff kid is much safer out here."

Shock took Timmy Tuff once he unveiled the covers from his victim. Laying under the sheets was a middle aged black fellow with glassy red eyes.

"Hey, what's going on man?" The man laying in the bed demanded to know. His stare fixed on the producer's stainless steel blade and pulsating hard on.

"And put that away...both of them!"

Timmy Tuff stuttered every other word uttered, "I'm...uh, I-I didn't-"

He swallowed hard trying to gather himself. "Look! I gots money, lots of it, just calm down ole' man, okay?"

"Who you lookin' for this time of night?" silence... "Nichole Wallace perhaps?" A wicked grin formed on the gentleman's face. His stare appeared sharper that Timmy Tuff's jig tooth knife.

"Hol' the fuck up! I know damn well I saw a woman in the window. Where is she?" His creepy stare darted around the room then settled back on the gentleman in front of him. "So this is Nikki's crib?" he asked, looking confused. "Who you? Her pops or something?"

"Nope! Nothing like that. In fact, I hardly know her." Then the man's eyes locked on the producer as he erected from the bed. He whipped a cigar from his pocket. "My name is Fish." Silence as he lit it up. "Detective Fish! I've been expecting you playa." His eyes shot back on Timmy Tuff. Cigar smoke followed.

Oh shit five-o! In an instant creepy eyes realized he'd been set up.

"That's right mutha fucka! It's over!"

Fear of finally being captured came over the producer. The awe turned into rage. Rage of a desperate man ready to fight his way out of a corner at any cost, even his life. With the blade in hand, Timmy Tuff drew it back, ready to attack.

Fish remained poise as he took another puff on his cigar, looking as if he were gazing up into the ceiling lost in his own thoughts.

Creepy eyes repositioned his feet and launched himself towards his prey. The detective did a triple spin, swiftly around the blade, slipping the attack with ease. "Damn white boy! I figured you to be much faster than that being you're so evasive and all." The detective parked against the wall and took in another swig of his cigar.

Timmy Tuff juggled the hunting knife as he stalked Fish. Once he started toward the officer, the quick-drawing Detective met Creep eyes halfway with the barrel of his .45 caliber extended out to the bridge of the producer's nose, stopping him in his tracks. "Negro please! I-wish-you-would." Timmy slowly inched backward. "That's it! Slow ya roll fatboy!" Fish's weapon drop to his side. "For you to be so slick you sure are stupid."

The jig tooth fell from the producer's leather grip. He turned and took off running out of the bedroom knocking down the female officer that sprung from the hall closet.

The Detective's radio flew up to his grill. "He's coming you all's way."

Once the undercover hit the floor she fumbled the pistol to the leg of the sofa. Creepy eyes gathered himself, scooped the burner and scrambled out the front door. To his misfortune, he was met by strobe lights and gun barrels extended out at him. The nervous stare surfed the front lawn. Damnit! They got me! Timmy Tuff lowered the gun to the ground upon command. After falling to his knees, he spotted Mitch Holley, Nikki and Keith Osbourne standing behind the SWAT team. The producer was instantly blinded by the many black uniforms that rushed him to the concrete.

The police cuffed the suspect and heave him by the arms. Stacy emerged from behind an unmarked police car. Their eyes locked instantly. Timmy didn't feel so tough at the moment. In fact, he wished he were dead. The look in Stacy's eyes told him they shared the same wish.

Three years ago, Stacy's older sister was sexually assaulted. Too embarrassed to report the incident to the authorities, Kentrale told only Stacy. Stacy almost believed her sister until Kentrale said she thought Timmy Tuff was the one who took advantage of her. Identified only by his pupils, Stacy dismissed her sister and her accusations as another one of her many deceptive lies and pleas for attention. Weeks after the incident, Kentrale moved to Concord, Connecticut. Stacy had not heard from her since.

I can't believe I didn't listen to her. Stacy scolded herself as her glare settled on her fiancé. This nigga raped my sister! Oh hell nawh…he ain't getting' off this easy! Stacy moved swiftly to one of the officers as they ushered Timmy Tuff to a nearby squad car. The patrolmen stopped upon request as Forensic Investigators took pictures of their subject. While they snapped shots Stacy's eyes were on a detective's holster. She lifted the service pistol from the officer, spun around the gathered badges and squeezed off a round.

"BLAAUU!"

A copperhead ripped through the producer's body. Before Stacy could spit another slug in her fiancé Keith Osbourne tackled her to the ground, hoping neither of them got blasted by one of the bad boys whose guns were now drawn on them.

"You raped my sister." Stacy cried out as she lay pinned under the rapper.

"I hate 'chu, I hate 'chu, I-hate-you!" her screams pierced through the midnight smog.

Detective Fish observed the incident from Nikki's doorway. He slid down the sidewalk as officers cuffed Stacy. Pataki met Fish at the parking lot.

"Hell no!" Fish snapped, already knowing what his partner was about to ask. "If he raped my sister I would've busted 'im in the ass too!" Pataki nodded. "Besides…he practically a dead man."

CHAPTER 25

Months had passed since the Timmy Tuff incident. He'd managed to pay all his victims two hundred thousand dollars not to testify against him. 7 of 15 victims showed up the day of his trial anyhow. The producer pled guilty to life, avoiding a consecutive sentence for each woman.

Stacy was slapped on the cover of every major woman's magazine in the country after catching wind of her story. Once the publicity bubbled down, she received 10 days in jail, which she served on weekends, and 6 years of supervised probation.

Since Timmy Tuff had no living relatives besides his child with Stacy, she automatically became the heir to his multi-million dollar estate. Sometimes Stacy pondered the idea of writing him. She couldn't deny the fact that she loved her baby daddy deeply. Eventually Stacy would reach out to the ex-producer, just wasn't going to be anytime soon!

Detective Fish and Pataki became the hot topic on CNN's Larry King Live and every other major newspaper in the country. Fish was later promoted to captain. Detective Pataki was promoted to Lieutenant which brought serious animosity within the department being that he was a new transfer. He and Fish's bond, no closer. In fact, since Fish was his superior, he'd talk shit and harass Pataki every chance he got, which was all the time.

Shawnte' recovered weeks after her surgery. During her coma she'd come to realize that life was too precious to be taken for granted. And that it was time to stop with the games and become a mature and responsible mother and loving wife. Before Shawnte could break the truth to her husband and Daisha, Hectic advised that he already knew and that he would love the two of them unconditionally forever. Hectic's baby momma Vicky 'Dee Dee' Edwards was sentenced to three years in which she recently arrived to a female prison in Goochland, Virginia. Big daddy married his baby momma, Shirley, just days after their visit to Hampton General Hospital. He and his wife would become good friends with Hectic and Shawnte'. Of course Hectic never learned the truth about them. Big Daddy and Shawnte' never sexed each other again. At least she said she didn't.

Nikki relocated days after the incident. She moved to one of the nation's safest cities, which happened to be ten minutes away in Chesapeake, Virginia. She hadn't heard from princess since her last visit to Richmond. Shawnte' and herself hadn't spoke in a minute. They fell out after Shawnte' confessed to knowing the truth about Princess's child all along. Nikki quit her job as a correctional officer and landed a gig as a paralegal with a local law firm.

Mont, Keith Osbourne, and Alfred were touring around the country at the moment. Some cities they were boycotted, yet the rapper managed to sell out every venue. Mont hadn't spoke directly to his cousin for the first couple of weeks. Upon arriving to the conclusion that MC K.O. did the right thing, he unquestionably started to perform a lot better. Even though Timmy Tuff was Mont's closest friend, the hype man found himself calling Stacy from wherever city he landed in. 'To check up on her' was the excuse he gave himself. Before long, Mont couldn't deny that he'd developed some strong feelings for his friend's ex. Although Stacy didn't admit it, she enjoyed Mont's humorous personality and looked forward to his calls. Didn't take long before they were exchanging 'I love yous".

Keith Osbourne was MC K.O. and MC K.O. was in a zone. Nothing seemed to distract the rapper when he was performing on stage. Even though the divorce wasn't final that didn't keep the millionaire from planning to propose to Nikki. Whenever Keith Osbourne could, he'd catch a private jet to Norfolk international just to spend a few hours with his woman. He hardly ever stopped to his mansion. He'd left the keys with Mitch so he could check up on things while he were away.

It was the third of September. Half naked and pissy drunk, Mitch Holley plopped in the sofa watching MTV Real World when the phone chirped. The P.I. took his time to the dining room bartop. Looks like the night isn't over just yet. He told himself after a young blonde stood him up. He answered with a loud belch. "Honey, where you at?" Mitch assumed it was his bikini specialist on the other end.

"Sorry, dude but I ain't your honey." A goofy voice responded.

I must be drunk? Mitch thought, "You got the wrong number kiddo." The P.I. didn't bother to ask the caller who he was looking for.

"Don' hang up dude." Mitch Holley paused, the voice rung a bell in his head.

"Mitch, it's me Randy. Forgot about me already, huh?"

No response!

"Randy Wright, remember? Federal Corrections Officer in Georgia. Ring a bell?"

"Oh, the young kid with the boy George shit all in his hair."

"Ha ha ha ha!" Randy said, unamused by the humor.

"Yeah, I remember you…sooo, wussup? whudda you need a date or something?"

"Being that your words are slurring of the road, I take it that you are on the drunk side of home. So I'll get straight to it."

"Get to what?" Mitch snapped, already tired of the voice in his ear.

"It's probably no biggie, but Psycho Johnson, he goes home in a few months."

"Yeah, so what? I knew that."

"Let me finish. Gosh! Before inmates are released to the community they are required to undergo a medical background for the B.O.P.'s central file.

"And so guys know their condition upon release. Look kid, I'm getting sleepy over here."

"Long story short." Randy took a long pause, "Well Psycho has AIDS! Full-blown-AIDS dude."

Mitch's alcoholic buzz diminished in an instant. "Kid, you ain't shittin' me are you?"

"Mitch, its been what, five months since I last saw you? What makes your think I'd up and call at 11 o'clock at night to shit 'chu around?"

He gotta a point there. The P.I. wondered. Still, there's something else here. Has too be. Why else would he bother to call? "Soooo, what, you callin' to inform me of this cause you's a loya; K.O. fan?"

"Negative dude! Its about money, of course."

"Figured that."

"Look, for ten grand I'll tell you how long Psycho has been infected and whom he was infected by. Most importantly, I wont go public with this."

"You got it Randy. Can I have your word on that?"

“No doubt!” the C.O. shot back. “Do you have internet access?”

“What do I look like, a fuckin’ retard or something?” Mitch snapped, emphasizing his frustration. His tone lowered soon after. “Gimme your account number and I’ll have the dough wired to you in five minutes.”

“I presume you want Psycho’s medical records in return?”

“Damn right I do. My fax number is 757-5555 double 0 seven.”

“Got it.”

15 minutes later, Randy was ten G’s richer and Mitch Holley was massaging his belly in disgust. Tears ran down his face as he gazed upon the blood tests. ‘POSITIVE POSITIVE POSITIVE POSITIVE’

“They’re all infected, Sheila, Keith Osbourne, Nikki, psycho, and his brother, all of them.” The P.I. cried himself into a deep depression then fell asleep. He’d wake up in tears only to fall back into a snooze. The following morning Mitch woke up feeling dizzy. His eyes were decorated with garbage bags beneath them. His hair looked like a Nick Nolte mug shot. The private investigator staggered into the kitchen and turned the coffee maker to brew. Afterward, he stood over the balcony overlooking the autumn birth of the trees. Sip by sip he drank his morning booster contemplating what his first move would be. First thing Mitch had to do was be sure that Sheila Osbourne was unquestionably infected with the virus before he went to the rapper with the bad news. The P.I. tossed the remainder of his coffee over the balcony and hurried back inside his condo. The mug landed on the bar top as he squatted in front of his computer.

“If this broad has AIDS, Melvin could definitely find out.” He mumbles to himself. He tapped a few keys, moments later he was on-line.

[Might Melvin hit P.I. real quick.] was the E-mail he sent too his old cellmate from prison.

Melvin was a short dark skinned brother with a lengthy neck and an oversized head. He adopted the name Mighty Melvin in prison after he rigged the ‘collect call’ phones up so everyone could dial straight home at the Department of Correction’s expense. Mighty Melvin was a computer hacker, one of the best, and he did it just for fun. He hacked into the Congressman’s checking account and transferred every single dime to the Children’s Hospital King’s Daughter Foundation. For that criminal offense, he was sentenced to serve five months in the joint.

Melvin responded with the quickness. [Mighty Mel in the hi-zouse, wussup?]

“That’s ma’ man.” Mitch said out lout after skimming over the E-mail.

Need serious info. Call me on the horn] the P.I. typed in. within a minute the phone rang. "Hello?"

"What's up, man. Wus good?"

"Everything is everything. I need your assistance." Mitch told him, moving briskly to the coffee table where Sheila Osbourne's information lay.

"Michael Biason, since everything is everything can you hook me up with that fine ass daughter of yours?"

"Hell no!" Mitch Holley snapped, giggling.

"I'm telling ya, I'll make a great son-in-law." The P.I.'s chuckled continued as he skimmed over the papers in front of him. "Mitch, I had this jungle fever for too long. Help me out, man. Let 'cho fine ass daughter cure a brother."

"My daughter's a lesbian stripper, you don' want 'er

"Foreal?" Mighty Melvin sounded amused.

"Fuck no! just get the message I'm trying to give ya." More laughs. "This is serious, Mel." His tone hardened. "I'ma throw you a name. I need you to tap into her medical records in Virginia and Georgia. I need to know if she's been diagnosed with the HIV virus or full blown AIDS."

"Okay, shoot."

"The name is Sheila Osbourne. Her maiden name is Sheila J. Mae."

"No problem. I'll have that for you in a jif, son." Mitch Holley remained on the line as his young friend rhythmically punched on his keypad. Silence for the next few minutes. "Mitch, I found something in Georgia's Department of Health."

The P.I. braced himself for the worst. "Alright kiddo, whadduya got?" his voiced almost cracked.

"It says here that she contracted N.G.U. Chlamydia and Gonorrhea." Melvin tapped a few more keys. But there's no sign of her contracting the bug. That doesn't mean too much considering she hadn't been to a clinic or private doctor in 18 months."

"Thanks Melvin, gotta go. Call me next week, we'll go fishing before the weather changes."

"A'ight Mitch, and-"

The P.I. hung up in his ear. He quickly darted to the front of his Dell and booked the next flight to Atlanta. Destination: Sheila Osbourne's new residence.

LATER THAT DAY...

Sheila had been living in Psycho's mansion ever since she left Virginia. She preferred to stay in his estate while in the city. Since Keith would call and check up on her at times, she settled in Betty Mae's. Being that there was nothing to hide anymore, Kayla and herself moved back into the huge property soon after Psycho gave her the okay.

Psycho Johnson had nine months left to serve on his sentence. Sheila expected him home in three with six months in a halfway house or home confinement. The coming home party he wanted had been put on hold. 5 weeks ago, the CEO of Psycho Records found out he contracted full blown AIDS. Now it appeared that all his hopes and ambitions of reuniting with his ex-wife would not be promised as he had planned. Of course Psycho was still going to be with Sheila. Things just weren't going to be the same. The CEO decided that he would not share his misfortune with Sheila. He planned on waiting six months after his release, then the two of them were to go get routine physicals where there would learn their fate together, so it would seem. Psycho planned on blaming Sheila for everything, knowing she was sleeping with other men beside himself.

Days after the CEO learned of his fate he managed to remain calm as if nothing was wrong. Jelly was the only loose end to his dark secret prison life. Psycho was convinced that his lover had passed the disease to him. So killing Jelly was a must! The CEO slipped into his lover's cell one night while the other inmates crammed into the TV room for Primetime Football. He had Jelly lie on her stomach and spread his legs. Psycho informed his lover that he was in the mood for kinky sex play and wanted to tie her up. Jelly complimented his wish. He tied one leg to the right side of the iron bunk and the other to the left. Psycho then scooped Jelly's sock and bonded his lover's arms behind her back. Jelly giggled as Psycho slid her boxer's down. The CEO commenced to smacking the homosexual across the ass a few times.

"Would my number one bitch ride or die for me?" he asked in a grim whisper.

"Yeesss!" Jelly moaned out.

Psycho's teeth grinded together as he drew back a ten-inch shank. "That's why I love you...because-you-down-for-me!" The CEO plunged the blade into his lover's back, piercing him through the heart. Jelly never had a chance to scream. Psycho crept back to his cell undetected.

Special investigative services declared Jelly's murder an attempted rape. The CEO was ruled out a suspect just as he anticipated. Now he walked the rec yard grieving. Not over the death of his lover, but the afterlife that stared him in the mirror. He slid to the weight pile and readied himself to rep a few sets. Pondering Sheila and their future seem to lead all thoughts at the present moment. I gave her a child…money…cars…and a big ass crib to live in. I gave her everything she wanted. So dying for me shouldn't be an issue if she truly loves me as she says. In three months we'll see….we will see!

CHAPTER 26

MC K.O. massaged his throat as he gargled salt water and spat in the hotel's sink. He would practice the common routine whenever he felt hoarse.

"You okay? You sounded kinda rough out there last night." Mont asked.

"Yeah I'm good cuz." Keith Osbourne cleared his throat and wiped his mouth with a complimentary towel.

"Me and the rest of the crew jettin' down too Time Square, parlay a lil' bit. You game or what?"

The rapper answered with a question of his own. "Wussup wit 'chu Gee? You ain't been the game since Timmy Tuff got knocked. You still mad with me?" Keith Osbourne tossed the cloth and walked over to the window. His gaze fell to Westside highway commuters.

"Iuno. I'm not mad at 'chu, just trying to move on I guess."

"Stacy! You've been talking to her a lot now." The millionaire interjected.

"What's up with dat?"

Surprised by the question, Mont perched on the bed thinking of a proper response.

Keith turned away from the window to face his cousin after he hesitated to answer. "Mont, is there something you want to tell me?"

Mont shook his head, a sly grin formed in the corner of his mouth. "I just can't believe it."

"Believe what?" the rapper asked, assuming he were referring to him turning the producer in to the authorities.

"I can't believe that white boy's dick was bigger than mine."

Keith let out a light chuckle before a serious face took over. Something else was on Mont's mind, the rapper knew it. Yet he reminded himself how reviving it was to hear his little cousin cracking jokes again.

"About Stacy?" Mont's tone lowered to a whisper. "I think I'm in love with-"the hypeman stopped in mid sentence. "No! I do love her. Not sure how It happened but it did."

"I see. That's what's been eating away at you? Feeling a lil' guilty?"

Mont shrugged, "A little."

"Don't be." Keith's arm landed on his cousin's shoulder. "Stacy and yourself were missing a void in yall's lives that Timmy used to fill. The two of you have common ground, which is pain and loneliness."

"So you think it's okay if I date Stacy?"

"HELL NO! I'd be furious as a mutha if my homie was creeping with my baby momma after I got locked up." Mont hung his head. "All I'm saying is…it's known to happen. And…I understand. Can't hide love, bro." Instant smiles from his hypeman. "Feel better?"

"Pretty much."

"Does that smile on your face mean I can count on your usual comical self again."

No response. Mont tried holding back his tears. Keith Osbourne met him with a much needed hug. "Go on…get outta here. Enjoy yaself."

"Thanks big cuz. I really needed that."

"Don't thank me, just stop by Jimmy Jazz and pick me up something to sport to the Gardens tomorrow night."

"Love you man."

The rapper recoiled, smiling, "Enough with that. Just know I love you too, Lamont." The hypeman exited the hotel room and headed down to the lobby where the Salt Water Boys awaited his arrival. Keith Osbourne locked the door behind him. He gazed down at his watch, reminding himself that he only had an hour to call Arlene as he always did. He whipped out his wireless phone and dialed her up.

"Hey momma, it's me."

“I know who this is. And why don’t you call me from your hotel room?” the rapper burst into laughs. “Momma, you know I’m always moving around taking care of business. Hotel phones have no mobility.”

“What ‘chu mean is that you calling me on that pocket phone so I won’t get the hotel number on the caller I.D.”

More chuckles. “Busted, okay momma you got me.”

“You ain’t slick. Arlene may be getting’ old but not dumb, keep on, God don’t like ugly.”

“Where’d you hear that from, one of the gospel plays?”

Silence.

“Matter of fact, I did. Mitch took me to a Willet Hall last week thank you.”

“Sounds like you enjoying yourself. Good for you momma.” Keith said, pulling his Sean John outfit from the suitcase. “Well momma, I just called to tell that I’ll be ending the tour on New York tomorrow. And I can’t wait to get home to those big Sunday dinners of yours.”

“You just be careful up there. And watch out for them Ben Latin Fellows.”

“That’s Osama Bin Laden, mom. Trust me, I’ll be fine. I’m pretty sure that Mr. Laden is somewhere in the mountains of Tora Bora.”

“Where?”

“A long ways from here.”

“Alright then. See you in a couple of days, son. Oh, are you still gonna introduce me to that new girl of yours?”

“Of course Ma, she’s having your first grandchild.”

“Okay, momma loves you.”

The millionaire hung up after his mother did. He tossed the jack on the bed and cuffed the hotel’s phone and dialed Nikki up.

“Hey love, I was just thinkin’ about ‘chu.”

“How’d you know it was me. I could’ve been Alfred or Mont delivering a message.”

“Yeah right,” Nikki replied unreceptive, “any ways, I’m glad to hear your voice. I brought you a present.”

“What is it?” excitement flooded the rapper’s voice.

“You know I’m not telling you. So don’t even start it.:

"Pretty please! Please!"

"You so crazy, boy. Oh yeah, don't forget-"

"I know baby." Keith chimed. "I wouldn't forget the day of my baby momma's first ultra sound."

Nikki growled at him. "Don't call me that!"

"Wus wrong love? I-"

"Am I or Am I not YOUR woman?" her undertone startled the rapper.

"Nikki baby, I love you. You're more than my woman, you are my everything."

"If you're sincere about your words then please do not refer to me as a baby momma. I wouldn't label you baby daddy because our relationship is supposed to have meaning and substance. It isn't just us having a child together."

"I understand, Nikki. And you're absolutely right. I'm sorry." His tone told Nikki that he was down on himself.

I hurt his feelings. I know just how to cheer him up. "Keith, I think we're gonna have a boy just as you wanted because my stomach is much bigger than the average 15 weeker. Plus my belly is really emphasizing more towards the top of my stomach."

"That's great, Nichole." The sudden energy in the millionaire's voice told Nikki her plan to elevate his spirits had worked.

Keith Osbourne talked about his plans to give his first born the world and how he would introduce the game of basketball to him. Nikki pretended to be interested in the story he shared of his childhood days of Pop Warner football.

"Oh snap. I almost forgot." Keith's wrist flew up to his face.

"Forgot what?" Nikki asked, glad he finally changed the topic.

"I'm supposed to be at the radio station in twenty minutes. Can't believe we were talking that long."

"You mean how long you were talkin'." Nikki corrected, giggling afterwards.

"Real funny, sweetie. Look, I gotta bounce. I'll try and call you tonight if it's not too late. Promise you I will be at the doctor's office the day after tomorrow. I love you."

"You better be there…I love you, Keith, now go ahead and hang up."

"You first."

"Together on three." The rapper said. "One-two-thr-" Keith slowly hung up. No time to shower, the millionaire undressed himself, dabbed his armpit with deodorant and slid into a fresh outfit. "Who's gonna know?" he said out loud after his guilty conscious kicked in. Keith Osbourne grabbed his wallet from the slacks on the floor. His gaze circled the room assuring himself that he hadn't left anything behind. 'Room card!' he reminded himself. The rapper scooped the card from over top of the television and scrambled out the room. In a minute's time, the rapper had sprinted downstairs through the lob and into a yellow cab.

"Where are you headed sir?" the Arab's accent was thick.

"To the Hot 97 radio station."

Maybe I should have told Keith I quit my job the other day? Nikki pondered. I don't have to tell him shit. He ain't my daddy. If my feet hurt then I simply cannot work. Nikki repositioned herself on the sofa's cushion after the phone rang.

"Hey Boo? Miss me already?" her tone was sexy, assuming it were her lover.

"Everything okay over there, Nik?"

"Sorry Mitch…I thought you were-"

"Mister K.O.?" Mitch finished for her. "No its just me. My nose is coming along just fine, in case you're wondering."

"Nikki forced a giggle, "What can I do for you Mitch?"

"I need the number to wherever hotel Keith's staying in. Got some need to know info for him."

Nikki's brows shot to the center of her forehead as an uncomfortable feeling took her. "I thought his divorce situation was almost final?"

"It is but it ain't."

"It is but it ain't?" Nikki repeated, exposing her suspicion. She conveyed the number to the P.I. anyhow. "Wait a couple of hours before you call. He's at a local radio station doing interviews." The line went dead. "It's probably nothing." She mumbled to herself. Yet that funny feeling continued to dwell in the pit of stomach. Before long, Mitch's phone call had become a memory. Nikki walked into the kitchen for a bag of chips and a bottle of water. As she headed back into the living room the doorbell rang.

"Unh-unh!" Nikki snapped. Don't nobody know where I live so why is my bell going off?" "Who is it?"

“Pee-Wee’s floral service, mam.” The delivery boy’s tone was pleasant and inviting.

Her stare met the peephole. Instant smiles as the front door swung open.

“How ya doin’ mam? Are you Nichole Wallace?”

“Yes, yes I am.” Nikki could not stop blushing at the wave of roses that perfumed off a romantic scent. “There must be at least a hundred roses here?”

“Quite a few of them, mam. 20 dozens calculates to 240 long stems.”

It took the delivery man five minutes to heave the flowers into her living room. Nikki tipped him a dub and he was on his way. “Keith shouldn’t have?” she peeled the card from one of the vases and crashed on the sofa. The envelope landed on tha table as the card glided up to her face. It read ‘Surprised? It’s me, Shawnte’. I just wanted to say I’m sorry. Its been three months and I think it’s time we talk. Love always, your friend Shawnte’.’

Nikki stared at the card a few more times then tossed it to the coffee table. I’m just not in the mood for making up right now. Her gaze fell on the bag of potato chips. She suddenly lost her appetite. Thoughts of Shawnte’ and the night of her rape replayed in her head. There’s always some fuckin’ drama going on. I’m glad its finally out in the open now. Because I couldn’t take anymore lies and secrets. Nikki’s gaze floated to the ceiling. She begin talking to God.

Dear Heavenly father…I’m praying for my friend as well as myself. She has some issues that need working out. Perhaps you can work it out for her. Dear God, please protect her from harm’s way and deliver her the strength she needs to be a better person…Amen…oh, and protect me too Lord. In your name, Amen.

CHAPTER 27

Mitch Holley located the CEO's mansion after professing to be a reporter when he approached some kids in Bankhead. Once he told them he was a journalist for Vibe magazine they didn't hesitate to point him down National Highway. The P.I. rented a black Corvette. He wanted to blend in the upscale community without incident.

Now he parked across the street from Psycho's mansion. There was no doubt it was the right estate. At the foot of the landscape was a bronze statue with of a man with a long butcher's knife drawn back. Underneath was an engravement that read 'Psycho's Place'. Plus the red Mercedes Sheila drove around town. Stood out over the average luxury car that resided in the driveway. Mitch Holley wanted to storm in the mansion upon arrival. The three vehicles on the property told him that Sheila had company. The P.I. had no choice but to patiently wait out whomever drove those rides. She's probably in there fucking Psycho's cousin or father. Mitch Holley chuckled at the thought. He flipped through the telephone book in search of a private doctor's office that performed their own lab work. His attention shot to the men that stood in the doorway. Finally leaving? His mini binoculars flew up to his face. The P.I. focused in on the two gentlemen as they jumped into their whips.

"Oh shit! That's Crazy Thumb and D.C. Snipes." Crazy Thumb and D.C. Snipes were Psycho's top selling artist. They were probably in there puttin' something down on wax? He guessed, assuming there were a studio somewhere in the mansion.

Once the Porche and Impala merked off into the street Mitch Holley slid down into his seat. Slowly he erected after the revving sound of the engines faded off. The P.I.'s gaze fell to his watch. It read; 8:15pm. The sun had started to settle behind the horizon. Mitch Holley had to make a move. Once darkness swallowed the sky there was no question in the P.I.'s mind that it would be almost impossible to get onto the property because that's when most rich folks security systems automatically armed themselves. One car remain in the driveway, Mitch Holley had no choice but to take that chance.

"It's now or never." He mumbled, riling himself up. The P.I. whipped out a Deringer pistol and checked the barrels to make sure there were two rounds inside. Thoughts of slipping past airport security undetected crawled through his head. Lucky for them stupid bastards I ain't no terrorist. Mitch ripped out a page from the phone book. He folded the yellow page and tucked it away in his breast pocket. The yellow pages landed on the passenger seat as he leapt out of the sports car. The P.I. moved swiftly onto Psycho's estate unnoticed.

Sheila Osbourne escorted Crazy Thumb and D.C. Snipes to the front door. The two rappers hung around pretending to be checking up on their boss's ex-wife. The multi-platinum selling artist had routinely ran trains on her twice a week. At Sheila's request, sometimes D.C. Snipes would bring other females along to join their private porn show. On occasions, Sheila Osbourne would give the rappers demonstrations on how to eat pussy and deep throat their protein deposits. Sheila hadn't expected thunder over until later on that night. Incidentally, the stripper showed up much earlier than expected. Now he were trying to wait out his brother's artist. They never suspected each other to be sexing the hostess.

"Come back in a few hours," Sheila whispered, "And bring me a nice lookin' bitch this time." She palmed Crazy thumb's ass he stepped out of the front door. "What was that all about?" Thunder growled after the doors swung shut.

"It's about money,why?" Sheila spun around afterward.

"You squeeze every rich nigga's ass fa money?"

Sheila Osbourne appeared to be giving his concern serious thought. "Not every rich nigga!" Her gaze climbed to the middle of the steps where thunder stood.

"You're evident of that."

The stripper's eyes tightened, yet he remained calm. He wanted what he had come for, and that was to taste Sheila's guilty pleasures. Thunder followed her upstairs into the bedroom. "Close the door!" Sheila commanded, he obliged. "Now take off your clothes." Her tone was aggressive and authoritative.

"I love it when you talk to me like that."

“Shut-the-fuck up, nigga.” Sheila’s bark echoed across the room.

“But….”

Sheila’s index finger flew up instantly cutting him off. “BUTT……is what you’ll be eatin’ out tonight.” Her sundress seductively slid down her body emphasizing every inch of his passive demeanor. “You used to be the shit…..Look at’chu! I turned you into my stripper bitch.” Sheila’s firm breast hypnotized Thunder as she sashayed over to him. Her dreamy eyes climbed down Thunder’s naked frame. She constricted his limpness and massaged it until it stiffened. “You like that?” Thunder nodded as he grasp for air that suddenly got thick. Sheila Osbourne dropped to her knees, her eyes still on his. Her tongue slid off her lips. Gently, she licked him around his chocolate head. Sheila’s seductive stare changed all of a sudden. “Nigga!” Her fingers released his pulsating dick. “How many times I toldju’ about them musty-ass-balls? Get’cho funky smellin’ ass in the shower.” Sheila’s finger extended out to the bathroom door. “You would’ve climbed ya stinkin’ self in my bed if I had’nt noticed, would’ntchu?” No response from Thunder. He quick-stepped behind the bathroom door and turned on the shower. “What a bitch!” She laughed wickedly at his manhood, “I really got this sucka trained.” Sheila walked over to the PC and armed the hidden cameras as she always did.

Thunder, Crazy thumb, and D.C. snipes had no idea Sheila Osbourne recorded every sexual episode. There was no doubt in her mind that Psycho’s artist would be on top of the music charts again. Sheila wanted a piece of all the pies. With these sessions recorded on compact disc, blackmailing the three was inevitable. Sheila Osbourne froze after spotting a man standing under her bedroom doorway.

Mitch Holley lightly tapped on the door hoping no one would respond. His eyes shot back to the street to see if anyone were watching his moves. Something told the P.I. that he should inform Keith Osbourne of his business in Atlanta just in case he got caught snooping. So he whipped his cellphone from his pocket and dialed up Nichole Wallace. He knew that Nikki would be able to locate the rapper’s whereabouts. As Nikki recited the number to the New York City Hotel Mitch unconsciously wrapped his hand around the door handle to find the front door unlocked. After the P.I. hung up with Nikki he looked over the driveway and slid inside. “Whoa this is nice.” He whispered, immediately overhearing a set of voices from upstairs. His gaze floated over the quiet scenery. This place is like MTV Cribs Live up in here. The P.I. arrived to the foot of the staircase and stopped to dial Keith Osbourne’s hotel room. No answer! He left a message on his answering service.

The cellular landed in his back pocket as he tippy-toed up the stairs. Mitch Holley followed the voices to the master bedroom. His ears pressed against the door, he could hear Sheila Osbourne and her acquaintance on the other side. Once he realized thunder was in the room he drew his two shooter. The P.I. waited for the shower to ignite before he walked in. The door slowly crept open, his stare circled the huge bedroom and settled on Sheila who sat in front of her Apple computer.

Mitch Holley stepped into the bedroom just enough to draw Sheila's attention. It worked! The look on her mug told him she had been startled by his presence. "Heyyy….What?" I know you from somewhere….and how did you get in here?"

Sheila's arms flew over her bosoms as she recoiled from the desk. "I recognize you….you're that mover guy." Mitch Holley hurried across the bedroom, his focus cut on the bathroom door. "Sure am."

"No you're that God damn Private Investigator." The P.I.'s hand arrived to her throat the other held a handful of hair. "Sorry to interrupt you're AIDS spreading convention but uh….we got some business to attend to."

"What do you want from me?"

"Just shut up, trick. I'm asking the questions here, already." Mitch shoved Keith's wife to the hardwood floor. "I didn't come here to shit around, you hear me. So hurry up and get dressed."

"If I were you I'd leave. My boyfriend's in the shower so don't try nothing."

"Don't you mean your brother –in-law, thunder?" Yeah right!" Mitch chuckled sarcastically.

"I'll give you whatever you want….money….pussy…..whatever you want."

"This isn't about money and I wouldn't fuck you with Satan's dick, honey."

"Well what do you want ?" Her dreamy eyes didn't work on the P.I.

"Look you nasty excuse of a whore…..I got reason to believe that you have contracted AIDS."

"And why would you think something like that?" Sheila Osbourne stared at Mitch Holley as if he just insulted her. "oooohhhh! I know, Keith has AIDS, doesn't he?"

Mitch's stare shot to the bathroom door momentarily, "Keith Osbourne does not have AIDS…..Psycho does ….." Sheila climbed to her feet, looking baffled. "Get dressed now! If Thunder comes out that bathroom and we're still here, I'ma have to explain to him why, trust me…..you don't want that." Sheila asked Mitch Holley to turn around while she slipped into her dress.

Mitch Holley stepped out of the room and waited. Moments later the P.I. was carrying Kayla, who was fast asleep, out the front door and into Sheila's Mercedes Benz. Mitch pulled the yellow page from his pocket and instructed Sheila Osbourne to drive there. She gave him a cold stare as the coupe shifted gears. When thunder exited the bathroom Sheila Osbourne was half way to the city.

The doctor's office was located in Fulton County. Doctor Leofwols had just armed his security system when the red Mercedes Benz turned into the parking lot. Leofwols was at the door of his Jaguar when the Private Investigator approached him.

"Excuse me. We come for emergency service."

"I only work by appointments, sorry." The doctor said, obviously in a hurry. "Besides, the emergency room is just a few miles that way," his arm extended down the hill. Mitch Holley whipped out $10,000 in cash and slapped it against the doctor's chest. "what's overtime costin' these days, Doc?"

"Oh why didn't you say cash was involved?" Leofwol's stare sailed over the parking lot for anything suspicious such as police. He snatched the money from Mitch's hand. "right this way Mister uh…?"

"Cash. Call me Cash." Mitch told him.

"Alright Mr. Cash follow me this way." The P.I. turned to Sheila and motioned for her to get out the car. He shook his fist at her after she hesitated. "I usually don't do same day results, but uh, for you Mr. cash, I'll make an exception."

For hours Sheila and the P.I. waited in the lounge while Doctor Leofwols processed her DNA. When he returned to the waiting room it were almost midnight. Leofwols didn't have to utter Sheila Osbourne's results, the frown on his face said it all. I'm sorry Mr. Cash.....your wife Mrs. Cash is indeed infected with the HIV virus. Her viral load doesn't look good."

"So it's not full blown AIDS?" Sheila chimed as tears formed in her eyes.

"No, not as of yet." Leofwols answered, "You can prolong the virus if you take the necessary prescriptions. Full blown AIDS isn't far along….YOU WILL DIE!" Doctor Leofwols handed Sheila a written prescription and his business card. "Make an appointment with my receptionist. You have no refills on that so make sure you pay me a visit soon." Sheila nodded. The Doctor escorted them outside into the parking lot. Mitch totted Kayla as Sheila Osbourne ran to her car in tears. "I'm sorry once again." Leofwols frowned. "I know how difficult this is for you and her." The doctor walked off.

The P.I. wanted to smack Sheila around just a few hours ago; now he found himself feeling sorry for her. Mitch Holley wanted to utter something uplifting but couldn't find the right words. Instead he said nothing the entire drive back to Psycho's place. Keith's wife's cries didn't let up. The sniffles and wincing started to effect Mitch. His eyes begin to water as thoughts of Keith Osbourne and Nichole Wallace's funeral services played out in his mind. After a while, the P.I. fell out of his daze realizing he were in front of Psycho's estate.

"I believe that's your ride." Sheila's tone was painted with bitterness. Mitch climbed out the coupe feeling like he should say something comforting to her. As he started to utter the words Sheila cut him off. Her voice lowered to a grim whisper. "If I'ma die.....at least. I'm not going by myself, am I?" A sarcastic grin perched in the corner of her mouth as she sped up into the driveway. Mitch Holley stood in the middle of the street, shocked. As much as he wanted to disagree with her, he couldn't. That bitch really is the devil!

CHAPTER 28

The outfit Mont copped for MC K.O. was nice but his cousin's looked much better. And Keith Osbourne wasn't about to be out fashioned by his hypeman. He woke up around noon and bounced down to Harlem. His first stop was Jimmy Jazz Clothing Store. He browsed through the designer wears until this ENYCE outfit caught his attention. The millionaire purchase the cream velour jumpsuit along with a pair of butter flavored S Dot Carters. The rapper's next stop was to pay his main man, Jacob, a visit.

Now he sat in the back of the store contemplating what type of engagement ring he were going to purchase. As Jacob attended to some out of towners Keith Osbourne's mind begin to drift. He pictured himself at the alter along side Nichole. The wedding took place in a park adorned with Botanical flowers and white roses that formed a vined aisle up to the bride and groom. The beautiful thought brought warmth to the rapper. He broke out his daze and focused on the diamonds that lay on a velvet cloth in front of him. A horrifying thought struck him from behind. What if Nikki says no?"She is on the stubborn side. The rapper whipped out his wireless and dialed 757 pound -1.

Nikki answered on first ring.

"Tell me you love me, Nikki" he asked before she could utter a greeting.

"I do love you."She said, sensing something bothering him. "Is everything okay? You sound kinda distant."

"I'm good. Really…I'm in love that's all."

Nikki chuckled, "hope it's with me."

“Of course it is. I love you more than anything.”

“Anything.”

Silence for a few seconds. “Yeah, that’s right! More than anything. That may change once our little boy is born. Love, I can’t talk long, just wanted to hear your voice in my ear. Wel....gotta go. I love you, Nichole.” Keith hung up.

His eyes fixed on the sparkling stones once more. A man dressed in an all black Armani suit and bronze skin caught his attention when he stepped in the office. Mr. Armani approached with his hands clasped behind his back. “So, my friend, what do you’z think about de stones?” Keith Osbourne’s head shook slightly. “You don’t like?”

“No it’s not that. They’re beautiful....Jacob, every last one of these diamonds are absolutely breathtaking.”

“I’m sure, Nichole is her name, correct?” the rapper nodded, “I’m sure that Nichole will love dese’ stones, my friend. “The jeweler picked up one of the 10 carat rings. “It has K-color with I-2 clarity. Fits perfectly.”

“It’s alright. I kinda was leaning toward this stone here. It has VS-2 clarity with H-color cut. But this diamond over here, “this diamond is SI-1 with J-color and the cut is excellent. Look at the way it blings under the dim lighting.” “Careful my friend, you could get frostbitten by a piece of ice that size.”

Laughs. Silence swept through soon after. Jacob fixed his stare on MC. K.O.’s I’m very impressed that you know your stones the way you do.” The jeweler turned and paced to the window. His eyes fixed on his brother as he attended to a customer. “Over the years you must’ve spent at least three mill tickets with me.”

“I was thinking more like four million, but who’s countin?”Keith shrugged drawing a light chuckle from Jacob.

“Yes, your pro’bly right. Over the years we’ve become very good friends,”his finger shot up in dramatic fashion. “That Sheila, I never liked her. As goes for that Psycho fellow. He always resold his jewelry back to us. You know, I no like that.” The jeweler turned around and walked toward Keith Osbourne, his fingers now positioned behind him. “I don’t know much about dese’ Nichole girl but she is the one for you. I see it in your eyes, the way you gaze upon those stones as if it were her, tells me a lot. My friend, zat ring.”

“This one here?”

“Yes, zat one. It’s yours, Good luck and God Bless.”

“Jake, this ring must we worth at least a half million?”

“750,000 thousand.” The jeweler offered.

“I can’t take this without giving you something.”

“You’ve given me enough. Your friendship to me is priceless.”

“Let me at least throw you $250,000 at least.”

Jacob spun away from Keith so he wouldn’t notice his grin. “If you insist.” The jeweler cleared his throat, “How will you be paying for zhis?”

“I’ll transfer the scrilla to your account soon as I get back to the hotel.” Keith’s gaze fell on his watch. It read thirteen until seven. “Holy shiiii.”

“What’s wrong?”

“I have to go. The concert starts at eight. Can’t believe I allowed myself to slip like that. Alfred’s gonna cuss me out for sure.”Jacob had the ring placed in a platinum barer before letting the millionaire leave with it.

“Thanks Jake.”

As MC. K.O. dashed out of the store the jeweler uttered, “No, thank you.” By the time Keith Osbourne flagged down a cab it was 7:02pm. “Hey, its MC. K.O.” the cabbie shouted out of his window into the traffic. “Hey you all, MC K.O. is in my cab. Can you believe it.?” “Calm down, yo.” The rapper demanded the young Arab driver.” Please, I’m in a hurry.” MC K.O. ?” the driver asked, trying to suppress his excitement.

“To the Westside highway.”

20 minutes later the rapper arrived to his hotel. He handed the cabbie an autographed napkin as he requested then darted out the back door. Just as the cab started to peel off Keith Osbourne stopped in his tracks and spun around.”Stttoooopp! Yo” the driver slammed on his brakes as Keith ran toward his cab. The back door flew open once more. “Almost forgot. “He let out a deep sigh as he scooped the engagement ring off the back seat. “Look, here’s another fifty. If I’m not back here when that runs out then leave.” MC K.O. didn’t wait for a response. He took off running into the hotel lobby.

His watch read 7:27 when he stormed in the room. On the bed was a note from Alfred. The millionaire spotted it immediately. It read: get your site seeing ass to the Gardens, ASAP!

Keith Osbourne dropped the note on the bed after being distracted by a blinking light. He ignored the red light flashing on the telephone. Got no time to be checking messages. Pro’bly that damn Alfred whining like always, he guessed. It took him 8 minutes to shower and climb into his concert wear. The red flash caught his attention once more. Wonder if it’s Nichole? I don’t have time. Besides, I just talked with her a little while ago. He contemplated as the room door closed behind him. Like an Olympic track star, the rapper jetted down the stairs leaping every other step with the railing as his support. Keith managed to arrive at the lobby in a minute's time. The cab remained parked where he last saw it. The rapped climbed in the front seat this time.

"I got twenty minutes to get to Madison Square Garden." Another hundred dollar bill landed on the cabbie's lap.

"I get you there in ten, my friend."

"Hey Nichole." Mitch Holley said, trying to disguise his depressing mood.

"Have you spoke to Keith today?"

"Briefly, why?"

"I've been calling him since last night. He hasn't returned any of my calls yet."

"Right now he's pro'bly in the middle of a concert. He's performing at the Madison Square Garden." The P.I. pondered catching a flight to the Big Apple. "I'm so happy that it's his final concert. Tomorrow we can finally spend some quality time together."

"If that's true I'd be wasting my frequent flyer miles. I'll just leave a message on his voice box. "Are you sure he's coming home tomorrow?"

"Of course he is. We have an appointment with the doctor tomorrow. He's meeting me at the doctor's office at three."

"Well, if you hear from him before I do, tell'em to holla at 'cha boy, already!"

Nikki hung up, giggling. If she knew what I knew she wouldn't be so jolly. The grim thought made the P.I. sick. He sat on the couch with a beer in hand. The can was open but he hadn't taken one sip. He began considering Keith Osbourne's reaction once he broke the bad news to him. He finally fathers a child…now the unborn is going to enter this world infected with the virus. "It just isn't right." Mitch cried out, hurling his beer across the room and into the wall. He closed his eyes weeping himself to sleep, only to be awaken by his chirping phone. "Hello." The P.I. slurred into the phone.

"Hi Mitchy bear, this is Katie. I was wondering if I could stop by."

"Not tonight. Ain't in the mood honey." He answered, anxious to hang up.

"I gotta friend, her name is Vivian." Silence.

Threesome? That's just what I need, he contemplated. Could use an extra hand to beat me off.

"Tell you what, you and your girlfriend come on over to Big Poppa's and bring maggy along, ain't try'na make no babies." Laughs.

MC K.O. put on his best performance of the tour. Novocaine stormed the stage in the middle of the show and ripped the microphone from Mont's hand. MC K.O.'s teeth grinded together as security rushed the stage to hold mint and himself from clashing with Novocaine and his clan. The arena fell silent. Moments later the DJ dropped the instrumental to the Richmond native platinum hit song 'In Ya Veins'. The crowd went wild.

Halfway through the song the beat stopped. The disk jockey then dropped the 'All Out' instrumental. The crowd erupted with more cheers. The high fives between the two rappers assured the concert goers that the entire incident was rehearsed.

Usually Keith Osbourne didn't go to after parties, but tonight he was feeling real good about the outcome of his tour, so he attended at Novocaine's request. This ain't bad, the rapper told himself as he surveyed the party goers. He turned to Novocaine. "So this is what the club's VIP section looks like these days?"

"Long as there's plenty uh bitches around, I don't care what the VIP look like." Novocaine said, emphasizing his southern accent.

"I heard that playa." Keith Osbourne's gaze surfed over the wave of New Yorkers that occupied the dance floor.

Novocaine cuffed the Moet bottle and did the same. "Whuuuuu Weeee!: the rapper whistled over the music, nudging MC K.O.'s shoulder. "Look at the salt on that shaker. Boy she phatter than grandma's blueberry muffin. She phatter than a Tyson's Turkey with stuffing. Whuuu Weee! She phat shawdy! I got to get me some city thighs. Baked, fried, extra crispy, don' matter long as I get the booty." Novocaine shot up from the table and scrambled through the crowd to some groupies that were giving him the eye. Keith fixed his stare on the three young ladies the Richmond rapper was spilling wine all over. One of the females excused herself from his acquaintances and sashayed over to his table. Her smile was warm and innocent.

"Can I sit down?" MC K.O. shrugged, "Hi, my name is Tommie."

"Hello Tommie." The rapper's hand extended out to hers. Keith tried his best to brush her off, but somehow he found her conversation more than entertaining. Forty minutes later, the rapper did the unthinkable. He escorted Tommie up to his suite. It was the millionaire's first experience to a weak moment.

(THE NEXT MORNING)

10:43 AM

Keith perched on the edge of the bed massaging his temple. For the last 15 minutes he scolded himself for cheating on his girl. Can't believe I invited a stranger to my room. "What was I thinking?" he snapped, rising from the bed. His naked frame moved across the room toward the bathroom. He stopped after his reflection from the mirror caught his attention. The rapper stared at the man in front of him with disgust. His palms parked on his waist as he gazed over his chocolate torso. "I hope you're happy with yourself playa." Keith growled at his reflection. "How could you do that to Nichole? On top of that…you let that bitch rob you fuckin' blind." The rapper broke away from the mirror. "Hi my name is Tommie." He mocked the groupie's voice. As he stepped into the shower. The phone went off. "Leave a message…Keith Osbourne is feeling like a played out sucka at the moment."

While the jet stream shower misted over the rapper he leveled himself against the marble wall with his palms. For thirty minutes he stood in the same position as he collected himself. He'd come to put last night behind him, forever. "I'm rich! Whaddu I care about gettin' jacked?" he scooped the complimentary soap and cloth and went to work.

Once Keith Osbourne stepped out of the tub the telephone rang again. Something told him to answer so he quick-stepped over to the bed and picked up the receiver. Dial tone! At least she left a message, he guessed, assuming it was Nikki calling to remind him about the three o'clock appointment at the doctor's office. Keith punched in the suite's number and access code to listen to his messages.

You have 17 messages. A computerized voice offered. He pressed three to hear first voice mail.

'This is Mitch Holley. I'm in ATL. Call at-'

What's Mitch doing in Atlanta? Keith asked himself, skipping to the next message.

'This is Mitch again. It's important that you get at me.'

The next 14 voice mails belonged to the private investigator. "What the hell is going on with him?" the rapper mumbled to himself.

Message 16:

'Hey baby. I just called you to say I love you and can't wait to see you later on at the doctor's office. I'ma be in the parking lot waiting on you. I want us to go in there together. I love you.'

As message 17 began to play he rushed over to the Gucci suitcase nearly ripping the zipper off track. A sigh of relief followed after confirming his one night stand hadn't lifted the diamond ring. Whew! Scared me for a second. With the platinum case in hand the rapper strode to the other side of the bed to check his final message. His eyes stared intently on the ice cold stone as the voice message played in his ear.

'I guess your private eye friend had already told 'ju, huh?'

Keith's stomach flipped backwards upon hearing Sheila's chilling voice. 'Looks like we both lose. Ha ha ha hah ha!'

What the hell is she talking about? And how'd she get this number here? All MC K.O. was sure of was, that wicked laugh of hers really bothered him. Whatever she's referring to, I'm sure Mitch will know. Keith Osbourne hung up and dialed Mitch Holley's cellular.

Just as he got an answer, loud knocks echoed off the door. "Yo, K, you ready?" Mont yelled from the other side.

The millionaire's palm octupused the horn. "Yeah, gimme a second." His hand slid from the phone. "Mitch, it's Keith, what's up?"

"I'm sorry. This is the front desk. All phones automatically transfer calls here after eleven, sir. Its twenty-five minutes after."

Keith Osbourne slammed the jack on the hook and dashed to the door with only a towel wrapped around him.

"Damn cuz! The limo's outside waitin' on us." Mont said. "And why does your room smell like pussy, balls, and cheap soap?"

Keith Osbourne ignored his humor. "My bad, Gee. Misplaced my watch last night and lost track of time."

Mont saw right through him. "It's okay man. I've been got a few times myself. Part of life, ya win some, ya lose some."

A sigh of relief overtook the rapper. "Can you gather my belongings while I get dressed?"

Mont didn't respond, he just rounded up the millionaire's wardrobe and forced them into the shopping bags and suit cases.

Minutes later they were in the elevator. The shaft was halfway to the lobby when Mont's stare cut at his cousin.

"So, how much did she jack you for?"

"You don' wanna know."

“Yes I do.” Mont shot back, grinning from ear to ear. “Maybe I wont feel so bad once you tell me you got robbed of more valuables than I did.”

“One thing for sure that trick didn’t get this.” Keith Osbourne whipped a huge diamond ring out of his pocket.

His cousin’s eyes lit up.”Now that’s, whoa! It’s for Nikki, ain’t it?”

“No doubt!”

Mont’s eyes widened as he produced a ring from his coat. “You ain’t the only one making moves.”

“You and Stacy?” the rapper asked, disguising his feelings.

“Yeah, she asked me yesterday. So I took the liberty of copping this joint early this morning.:

“That’s, that is beautiful, man.” Keith forced a smile afterward. He couldn’t fathom his cousin marrying anyone, especially his best friend’s ex. The negro has surely lost his mind, Keith Osbourne pondered as they met up with Alfred and the rest of the crew in front of the Escalade limos. They arrived at Newark International Airport around 1:30 where the Salt Water Boys private jet awaited them. By 2 o’clock the G-4 was gliding south through the clouds. Destination: Norfolk International.

CHAPTER 29

"You got five minutes Mister Osbourne." Nikki huffed, as her stare leveled with the clock over the dashboard. She cuffed her purse and scanned the parking lot of the doctor's office after a dreadful thought crept up behind her.

Maybe his jet crashed somewhere in the ocean. Maybe he was in an automobile accident. He's probably getting a speeding ticket right at this very moment. Nikki reached for her cell phone and dialed his number. Her gaze settled on the clock once more. It read 2:59pm. "Hey Keith, where are you? If you Miss this appointment then you better be dead cause I'ma kill you." The message ended. "Shit!" frustration overtook her. "Where the hell is he?" Nikki grabbed her insurance card from over the visor, opened her door and carefully stepped down from the SUV. She spotted her facial expression off the window's reflection as she locked the door. A disgusted woman who appeared to be tired and worn stared back at her. Nikki stepped back just enough to observe the dirty vehicle shed been taxing around the past few months. Nichole Wallace, get it together girl. Her eyes glided over the parking lot and fixed on the entrance, hoping Keith Osbourne would turn inside at any second, he didn't! She shrugged and started across the lot towards the private M.D.'s entrance.

11 MINUTES EARLIER...

Keith Osbourne's jet landed where his Bentley waited unmolested for him.

"Alfred, Mont, I need you to gather my belongings to take to my place." He tossed the road manager the keys to his mansion. Once the aircraft's exit descended the rapper leapt down the small flight of steps and made a dash for his ride. He peeled off the terminal without saying goodbye. As he arrived to Military Highway his wrist flew up to his face. The millionaire sucked his teeth afterwards. It occurred to him that his Jacob & Co. wristwatch had been donated to the 'trick uh ho' fund. As the Bentley coasted I-64, Sheila's message began replaying in his head. Without hesitation, he dialed Betty Mae's number. Kayla answered on the second ring.

"Hello there?" Keith greeted, forcing an uplifting tone after realizing his step-daughter was on the other end. "Is mommy there?"

"Hol' on please." The little girl replied. The line fell silent.

He hit the brakes after spotting a trooper's vehicle parked in between some trees. His stare shot on the cruiser as he drove by, hoping the trooper hadn't clocked him. He's on his lunch break. A sigh of relief. As the luxury sedan started to accelerate a voice spoke on the other end.

"Yeah, who's this?" The bitterness in the woman's tone confirmed that the rapper's ex-wife was on the line.

"Hello Sheila, its me Keith. I got your message and I-"

Sheila growled at Keith. "And what?"

Keith Osbourne took a deep breath. "And I just wanted to know exactly what do you mean by it?"

Sheila huffed into the receiver, "Just what I said."

"I'm not following-"

Sheila cut him off, "Die muthafucka! Die!"

The dial tone hummed in his ear soon after. That woman has some serious issues. The cell phone landed in the passenger seat. I'm about to get married and have a baby, he assured himself, pulling the engagement ring from his pocket. I don' got no time for her animosity. With the rapper's attention focused on the highway he flipped open the platinum case and held it over the steering wheel. She's going to love this. The Bentley switched into the exit lane after spotting the Greenbrier exit. Keith Osbourne was just three blocks from the doctor's office when his cell phone went off. "Chill love, I'm just a few lights away."

"It's Mitch kiddo."

"Thought 'chu were-"

"Don' sweat it man." Mitch's tone filled with urgency. "Keith, I've been trying to call you for a couple of days."

"I know, Gee. Been ripping and running with the tour and all."

"Yeah Nichole told me." The P.I.'s voice lowered to a somber whisper. "I got some bad news, kiddo."

"Does it have something to do with you in Atlanta? Because I just spoke to Sheila at her mother's to ask about a disturbing message she left in my voice mail. The bitch hung up in my ear." Now the millionaire was just a half block away from the M.D.'s private practice. He waited for the traffic signal to turn green.

"It has a lot to do with my trip to Atlanta." Mitch Holley fell silent.

"Mitch?"

"I'm still here." Silence as the P.I. took a deep breath.

"Mitch, what the hell is going on?" Keith Osbourne felt that uncomfortable chill swarm him again.

"Sheila...she...uh-"

"What about 'er?"

"She has AIDS Keith. Sheila is infected with the HIV virus."

The traffic signal turned green. The Bentley slowly rolled forward. The doctor's office soon fell into view. Keith Osbourne couldn't allow himself to turn into the parking lot. He spotted Nikki's Cherokee, then her as she stepped into the one story sandstone unit. The luxury sedan sailed past and stopped at the next light.

"How can you be so sure?" Keith asked, swallowing hard afterward.

"She is infected...I personally had her checked. Sorry man."

Beads of sweat formed over the rapper's forehead.

Green light.

He veered into a shopping plaza , nearly sliding into the rear of an old Plymouth. "Meet me at my place in twenty minutes." The millionaire demanded. "And bring me some facts." Mist filled his eyes as thoughts of a picture perfect family diminished before him.

"Nichole Wallace?" the receptionist called out. Nikki walked over to the woman who'd been admiring the new design on her nails the entire wait. "Yes, I'm Nichole Wallace." She answered, knowing the clerk already knew.

"Doctor Pierre is ready to see you now."

Nikki strode through the double doors where the M.D. met her. "Here's the videos and photo copies you requested." He handed Nikki a laser disk and some photos and suggested that she pay him a visit in three weeks.

"Thanks Doctor Pierre."

"Thank you Miss Wallace. And remember what I said. A little sex is good for-"

"My pregnancy." Nikki finished. "Thank you again Doc."

Dr. Pierre nodded and escorted her back into the waiting area. After she walked through the exit he informed the receptionist to send his next patient.

Nikki was well aware of the many obstacles an artist such as MC K.O. probably had to face on a daily basis. That didn't stop her from being upset. She told herself whatever excuse Keith uttered would not be good enough for her. Nikki cranked the engine, then the air conditioner, hoping to cool off her temper. It worked! Happy thoughts arrived.

I can't believe it. I'm having a baby boy. Keith is going to be so excited when I tell him. A smile formed on her face as she pictured herself breaking the news to him.

"He's going to be so happy." She sang out loud, merging into traffic. Gotta call him again. She scooped up her wireless without taking her eye from the car in front of her. He better answer!

'Yo this is Keith-'

Nikki hung up on his voice mail and dialed the rapper's home number. Keith answered on the second ring.

"Yeah."

"Keith? What's wrong? Why are you sounding like that? And why-"

"I'm good." He chimed, trying to prevent his voice from cracking. Nikki sensed trouble. She was starting to get that feeling again. Her instincts told her to drive over to her man's place. "I'm on my way over there, okay?"

"No! It's-not-okay."

Nikki's cellular shot to the front of her face. She stared at it momentarily before placing it back to her ear. "My phone actin' up. Sounded like you said-"

Keith Osbourne cut her off again. "You heard me correct." His whisper was barely audible.

"What 'chu mean it's not okay?"

"I'm just not ready for your company right now. I can't explain it but-"

"Keith, I don' understand."

The millionaire forced an exaggerated sigh. “Look, something’s come up.” His tone elevated with every word. “And I don’t need you around me right now.”

“Don’t chu at least wanna know if you’re having a boy or girl?”

Silence.

Keith was trying his hardest not to choke up but the tears had started to flow. He wanted to say those three special words of love to Nikki and tell her that he already knew it was a boy because that’s what he’d prayed for all these years. He could not come to utter a single word. How could he tell Nikki he loved her so dear then inform her that she contracted the HIV virus from him. “Boy…girl…don’ matter. A baby’s a baby, nahh uh mean?” the rapper was shocked by his own words.

“No Keith, I don’t know what you mean!” Nikki could not believe his cold heartedness. Never had he spoke to her with that kind of tongue. “What’s gotten into you?” She burst into tears.

“What….you and your bitch of a wife getting back together, is that it?” Nikki’s cry had begun to distort her words.

“Is this what it’s all about?”

Keith Osbourne didn’t respond.

“You know what...You’s a fake ass nigga. “You know that?” Nikki broke down and cried into the phone.

Tears ran down the rapper’s face as well. He quickly collected himself, drying his eyes. “Look Nichole I…uh, I gotta go.” Before Nikki could ask why the line went dead. She sat behind the wheel listening to the dial tone, shocked. The Cherokee made a U- turn after she regained her composure. I hate chu’ Keith Osbourne!

Mitch Holley turned the door handle after knocking to find the entryway to Keith Osbourne’s mansion unlocked. His gaze drifted over the dust covered furniture before ascending the stairwell. Too quiet! Hope he hasn’t done anything stupid. The P.I. yelled out the rapper’s name. No answer. He darted upstairs searching every room. “Where are you man?” He screamed as thoughts of finding his lifeless body crawled into his head. He jetted back to the first floor, a heat flash swarmed him as he stepped through the game room for the pool area. The glass door slid back, Mitch Holley stepped through it. His stare darted over the small swells in the water to find Keith Osbourne perched on the edge of the pool with his feet dangling inside. The P.I.’s hands flew up in grief as the rapper stared blankly into space.

"Hey man, why didn't you answer me when I called out for you? You had me shittin' in my pants already." Keith snapped out of his daze after Mitch's anger echoed of the walls. His eyes followed the moving reflection on the water until Mitch Holley came into view. His head shot sideways, "Whudda thought I was gonna do….kill myself?" Mitch looked him off, scratching the back of his head, "yeah…I did to be honest."

The rapper chuckled, "I can't go out like that, Gee. A brother try'na go to heaven. Damn sure can't make there by way of suicide."

"Where'd you hear something foolish like that?"

"From James Van Praagh's book Messages from the Heavens."

The P.I. shrugged, "Whatever! Here are the documents you requested." Mitch walked to the other side of the pool and placed the folder in Keith's hand. The rapper shuffled through them, skimming here and there.

"I see…unh hunh." He mumbled as he studied the final page on Psycho and his wife. "They definitely got the Ninja."

"Ninja?" Mitch never heard that before.

"Means one has AIDS."

" I know what it means. Just never heard that terminology. I heard people use words such as 'That Thang' or 'The Bug' and 'The Midas Touch' but never 'The Ninja.' Keith Osbourne shrugged off his humor. His stare was still in the P.I. "How do I tell my mother that her only son is going to die of AIDS one day?" How do I explain to Nik.."

"Wait a minute." Mitch Holley chimed, "You don't know for sure that you're infected." The millionaire rolled his eyes and tossed the folder at Mitch's feet. "There's the evidence right there." "Alls I'm saying kiddo, is you gotta believe. Have a little faith. It's possible; it's very possible that you do not have it at all. Certain blood types have scientifically proven to reject the virus."

"Difficult but not impossible!" Keith Osbourne corrected, "And what if I do have it….then what?"

"I can't answer that kiddo, you know I can't. First thing we need to do is go see a doctor. I know one; he owes me a huge favor. He can have your results in a matter of hours, just as Sheila did."

"That's a good idea." He was still talking in a whisper, "but is your guy cool? Can't afford to have my personal business dragged through the media. I just can't, this is too personal, too humiliating."

Mitch Holley nodded, “We can trust this doctor. I promise you nothing will leak out of his office. He has the virus as well so I know he wouldn’t cross me, his situation isn’t exactly public information.” Keith climbed to his feet and walked over to the linen rack. He slid into a pair of socks and tennis shoes after drying his feet. His thoughts suddenly fell on Tommie, the groupie he had unprotected sex with last night. Thoughts of Nikki came barging in soon after. “You know I…I talked with Nichole minutes before you arrived.” His somberness told the P.I. that things didn’t go so well for him. “I was supposed to meet’er at the doctor’s office today.” Keith was drowning in his own tears. “ I said some things that I really didn’t mean. I didn’t know what else to say, she was on her way here. Had to say something. Couldn’t let her see me like this. She even tried telling me about our unborn but I continued to push her away.” Silence… I really wanted to know.”

“I know you did kiddo.” Mitch Holley’s arms landed around the rapper. That’s when Keith Osbourne let everything out. Everything that burdened his soul was being released through his cry. The anger, his fears, all his pain, anguish, and love came down in a herd of tears. “I-love-her-so-much. I don’t wanna lose her, Mitch.” The P.I.’s hug loosened. His stare leveled Keith’s. “No matter what your results turn out to be, you make sure that you stand strong…..as a man. And that you are there for Nichole and your child, no matter what. If you can’t be strong for the ones you love then you might as well lay it all the way down. Drown yourself right now, kiddo.” The look on Mitch’s face told the rapper that he meant every word.

“You’re right.” Keith Osbourne nodded, gathering himself afterwards. The two made way out the front door and into the P.I.’s Corvette. “Mitch, I don’ want my results today. I’d rather wait the three weeks it takes to process them.”

“Why?” Mitch asked as if it was the dumbest thing he ever heard. “Thought you needed to know as soon as possible?”

“I do wanna learn my fate, just not today. Negative…..Positive! I can’t bear to hear either of them right know.” Mitch shrugged, “but why?”

“Because I’m scared Mitch.” The millionaire confessed, his voice lowered to a whisper. “I’m scared! I need some time to build up courage within me. I wanna be strong for Nichole as well as myself. Right now…..I can’t be that. When I get me results back I will confront Nikki with the truth. We will learn them together.”

“So what do you plan on doin’ in the meantime, avoid her?”

“I’ma try my best.” The rapper shook his head in grief. The P.I. gave Keith Osbourne this funny look as he cranked the engine. They drove in silence the entire trip to Newport News.

Thirteen days had passed by and Nichole Wallace had been pushed over the edge. She called her Baby Daddy's phone only to receive the dial tone every time. When the rapper didn't answer Nikki would leave messages. Some were compromising while others expressed her bitterness and rage. One day she drove out to his estate and kicked on his front door.

"Go a-way!" Keith responded by intercom.

Nikki's temper soared beyond her imagination. She picked up one of the larger rocks that manicured the entryway and shot-put it through the front windshield of his Bentley. After Keith Osbourne refused to come outside and confront her she gathered some more stones and shattered ever piece of glass on the luxury vehicle. Still the results were the same. No Keith! Like a possessed maniac, she scooped a piece of the window from the driver's seat and ran the glass across his glossy paint job. Again and again and again.

The millionaire witnessed Nichole administer the damage to his ride. He wanted so badly to hold her in his arms but couldn't muster enough strength to open the front door. Instead he peeped through the living room window drowning in his own misery. Blood seeped from Nikki's palms as she slit the last of his tires. The angry woman disappeared soon after. Assuming Nikki's destructive temper has simmered, Keith sighed in relief. He was wrong!

Nikki returned threatening to burn his mansion down. The gasoline drum in her hand supported her loud bark. "I know you got another bitch up in there, nigga. But it's all good though 'cause you picked the right bitch to fuck wit! What…you thought I was Miss Community Pussy or something? You ain't gon' knock me up, tell me a bunch of lies, and then bounce to the next chick…oh hell-to-the-nawh!"

Before Nikki could utter another word police bum rushed her to the pavement. They soon discovered that the gasoline container was empty. They quickly recoiled upon learning that she was pregnant. A nosy neighbor witnessed Nikki's anger unravel and dialed 911. Keith Osbourne insisted that Nikki wasn't the perpetrator that damaged his vehicle and had no intentions of filing any charges against her. All the rapper asked was that they escorted her off the property.

Now Nichole Wallace lay across her bed staring blankly into the ceiling. The phone rang breaking her out the trance. "Hello?"

"Hey girl, it's me Shawnte'. Just called to let you know I was thinking about you and to say I Miss you like crazy."

Nikki tried to prevent her voice from cracking but found it difficult under the circumstances. Hearing Shawnte's voice was the best thing that happened in the past twenty days. "I miss you too, Shawnte'." she broke down into tears.

"Nikki, are you okay?"

Silence.

"Shawnte', I need you right now. I really do." Nikki collected herself before reciting directions to her apartment.

"I'm on my way. Everything is going to be okay. Gimme forty minutes."

Nikki hung up after Shawnte' did. Before long she dozed off into a light nap. The ringer woke her up, she answered, "Hello?"

"Look here bitch, stop calling my fuckin' crib. I don't want 'chi or ya raggedy ass pussy!"

"Keith, why are you talking to me like his?" Nikki cried out. "I love you."

"I love me too." The rapper said. "Call my house one more time and I'ma finish what Tony Gangsta couldn't."

"Don' hang up, please! I know we can work this out, Keith." Dial tone! Nikki screamed at the top of her lungs until she woke from her dream.

Enough of this! I can't take it anymore. She cuffed the phone as her gaze landed on the clock near the mirror which told her she had been snoozing over an hour. "Where is Shawnte'? She should've been here." She whispered as she dialed Keith's number. Nikki waited for his voice mail then left a message.

"Keith, it's me Nichole." She took a deep breath then sighed. "I don't know what's going on with you or how we got like this but I can't do this…I can't play this game of cat and mouse with you anymore. I just can't. I never felt for any man as I feel towards you. And I never had to stoop to such a drastic measure to prove it. I believed you when you said you would be by my side…forever. You're forever ain't worth shit! You hear me?" Nikki was crying all over again, yet she remained strong and determined to speak from the heart.

"What happened to 'trust me'? Member that? Trust me is what you said…now that I need you, I," Nikki paused, the doorbell echoed through her apartment. She sprung from the bed and quick-stepped to the front room to let Shawnte' in. Nikki concluded her message before opening the door. "I just wanted you to know that I've decided to get an abortion. That way we can both move on."

The line went dead. Nikki hung up as she reversed the bolt lock. The front door swung open in a hurry. Nikki's heart tumbled a hundred times over as her surprising stare leveled with Keith Osbourne's.

CHAPTER 30

The phone glided up to Keith's face. He hesitated before speaking into the receiver. It was the clerk from the doctor's 'office calling to inform him that his test results were back. After the rapper hung up he walked over to the mirror and gave himself a close observation. "Look at 'chu!" he huffed, staring upon the whiskers that grew haphazard on his chin and around his head. "You-look-like-shit, Mista Kay-yooh!" he tried looking away. He couldn't. In fact, the rapper refused to. I'm tired of running from love. Today…I'm going to get my woman back. The thought of Nichole drawing her pistol on him once she learned that the results were positive was a chance Keith Osbourne was willing to take.

The dressed drawer recoiled; he pulled the platinum barer out and gazed upon the platinum ring. Just staring at the stone uplifted him. A smile formed on Keith's face soon after.

ONE HOUR LATER

The millionaire had manicured himself from head to toe. It was fairly humid on that particular morning but that didn't stop the rapper from climbing into a dark-blue pinstriped suit. He stood in the mirror adjusting the cuff links on his sleeve. MC K.O. then surveyed himself one more time. This is definitely a good suit to get married in. His gaze followed the mirror down toward the dresser until it landed on the engagement ring. He found himself mesmerized by the many colors that glistened off it. Finally, he smothered the barer close, grabbed his keys and dropped the case in his hip pocket and walked out the front door.

Doctor Clark's Office-Newport News, V.A.

Doctor Clark escorted Keith Osbourne into his office where they both took a seat across from each other. The rapper's odd behavior told the physician that he was undoubtedly nervous.

"You're nervous, Mister Osbourne. Can't blame you, I felt the same way."

Beads of sweat formed over the top of his head. "I wasn't suggesting that you are…uh, you know. Because you test results are sealed just as you requested." His voice lowered. "If you are positive I recommend that you seek counseling. If your test results are negative, I recommend that you get tested every six months for the next five years. The virus may occur later on."

Keith loosened his tie from around his neck as perspiration seeped through his collar. "Is it me or is it hot as a mutha up in this piece?"

The doctor's cheek shrugged, "its 65 degrees in her Mr. Osbourne. I assure you, this current situation is the reason for the sudden hot flashes." Keith Osbourne swallowed hard then took a deep breath as Dr. Clark handed him the sealed document. "I see you're all dressed up. Is there a special event you're attending on this fine day?"

The millionaire nodded. "Yeah…there is." His whisper was barely audibly.

"I'm either attending a wedding or a funeral…it depends."

"Depends on what?" the physician was curious.

Keith Osbourne's stare floated down to the envelope in his hand. "Depends on these results."

Back to the present time…

Keith Osbourne stood helplessly under Nikki's entryway with his head hung. He hoped and prayed that every word uttered came out his mouth correctly. The cordless phone fell from Nikki's hand as she stared in awe.

"Nichole…I uh…I." the millionaire paused to clear his throat after fumbling his words. "I know things have not been the way they should … but…uh, I…uh, I'm here to make…I mean try and explain myself."

Nikki gathered herself in a hurry. "What's the matter? Wifey dump you again?"

The rapper cleared his throat, his voice elevated slightly. "It isn't about Sheila, never was. It was always about you and my love that is deeply rooted in me for you."

“Love doesn’t treat people like that!” Nikki shot back, “I needed you… but all you did was reject and neglect me, the mother of your first child. Tell me Keith, how is that love?”

“You’re right, Nichole, and I am a hundred and ten percent wrong. But right now, baby, I need you to hear me out just this once. I’m kinda in a hurry. There’s a wedding jumpin’ off at five o’clock. It’s already 4:15.” His fingers slid into his tuxedo pocket. An envelope was clutched in between his fingers. “It’s my HIV test results, open it.”

As Nikki peeled back the envelope’s flap Keith Osbourne began explaining to her the reason for his sudden behavior and how he wanted to learn of his fate with her, the woman he loved. Nikki stared upon the results as she took in her every word. Her eyes seemed to be transfixing on the bottom of the page. Her expression told the rapper nothing.

Keith Osbourne pulled out the platinum barer and opened it. The sparkling stone slowly ascended up toward Nikki. She hadn’t noticed the huge diamond ring–winking at her until Keith whispered her name. Nikki’s stare shot up. She appeared to be angry and engulfed with hatred until her stare met the twelve carat engagement ring. The lab results dropped to her side.

“Nichole Wallace, I love you. I want you to be my wife more than anything in this life.”

Nichole’s gaze floated on Keith Osbourne who nervously trembled. Her eyes then returned to the diamond ring that extended out to her. “Marry you hunh?” Keith Osbourne managed a smile over his face as Nikki’s dreamy eyes finally fell back on his. She wiped the tears from her cheeks and returned the gesture with a smile of her own. Thunder erupted. The front door shook the walls after it slammed in the rapper’s face. He simply turned around and walked away.

24 MONTHS LATER…

Nichole was sitting in church with Keith Jr. perched in her lap. Beside her was Keenan, her newborn daughter that Keith Osbourne cradled in his arms. She and the millionaire stood at the pastor’s request.

“I’d like to congratulate Mr. Osbourne and his wife, Nichole, on this fine and glorious day. They had just had their second child, a beautiful baby girl. Amen! And let the church say amen. And the church would also like to thank the Osbourne’s for their substantial contributions towards the church’s renovation fund. Amen…and amen…finally Pastor Thomas would like for you to explain to the church why he was the person to receive an invitation to your 2nd wedding anniversary party.”

The congregation broke out in laughs and applauded as the couple maneuvered the little ones in their arms to shake hands with members that sat beside them. Before long their gaze met each other's. In unison they whispered 'I love you'. Their lips met with desire and passion

24 MONTHS EARLIER...

After Nikki slammed the door in the rapper's face he started toward his car. It didn't take long for her to realize that she loved Keith with all her heart and soul. Nikki wasn't about to let love slip away so easily. Her front door swung open. "I love you too Keith."

The rapper stopped in his tracks and spun around to find the love of his life standing in the doorway. "Did you say somethin'?"

Nikki nodded. "Yes, yes I did. I said bring me that ring before somebody robs you."

Keith's face lit up with a smile. "Somebody like who?"

"Somebody like me!"

Shawnte' pulled up in a parking space in time to witness Keith and Nichole meet each other with a wet kiss. The millionaire recoiled from her and knelt down on one knee. His watery gaze floated up into Nichole's sparkling eyes.

"Nichole Wallace, will you marry me?"

"Yes, yes Keith, I will. I love you so much."

Before the millionaire could climb to his feet Shawnte' had run to Nikki and met her with a hug. As they spun each other around Keith Osbourne's tailor made suit sparked her curiosity. Her arms fell from Shawnte'.

"Keith, whose wedding were you going to anyway?" she asked.

The rapper's stare transfixed her. "Ours! He answered. "And Shawnte', you're invited." Their lips touched as if it was the first time in years. "But before we get married I have to introduce you to a very special person in my life. I want you to meet Arlene, my mother."

Nichole and Keith joined each other in union later that day. They continued to grow through friendship, desire, and honesty. Nichole Wallace quit her job and published a book about her traumatic life.....you just read it. My husband hooked up with Hectic and produced two successful albums. Not without scrutiny of course. His cousin, Mont and Stacy married not long after we did, which made him an instant millionaire. Mitch and Keith's mom moved into his estate....which didn't work out to well being that Mitch wanted to party with the young girls and Arlene only wanted to party with him.

Sheila, Psycho Johnson and his brother, Thunder all died of the AIDS virus. Crazy Thumb and D.C. Sniped lived on. They were smart enough to wear protection whenever the two tricked around. Everyday Keith and I continue to pray to the Almighty that we never come in contact with the deadly disease……and we never will……because this is a happily ever after story!

THE END

FROM THE AUTHOR

Although this novel concludes with a happily ever after ending the grim reality in our community is that we, continue to ignore the epidemic that plagues. Statistics show that black woman from the ages 25 to 44, a small percentage of the U.S. population; lead all gender and race with the highest percent of AIDS and HIV cases.

Yes, I despise the way television portrays men behind bars. Voluntarily! Black men are falling prey to the manipulation of the crafty, articulate homosexual. I write this with no disrespect to the majority of men behind bars but all women must and shall be put on notice. Some men, especially men of color, allow our ignorance to be our weakness. Therefore, you, women of all colors have to be strong and smart by way of responsibility. All I'm saying is Have that ass tested.....ex-cons....professional businessmen, and celebrities do not be fooled. No one is immune!

Before I conclude I have to recognize the original Tony Gangsta' of Portsmouth, Virginia. Yes, Tony Gangsta' is real. How he's portrayed in this story is a work of fiction. However, the fact is, there's way too many Tony Gangsta's in our community doing more harm than good. Far more times than often young men are losing their identities to the lyrical lifestyle of some rapper who does not carry on in the manner of his rhymes. It is sad to witness grown men, fathers, bopping around looking like.....dressing like....talking like the hottest rapper of the week. "NEWS FLASH NEGRO" A rapper, artist, or actor's main objective is to appeal to his demographics (that's you) through marketing and promoting him or herself. At the end of the day I can almost guarantee that your favorite entertainer goes home and carries on in a responsible manner. Life isn't about ball'n, and thug'n-and bein 'A boss'- brothers. To my beautiful black sisters, in order to demand respect you must first respect yourself. There is much more to you than your designer shoes and healthy apple bottom.

Be entertained....Be inspired.......BE mindful.....DO not be fooled! There is only one Denzel Washington.....There is only one Jay-Z.....One Oprah Winfrey....One Tupac. I may need to say that again for all the wanna be thugs that believe ignorance is hip. There was one Tupac, great as he was we do not need another one. There is only one Michael Jordon. One Mary J.Blige. One Minister Farrakhan.....thank you for awakening me from my dead state of mind. I will always love you for that. There is only one Missy Elliot. Wussup homegirl? There can only be one Dr. Cornell West or Dr. Connie Rice for that matter.

"Yeah, yeah, yeah! So what's your point,Gee?"

My point is……there's only one you!

SO BE YOU!

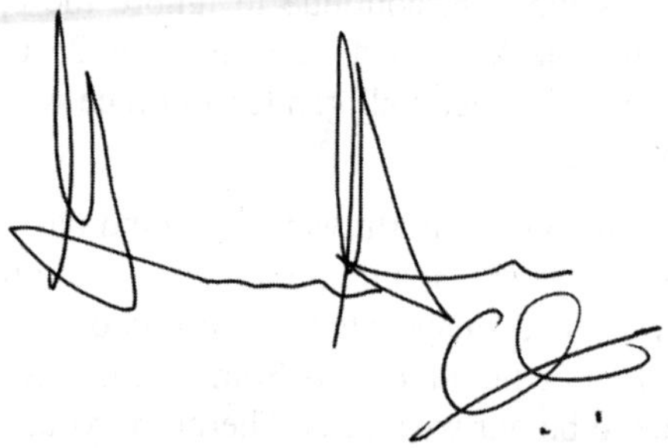